THE DEATHLY
GRIMM

THE DEATHLY
GRIMM

KATHRYN PURDIE

MAGPIE

Magpie Books
An imprint of HarperCollins*Publishers* Ltd
1 London Bridge Street
London SE1 9GF

www.harpercollins.co.uk

HarperCollins*Publishers*
Macken House
39/40 Mayor Street Upper
Dublin 1
D01 C9W8
Ireland

First published in Great Britain by HarperCollins*Publishers* 2025

1

Designed by Devan Norman

Kathryn Purdie asserts the moral right to
be identified as the author of this work

A catalogue record for this book is
available from the British Library

ISBN: 978-0-00-858838-0 (HB)
ISBN: 978-0-00-858839-7 (TPB)

This novel is entirely a work of fiction.
The names, characters and incidents portrayed in it are
the work of the author's imagination. Any resemblance to
actual persons, living or dead, events or localities is
entirely coincidental.

Printed and bound in Great Britain by Clays Ltd, Elcograf S.p.A.

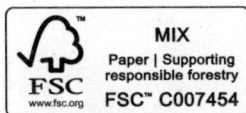

MIX
Paper | Supporting
responsible forestry
FSC
www.fsc.org
FSC™ C007454

This book contains FSC™ certified paper and other controlled sources
to ensure responsible forest management.

For more information visit: www.harpercollins.co.uk/green

For Aidan,

who, like his name, has always been

my help and little fire

PROLOGUE

BEFORE THE CURSE

The first snowfall of the season was a dangerous time for a ten-year-old girl to sleepwalk in the Forest Grimm. To her grandmother's knowledge, this was the only occasion Clara had ever walked while asleep. If it had been a habit, Marlène Thurn might have bolted the front door of their cottage shut or sent Clara to bed wearing a fur mantle, sheepskin boots, and woolen stockings.

As it was, the wisp of a girl was bare-legged, with only the linen of her nightgown to protect her from the bitter cold. Clara had fallen asleep curled up on a fleece in front of the kitchen hearth, and she looked so warm and contented that Marlène hadn't wanted to disturb her. The old woman had nodded off herself, her head tucked against a wing of an armchair mere inches away.

Clara's mother and father were dozing in another room, so when the snow swirled inside past the open door and tapped Marlène's shoulder with its frosty fingers, only she had awakened to find Clara missing.

Marlène searched the cottage to see if the child might be elsewhere, and when she wasn't, she grabbed a shawl from a peg, shoved her feet into slippers, and raced outside. She didn't dare wake anyone else. The Grimm wolf had been prowling around these parts, and Marlène had a careful relationship with the creature.

Once a year, the old woman allowed the wolf to snatch one of her lambs for a meal—a sad loss for the family, but Marlène considered the beast's feelings as well, and it must have been hard for a predator to be bonded to a shepherdess. It was only fair that the wolf reap some of the benefits, especially since Marlène had the ability to slip into its skin and possess its body at will.

Marlène considered doing so now. Would she be able to find Clara faster? But what if Clara's father or their farmhand *did* awaken and bring weapons? If anyone killed the wolf, they would also unwittingly kill Marlène. She had a better chance of protecting Clara and the wolf as a woman.

No one knew about the bond Marlène shared with the animal that sealed their fates together. It was safer that way. When Marlène's family of Anivoyantes had been massacred in a foreign land, she'd learned an unforgettable lesson: most people feared magic, especially when it presented itself as seers who wore the skins of wolves. Alone, she'd escaped to Grimm's Hollow, and all she claimed to be now was a simple fortune-teller.

Following her granddaughter's footprints in the snow, Marlène dashed past the herb garden, the north sheep pasture, the woven fence, the hedgerow, and, beyond it, the frozen stream that divided her farmland from the Forest Grimm.

Her heart thumped when she spied large canine paw prints that merged with Clara's tracks. She hastened, willing the wolf not to harm her only grandchild. But no amount of inward pleading could penetrate the wolf's mind. Marlène's bond didn't include that ability.

At last, Marlène clapped eyes on Clara. Twenty feet away, the child stood in a moonlit clearing beside a lone aspen with only six golden leaves clinging to its branches. If only there had been seven, they would have made a lucky number.

Clara's expression was distant, her gaze unfocused, her mind lost in a dream. Perhaps a nightmare. For that's how this moment felt to Marlène—because looming a few feet to Clara's left, opposite the skeletal aspen, stood the Grimm wolf.

The girl and the beast looked eerily disproportionate, Clara being smaller than other children her age, and the wolf twice as large as common breeds.

The old woman froze, as transfixed as Clara, unsure what to do. The Grimm wolf stared down at the girl, and while it didn't bare its fangs, the tip of its tail elevated slightly, indicating its uncertainty about the child. Perhaps it was trying to determine if she was a threat or a tasty midnight snack.

What must have confused the wolf most was the fleece Clara was holding—the same fleece she'd lain on by the hearth. It gave her all the more appearance of an offering come willingly from the Thurn sheep farm.

Marlène strained to breathe. She couldn't stop thinking about two fortune-telling cards she'd drawn over and over for Clara: the Midnight Forest for a forbidden choice, and the Fanged Creature for an untimely death. Clara's fate seemed to be playing out this very night.

No, it can't. Not yet.

"Adiah." Marlène spoke to the wolf, and it turned its great head. Marlène had never ascertained if the wolf knew the name she had given her. Wolves couldn't be domesticated like dogs. The only thing Marlène could trust was how the Grimm wolf had always tolerated her presence. They were halves of a strange whole even she couldn't comprehend fully after all these years. "Adiah, come to me."

The wolf didn't understand the command, but perhaps the primal gesture of Marlène's open hand might stir some buried instinct to press forward.

It didn't. The wolf looked away and fixed its large brown eyes on Clara again. Thankfully, the girl didn't return the stare directly, but if she were to awaken, she most certainly would, and the wolf would attack.

Marlène made herself look small, bowed her head, stooped her posture, and tentatively advanced five steps, cringing as the snow crunched beneath her slippers. On her sixth step, a low growl reverberated from the Grimm wolf. Marlène halted.

She knew what she must do—slip into the skin of the wolf. Doing so should be safe now. No one had followed her. No one would try to kill the beast.

Still, she hesitated. Marlène had never determined how quickly her spirit could leave her body and take possession of the wolf. Until now, she'd never had reason to time it. Could she shift fast enough to protect Clara? Any sudden movement might provoke the wolf.

The Grimm wolf growled again, throwing the sound at Marlène, as if it could sense her intentions. It curled back its lips and bared its fangs at Clara.

The girl's emerald eyes began to focus. Frown lines formed between her brows. She staggered, disoriented, and addressed the wolf: "I-I'm looking for the boy in the forest. He's very cold. I've brought him my fleece."

The Grimm wolf's jaws gaped wide. It snarled and lunged.

Clara screamed.

Marlène released her spirit. Her body collapsed. The world went black. Silent.

Then color and sound burst into her awareness. Her mind

raced to discern her new perspective. Blurring vision. Rushing cold. She hurtled through the air. A shriek pierced her eardrums.

She crashed into something and fell on all fours, stunned by her own massive size. She wasn't yet acclimated to the body of the wolf. Her open mouth pressed against flesh, where a pulse thundered. Clara's neck. Her jugular vein.

It took all of Marlène's willpower to prevent her jaws from snapping shut. She had no desire to kill her granddaughter, but her spirit was still fresh in the wolf, and the wolf had been in the midst of fulfilling its strongest animal instinct.

Marlène forced herself off the girl, who lay stunned and terror-stricken. Tears welled in Clara's eyes. Her body shook violently.

Marlène lowered her tail and flattened her ears, but Clara didn't understand the signs of submission. To make matters worse, no red rampion was growing nearby. If Marlène could have eaten some, she would have been given a human voice to speak soothing words.

Clara regained her composure and scrambled to her feet. She grabbed the fleece she'd dropped in the scuffle and darted her gaze to the forest. A look of confusion crossed her face. Was she remembering her dream?

Marlène backtracked to the trees surrounding the clearing, showing Clara that she would leave her alone now. *Go home,* she thought. *There is no boy out in the cold. You are the only child who is freezing.*

Clara bit her lower lip, which was swiftly turning blue. Hesitating, she glanced about her again, and gasped. "Grandmère?"

Marlène cursed inwardly. She hadn't anticipated Clara seeing her human body, especially in its spiritless state—not breathing but mystically preserved, as if frozen in time.

Clara rushed over and shook her grandmother's lifeless arms. "Why won't you wake up?"

Marlène deliberated. If she pulled her spirit from the wolf, the beast would be free to attack again. Yet if she didn't, how long would Clara remain in the forest, worrying over her grandmother's body? If Marlène delayed much longer, Clara would catch her death out here. Her two-card fate could still come to pass tonight.

Marlène sprinted across the clearing, bolting toward what she knew lay a half mile in the distance—a deep ravine with sheer walls, difficult to climb, even with sharp claws.

Once she reached the edge, she skidded to a halt. She scouted for the best place to take a tumble, one that wouldn't kill the wolf—and her human self within it. She spied a promising path downward with fewer rocks and patches of soft moss peeking out from the snow.

Remember my one wish, she thought, a sort of prayer to the Book of Fortunes. She'd made that wish when she was twenty-five, a newcomer of two years to Grimm's Hollow and pregnant with the babe who would become Clara's mother. *Protect my bloodline,* she added, craving reassurance in case this ended badly.

Of course, the book wasn't there to give its answer, and even if it were, *Sortes Fortunae* might not have written a reply. No one dared to petition the book twice. Doing so would be tempting fate, which was most forbidden.

All Marlène could do was hope for the best as she threw herself into the ravine and pulled her spirit from the Grimm wolf.

Blackness overcame her again. When she regained consciousness, she felt as if she'd been sucked into a whirlpool, beaten against a riverbed, and spat out onto hard, dry land. Through her bond, she felt the wolf's injuries. She'd wounded the poor creature viciously.

"Grandmère?" A fresh sob burst out of Clara, overflowing with relief. "I thought you were dead!"

"Oh, *ma petite chérie*." Marlène sat up and held her granddaughter fiercely. "I fainted from seeing that wolf."

"It was a *Grimm* wolf," Clara said, shuddering.

"Indeed?" Marlène brushed snowflakes from Clara's dark hair. Villagers in Grimm's Hollow spoke of Grimm wolves as if there were many in these woods. But Adiah was the only wolf of her kind here. Bonded with Marlène, Adiah had followed her from their homeland to these forested mountains years ago. "However did you survive?"

"I don't know." Clara's forehead puckered. "The wolf just ran away. I hope it didn't go after the boy."

"Boy?" Marlène recalled too late what Clara had murmured while sleepwalking.

"He's traveling here, and his clothes aren't warm enough. His father says they must hurry. Winter came too soon. I want to give him my fleece."

"You are a sweet girl." Marlène rubbed Clara's arm. "But that was only a dream."

"No, he's real. I saw him yesterday before the snow started falling."

"Yesterday? But you never left the cottage."

"I saw him tonight, I mean. But for him it was yesterday." Clara scratched her head. "It's confusing."

"I see."

"His name is . . ." Clara sighed. "Well, I've forgotten it."

"Ah, there's the catch—the true sign of a dream. They are always missing pieces, you see."

"But—"

"Come, now." Marlène pushed her aching body to its feet and scooped up her granddaughter. She may have been old and sore, but she had always remained strong. "I'm going to make us a nice pot of tea." She didn't mention all the strong herbs she planned to steep into it.

Clara needed to forget this night, Marlène determined. She was a curious child, one who had too many questions and sought answers at any cost. Marlène didn't want her drawing any conclusions about the Grimm wolf, especially if they were true.

And so it was that Clara never remembered the one time she had sleepwalked as a child, nor the cause for her frostbitten toes, nor her first thoughts of a boy named Axel who was about to arrive in Grimm's Hollow and change her life forever.

Fortuitously, he survived the bitter cold and never crossed paths with the Grimm wolf. At least not on that journey.

As for Marlène, although she was a seer, it wasn't until many years later that she pieced together what Clara had accomplished that night. The dream Clara had while sleepwalking was, in fact, a vision. Not a vision of the future, like Marlène had when she read someone's fortune, but a vision of the past.

This was the first demonstration of Clara's gift—proof that some of the magic in Marlène's bloodline had passed on. But even among Marlène's slaughtered family, Clara's gift was rare. Seers who could see into the past were known as Voyantes of the Bygone, and unlike Anivoyantes, they didn't shift into animals. Still, magic was magic, and people were threatened the most by forms they understood the least.

Marlène wished Clara's gift had never manifested. That way no one would have cause to endanger her life. Clara's fate was already spelled out, but that didn't mean her destiny should be encouraged.

As the years passed, Marlène's only consolation was that Clara's magic remained dormant. By and large, it stayed so until Clara's two-card fate played out, even though Marlène hadn't foreseen everything that would precede and follow her granddaughter's death.

She didn't know the boy Clara had wished to warm with her fleece would grow up to fall in love with her. And when Clara died, he would use a spindle to plunge red rampion into her heart. It would give her back her life, and with it, greater access to her magic.

But Marlène still had reason to fear, for the fortune-telling cards revealed a new story for the girl, and Clara's flourishing magic would only make it more dangerous and heartbreaking.

A troubling fate also awaited Marlène, made all the more real now that Clara had her life back. Marlène began to understand how their destinies would tangle.

And Clara's destiny—Clara's life—was one Marlène swore to die protecting.

CHAPTER 1

SIX YEARS LATER

I stand outside the village meeting hall, perspiration soaking the linen of my day dress as I await the call to be admitted into the inquisition. I wish Grandmère were here. I could use her courage. Still ill and barely coherent, she's the only company I've had this week. The council hasn't allowed me to see any of my friends. They don't want us comparing and later corroborating one another's stories about what happened in the Forest Grimm.

Beside me, Karl Wagner, a middle-aged farmer, serves as my guard. Tan lines surround the wrinkles radiating from his eyes. He removes his straw hat and rubs the mark it left on his brow. "My Geraldine," he hisses, his voice warbling with grief. "Did you ever see her in the forest?"

My chest sinks. Since I've returned, he isn't the first person to ask about a Lost loved one. "I'm sorry. I didn't see many villagers." I won't tell him about the ones I found dead, most of them unrecognizable. The ones my mother killed.

What little light is left in Karl's eyes extinguishes.

"Perhaps your wife is still alive," I say. The old Clara would have sounded more hopeful. But this Clara, the Clara who killed her mother and brought back a book that couldn't break the curse, can only offer him weak reassurance.

One of the doors to the meeting hall cracks open. Karl turns his empty eyes on me. "It's time."

Before I can take a calming breath, the double doors open wide. It's a sweltering day, and the stench of sweat and wood polish hits me square in the face, along with the gazes of over fifty villagers sitting in the pews.

This must be what a bride feels like on her wedding day. Except if the aisle I'm about to walk down led to an altar, it would be for a slaughter.

No one will believe the truth. I can already see it in my best friend Henni's eyes, bloodshot from crying, and the look Axel gives me, strained with worry.

"Clara Thurn, come forward and take your seat," Herr Oswald, chairman of the governing council, commands. He smooths his thinning hair with bony fingers and indicates the chair, positioned to face the assembly. To its right sit the five members of the council.

I walk the aisle, feeling my doom descend, a strange sort of fear since I've been confronted by far more dangerous people in the forest.

Then why am I so afraid?

The chair is unforgivingly hard and wobbles as I shift to sit taller. *Look confident for Henni's sake.* This inquisition has, overall, been targeted at her. The gratitude first shown us when we returned from the forest was rescinded the moment Henni's one wish on the Book of Fortunes failed to break the curse on Grimm's Hollow.

It wasn't enough that we *partially* lifted the curse, the result of my one wish gone awry. Because of it, more rain falls. More crops flourish. But what everyone really wants is for their loved ones to return home from the forest. And for that, the curse must fully break.

Herr Oswald sits in the center of the councilors behind a long table. He dons a pair of wire-framed spectacles and peruses his notes. "Clara, since the day the curse fell three years ago, you and your friends, Axel Furst and Henrietta Dantzer, are the only people to ever enter and return from the Forest Grimm."

"Aside from Ella Dantzer, Fiora Winther, and Fiora's children, Hansel and Gretel," I reply, spotting Ella and Fiora in the crowd. Ella is seated next to Henni, her hand over her sister's, and Fiora is two rows behind. Hansel and Gretel appear to be absent, which is a relief. This is no occasion for children.

"True, true," Herr Oswald concedes. "Although we consider them to be among the Lost, thankfully found, unlike you, Axel, and Henni. I believe we can agree you three were never Lost?"

I nod, not wanting to hash out how we actually became lost—though only lost in our travels, not Lost to ourselves. Being Lost like that changed Ella into Cinderella the poisoner, Fiora into Rapunzel with miles of strangling hair, and Hansel and Gretel into cannibalistic captors.

"Very well. Back to the matter at hand." Herr Oswald's voice is neither kind nor condescending. He can rule pragmatically as the closest person we have to a mayor. "Will you explain how you three accomplished the feat?"

"I can try." I clear my throat, stalling. Henni and Axel have already been interrogated. How much would they have shared? "Before my mother went Lost, she made me a cape."

Henni rounds her eyes. Axel shakes his head slightly. They didn't share about the cape's magic, then—how my mother dyed it with protective red rampion, which allowed me to enter the forest. They achieved the same with a scarf and a kerchief I made from my cape.

"The cape is vibrant red, and I hoped my mother could find me if I was wearing it," I go on, improvising a new excuse. "Perhaps the forest let me enter because it sensed that connection to her. She had already been welcomed, when I had not been, not until then."

"And how do you account for Henni and Axel being welcomed?" Herr Oswald asks.

"We traveled together, so perhaps the forest viewed us as an entity."

Hazel Roth, a councilwoman, harrumphs, her frown accentuating her double chins.

"Isn't that explanation a bit far-fetched?" Herr Oswald asks.

"Possibly." I fold my hands in my lap to hold down my trembling knees. "I'm only speculating, sir. But my best guess is the forest finally wanted the Book of Fortunes to be found, so it gave us passage. It must have wanted all three of us to accomplish the task."

Herr Oswald peers at the other council members, and as there are no more harrumphs among them, he moves on to his next points of interrogation: where I found the book, how we discovered the Lost Ones we brought home, and how we managed to come home at all.

I'm honest about the book's location near a subterranean waterfall, as well as how we navigated the forest following rivers and streams. As for Ella, Fiora, and Hansel and Gretel, I share how we came upon them, but not how they tried to kill us and likely killed others. They're innocent of any monstrosity triggered by the forest's tainted magic.

"So you set out on your journey in search of your mother, Rosamund Thurn," Herr Oswald continues. "How did that search end?"

I see myself as a ghost hovering over my own dead body, a terrible gash at my neck and blood blooming from the wound. "I found her but couldn't save her." Axel's and Henni's expressions are pensive but supportive. I trust they haven't betrayed the killer my mother was, deadlier than any of the Lost we encountered. "She was living in an abandoned fortress and . . ." Axel nods at me. Henni's eyes well with fresh tears. ". . . it was unstable. It collapsed and buried her in the rubble."

Herr Oswald studies me for a drawn-out moment, his wiry brows lifted. "If that is true, child, you have our deepest condolences."

I sink a little in my chair. Perhaps I'll get out of this inquisition unscathed—and more importantly, my friends will.

"Now about the villagers you didn't find. Are we to believe, of the sixty-seven villagers who have gone Lost, you only met with five?"

"The forest is vast, sir. A difficult place to survive in, even when you've been admitted. We barely had food to eat. Deer hid from us. Fish were scarcely found. Many villagers must have already . . ." I lock gazes with Karl Wagner. His face is haunted, devastated, a reflection of so many. Everyone has a Lost loved one. "They would have had great trouble staying alive."

"Yet you found no graves, no markers from other villagers who might have buried them?"

"No graves, sir."

"Nothing in the trees, then?" he prods, one eye squinting.

Why is he mentioning the trees? Someone must have revealed the truth about them. A quick glance at Henni confirms it was her. *Sorry,* she mouths, though she has no need to apologize. We weren't allowed to correspond, to decide what to share or keep secret.

Unfortunately, the more bizarre our stories are, the more unlikely the council is to believe the fundamental reason we're here: to explain why Henni couldn't break the curse.

"We did see faces in the trees," I answer reluctantly. "It was as if the dead had been absorbed in them."

A woman in the crowd gasps.

"But they could not be identified," I rush on. "They might have been fallen soldiers, like in the legend." The legend no one really believes in. A scary story shared when people gather around hearth fires and want a thrill. It speaks of a great battle that took place long ago, in which every dead soldier became a tree, and those trees became the forest.

I believe that story now.

Herr Oswald gives a small grunt. "That brings us to Henni's wish ceremony." My heart gives a hard thud. "You say the forest allowed you entrance because it wanted the Book of Fortunes to be found. One would therefore assume it wanted the curse to be broken. How do you explain why it wasn't?"

Henni clasps her hands, as if in prayer. Axel leans forward, his elbows on his knees.

"I'm unsure how to answer, as I don't know what Henni wished for." This time my words are calculated. I've prepared myself for this line of inquiry, and I'll begin by throwing a village law in the faces of the council: "Sharing what one wishes for is forbidden, after all. Henni would never tempt fate by breaking that rule, even for me."

Herr Oswald knows as well as I do that she would have wished to break the curse. Henni's too good-natured to do otherwise, being the only person of age in Grimm's Hollow who hasn't made her one wish, the only one the village can depend upon to end their suffering.

Herr Oswald levels a glare at me. "Very well, then, Clara. Recount for us what you witnessed that day."

"Do you mean from the time *you* let me go behind the pavilion curtain to join Henni?" I answer, careful to keep my tone courteous. This was another breaking of customs, and Herr Oswald was the one who allowed it.

His face reddens as the other council members grumble. "Continue," he says past thinning lips.

"Henni was in a state of shock. She said she'd kept making her wish, but every time she opened the book for an answer, *Sortes Fortunae* kept turning to a spot where a page was missing. I saw for myself the remnants where it had been torn out."

"Then you didn't see any words on the page?" Herr Oswald squints one eye again, like he's trying to hint at what someone else revealed.

Axel wouldn't have said anything. He doesn't even know what happened. I haven't been allowed to speak with him. And Henni wouldn't have exposed that I did something forbidden.

I made a second wish on *Sortes Fortunae*. Second wishes are unspoken of, unforgivable, the worst way a person can tempt fate. Nothing is more sacred than the Book of Fortunes, especially now that it's finally back in Grimm's Hollow.

But when I made my second wish, I wasn't thinking about laws or blasphemy. I'd felt strangely bold and untouchable—even angry. I was someone who'd died and come back again, someone who'd killed her own mother, and I wasn't going to allow the curse to remain unbroken because of a missing page. So that's what I wished for:

I wish to know where your missing page is. The one meant for Henni.

"When I found Henni, no words were written in the book," I answer carefully.

"And *after* you found her?"

I briefly close my eyes, and the magicked green ink of *Sortes Fortunae* seems to burn through my lids, a blazing reminder of the answer it wrote on a page that *wasn't* missing:

Only one page holds the secret to finally restoring peace.
Only one person is to blame for breaking it.
Both must be found, for one has the other,
And together they hide in the Forest Grimm.

"The book made it clear that it wouldn't give Henni an answer until the missing page was restored."

Henni breaks into a coughing fit. Her eyes are overbright as she stabs me with a look that says I've confessed too much.

"And how exactly did the book make this clear?" Herr Oswald demands.

Henni coughs again. Herr Oswald motions for Karl Wagner. "Escort Miss Dantzer from the room."

"I've told you already," I reply, trying to stall him. "The book is missing a page. It's simple enough to draw the conclusion that it needs to be whole to answer Henni."

What I can't explain, even to myself, is why the book answered *me*, though I believe in my bones that if I'd asked to break the curse, I would have been met with the same missing page.

I'm convinced the curse won't be broken until the person who murdered Bren Zimmer is found and the page is returned. That's what the riddle must mean. Whoever brought about the curse by using our sacred book to make a murderous wish to kill the prominent blacksmith of our village is in the forest with the missing page, and they need to be brought to justice.

Karl reaches Henni and prods her back.

"She isn't leaving." Ella clutches her sister's hand. "Clara is the last one being questioned. Henni has every right to hear her testimony."

Councilwoman Hazel Roth raises her double chins. "It is *we* who give permission to stay, and Henrietta's time is up."

Ella looks to her parents for help, but they urge her to let

Henni leave. I see the fear in their eyes. They don't want to make matters worse for their youngest daughter. I've been told Henni was questioned for three days. Shy Henni, sweet Henni, barely sixteen-years-old Henni, was relentlessly interrogated over something that wasn't her fault.

It's more than ridiculous; it's insulting. What does the council imagine her ulterior motive could be? Or any of ours? They're acting as though we returned to Grimm's Hollow, Book of Fortunes in hand, to bring our village into utter ruin.

Ella releases her sister's hand, and Henni rises. I ache to see how wilted she looks, especially when she'd grown so much bolder on our journey.

"She's done something to offend the book!" a woman calls. "Now the forest is angrier! I'll never see my son again!"

A man whips a finger at her. "She's made the curse worse!"

"What? No!" Henni blanches. "I *tried* to make a wish."

"She needs to be punished!" yells another man.

I jerk up from my chair. "She needs to be *protected*! She's the only one who can break the curse. No one else will come of age for another year."

More shouts erupt. More people cry for Henni to be reprimanded. They weep over their Lost Ones. They rage that Ella and Fiora, with her illegitimate children, have returned, but not anyone else. They see our coming back as a conspiracy. The unbroken curse is proof.

"Order, order!" Herr Oswald calls, but no one listens. Everyone is on their feet now. Karl struggles to escort Henni outside while villagers elbow closer. Fists clench. Spittle flies. Faces redden.

I bolt for Henni, but two council members hold me back while the others struggle to calm the assembly. I watch, openmouthed, as the chaos intensifies. My once gentle neighbors, farmers and craftsmen, millers and tradesmen, morph into a terrible mob. If only they could see themselves, the monsters they're becoming, worse than any Lost Ones.

"Stop! Please!" No one hears me. Not until I hurl my chair against the wall. "You're acting no better than murderers! Have you forgotten why our village was cursed in the first place? And that was due to one murderer. What do you think the forest will do if you all become killers?"

Heads lower. People shuffle back. Not everyone has the grace to look ashamed, but I've at least given them pause, and that brief time allows Karl to finish escorting Henni from the meeting hall. Ella and her parents swiftly follow. Axel weaves his way to me and pulls me into his arms. Only then do I realize I'm shaking and clawing at the rose-red strip of wool I wear around my wrist. My remembrance of my mother from the Tree of the Lost.

I can't have any more death on my hands.

Over Axel's shoulder, I take in the crowd through my blurred-hot eyes. If any of them *did* harm Henni, would I hold them as blameless as my mother? The curse drove her to madness until she was no longer Rosamund, but Briar Rose, a blood-sucking monster, the Fanged Creature my grandmother had foreseen in her cards.

I couldn't save her, but I can save this village. If I do, maybe I'll find some redemption. Maybe my mother will.

I *will* return to the forest. I'll discover the murderer. I'll bring that person back—and with them, the missing page. I'll save Henni, and Henni will break the curse.

CHAPTER 2

SEVEN WEEKS LATER

Though the night is dark and this room is dim, I veil my face in black and struggle to conjure a vision of the past. I'm sitting cross-legged on the floor of Grandmère's bedroom in our cottage. Her snores drift to my ears, but I imagine the rattle in her chest isn't wet from the cough in her lungs. It's the sound of a summer storm or the rustle of wind through damp autumn leaves. Nothing to worry over.

I concentrate on the fortune-telling cards I've spread facedown and the token clutched in my left hand. This is how Grandmère divines someone's future, or at least as close as I can replicate. If my magic is anything like hers, then her trick for sparking her ability should also spark mine.

I won't think about how many times I've attempted this ritual and failed. Since I returned from my journey, I haven't had any more glimpses of the past. But I'm determined to change that. I need to if I'm to solve who murdered Bren Zimmer.

In the weeks since the inquisition, I've worked endlessly at having visions and gathering clues. I have so much more work to do, so many more skills to develop, but I feel my time running short. I hoped Grandmère would recover first, but I can't delay my second journey much longer. The village has reached a tentative peace with me and my friends, but it's like a broken teacup pieced together without glue. A sneeze could shatter it again.

I refocus on the vision I'm trying to summon. When Grand-mère reads someone's fortune, they place their hand atop hers. Through that touch, she feels their blood "sing," which guides her to pick each card. She does so blindly, veiled in opaque black, like I'm veiled now.

I don't have the luxury of someone's touch—not when I'm trying to connect to Lost Ones—so I've been experimenting with tokens, tangible items special to that person.

Johann Schade is the Lost One I'm currently trying to channel. I picture his long, gaunt face. His lanky frame. According to the glassblower he apprenticed for in Grimm's Hollow, the green marble I'm holding was his prized possession: a beautiful clear globe with a ribbon swirl of green in its core.

I'm not sure how closely Johann knew Bren Zimmer. Johann was a quiet man in his midtwenties who kept to himself, though he attended occasional festivals. In the days before the curse, celebrations were held frequently. Johann never danced at them, but he watched the couples with a furrowed brow and his hat bent from wringing the brim.

I squeeze the green marble. "Speak to me," I murmur to Johann, or his marble, or the cards—anything that might open my mind to see his past.

Johann went missing in the second year of the curse, after he journeyed into the forest of his own accord, for what reason I can't say. Back then, the forest admitted people on occasion, though I never understood why some were allowed while others were barred, like Axel was when he ran after Ella on the eve of their wedding. Like I was every time I ventured past the ash-lined border until I had the protection of red rampion.

I strain harder to focus. A headache throbs between my

pinched brows. I glide my hand over the cards. I wait for any unusual sensations. A firing nerve. A rush in my veins. A flutter in my belly. Grandmère never clarified how she felt blood "singing."

I crack one eye open to peek at her, as if that can help solve my dilemma, but I can't see anything past my silken veil.

One minute passes. Two. The clock in our front room cuckoos eight times.

No one's blood is singing. If it did, I've missed it.

I'm probably overthinking this.

Just draw the cards, Clara.

I flip over three, lift away the veil, and stare at what I've chosen. The Fanned Tail for irrepressible confidence. Coins in a Pocket for a sudden inflow of wealth. The Lady with the Lily for untarnished beauty.

I burst into laughter, but the sound is mirthless, pathetic. I couldn't have picked cards more at odds with Johann. How will I ever discover the person who committed murder and triggered the curse? My magic is the only advantage I have in this impossible task.

Grandmère coughs and shifts uncomfortably. I go to her bedside table and pour a spoonful of elderberry syrup, which is more like strained puree, as we have no honey. Hopefully it still helps.

I sit on her mattress and bring the spoon to her mouth. She grimaces but forces down the concoction. A few moments pass, and her cough settles. She relaxes into a deeper sleep.

I smooth her flyaway gray hairs into the long braid resting atop her patchwork quilt. When Grandmère was in the body of the Grimm wolf, she was injured, and while that wound healed, she's been ill ever since.

My hand gravitates to the rose-red strip of wool I've fastened around my left wrist. *Mother isn't Lost anymore*, I remind myself. She isn't the monster who attacked her own mother and killed me. I found her like I'd set out to do, and for one beautiful moment she recognized me before she died.

Grandmère said I saved her. But perhaps she only meant to console me, her last remaining family member, even though I killed her daughter.

The candle flame on the bedside table flickers, its light reflecting in the leaded glass of the casement window. My gaze lifts to my own reflection, a younger copy of my mother, the same green eyes and sable hair. It hangs loosely about my shoulders, but doesn't hide the scar on my neck, where Briar Rose bit me and drank my blood dry.

With shaking fingers, I touch the scar. It's not a simple imprint of teeth; Briar Rose tore a chunk of my flesh away. She killed me . . . but did that justify me killing her?

My fingers trail down to another scar, one I can't see but can feel past the linen of my dress. Axel brought me back to life by plunging a red spindle into my heart, a piece of my magical cape with it. But what brand of madness made me believe I could save my mother from her Lost spell by doing the same? She was alive, not dead like I'd been.

Deep down, did some part of me want her to die?

No, how can I think that?

I blow out the candle, and my reflection vanishes. I look through the window and see one of the sheep pastures in its place. A few ewes are grazing on the scant grass. Past them, in the distance, stand the trees bordering the Forest Grimm, only hazy silhouettes in the dark of the night, yet the longer I stare, the more that darkness sharpens and separates into different casts of gray.

Then the gray moves.

It sneaks, skulks, stalks. I see a tail, a snout, peaked ears.

My heart kicks a heavy beat.

The Grimm wolf.

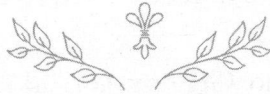

CHAPTER 3

on't be ridiculous, Clara. You can't see any animal in the forest this far away.

I blink, and the illusion is gone. I rub my brow and release a slow exhale. I'm still living in the past, still remembering how I sensed the wolf when she trailed me on my journey. I'm sure I only noticed her because Grandmère was in her skin.

I pocket Johann's green marble, wrap a knitted shawl around my shoulders, and stride outside with a lantern. Nightingales sing. Crickets chirp. A frog croaks. The air is brisk, cooler than it's been in ages. It carries the smell of damp fallen leaves and sharp pine resin. For the first time in three years, autumn has arrived.

Until now, Grimm's Hollow has been stuck in a dry spell of endless summer, but with the partial lifting of the curse, the seasons are finally shifting.

I glance over my shoulder and sneak inside the barn, closing the door firmly behind me. I don't want anyone to discover what I'm hiding in here.

The barn is empty of animals. We only shelter sheep when the weather becomes harsh.

Balancing my lantern in one hand while hitching up a fold of my skirt, I climb the ladder to the hayloft, then slip between hay bales as I work my way to the far wall. The window shutters are already closed, but I hang a dark cloth across them and stuff extra fabric in the gaps to hide the glow of my lantern.

I can't shake the feeling that I'm not alone, but I try to reason with myself. There's no Grimm wolf here, no feral Rapunzel, no poisoner Cinderella, no cannibalistic Hansel and Gretel, no vampiric Briar Rose. No one is stalking me or trying to kill me.

I set down my lantern, stand on tiptoes, and reach into a nook between a wooden beam and a crooked board. I can't find the strings of my cinched bag. I've tucked it back too far. I hop and swipe. I feel it, but I can't—

Arms snake around my waist. I'm yanked back, shrieking. A hand clamps over my mouth. I squirm and buck. Strike my heel. I'm released before the kick lands. I spin around, hands fisted.

River-blue eyes twinkle back at me. Yes, *twinkle*. This boy is maddeningly charming in any situation.

"Axel!" My shoulders collapse. "What are you thinking, sneaking up on me like that?"

He cracks a sheepish grin. "I thought it might be romantic." Taking in my unimpressed glare, he adds, "In a surprising way."

"Not romantic. Not surprising. More like horrific and terrifying." I lean back against the wall to steady myself. "You're lucky there wasn't a scythe nearby. I could have mauled you to death. Or scarred your beautiful face."

He swaggers closer. "Beautiful?"

"Stupidly beautiful."

A soft chuckle slips past his crooked smile. "I can live with that." His nose brushes mine. "Is there anything I can do to earn your forgiveness?"

"No." I squeeze back another inch.

"Does this help?" His hands trace my hips and rest on my waist. He twirls a lock of my hair and places a gentle kiss behind my ear.

My heart pitter-patters. "That's cheating."

"How?" His lips slide from my ear to my jawline and down the column of my throat.

"You know I can't think when you . . . when . . ." I sigh and arch my neck. His kisses travel over every place my skin is exposed above the loose neckline of my dress. My shawl falls to the floor. I curl my toes in my shoes. My body is awash with prickling heat.

Axel's mouth finds its way up the other side of my neck, the left side where—

I stiffen and push against him.

He immediately draws back. "What?"

I cover my scar, cheeks burning. "Sorry, I don't know why . . ." I take a measured breath. "I know it's ugly, but—"

"It's not ugly."

"It's just the place where she . . ." My throat closes. I can't meet Axel's gaze. I stare down at the hay scattered across the floor, the way it shines golden in the lantern light, stark in contrast with my scuffed leather shoes.

"I remember," Axel murmurs. He's patient, not prying. If I say nothing more, he won't press me. He hasn't since that day at Briar Rose's castle.

I peel away from the wall and glide around him, eager to change the subject. My gaze snags on a few rucksacks by a large pile of hay with a body-shaped indent, like a down-filled mattress. I frown. I never asked Axel how he was able to surprise me. "Have you been sleeping in here?"

Now his cheeks turn red. "I was going to tell you."

"But your house—"

"The Dantzers asked me to leave."

I can't speak for a moment. For the past year, Axel has been living in a small house on the Dantzer farm, a place he was supposed to share with Ella once they wed. But then she became Lost in the forest, and Axel remained with the Dantzers. The family was hoping for a happy ending, and he was hoping to bring back Ella. Now that she *is* back and Axel isn't marrying her . . . well, I suppose he was bound to have to leave at some point.

"What about the Tragers' cottage?" It's been abandoned for almost two years, ever since the couple went Lost. "They were so fond of you. I'm sure they wouldn't mind if—"

"I'm not moving into their cottage." Axel sets his jaw. "That wouldn't be right."

I don't fight him on this, though his unshakable sense of honor rarely does him any favors. "Where will you go then?" I know he won't consider moving back with his uncle, not after the beatings he took growing up. "We'll have to shelter the youngest of the flock in the barn if the weather takes a bad turn. Conrad is bound to find you."

Axel nods, nibbling on his lip as he steals a shy glance at me. I don't understand. Is he hoping that—?

Oh. I suppose Grandmère and I do have an extra bedroom in our cottage. But it would cause a scandal if Axel moved in with us, he being unmarried and—

Oh.

Can marriage really be what he's hoping for? I'm only seventeen. Village girls get married at that age aplenty, but . . . I'm only just alive again. I'm not sure if I'm ready for that. Besides, how can I think of marrying when another dangerous journey is ahead of me?

"I'll figure something out." Axel forces a chuckle, raking a hand through his tousled, golden hair. He casts his gaze about the loft, as if looking for something else to talk about. He gestures at the nook. "What were you searching for up there?"

"Oh, um . . ." The bodice of my dress suddenly feels too tight.

He cocks his head, and his eyes slowly narrow. "Clara?"

"It's just a little collection."

"Of what?"

"Things."

"What kinds of things?"

"Special things."

His frown deepens. He skirts around me and strides to the wall.

I clutch his arm as he reaches into the nook. "I'm going to give them back, I promise."

He pulls out the drawstring bag. It's large enough to fit five apples. Apples would be so much easier to explain.

Axel gives the bag a shake, and its contents clink and jangle. "So you *stole* whatever is in here?"

"Just temporarily."

He opens the bag, and his eyebrows dart upward. I know what he's gawking at: rings, brooches, bracelets, cuff links, tiny figurines. . . . "Clara Thurn, you are a right and proper thief. You have a small fortune in here!"

"I can't help it if prized possessions are worth more coin."

He rolls his tongue in his cheek to tamp down a smile. "And what do you intend to do with all of this—just temporarily?"

I turn away, stalling like I've been stalling for weeks to tell him. Why does my perfect plan suddenly feel so ridiculous? "I'm going to solve the murder that brought about the curse."

He doesn't laugh, which is slightly heartening. "How?"

"The curse won't break until Bren Zimmer's murderer is brought back from the forest. He or she will have the missing page and—"

"So what's all of this then?" He shakes the bag again. "Evidence? How could it be?"

I sit on the hay he's been using for a bed. "Think of them as clues for Lost Ones. Not that I have a token for each of them yet. But every Lost One needs to be considered a suspect."

Axel pulls out a tiny silver jar and looks at me questioningly.

"That belongs to Edwina Braun," I explain. "It's filled with beeswax perfume."

"And it can tell you if she committed murder three years ago?"

"No. But it can help me connect to her . . . so I can have a vision of her past."

Axel's face splits into a wide grin. "Clara, that's brilliant!"

"You think so?" A flicker of pride kindles inside my chest.

He plops down beside me. "So what have you discovered so far?"

"Discovered?"

"In one of your visions." He gives my arm a rattle. "I can't believe you haven't told me about this!"

I cough up a laugh and shrink back into the hay. "Well, I've been more focused on collecting the tokens."

"Stealing them, you mean." He winks.

"Mm-hmm." I want to bury myself deeper until all the hay smothers me.

"Wait, do you mean you haven't had any visions? At all?"

I throw my arms over my eyes, not withholding any theatrics. "The village is going to find out what I stole and exile me to the lower valleys!"

Axel lies back in the hay with me and pokes my ribs. "Why did you keep stealing them if they weren't helping?"

"Because I was sure they would. Eventually. Maybe the problem was finding the right token, one special enough to trigger a connection. I *have* been practicing at having visions, but it's so difficult. And, of course, Grandmère can't help." I moan and fold my arms tighter over my face. "It's only a matter of time before I'm caught. I can't face another inquisition."

"Well . . . then we'll have to leave sooner."

"To the lower valleys?"

"To the Forest Grimm."

I'm quiet for a moment. Axel and I haven't talked about taking a second journey together. I've known he wouldn't let me leave without him. That's why I've delayed this conversation.

I pull my arms down and peer at him. "You're not going to tell me I should give away my cape so someone else can enter the forest instead?"

"Not if you're not going to tell me I should give away my scarf so I can't take the journey with you."

I curl on my side to see him better. "And you're not going to say I should just live for myself now that I have my life back and let breaking the curse be someone else's problem?"

Axel tucks closer. "I know better than to start an argument I won't win. Besides, breaking the curse is going to save our village. That means you'll be saved too. You'll be able to live fully. I want that for you."

"But what if I die?" I whisper. "Permanently this time."

He presses a soft kiss to the scar on my neck, then above my heart, where I bear the scar from the spindle. "I won't let that happen."

I rest my brow against his. "What if *you* die?"

"We're all going to die someday, Clara. When I do, all I want is for you to be there with me."

I drink in his smell, freshly cut wood and mountain pine. "You were there for me," I whisper.

He kisses my forehead, and an owl hoots in the distance. I should go back to the cottage, but I miss sleeping beside Axel like we did in the forest. "Can I stay with you tonight?" I ask shyly.

His eyes warm a shade deeper, and he rises to blow out the lantern.

We trade kisses to the *baa*ing of ewes in the pasture and the whistling autumn wind. We don't talk about when we will leave for our journey. I sense our desperation to delay in the strength of Axel's arms and mouth and the spread of his hands against my back. I feel it mirrored in the way I want to lose myself in him . . . or perhaps find myself.

Since I died and came back again, it's like I'm in a stolen body, like I'm wearing the wrong clothes. I don't know how to be the same Clara anymore. That was a girl who lived to save her mother, but now my mother is gone. And I'm still here.

I will break the curse or die trying—that much I know. But if I succeed, what follows? What will give my life meaning?

That's what I can't explain to Axel without hurting him. In struggling to reclaim my life, I don't know how to make it as simple as just him and me.

But here in the darkness of this hayloft, it is that simple, and I keep him close, afraid of what tomorrow will bring.

CHAPTER 4

Axel and I meant to wake up earlier than Conrad, who rises early indeed, but we're so comfortable in the warm hay and each other's arms that we oversleep. When Conrad enters the barn, we startle and smother our laughter as we clamber for a way that Axel can escape unnoticed.

I remember a fresh haystack outside the loft window. Axel grabs a rucksack with clothes, gives me a peck on the mouth, and whispers, "See you at the festival," then jumps outside.

I stuff Johann's green marble in the drawstring bag, cram it in the nook, and comb the hay from my hair. As I descend the ladder, I shoot Conrad my most innocent smile. "None of the hay is moldy," I announce, as if reporting something that's been weighing heavy on his mind.

Before he can untangle his brows, I breeze past him and exit the barn.

I perform my morning chores and warm some broth for Grandmère, forcing her to take a few swallows before she shoves my spoon away and drifts back to sleep. I wipe a bit of dribble off her chin. "Please fight and get better," I whisper. "I need you."

She coughs and moans, rolling onto her side with her back to me. I hang my head. What if she dies while I'm gone to the forest? What if I can't succeed without her help?

I force myself to stand, to keep moving, keep doing. Tending to our farm and preparing for my journey are all that's holding me together right now.

I check the clock. It's early in the afternoon. I have just enough time to obtain another token.

I remove my apron and head outside, trying to make a quick decision about where to go. Of the sixty-seven villagers who have gone Lost, I'm aware of only seven who are dead, including my mother. Others were also dead at Briar Rose's castle, but their bodies were so decomposed I couldn't recognize them. Among them were at least two more from Grimm's Hollow. Then there's Fiora and Ella, who are no longer Lost, and Fiora's children, Hansel and Gretel, who don't count since Fiora kept their existence secret until she returned. That leaves fifty-six Lost Ones who might be alive—and suspects in Bren Zimmer's murder. I've only collected tokens for thirty-four. I still have a lot of work to do.

I follow the road from my cottage until it meets the thoroughfare that connects to other farms. From here, I can go either left or right. A beech tree rests in the middle, burnished copper for autumn. Two round leaves snap away and flutter down like glittering pennies.

Pennies . . . two of them . . . just like the two Ollie needs. It feels like a sign.

I turn left and set off for the house of Axel's uncle, Ollie's father. I may not get the chance to obtain tokens for every Lost One before I leave on my journey, but I need to do better for Ollie. He isn't Lost like the others, but he's still trapped in the forest.

Ollie stole two pennies he was meant to give to a poor man, and then hid them in the forest. Before he could think better of his choice, he became ill with consumption, forgot where he hid the pennies, and passed away. That was thirteen years ago, well before the time of the curse. Ollie was only seven years old, and that's how he appeared in the forest—as the ghost of a little boy.

Ollie's soul can't be set free until the pennies are found again and given to the poor man. I promised to help him do that.

I travel a few miles until I reach the place where Ollie grew up, a rocky farm that's failed to thrive. Even before the curse, Rudger Furst was more intent on finding silver on his land than taking care of his fields of rye and millet.

I dodge precarious spots where his mines have collapsed or the land is unstable from poorly dug shafts. Needless to say, Rudger wasn't a talented miner and never found any silver.

As I approach the ramshackle house, I picture Axel's uncle. Mother told me, in his younger years, Rudger was considered one of the handsomest men in the village, though his callous personality makes that hard to imagine. Rudger's thick, dark brows are his most distinctive feature—harsh lines that frame gloomy brown eyes.

Stepping onto the porch, I listen for any sounds within. I hear nothing, but Rudger is a lazy man who drinks and sleeps most of his days away. He could still be home.

I knock on the door and square my shoulders. A sharp twinge shoots through the S-curve in my spine. Sleeping on hay didn't do my crooked back any favors.

Rudger doesn't open the door or yell for me to go away. I knock a few more times, and when I'm greeted with only silence, I do what I've done best these past few weeks. I sneak inside. Tokens—or pennies—are easiest to steal when no one is home.

"Hello?" I take a tentative step into the dark and dank room. The air smells as musty as a cellar and as stifled as a chicken coop. "It's Clara Thurn," I add, though I'm starting to trust he isn't here. I push open the shutters in the kitchen to let in some light and better survey my surroundings.

I expected Rudger's house to be untidy, but this is something more. A thick layer of dust coats every surface, cobwebs cling to cupboards hanging open, and in the corner behind a rocking chair is a pile of rubbish that looks like the nest of some rodent.

By all appearances, Rudger has been absent for a long time.

I wander about, puzzled. Axel hasn't mentioned seeing his uncle lately. The last time I remember him coming here was three days before he was supposed to marry Ella. That was a year ago last summer, when he moved into the little house on the Dantzer farm. He said he wanted to gather a few more belongings. If any villagers have seen Rudger since then, they haven't spoken of it.

Is it possible Rudger became Lost without anyone noticing his absence—and for as long as a year? Or could it be that he's dead and somewhere on this farm, perhaps in one of his dangerous mines? He couldn't be in this house, or I would smell him rotting. I suppress a shiver and remind myself why I came—Ollie. The mystery of Rudger's absence will have to wait.

I poke around the two bedrooms, Rudger's and Ollie's, which later became Axel's. But I don't see anything to indicate that Axel ever lived here. He either took everything he owned, or Rudger threw it out.

There isn't much to show for Ollie either, only a juvenile etching on a wall, carved with something sharp like an awl or a nail. It shows a little person with a wide smile holding hands with two people. They must be Ollie's parents.

It's difficult to imagine anyone having led a happy life with Rudger, considering Axel's history, but perhaps Ollie had, and whatever love Rudger had in his heart died when his wife and son passed away from the same illness in the same week.

I sigh and turn in a circle. I didn't really think I'd find Ollie's pennies here. I just hoped to discover a clue as to their whereabouts, like a diary Ollie might have kept, though that seems a stretch for a seven-year-old.

I return to the front room, my gaze drawn to the pile of rubbish. In the forest, Ollie mentioned something about that spot. He was trying to prove his existence to Axel, who couldn't see him as a ghost like I did. Ollie had me relay a message: *There's a loose floorboard by the rocking chair where Papa hides his hard cider.*

It would make a good hiding place for other things too.

I kick away the nest of rubbish and tap my shoe on the floorboards until I find one that wiggles. I remove it and peer in the hole below. Dust floats around dingy bottles half-full with brackish-looking fluid.

I press myself to the floor, dig past the bottles, and reach farther back, hoping I don't get bitten by rats. My fingers brush a bit of cloth. I grab a corner and tug it out. A handkerchief. One with a faded blue-and-yellow diamond pattern. It's wrapped around something hard.

I unfold it and discover a beautiful key-wind pocket watch with gilt hands and a case of engraved silver. The face of the watch rests under a dome of crystal glass.

I brush my thumb over the watch. It's in pristine condition, without even a scratch. Why did Rudger hide it away?

I check for any inscriptions—there are none—but as I examine the handkerchief again, I spot two embroidered letters in the upper-left corner: *O.F.*

Ollie's initials.

Was the pocket watch meant for him?

Maybe Rudger intended to give him the watch when he was older, but then Ollie died and Rudger couldn't bear to use it for himself.

I wrap the watch in the handkerchief again and slip it in my pocket. I'm not sure how it can help me find Ollie's pennies, but it can at least serve as a token for Rudger, assuming he *is* Lost in the forest.

My stomach twists. If that's true, I have to count him among the others who are missing from Grimm's Hollow.

Which means Rudger is also a suspect in Bren Zimmer's murder.

CHAPTER 5

I stand in front of the looking glass in Mother's old bedroom, wondering what she'd think of me wearing another one of her dresses. It's common to repurpose clothing. No one in Grimm's Hollow is wealthy like the nobles who live so far away that they may as well be make-believe. But I still feel strange, like I'm donning the dress of some other girl's mother.

The older I become, the more out of touch I feel with myself. And I feel so much older since my journey into the Forest Grimm.

The dress is an oatmeal shade of linen with billowy gathered sleeves and floral embroidery at the skirt's hemline. Fiora altered it to fit me. It's a lightweight dress meant for a sunnier season, but I'm wearing stockings and an extra chemise for warmth. The burgundy bodice laced over the top will also keep out the chill. Its matted velvet has lost its luster, but it's still one of the finest pieces in Mother's wardrobe.

She wouldn't mind me wearing this dress, I decide. It's harder to convince myself she'd recognize me when I barely do.

If anything grounds me to my identity, it's the dull ache in my lower back, the ever-present reminder of my S-curved spine, the reason I can't wear prettier shoes. My sturdy pair lace up to my ankles and have a wedge-lift under my left heel, which straightens my hips and alleviates my pain.

When I'm finished getting ready, I wander into Grandmère's bedroom, wishing she could come. Maybe then I wouldn't feel like I'm wasting precious time at a festival. But I'll go for Henni's sake. She's looking forward to a happy occasion when she isn't under scrutiny.

I sit on the edge of Grandmère's mattress and adjust a few things on her bedside table. Her water glass sits too close to the edge, and a tincture bottle has its stopper removed. Did I forget to replace it? And where are her fortune-telling cards? I swear I left the deck here.

A light snore rattles from Grandmère's chest. She's sleeping as always, but a new pinch of rosiness warms her cheeks and helps me breathe easier. "You'll be back to your old self before you know it," I murmur.

A few seconds pass, and then a soft laugh tumbles out of her. Her violet eyes crack open and her mouth flits upward, tugging at a host of crisscrossing wrinkles. "That is the problem, *ma chère*. My 'old self' is that very thing: old."

I gasp to see how alert and articulate she is. "Grandmère!" I lean over and throw my arms around her.

"Careful, child. You'll crush the marrow from my bones."

I laugh, but don't pull away. She was never one to give hugs freely, but she'll have to put up with me. I'm not letting her go. At least for a good thirty seconds.

Finally drawing back, I bombard her with questions. "How are you feeling? Do you need something to eat? Or would you like to stretch your legs? We could take a turn around the pasture. Unless that's too much? What if I open the window for—"

"Clara, dear, I am quite all right," she grumbles, regaining some of her old fire. "You should be getting along to the festival. I can take care of myself." She shoos me with her hand.

I'm astonished she's even aware of the festival. "I don't have to go."

"Nonsense. Grimm's Hollow hasn't had a festival in over two

years. You are not going to miss this one because I woke up from a long nap."

That's a mild way of putting the last few weeks. "But—"

She *tsk*s at me. "Look at how pretty you are, like a vision of your mother. Axel will want to dance with you, and Henni will desire your company. You three deserve happiness while you can."

I open my mouth, ready to spout a fresh argument, when my mind snags. "What do you mean, *while we can?*"

The lines around Grandmère's mouth purse with deeper wrinkles. "The days of your youth are as fleeting as mayflies. Do not waste any opportunity to live life to its fullest."

I narrow my gaze. "But you're hinting at something more."

She searches my face and shifts to sit taller. "Now that you mention it, I would like to read your fortune again."

"Oh." I laugh, but it comes out strained like a frog's *ribbit*. "I don't think so."

She grabs my hand. Her skin is startlingly cold. "Your fate could have changed, given that you died. A reading would ease my heart. It might ease yours."

"I doubt that." I move to pull away, but her grip forges to iron.

"I've been having strange dreams, Clara." She speaks in a rush. "Visions of you returning to the forest. I know I won't be able to stop you. I only ask that you give me a better glimpse of what awaits."

The pulse at my wrist thuds under the pressure of her thumb. "Knowing my fate gives it too much power over me and . . ." I trail off. The blankets rustle where her other hand is hidden.

I yank the covers back. Her deck of fortune-telling cards is spread facedown on the mattress. Except for two cards: the Midnight Forest and the Dueling Rings.

My mind reels. The Midnight Forest I'm all too familiar

with—it represents something forbidden. And the Dueling Rings depicts two circles in a vertical stack, one golden circle for the sun and one silver circle for the moon. A symbol of a solar or lunar eclipse, depending which way the card is drawn, whatever "ring" is on top.

With the sun on top, it's a solar eclipse for an epic beginning.

With the moon on top, it's a lunar eclipse for a dramatic ending.

But I don't know which way the card was drawn. I knocked it askew when I threw back the blanket. Now it lies horizontally.

I spring away from the bed. "You shouldn't have done that! I didn't give my consent!"

"Please understand. It is better to know, *ma chère*." Grandmère's kind tone is harmless, but she doesn't fool me. She's a powerful woman, an Anivoyante who can shift into the most terrifying creature in the Forest Grimm. "Sit down again, and we will do a proper reading. I wasn't finished."

"*I'm* finished!" My furious voice takes me by surprise, but I don't want any part of this. I can't deny I've wondered about the Red Card—whether I'm still the Changer of Fate—but I don't want to live my new life with my destiny looming over me. I won't be a puppet on strings. I want my choices to be my own. "I'm leaving for the festival. You're right—I don't want to miss a moment."

"Clara, dear, stay a little longer. You have always been the child who wanted to know more."

"I've changed," I snap.

"Please allow me to try again. The Dueling Rings are important. Don't you see? You will either break the curse or make it final. I must draw again to know."

"Stop!" My voice drowns to a whisper. My mind is racing ahead, fitting myself into the role of either the curse breaker or the person who ruins the lives of everyone I love. Dizzily, I stumble to leave.

"Do not be angry, *ma petite chérie*. Somewhere in your heart, you desire to know. Otherwise, I could not have felt your blood sing so strongly. There are more cards waiting for you, more of your story that needs unfolding. Look, I was already holding one of them."

I can't say what possesses me to glance over my shoulder. I barely register turning my head, when my vision tunnels on the card. My knees threaten to buckle as I take in the faded red heart with a wash of blue painted over it, making the heart appear underwater.

Love Lost.

It represents lovers parted by a tragedy. A card drawn for my father before he went missing and was later found dead in Mondfluss River, tangled in his fishing net. Mother didn't know about his accident before she embarked into the forest for him and never returned.

My heart pounds like the roll of a kettledrum. I don't want Love Lost drawn for me. Not when the person I love is Axel. But it's too late. Grandmère *has* drawn it. Now it *is* part of my destiny.

My eyes burn as I trip back another step. "How could you?"

Grandmère's gaze holds sympathy, but no apology. "I do not choose your fate, Clara. I only reveal it. It is better to know and prepare. If you will only let me read the other cards—"

"No!" I rush out the door. I won't hear another word.

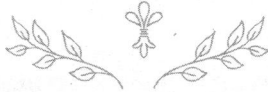

CHAPTER 6

I splash water on my face from a sheep trough. *Calm down, Clara.* Love Lost doesn't have to represent death. Lovers parted by a tragedy could mean they split up due to a heated argument. Axel and I have had plenty of those. We can survive another one, even if it separates us for a time. I'll make that time short. Solvable. And I'll make sure we live through it.

As for the Midnight Forest, well, doing forbidden things has become second nature. And when it comes to the Dueling Rings, I may have knocked that card askew, but I'm determined it was drawn with the sun stacked on top of the moon—a solar eclipse for an epic beginning. It will be an epic beginning for everyone in Grimm's Hollow.

I shake out my hands, lift my chin, and set off for the autumn festival.

Dusk is falling when I arrive on the fringes of the village square. Its focal point is the Cuckoo House, our meeting hall that features a giant cuckoo clock on the front facade. Every hour, a bird pops out of painted shutters and cuckoos the time as figurines of dancing couples twirl in and out of balcony doorways.

The villagers are amidst their own twirling dance, accompanied by pipes, fiddles, and clapping hands. The air is fragrant with apples, cinnamon, and roasted pumpkin. People drink mugs of freshly brewed ale and mulled cider. Children chase each other, rolling hoops with sticks. Lanterns hang from the eaves of half-timbered shops, and a great bonfire bounces light off the cobblestones.

The autumn festival is in full swing.

In the past, the villagers waited another month until the wheat was reaped and held a harvest festival. But the council wanted to celebrate sooner, so we're celebrating the return of the Book of Fortunes and the partial lifting of the curse.

What a different tune they're all whistling since the inquisition. As soon as the long-overdue autumn arrived, everyone's spirits lifted. The council ultimately decided to give Henni more time to make her one wish. Perhaps *Sortes Fortunae* needed to test the goodness in the hearts of the villagers before it allowed her to do so.

That's the real purpose of this celebration—to show our goodwill. It won't be enough to allow Henni to break the curse. Only bringing Bren's murderer to justice and restoring the missing page can do that. But at least my friends are allowed an occasion to enjoy themselves.

Fiora is standing near her children, her vibrant red hair tucked beneath a cap, while Hansel and Gretel frolic with a few boys and girls. From the handkerchief Gretel is tying over Hansel's eyes, it appears they're about to play blind man's bluff.

Ella dances with a group of girls who hold hands in a circle and step inward and outward, like a flower withering and blooming. Ella's chestnut hair shines in the light of the bonfire, and her complexion glows radiantly. She hasn't lost any beauty from her year spent in the forest.

Henni basks in the gaze of a sweet and bashful-looking teenaged boy. Ribbons flutter from her braided buns and match her lavender dress. The two of them converse near the pedestal that holds the Book of Fortunes.

For the occasion, the book has been moved from the meadow pavilion near the forest border and brought here by four night watchmen. Each wears a black cloak and wields a halberd. The boy flirting with Henni is one of them.

A group of villagers circles a man juggling knives. Boys chase a frog that leaps across my path. Girls weave heather into hair wreaths. I drift closer to all the revelry and survey my surroundings for Axel. I can't find him anywhere.

Love Lost.

No, not yet. Be reasonable, Clara.

I wander toward Henni. My path takes me by Ella as she breaks away from the circle of dancing girls.

"Ella, come back," Geneva Sommer calls. "We make an unlucky number without you."

Ella shoots me an exasperated look. "Goodness, these Sommer girls could dance all night. I swear they never tire." She turns to Geneva and imparts a diplomatic smile. "I'm afraid I need to give my feet a rest. But take my luck, dears. Six is as lovely a number as seven."

She waltzes away before Geneva can stop her. I should have waltzed away too, because Geneva turns her hopeful russet eyes on me. She smooths back a dark curl. "Clara, you'll help us, won't you?"

"Oh, um . . ."

"We're paying a special tribute to our sisters and friends. If we dance beautifully enough, the forest might send them back to us."

Guilt twists inside me as the other dancers' expectant faces crowd my vision. The Sommer girls, as the villagers call them, range in ages from thirteen to nineteen. Most are related, and those who aren't are still as close as family. The girls who share blood have ebony hair and bronze skin. Their grandmother came from a foreign land, like mine, although Ekhoe's journey to Grimm's Hollow took months, not weeks like Grandmère's.

There were once five sisters in the Sommer family, granddaughters of Ekhoe. Now two are Lost in the forest. Three remain in the village, along with two Sommer cousins and a dear friend.

The first Sommer girl who went Lost was the oldest, Lila. At the last harvest festival, Lila was crowned with wheat sheaves and proclaimed the harvest queen. Over the next several months, five more Sommer girls vanished into the forest, among them a friend, three cousins, and one of Lila's younger sisters.

I can see why Geneva is so eager to form a number of seven. For the Sommer girls, luck runs exceedingly thin.

"I'm so sorry," I say. "I never learned the circle dances." While other girls in Grimm's Hollow took up embroidery, learned an instrument, or mastered special dances, I was too busy obsessing over the two-card fate I shared with my mother and the one wish I hoped to make on *Sortes Fortunae* to save her.

"We can teach you." Geneva's tone verges on desperation. "And what a difference you'll make, you being favored by the forest." My gaze flicks past the circle, where Ekhoe, the Sommer family matriarch, pins me with an unforgiving stare. Her resentment seeps into my pores. She loathes me for not bringing back her Lost granddaughters, like I brought back Ella and Fiora.

"Maybe I'll join you at the next gathering," I say. "Excuse me."

As I hasten away, I vainly search for Axel. He was looking forward to tonight. I expected him to arrive first.

I sink onto a bench, my stomach cramping into knots. What if Love Lost means I never see him again? That's how my mother lost my father. One day, without warning, he just disappeared.

I release a slow breath and strive to relax. This is the very reason I didn't want my cards read. I can't live like this again, worrying if every happenstance might be manifesting my doomed fate—and Axel's fate, tangled with mine.

Nearby, the musicians play a folk song that jeers at my mood, all bright notes and whimsical beats. Herr Oswald, the village chairman, plays a simple willow pipe, while a few feet away, I spy another pipe of far better craftsmanship. It pokes out of a satchel in a pile of the other musicians' belongings.

The base of my neck tingles. I recognize that second pipe. I've heard it played before. It has a double reed and produces a rich, mellow sound. It belongs to Harlan, Herr Oswald's son and only child. Another Lost One. I sit taller, realizing Harlan's pipe can serve as a token in my collection. Claiming it is just what I need right now, something important to do rather than stew over the maybes of my destiny.

I wait until the chairman is distracted with a complicated string of notes, then meander over to the satchel and circle closer. My palms sweat. I don't want to get on Herr Oswald's bad side if he catches me. And he might. I haven't brought a bag of my own to hide the pipe. But I *could* tie it beneath my dress, use some of the length from my chemise to—

"Clara?"

I whirl around and nearly jump out of my skin.

CHAPTER 7

xel. I wait for my frantic pulse to settle, then smack him in the chest before throwing my arms around him. "Please stop scaring me like that!"

He chuckles and holds me tight. "Goodness, you're trembling. I swear I didn't mean to frighten you. I didn't recognize you right away. Your hair is different and . . ." He pulls back, his lower lip jutting in a mock pout. "Honestly, I just said your name."

He's right. I'm horribly overreacting. I flop my head against his shoulder. "I'm sorry. I didn't know where you were and . . ." I exhale and peek up at him. "Well, I was about to claim another token when you surprised me."

"Ah, now it makes perfect sense." He smirks, far too charming and handsome for his own good. He's dressed in his nicest pair of trousers, a crisp linen shirt, and a smart clover-green vest. Someone must have helped him press his clothes, homeless as he is. And from the soapy smell floating about his natural woodsy-pine scent, he also somehow snuck a bath. "I think it's time to admit you have a serious problem, Clara Thurn." He plays with one of the dark ringlets framing my face. "The good news is your hair looks very pretty."

I snort, but bless the hour it took to wrap each lock around heated curling tongs. I was hoping he'd notice. "What took you so long to arrive? I thought something terrible had happened."

"Why would you think that?"

Love Lost. The Midnight Forest. The Dueling Rings.

But I'm not about to tell him I received a new and dreadful fortune, even if I was hoodwinked into having my cards read.

"What is it?" he presses.

"Nothing, I just—"

"Clara, Axel." Herr Oswald strides over. I realize too late the music has stopped. "How fortuitous it is to see you. I was hoping you might . . ." His gaze drops, and I become painfully aware of how near I am to the satchel with his son's pipe. One of my shoes is planted within its strap.

"Oh . . ." My cheeks flush. "We were just admiring Harlan's instrument." I step away. "I remember how beautifully he used to play it."

"Yes, he did." Herr Oswald's face brightens, and he rakes his spindly fingers through his thinning hair. "I taught him, you know."

"Did you?"

"There isn't a woodwind I've met that I haven't mastered."

Axel stifles a laugh, and I want to smack his chest again because when he laughs, I do too. I have to bite the inside of my cheek to keep my face straight. Herr Oswald is not the humblest of men, but he generally means well. At least he wasn't cruel to Henni like some other council members during her inquisition.

"I've never heard you play a pipe like Harlan's." I'm simply making small talk, so I startle to see the chairman's eyes rim with tears. "I hope you see your son very soon," I add, sorry I upset him. "The Book of Fortunes will surely allow someone to break the curse before long." I omit Henni's name as that curse breaker so no more pressure is directed at her. I'll be the one to ensure it happens.

"Thank you, my dear." Herr Oswald dabs at his eyes. "Perhaps you are correct. The Forest Grimm has already granted a little forgiveness, has it not? And with this festival, perhaps it will grant more."

"Yes." I rock back on my heels. "Though, I have to admit, sometimes I wonder if the forest can forgive something as terrible as the murder that set the curse in motion."

"Oh?" Herr Oswald's wiry brows catch together, and Axel throws me a pointed look. The council doesn't know what the missing page told me. But this moment strikes me as an excellent opportunity to learn more about the investigation they conducted years ago.

"Do you think if you'd discovered the identity of the murderer, Henni would have been allowed to make her one wish? Perhaps that's what *Sortes Fortunae* really wants—restitution."

Herr Oswald balks. "I sincerely hope not. The council and I exhausted every line of inquiry. It took several long months. I'm afraid the murder is unsolvable."

"What a shame."

His gaze returns to Harlan's pipe, and his throat contracts. "Of course, it's not easy to forget the night Bren Zimmer was killed. And it had started as such a pleasant evening." He musters a wobbly grin. "My son and I were home practicing a song— Harlan had just replaced his double reed, you see—when I heard a commotion. I went outside to see what was happening and . . ." He turns away from the bonfire, and his eyes go flat, no longer reflecting its sparks. "That's when I found Bren's body."

I suppress a shudder. This part of the story I know. Everyone in Grimm's Hollow does. Herr Oswald, along with three others, were the first to discover Bren Zimmer in a forest stream, one near the village. Bren was lying facedown with a kitchen knife thrust in his back.

"What a terrible time that was." Herr Oswald draws a labored breath. "The curse began, and then your father was found dead only six days later."

I stiffen. Herr Oswald can't be implying a connection, but it reminds me of how many villagers suspected Father as Bren's murderer. When Father went missing, they supposed he'd escaped into the forest to dodge punishment—until he also turned up dead, though not murdered. "Did you say you wanted me and Axel to do something?" I suddenly have no more desire to discuss who died three years ago.

"Ah, yes." Herr Oswald straightens his waistcoat. "As both of you are in the forest's good graces, having survived your journey and whatnot"—he bats a hand as if he can also bat away the inquisition—"I was hoping you would do the honor of crowning our autumn queen."

Crowning a queen is a silly tradition that too many girls cry over when they're not chosen, but I suppose I should oblige. "Of course."

"Wonderful!" Herr Oswald claps his hands. "If you'll follow me."

Reluctantly, I leave Harlan's pipe behind, and join Herr Oswald and Axel on a platform near the Cuckoo House.

Herr Oswald waves his arms to gain everyone's attention, and soon the gathering quiets. "I have enlisted the help of Clara Thurn and Axel Furst to announce our autumn queen!" His voice reverberates off the surrounding shops.

Henni squeals and points at Ella, clearly hoping we'll declare her sister.

Two towheaded children emerge from the crowd. "We want to help!" Gretel bolts forward with Hansel, and they scramble onto the platform.

Fiora's cheeks are as red as her hair as she scurries after her children. "Come down at once!" she hisses, but Hansel has already leapt into Axel's arms, and Gretel paws for me to pick her up.

"It's all right," I say, hoisting Gretel on my hip. Fiora's children have a lot to learn about village etiquette, having spent more than two years on their own in the forest, but they mean no harm.

Herr Oswald shuffles to the back of the platform, unsettled by the twins. I try not to snort. He should have met them when they were Lost and intent on eating human flesh. They're practically angelic now.

After composing himself, he rejoins us and whispers the name of the autumn queen.

Axel looks to the children and grins. "Would you like to say it with us?"

Herr Oswald frowns. "No, that's not—

But Gretel is already blurting, "Geneba Sommer!"

A beat behind her, Hansel calls, "Geneea . . . Ommer!"

I laugh and declare with Axel, "Geneva Sommer!"

The square fills with ardent shouts and applause. Heads turn to locate Geneva. I also crane my neck, searching for the oldest Sommer girl still remaining in the village. As much as I dislike this tradition, it was a kind gesture for the council to choose one of the sisters of Lila, our last harvest queen.

The happy chatter dissipates, replaced by annoyed huffs that build into worried murmurs. Geneva is yet to be found. Her grandmother, Ekhoe, presses her hand to her heart and casts her gaze all around her.

Below the platform, a mess of black, white, and red catches my eye: a dead raven lying on the whitewashed cobblestones, its black wing feathers bent and its crushed body pooling with blood.

An icy chill racks me. I nudge Axel and show him. We turn the children away before they can see. Hansel and Gretel are no longer Lost and drawn to gruesome things.

Something very bad has happened. Ravens represent lost souls, and a dead raven is an omen of terrible misfortune.

Eloise Sommer, the mother of Lila and her sisters, dashes into the square. Her bun is loose, and dark strands fly wildly about her face. "Help! Please, someone help! I can't stop them!"

"Who?" Herr Oswald steps forward.

"All of them—all who are left! My daughters! My nieces! Their dear friend!" She sways like she might faint. Two people rush to support her. "They won't heed me!" Her nose runs as she sobs. "They're in some kind of trance." She spins and wags a finger at the road she came from. "They're headed for the Forest Grimm!"

CHAPTER 8

Apart from the night watchmen, who must remain guarding *Sortes Fortunae*, everyone at the autumn festival rushes from the village square to the meadow where Devotion Days are held, where lottery winners are chosen, where many people have died in their attempts to enter the Forest Grimm.

Axel and I aren't the first to arrive, having been briefly stalled by returning Hansel and Gretel to Fiora before racing the mile to the meadow. We took a shorter route, hoping to cut off the girls from the side. Now I see all six Sommer girls in profile:

The sisters, Geneva, Ilsa, Liese; their cousins, Sibilla and Helene; and their friend, Tildy. Their skin glistens feverishly. Their hair billows in the wind. The ruffles of their dresses flap in a riot of autumn colors: gold, rust, and umber.

They're only a few feet from the line of ashes, the demarcation between the village and forest that runs the perimeter of Grimm's Hollow. Under the light of the almost full moon, those ashes glow eerily, as if they're the residue of something unnatural.

"Geneva!" I call. My voice is drowned out by many others also crying after the girls. "Geneva!" I use all the air in my lungs. If she hears me, she makes no indication. She's the nearest girl to the line. Her gaze remains transfixed on the forest.

I dash forward. My ears ring from the screams multiplying around me. More villagers pour into the meadow, moths drawn to the flame of this horrible spectacle. Sixty-seven villagers have gone Lost in the forest, but until now never more than two at once. Six is unfathomable.

Axel and I are still several yards away. We'll never reach them in time. Garrick Unger, a spry man in his twenties, is the closest to the girls. He dives for Tildy, but falls short and takes a hard tumble on a large stone.

Berdina Fischer, lean and tall, is gaining on Helene. She grasps her by the sleeve, but it tears at the shoulder. Helene's arm slips free. Her expression remains serene, her gaze latched on the forest. Berdina swipes again, but trips and loses momentum.

"Geneva!" My lungs burn from yelling. She's heartbeats away from the line of ashes. Her mother, Eloise, and grandmother, Ekhoe, also scream for her to stop. They're nowhere near her, even more helpless to make a difference.

Axel picks up speed, running impossibly fast. I glimpse his panicked eyes as he outdistances me. He's the closest to the girls now, just a few yards behind. This is a nightmare relived for him. It's how Ella went Lost last summer. Like the Sommer girls, she was also overcome by a strange trance. When she crossed the border, the forest welcomed her, but it shut out Axel.

Geneva steps over the line. I curse. Ilsa and Liese follow, crossing at the same time. The villagers' screams turn to wails. Sibilla moves across the line. Then Helene. Axel stretches out his arm. He's inches away from Tildy, the youngest girl, only thirteen years old.

Please, please, please. Let him at least save one.

Tildy's foot lifts. Axel lunges. He reaches. Misses.

Tildy crosses over.

Axel can't stop barreling forward. He tumbles over the line. The wild grass writhes and coils around his ankles. He crashes to the ground.

"Axel!" I catch up to him, but halt before I step over the ashes. We reach for each other. Our hands clasp. I tug with all my might. *Don't take him, don't take him.* He's unprotected. He isn't wearing his scarf dyed with red rampion. *Don't let this be Love Lost.*

I curse myself for not listening to Grandmère. She read my cards and warned me to prepare. But I didn't bring my cape. I didn't tell Axel to get his scarf. I didn't do anything.

He manages to stand, but the wild grass grows unnaturally fast. It snakes up his arms and pins him in place.

"Don't let go!" I harden my grip, but I'm losing strength.

Ella appears beside me with a long knife. She cuts the grass tethered to his ankles. Henni arrives holding a halberd from one of the night watchmen. She hacks at the grass binding Axel's arms. Like me, the sisters are careful not to cross the ashes on foot, but we're forced to reach across them. Weeds sprout and grasp for us. Berdina, recovered from her fall, races to help. Garrick limps toward us too.

It turns out we don't need them. All at once, Axel is released. He and I fall backward, along with Ella and Henni. We land in a heap on the meadow side of the line.

I haven't caught my breath when the earth starts shaking like it did when Briar Rose's castle crumbled. We're shoved toward the line. No, the line is moving toward us—at an alarming rate.

We clamber away. Crawl, scoot, roll. We yank each other up. Fissures open in the earth, left and right. We run around them, but careen and stumble.

The quaking must last only thirty seconds, but it feels like an eternity. I cling to Axel for fear he'll still be stolen away.

Abruptly, the ground settles. We stop running and gasp for breath. We look behind us to absorb what's happened. Rolled forward by the earth and remarkably intact, the line of ashes has drawn inward over most of the meadow, a distance of nearly fifty yards.

The villagers shout the names of the Sommer girls again. The earthquake has knocked the girls down, but they're rising once more, their bodies stiff and mechanical, like the clockwork dancers of the Cuckoo House.

"Geneva, come back!" I cry. "Bring the others!" My voice sounds strangely foreign and hysterical, as if it belongs to someone else. "I'll dance with you! I want you to teach me!" I'm one of over a dozen people screaming, and the Sommer girls have ears for no one. "Please!" Despair caves in on me. "I want to help you form a number of seven! I want—" My voice breaks, going hoarse. I dig my hands in my hair. This is all my fault. Had I not refused Geneva, I could have prevented this.

Some of the Sommer girls stare back at us blankly. Others are already turning, moving toward the deeper reaches of the forest. Soon all have pivoted away. They drift into the darkness until the needle-tipped boughs and skeletal branches close over them and cut them from view.

They are gone. Lost.

Lost like my mother went Lost.

Lost like so many others I couldn't save, who are probably dead.

It isn't right, but I'll make it right. I can't have lived for nothing.

Breathless, I turn in the direction of my cottage, holding fast to the rose-red ribbon tied around my wrist. I need to take my journey now. I can't wait for more tokens or hope of guidance from Grandmère. If I'm quick enough, I can pick up the girls' trail.

"Clara?" Axel catches my arm.

"I need my cape," I stammer. He nods and takes my hand.

Councilwoman Hazel Roth calls out to the gathering. Her

voice pierces the shattered quiet that's overtaken us. "Everyone, back to the village square! Herr Oswald has declared an emergency meeting!"

Karl Wagner, the council's lackey, heads in my direction, no doubt to steer me and Axel there. I tense, ready to bolt and outrun him, when my gaze rivets to Henni. Two large men are already ushering her away.

Panic swarms me. I feel the inquisition happening all over again, the joy and hope from the change of seasons forgotten in the wake of losing the rest of the Sommer girls.

Axel and I exchange a grim look and allow Karl to guide us to the village square.

CHAPTER 9

Situated near the village council, I sit on a bench in between Henni and Axel, my shaking hand gripped around his like a vise. Hansel sits on Axel's lap. Gretel is on his other side, her arm linked through his. They must have seen him almost be taken. I didn't realize how attached they'd become to us.

Fiora and Ella stand at our backs. The seven of us gravitated to each other and formed a protective bubble. But from the gnawing feeling building inside me, I feel that bubble about to burst.

"This is your fault!" Eloise Sommer points at Henni. "If you had tried harder, *Sortes Fortunae* would have listened to your wish. You could have prevented all of this from happening! My daughters would still be with us!" She cries openly, her sobs harrowed and raging.

Henni blinks back tears. "I'm sorry."

"Don't apologize." Ella clamps a hand on her shoulder. "This isn't your doing. It's a terrible tragedy, and that's all."

The council members murmur, gathered on the platform near the Cuckoo House. More people raise their voices to blame Henni. Mr. and Mrs. Dantzer plead with them to see reason, but the crowd won't relent.

"Enough!" Herr Oswald holds up his hands, but the villagers only grow louder. The corners of his eyes droop as he looks to the night watchmen. "Bring forward the Book of Fortunes."

At last, the people hush. The night watchmen set down their halberds and lift the pedestal that holds *Sortes Fortunae*. Per custom, no one is allowed to touch the sacred book. That act is reserved for those ready to make their one wish.

Once the pedestal is moved onto the platform, the watchmen back away, and Herr Oswald motions to Henni. "Come, dear. You must try your luck again."

"No!" Henni pales, even in the warm light of the bonfire. One of her hair ribbons has come undone, making her appear fifteen again. "I can't! Please, it won't work. The book is still missing a page."

"Don't ask her to tempt fate!" Ella's naturally airy tone turns vicious, a stark reminder of how furious she became as Cinderella when we raced away from her forest wedding ball.

"I fear it is the forest asking," Herr Oswald replies. "What happened tonight is a clear sign—it's the forest demanding that someone fully break the curse. You are the only one who can, Henrietta. You are the only person of age who hasn't already made a wish."

"But this isn't a proper wish ceremony," I interject. I've seen for myself how swiftly the villagers can form a mob, and I'm sure that's what will happen if Henni fails to break the curse again. "There is no curtain. She has no privacy! No one can be allowed to hear her make her wish."

"We will find a solution." A growl punctuates Herr Oswald's normally even-keeled voice. He fixes a sterner look on my friend. "Henrietta—"

He's cut off as *Sortes Fortunae* flies open. Its front cover slams over onto the pedestal's tabletop. He hasn't even touched it. No one has. There isn't so much as a breeze to stir a leaf. But the pages fan forward in a gust, as if invisible fingers are rapidly flipping through them.

Herr Oswald backs away, blanching. The book finally stills. The crowd holds quiet, scarcely breathing. There's only the crackling of the bonfire, the baying of a hound, the buzzing of an insect as it flits past my face. Herr Oswald inches forward to the book again and gasps. "Words are forming! *Sortes Fortunae* is writing to us!"

I jerk to my feet. Henni and I exchange a wide-eyed glance. Will the book share the clause about the missing page again—but this time tell everyone? They'll finally believe us.

But the villagers have other theories:

"It's revealing how to break the curse!"

"The forest is showing us mercy!"

"Our Lost Ones will come back!"

A few council members gather around Herr Oswald, also witnessing the book's magic. I drift closer, overcome with sharp possessiveness for whatever those words are. The last two times *Sortes Fortunae* wrote something, it wrote to me. As I stop just shy of the pedestal, I glimpse the hope draining from the council members' faces.

"What has the book written?" someone in the crowd demands.

Herr Oswald grips the edges of the pedestal and reads:

"A partially broken curse
Is a truce with a crack.
Soon it will shatter
And claim Grimm's Hollow back."

His eyes lift, heavy and somber. "It's a warning. It's telling us that, unless the curse is fully broken, what happened tonight will happen again. More people will become Lost, and the line of ashes will continue to encroach upon our village . . . until Grimm's Hollow is no more."

For a staggering moment, no one speaks. Horror spirals inside me. I can't fathom losing this village forever—having my cottage, my farm, all the places filled with memories of my parents taken away. I'd be losing them all over again, but worse. It would be as if they'd never existed.

Herr Oswald rubs the space between his eyes, like all the weight of saving the village rests upon his shoulders. But it's not his burden. It's mine.

The Midnight Forest and the Dueling Rings are calling for me. I'm the one who must do the forbidden and enter the forest again, then either solve the murder and return the missing page so Henni can break the curse, or fail in my quest and make the curse final.

Whoosh.

The pages of *Sortes Fortunae* flip forward again. Herr Oswald startles backward and bangs his leg against the pedestal. It teeters and the book slides off . . . toward the ground . . . toward the mess of the dead raven. No one's cleaned it up.

I dive for the book. I can't have it land in the blood of a bad omen.

The book thuds into my arms and remains open, as if its magic holds the binding stiff. In a flash, a flood of new words spills over the page in green ink:

The time you have left
Is as a clock's gilt hands.
Measure it wisely
Lest the killer seize command.

Before I can reread them—or even blink—the words vanish. "Clara Thurn." Herr Oswald moves to the edge of the platform and stares down at me. "Return the book to the pedestal at once."

Dizzy, I do as he bids, but scarcely track my movements. My mind is awhirl. No one saw the second riddle but me. Should I share it? Would that help Henni or make her predicament worse?

"What are we waiting for?" someone calls. "The Dantzer girl must make her wish!" The demand echoes, repeated by others across the square. A man grabs a torch from a sconce. Another one snatches a scythe on display.

My heart clatters. I rush off the platform and beeline for Axel. "We have to get Henni out of here!"

Fiora overhears us. "Follow me now!"

My friends rise quickly. Axel carries Hansel. Fiora scoops up Gretel. Ella grabs Henni's hand.

We launch into a dead run.

Mr. and Mrs. Dantzer push back the villagers that pursue us. The night watchman who had eyes for Henni assists them. Even Conrad, my farmhand, along with workers from the Dantzer farm, step in to help us escape.

We sprint past the pile of bags and satchels that belong to the festival musicians. I spy Harlan's double-reed pipe. I seize my opportunity and steal it.

Once I touch its polished barrel, the world rocks. My eyesight flickers in and out. I glimpse a young boy with beautifully down-turned eyes. He's stacking wooden blocks to form a toy castle.

I stumble as the world rights itself again and my eyesight levels.

The boy is gone.

Axel wheels back for me. He wraps his free arm around my waist. "Are you all right?"

Shaken, I glance at the pipe.

"Clara?" Axel's urgent tone brings me back to reality.

"I'm fine." My body flushes as I race away with him and the others.

It was only a flash, a stolen moment of the past, but I think—I dare to hope—I just had a vision.

CHAPTER 10

"We can't stay here for long," Fiora says, wisps of red hair glued to her perspiring face. We're hiding beneath a small bridge on the outskirts of her father's land. The canal beneath it that's used to irrigate the orchards has run dry for the season. "They'll search all our homes and farms. We need to find somewhere to hide Henni, and then separate and pretend not to know her whereabouts."

"Axel and I intend to leave for the forest," I say. "If Henni came with us—"

"No," Ella says flatly.

"But no one can pursue her in the forest." Only we know the secret of red rampion.

"Lost Ones can pursue her." Ella crosses her arms. "They can kill her," she whispers, sensitive that Hansel and Gretel are in our company. "She's lucky to have survived the four of us when we were Lost."

Henni lets out a loud breath. "Do I get a say in this?"

"No," Ella snaps. "Not when Father and Mother just got both of their daughters back."

"So what am I supposed to do?" Henni throws up her hands. "Hide until Clara and Axel return?"

"Yes."

"Then Mother and Father will think I've gone to the forest anyway," Henni mutters.

"That's better than you being there."

"Wait." I scoot closer to the sisters. "This is actually a good plan."

"What is?" Ella asks.

"Telling everyone Henni has left with me and Axel. They won't doubt it since she did it before. Meanwhile, you hide her somewhere in the village. If people believe she's gone, there won't be a search party."

The group falls quiet as they warm up to the idea. Hiding will be miserable for Henni, but it will keep her safe, and as the only person who can break the curse, she needs to stay safe.

She stares at her beautiful slippers she's painted with lilacs to match the lavender of her festival dress. "What if . . ." Her voice quavers. ". . . you don't come back."

"We'll come back." Axel imparts a reassuring smile. "We know how to navigate the forest now. We'll stick to the water. Plus, Clara already has a strong plan for how to solve the murder."

"What plan?" asks Ella.

"Oh, um . . ." My cheeks heat. My scheme to rely on visions of Lost Ones makes me feel like a fraud, unsure as I am if I can have any more. Even if what I saw when I grabbed Harlan's double-reed pipe was a vision, I don't know how to make it happen again or how to direct it to a specific moment in time. "I've collected tokens for—"

Faint shouts drift in our direction. The villagers are coming. It's time to separate.

Fiora steps out of the canal. "We still haven't thought of a hiding spot for Henni."

Ella rises after her. "There's a crawlspace under our pantry."

Henni balks. "I can't live down there!"

"It will only be for a day or two." Ella lifts her up. "Then we'll find somewhere better."

I climb out and hug Henni fiercely. "Don't worry. I promise to make everything right."

Her eyes glisten. "Take my luck, Clara." She hiccups on a soft sob. "Please come back."

"I will." *I have to.*

I hug Ella as well, an unusual occurrence in our tentative friendship, but it allows me to whisper, "Rudger's home could do as a hiding place. It's been abandoned." She draws back with a questioning stare, but I can't say more. I haven't broken the news to Axel.

Fiora takes her children's hands. "Clara, will you join me at the house? It'll be quick. I've made something for your journey."

"Of course. Just a moment." I cross to Axel. "Let's meet in an hour in the north pasture, all right?" The last riddle from the Book of Fortunes etches across my mind:

The time you have left
Is as a clock's gilt hands.
Measure it wisely
Lest the killer seize command.

"Actually, make that forty-five minutes. Can you get my tokens from the hayloft?"

"Planning on it."

"And pack warm things and food and—"

"I know what to do." He gives me a peck on the mouth. "See you soon."

As he rushes off with Ella and Henni, following the same path, I hasten away with Fiora, Hansel, and Gretel. A couple of minutes later, we reach the home they share with Fiora's hermit father. I can count on one hand the times I've seen him. Apart from tending to his orchards, he keeps to himself.

Hansel and Gretel hug me goodbye, and Fiora hurries them inside and returns with a bundle of cloth. The faraway shouts grow nearer. We need to hurry.

"Remember how I took your measurements when I altered your dress?" she asks. "I know you have the lift in your shoe, but I thought a corrective corset could also ease your back pain."

"A corset?" I take the bundle she presents me.

"A bodice to wear over your dress."

"Oh . . . that's very kind of you, but corsets and bodices usually worsen my pain." The one I'm wearing, meant for my mother, is a case in point. My lower back and right hip throb with a vengeance.

"This one is tailored to your shape. It will stabilize you and only straighten your spine a little."

Curious, I unfold the bodice and quickly examine it. The fabric is a sage-green brocade, beautiful in its subtle floral pattern and practical in its sturdiness. The bodice is cut in a lovely shape as well, like a vest with a low-scooping neckline. Laces tie up the middle and along each swell of the hips to customize its support.

Fiora shuffles in place. "But if you don't think it will—"

"It's perfect." I kiss her cheek. "You thought of everything. Thank you."

She smiles shyly, but then her jaw muscle tightens. Rarely does she remind me of Rapunzel, but now, under the intensity of her gaze, I feel like I'm back in her tower and within the reaches of her strangling red hair. Her hand fastens around my wrist. "Show the murderer no mercy."

My mouth goes dry. She may as well have said *Don't hesitate to kill.*

In a rush, I'm taken back to Briar Rose's castle. Striding toward my Lost mother, gathering my mettle. I plunge the spindle into her heart. She falls to her knees. Blood sputters from her mouth, she collapses to the ground, her eyes lose focus, and—

Fiora lets go of me. "You better run."

I take a ragged breath and dart away.

My memories keep barraging me. Blood pours from a gash

on the Grimm wolf's throat now, Grandmère's wound from my mother, much like the fatal wound that killed me.

I spin back to face Fiora. "My grandmother hasn't been well. I think she's turned a corner, but—"

"I promise to check on her often."

"Thank you," I breathe.

The villagers are almost upon us. I slip behind the trees. Fiora situates herself on the porch's rocking chair, her chin high, her posture queenly. For as timid as she appears sometimes, her bones are made of iron. She will be a force to reckon with.

A second before the villagers barge into the clearing, she sends me a look that assures me she'll fare fine on her own.

I tuck the bodice against my chest and rush homeward.

By the time I reach the cottage, my lungs are burning. I hurry into Grandmère's room. I need to warn her about the villagers and—

I skid to a halt at the foot of her bed. Her skin is flushed and damp with sweat. She fidgets restlessly, eyes closed. My shoulders fall. Her fever is back.

I sit on her bed. "Grandmère?"

She moans.

My gaze shifts to the deck of cards on her bedside table, and my stomach knots. In the past few weeks, she had one moment of wellness and clarity, and I ruined it by arguing with her.

I brush my thumb over the back of her hand, the skin loose and age-spotted. "I'm so sorry we fought. I know you were only trying to help."

Unbidden, two cards I've labored to forget surface to mind, cards Grandmère drew for herself weeks ago:

The Fanged Creature for an untimely death.

And Fortune's Cup, drawn upside down, foretelling a tragedy.

"How can I leave you like this?" I whisper.

"Curse . . . break it," Grandmère murmurs.

"It's Henni who will break the curse, not me."

"You . . ." Grandmère's violet eyes flutter open, barely long enough to capture mine. ". . . are necessary."

Impossible. I know too little about the magic in my bloodline. "I wish . . ." My voice catches, and I hang my head. *I wish you could have taught me more about my ability.* But I can't say that, not when it's a regret there's no time to solve. "I wish to make you proud."

She drags her free hand across her quilt and rests it over our clasped fingers. "You will, *ma petite chérie.*" Her voice rattles like it's clawing through gravel. "You will live. I will die to make it so."

"Please don't say that."

"Go," she prods. "They are coming."

I look out the window. Nothing stirs in the darkness. I rush from the room to peek out the front door. I see no one, but I believe my seer grandmother.

I race outside and find Conrad in the smokehouse. I bless his trust in me as he listens to every word I blurt about Grandmère's worsened illness, the villagers coming, and how Henni will be leaving with me and Axel to the forest—a lie he must believe.

His brow hardens and he nods. "Gather your things. I'll pack food."

"Thank you!" I hug him and run back to the cottage.

I grab everything I can think of. A new map, focused on the waterways of the Forest Grimm. My lantern, candles, flint kit. A notebook and graphite stick to record thoughts about the murder. A handheld crossbow for bird hunting and tackle for fishing. My emergency apothecary supplies. A warmer bedroll of fleece. A small purse with a few coins on the off chance I need them. Ollie's pocket watch, still wrapped in the handkerchief.

Harlan Oswald's double-reed pipe. Axel will bring the other tokens from the hayloft.

I change into a brown woolen skirt and pale blue blouse with roomy sleeves. I tie up the bodice Fiora made me over the top, amazed at how perfectly it fits and the comfort it lends my spine. I throw on a belt with a sheathed knife. I'm already wearing my best shoes for travel—the pair with the wedge-lift underneath my left heel.

I hurry to the front room and open the large chest carved with evergreens and woodland animals. I dig past the linens and knitted blankets until I find a mantle made from a wolf pelt and my red-hooded cape.

My throat tightens. I lift the cape from the chest and skim my fingers across the hole I've mended, the spot where Axel slammed the spindle of a spinning wheel inside my heart. Around the stitched threads are two stain rings from my blood and my mother's. I was able to wash out the rest, but those spots never came clean.

Shouts float toward me. The villagers are arriving.

I fling on the cape, throw the fur mantle around my shoulders, and hasten into Grandmère's bedroom one last time. I remove the rose-red strip of wool from my wrist and tie it around hers, our remembrance of Mother from the Tree of the Lost. It can serve as Grandmère's remembrance of me too.

"I won't fail," I promise, though she's too deep in feverish sleep to comprehend me.

Eyes wet, I kiss her brow and stuff her deck of cards in my pack, hoping she'll forgive me for taking them—they may help me conjure visions—then I go outside and meet Conrad, who shoves another pack of food into my arms. I sprint to the end of the north pasture, where Axel is waiting, his red scarf wrapped around his neck.

I embrace him and try to steady myself. Our plan feels more fragile by the moment. I wanted more time to prepare, to gather tokens, to hone my ability. But by leaving now, we have a chance to catch up to the Sommer girls. Perhaps they aren't Lost yet, only lost in the forest, and the trance that lured them has broken. We could guide them back home.

"We can do this." Axel takes my hand.

I nod. Breathe my last breath of village air. Thurn farm air.

Falling into step with him, I cross the encroaching line of ashes.

The forest welcomes us with a breezy sigh and a gentle twirl of autumn leaves, as if it hadn't attacked us hours ago. A truce I won't trust.

We hurry onward, and I pray that Henni will be safe, that Grandmère will recover, and the words I vowed will somehow come true. . . .

I won't fail.

CHAPTER 11

I inhale the heady scent of cloistered pines, perfumed with the musk of brittle autumn leaves. It's a beautiful smell, a dangerous smell. I'm in a place that would kill me the instant I let my red cape fall from my shoulders.

Clara, Clara, the boughs of pines and oaks seem to call to me, writhing above in the darkness. *We've been waiting for you.*

I'm sure I'm only imagining it, like I once imagined my mother's voice on the wind, beckoning me to save her when I was stuck in the village. But what if I was never dreaming? What if I've always been called here, the woods where I was meant to die?

Hand in hand, Axel and I rush through the tall grass, circling the village on the forest side of the line of ashes. We keep those ashes in sight as we weave around trees and underbrush, working our way back to the spot where the Sommer girls were lured into the forest. Until we find a stream or river—unmoving anchors, unlike the trees that like to shift in the night—we need to moor ourselves to something else.

I tell Axel about *Sortes Fortunae*'s latest riddle as we reach the place where we last saw the girls and scour the darkness for their trail.

"The time you have left
Is as a clock's gilt hands.
Measure it wisely
Lest the killer seize command."

Frown lines pucker Axel's forehead, underlit by the lantern he's carrying. "How would the killer seize command? Command of what? The village? But how would ruling Grimm's Hollow benefit anyone, especially if the curse doesn't break?"

"Maybe it's command of something else, then." I crouch to examine what might be a footprint. Most of the ground has been disturbed by the earthquake, marred by deep fissures and root-ridden mounds. "Like command of the forest and its magic."

"But would the forest ever allow that? It wrought the curse in the first place because of the killer."

"Maybe it doesn't matter *how* the killer could seize control. What's most important is the warning to hurry up—find out who that person is and where they're hiding the missing page." I vainly search for more footprints. "Although finding anything right now seems impossible."

Axel stops short in the wild grass. "I've lost set of the footprints I was following. We should put this off until daylight, Clara. There's no sense in losing sleep over a task that's hopeless in the middle of the night, no matter the warning to hurry."

My stomach clenches. I hate that by halting, we might fall behind the Sommer girls even more. Pursuing the girls can't help us solve who murdered Bren Zimmer, but Axel and I wouldn't be able to live with ourselves if we didn't try to save them. Besides, we have no idea where to set out searching for the murderer, so we may as well be traveling somewhere.

Resigned to set up camp, we drift away from the ash-lined border and settle farther into the forest, though we keep a distant view of the village meadow to hold our bearings.

"Is it horrible that I'm grateful for dead trees?" Axel says, hacking at the limbs of a beech that isn't just leafless and dormant for the season; its wood is also dry and ready to burn, another strange occurrence of the partial lifting of the curse—or its worsening, depending on how you look at it.

Dead trees normally take two to three years to season like this, but in the weeks since we were here last and returned, dead trees actually exist now, where all were eerily alive before. Thankfully this one doesn't have a dead face in it. Those seem to be lost deeper in the woods.

"I think you're mostly grateful you have an excuse to swing that hatchet around." I smirk, trying to match Axel's lighthearted tone. Knowing him, it's to bring some positivity to the end of a long and harrowing day. He's gifted like that, a veritable walking ray of sunshine. I watch him play with the short-handled ax he's brought. "You remind me of a fortune-telling card in Grandmère's deck. The Woodsman's Hatchet."

He tosses his hair back and throws me a smolder. "So the woodsman is ruggedly handsome, then?"

"No." I snort. "He's painted with a gnarled beard and bulbous nose. But you share the same manly pride for felling trees."

"Manly pride?" Axel takes another whack at a thick limb. "Is that what that card means?"

I lay out my bedroll. "No, it represents temporal needs being met."

"I can live with that."

I shake my head with a little laugh. "You act as if Grandmère drew the card for you."

"She couldn't have." He winks. "I've never let her read cards for me. But I can pretend." With another deft swing, he cleaves the branch from the trunk. "You have to admit"—he nods at his work—"that was impressive."

I hold my smile for his sake, but what I'm really thinking about is how Grandmère actually did draw cards for someone without permission. Me.

"Clara?"

"Yes?"

Axel's river-blue eyes squint, glittering in the glow of my lantern. "I just asked if you were happy we didn't have to light any more pine cone fires. Not that it matters." He sets down his hatchet. "Are you all right?"

The Midnight Forest. The Dueling Rings. Love Lost.

I can't fathom what else Grandmère would have drawn to divine my future.

I brush leaves off my bedroll. "Yes, I was just . . . thinking about the murderer again." I will never tell him about Love Lost. Ever. Fate doesn't need an amplifier. It's better that he doesn't know, better that he loves me without feeling like he needs to cast up walls around his heart. "The more I mull over everything, which isn't much, the more I wonder if I'm missing a clue."

"Let's talk it over then." He carries a stack of freshly chopped wood to the hole I've dug to build the fire. With the help of my flint kit and a little dry moss for tinder, we soon have a blaze of crackling flames.

I pull out my notebook, open it to a dog-eared page, and take a calming breath. "A comet appeared in the sky on the night Bren was murdered," I begin. Many people in Grimm's Hollow saw the sign. They said they should have known it was an omen of something dreadful.

"The Book of Fortunes went missing that same night," I continue. "Which means the murderer must have already torn out the missing page." According to the riddle the book gave me at Henni's wish ceremony, it had to be the murderer who did it.

Only one page holds the secret to finally restoring peace.
Only one person is to blame for breaking it.

Both must be found, for one has the other,
And together they hide in the Forest Grimm.

"Although the page could have been torn out a different night," Axel notes.

I'd already thought of that. "But why would anyone tear out a page unless they hoped to make more wishes with it? I bet they couldn't."

"Why?" He warms his hands over the fire.

"Henni couldn't make a wish because the book was missing a page, so it stands to reason that it wouldn't work the other way around—with the *page* missing the *book*."

"But *you* were able to make a second wish," Axel says.

"I'm not so sure. I spoke the incantation, and I asked the book to hear my wish to know where its missing page was, but I don't know if it really counted as a wish."

"Then why did *Sortes Fortunae* give you an answer?"

"I think the book would have shared the riddle anyway, like it did in the village square tonight. It wants its missing page to be found. And quickly."

He still doesn't look convinced.

"All I'm saying is it was more like the book was just speaking to me." I shrug, unable to explain it any better. "I don't think the book grants second wishes. Real wishes. For bigger things."

His brow is still screwed up in confusion. "So what else have you written in your notebook?"

"Bren was stabbed in the back with a kitchen knife, according to the first four witnesses who found him dead in the stream. Then those people left—some to get more help, and some to hunt for the murderer—and when others returned, the murder weapon was missing."

Axel scratches his jaw. "Did the witnesses describe anything unique about the knife?"

"They never took the time to examine it." Residents of Grimm's Hollow aren't accustomed to crime, so they don't make the best sleuths. "They were more thorough when they discovered my father's body," I add, trying to maintain a casual air. I have no wish to revisit my father's death.

When Herr Oswald came to our cottage to bring the news, Grandmère shooed me away so I wouldn't hear the grisly details. But I hid in the hallway and gleaned everything. Father's body was horribly decomposed, not only from the river, but also from water scavengers and carrion-eating birds. He was only recognizable because of his engraved wedding ring.

Love Lost.

My chest aches, and I close the notebook with trembling fingers.

Always keen to sense anything amiss with me, Axel runs his fingers down my hair. Some of the curls have held from how I wore them for the festival. "I never had the chance to explain why I was late to the village square tonight," he says.

I meet his eyes, which have become shy, his natural confidence shifting into something more vulnerable. "What happened?"

He slips his hand into his pocket. "I was making something for you, and it took longer than I thought to finish." He lowers his head, and a lock of tousled hair drops across his brow. "I wanted it to be more beautiful . . . but I hope it's the thought that counts." He withdraws his hand and uncurls his fingers.

A little carved and varnished object lies in his palm, bathed amber in the firelight. An acorn. Its stem is wrapped in fine twine and looped onto a length of thin red ribbon.

"When your mother passed away, you left the acorn she gave

you with her," Axel says softly. "So I wanted you to have another one to remember her by."

My eyes grow hot and blurry. "Axel . . ." Warmth spreads through my body. "It's beautiful. Thank you."

He fidgets with his scarf. "The crosshatching on the acorn's cap is a bit crooked and—"

"Stop." I bring my arms around him. "You're the most thoughtful boy in the world. What did I ever do to deserve you?"

Pressed close, he kisses my earlobe and whispers, "I ask myself the same question every day."

I snort with laughter. "You're ruining the moment."

"Am I?"

No. Nothing could ruin this. Love Lost be damned.

He pulls back a little. "May I tie it on you?"

I nod, utterly smitten with him.

He draws my hair to the side and strings the red ribbon around my neck so the acorn rests in the hollow of my throat, just above the laces that tie my cape together. His fingers brush over the charm and drift across my collarbone. "You make it more beautiful."

My stomach is aflutter, and I kiss him tenderly. "Will you make a pact with me?"

"All right. But go gentle on me. I would promise you anything right now."

"Let's be smarter than we were the last time we came to the forest. Let's swear not to trust anyone we meet here." I cup his face in my hands. "Let's only trust each other."

"I can promise that. Gladly." He presses his lips to my brow. "I promise to trust no one but you, Clara."

I take a cleansing breath. He's all I could ever want. I won't let anything change that. "I promise the same."

Our mouths touch again, and his hands thread into my hair. He slips the pins loose from the bun holding the top half of my curls up. Locks cascade around my shoulders. I draw my arms around his neck, and his hands sweep under the folds of my cape. He scoots me back to our bedrolls, their fleece baked warm from the fire.

Hoot, hoot. An owl calls as we're about to lie down. I barely register the noise. Two hoots mean nothing. Only three hoots close together forebode danger.

Hoot, hoot, hoot.

I stiffen. Axel pulls back. "What is it?"

"Did you hear—?"

Maniacal laughter pierces the night. Dread cuts me to the bone.

Trust no one.

I jerk to my knees and scramble for my crossbow and knife.

Before I can grab either, something fist-sized and wet strikes me square in the face.

CHAPTER 12

Shrieking, I reach to pull whatever has struck me off my face. It could be poison or acid—I wouldn't put anything past this forest and a Lost One—but before I can cast it away, the ground shifts and the light of the campfire extinguishes. Everything goes black, soundless. I try to shout Axel's name, but I have no voice to cry with, no air to draw from my lungs.

The campfire flares to life again. Noise rushes into my ears. The wild, freakish laughter returns, and the wet thing still clings to my face. I grasp hold of it, but it wiggles. And has legs.

Whoosh.

The campfire darkens once more. Sound silences. An instant later, my sight and hearing flicker back, but they're dimmer, duller, quieter.

A giant of a man materializes in front of the campfire. He wears a knee-length patched coat, floppy-brimmed hat, and boots in a state of shambles. A dirty handkerchief covers his face, except for his eyes, which are raving mad and unfocused.

He's transparent too, I realize with a start. The logs from the fire are burning right through him. But he isn't blurry, like Ollie. What is he, then, if not a ghost?

His deep-throated voice rasps and crackles as he speaks:

"A curse is a riddle,
One that doesn't forgive.

Answer me this riddle,
And I'll let you to live."

The slimy thing in my hand squirms. I yelp, tossing it aside. The ground rocks again. No, it's my eyesight that's rocking. It flickers in and out like all sound in my ears. Then, at once, everything steadies, and the raving man vanishes.

I brace myself on my hands and knees, reeling.

Was that a vision?

A frog hops away from me. It must have been what struck my face. It's only a common frog with a spotted body, striped legs, and a V-shaped splotch on its back, but something about it sends a chill up my spine.

"Axel, did you see . . . ?" I look beside me, but he's gone. I shove to my feet and turn around. I can't find him anywhere.

"Axel?" I shout. Nothing makes sense. Barely any time could have passed. The fire isn't burning lower. Where has he disappeared to so quickly?

My heart kicks, and I rush to our packs by the woodpile, searching for my belt with my knife and small crossbow for bird hunting. I halt, noticing Axel's hatchet and a lantern are missing. Did he take them or did someone else?

I find my weapons. "Axel!" I have no idea which way he's gone, but I light a lantern and make a fast decision, setting off in the direction where I heard the wild laughter.

The forest grows dense. Tall evergreens blot out the light of the moon and stars, and the glow of my lantern only bleeds so far past the tightly knit trunks, needled boughs, and brambles.

A twig snaps to my left. I startle, drop my lantern, and fumble to nock an arrow. "Axel, is that you?"

An object whooshes past me, just shy of my head. A rock the

size of a melon. It hits the ground on my right. Cold sweat flashes over me. A stone that big could have crushed my skull.

Raucous laughter comes from my left. A tall, shadowy figure with a brimmed hat streaks by, racing behind the nearest trees, his long coat flapping. I train my crossbow on him.

He jumps out from the darkness. I scream and fire. "Don't shoot!" he shouts.

Too late. The arrow sails and passes *through* him. I gasp. It isn't the tall figure with the hat who sprang out, but a little boy who emits a glow as if he's standing in broad daylight.

"Ollie!" I fight to catch my breath. "What are you doing?" My hands rattle, and I lose grip of the crossbow. It thunks to the earth. "I could have killed you, if you weren't already . . ."

"Dead? It's okay if you say it. It's been thirteen years, so I'm used to it."

I gape at him. I haven't seen him in weeks, but he's the same beautiful boy I remember, elfin-looking with large hazel eyes, a small nose and mouth, and a mop of glossy chocolate-brown curls. His appearance is blurry, always slightly out of focus. It must be a ghost thing, though I can't be sure. He's the only ghost I've ever seen. At least I think.

I pluck up the crossbow.

Ollie grimaces. "You shouldn't use that if you don't know what you're aiming at."

"There's a hostile man out there."

"But you shot at *me*. What if I had been Axel?"

"Have you seen Axel?"

Ollie kicks uselessly at the ground. "Maybe."

"Where is he? Is he all right?"

He crosses his arms. "You haven't even looked for my pennies, have you?"

"Are you really holding that against me right now? Axel could be in danger!"

"He isn't." Ollie ambles across my path and jumps onto the rock that nearly crushed my head. He lands without a thud, his shoes hovering slightly above the surface. "Not tonight, anyway."

"How can you be sure? That man out there—"

"Never kills or captures people on the first night."

"Well, that's a great comfort." I shudder and pick up my lantern.

Ollie hops off the rock. "You and Axel should hurry away from this part of the forest. The raggedy man likes tricks, and they aren't the fun kind."

I swallow hard. "I'll be sure to do that once I find Axel. Did you see where—?"

"I'm being nice to warn you." Naked hurt floods Ollie's eyes. "Especially when you still haven't helped me."

"Oh, Ollie, I couldn't. I've been in Grimm's Hollow. You said your pennies were buried in the forest."

"Then you should have come back sooner."

"I promise I haven't forgotten you. Remember that spot you told me about in your house, where your father likes to hide his hard cider? I found something there."

"You wasted your time." Ollie tips his head back, exasperated.

"But your father kept a special gift for you. A pocket watch wrapped in a—"

"A pocket watch?" Ollie groans. "I can't use a pocket watch! I never even learned how to tell time. I can only count cuckoos. I can't even hold a pocket watch. I can't hold anything."

Pity sweeps through me. "I'm sorry. I didn't mean to make you sad. I simply hoped something from your house might stir some memories about the pennies."

"I don't remember any pocket watch." Slump-shouldered, he wanders back toward the place where he first appeared.

"I'll keep looking," I promise. I've no idea how to find two buried pennies in this vast forest, but there must be a way.

He doesn't answer. He just swats at a branch his ghostly hand can't rustle.

"Wait." I rush after him. He has a habit of disappearing prematurely. "I don't suppose you know anything about the murder of Bren Zimmer?" It's a terrible thing to ask a boy of seven, and Ollie must think so too, because he throws me an appalled look. With no dignity left to lose, I add, "Your house looked abandoned. Could your father be in the forest?"

"It's not nice to ask for help if you're not willing to give any."

I wince. "That's fair. But—"

He vanishes into the darkness.

I sigh and rub a hand down my face. "Well done, Clara."

Someone shouts in the distance. I stiffen and strain to hear the voice clearer. It's coming from the direction of the camp.

"Clara!"

Axel.

I backtrack and, a couple of minutes later, emerge into the small clearing with our bedrolls and campfire. I practically melt to see Axel unharmed. Dropping the crossbow and lantern, I throw myself into his arms.

"You're safe!" Axel squeezes me so hard he lifts my toes off the ground. "When I came back and you weren't here—"

"But *you* weren't here! Where did you go?"

"After the wild man, of course."

"You saw him too?"

"How could I miss him? He set a poisonous snake upon us."

"He did?" I draw back, and Axel's brow furrows. He points to a coiled but motionless viper on the ground behind our

bedrolls. Its head is severed from its body. Surely the work of
Axel's hatchet, although I don't remember a thing.

"Clara, are you all right?"

I slowly piece together what must have happened. "I caught
a glimpse of the man when I ran to find you, but I also saw him
before then. Not with a snake, though. He was standing right
there." I turn toward the campfire. "He was transparent, and he
spoke a riddle:

> "*A curse is a riddle,*
> *One that doesn't forgive.*
> *Answer me this riddle,*
> *And I'll let you to live.*'

"That's when I lost track of everything." I steal a glance at the
woods. "Axel, we need to leave here tonight. I saw Ollie and—"

"Ollie? You said it was the wild man."

"Ollie called him the raggedy man, and I saw them both. But
the first time I saw the man, I think I was having another vision."

Axel struggles to speak for a moment. "*Another* vision?"

I realize I never told him what happened when I touched the
double-reed pipe of Herr Oswald's son. "I promise to explain
everything—while we travel." I kneel and start folding my bedroll.

"What about the Sommer girls? If we leave tonight, we'll lose
the chance to find their trail."

I hadn't thought of that.

"And is it wise to run from someone we should consider as
a suspect? Discovering the murderer is the whole point of this
journey."

"But Ollie said he'll try to kill us."

"That puts him on par with every Lost One we've met in this
forest."

I let go of the bedroll. "What do you propose, then? Waiting around like bait while I try to have another vision? How? I don't know who he is or if I have any tokens for him."

"What spurred the vision you had tonight?"

"I have no idea."

Axel crouches beside me. "Look, we'll keep moving once it's daylight. We'll keep tracking the Sommer girls and stay on guard for the raggedy man. He won't let us leave so easily, not if he's anything like Fiora and Ella and Hansel and Gretel. Maybe we'll discover who he is along the way. Meanwhile, try your best to have another vision, one that tells us if he's guilty of murdering Bren."

My stomach feels like it's eating itself with worry, but I nod. "Ollie *did* say the raggedy man won't kill or capture us tonight. It's not the way he likes to play tricks, apparently."

Axel's grip tightens on his hatchet. "Then I'll take the first watch. You should get some sleep."

That seems impossible, given how fast my pulse is racing. "All right."

I keep my shoes on, in case Axel and I need to make a run for it, but I also tie my ankle to his—counterintuitive to running, but I don't want to lose him among any shifting trees if he accidentally falls asleep. It wouldn't be the first time the forest has separated us that way.

As I lie down, a quiet *ribbit* draws my gaze to the trees. Axel throws a log on the fire, and the sudden blaze illuminates the gnarled root of a pine tree, where a frog rests. A frog with a V-shaped splotch on its back.

A frog that stares directly at me.

CHAPTER 13

I awaken to Axel's kiss, like a princess when a prince revives her from death in children's stories. My eyelids bat open, and I gaze at him, his golden hair and tawny skin softly framed in the warm and misty predawn light. His beauty is mythical, and he *is* a saving prince. He did bring me back from the dead.

"We should go now," he whispers, and those words along with his careful tone slam me back to reality. The events of last night crash into my mind. Ollie. My vision. The raggedy man.

My stomach tightens. We'll have to move quickly if we want to stay one step ahead of him.

Trying to walk quietly but swiftly, we travel back toward the meadow in Grimm's Hollow. The trees have rearranged themselves in the night, but a little luck is on our side. Not too far from our campsite, we spy the footprints of the six Sommer girls.

"It looks like they walked single file," Axel says, and while that pattern stays consistent, their tracks meander off the beaten path whenever it curves, remaining straight regardless of streams and prickly brambles. They only veer to weave around trees, boulders, and rifts from the earthquake.

The girls were still in their trance, then, lured to whatever destination the forest has in store for them.

We pick our way onward. When our hunt leads us away from the stream we've been traveling near, my nerves flare, but I remind myself we're bound to find more water again, and when we do, we can trace it to one of the main rivers that intersects through the forest.

Axel holds his hatchet at the ready, and I keep a firm grip on my knife. The raggedy man is probably following us, and Ollie warned me how he likes to play nefarious tricks. I need to have another vision of him. But without knowing his identity, I don't know how to form a connection.

Midday, Axel and I pause to eat, and I sit on a stone with my drawstring bag of tokens. If I do have a token belonging to the raggedy man, perhaps I can figure out what it is by the process of elimination.

I sift through the tokens belonging to men:

A marble with a green ribbon swirl at its core belonging to Johann Schade.

A straight-edge razor with a ram-horn handle belonging to Leo Halm.

An engraved brass tinderbox belonging to Fitch Ebner.

This isn't helping. Any man, young or old, could be the raggedy man. He's too hidden by his handkerchief mask, low-lying brimmed hat, and hair so grimy I couldn't tell its color.

"Any luck?" Axel drinks from his waterskin.

"I've never had a vision intentionally. What if it isn't possible?"

"Sure it is." His tone doesn't make any room for the smallest doubt. "Think of the circumstances surrounding each of your visions." He helps me to my feet and continues as we keep tracking the Sommer girls, "What did they have in common?"

"Not much." I consider the four times I've had visions. "When I glimpsed your past during Ella's wedding ball, I was under the influence of red-spotted mushrooms—poison too dangerous to ingest again."

"Agreed."

"And when I saw my mother's memories, she was seconds away from dying." I bite the inside of my cheek against a rush of guilt and regret. "That's another situation I don't wish to repeat."

Axel laces our fingers together and squeezes.

I inhale a steadying breath. "My third vision happened when I touched the double-reed pipe." I tell Axel about the young boy I saw building a toy castle from blocks, presumably Herr Oswald's son Harlan.

"Which supports your theory that tokens can trigger visions," Axel says.

I nod, although it's the only time it's happened. "The last vision makes the least amount of sense. I caught a moment of the raggedy man's past when a frog hit my face."

Axel slows his footsteps. "Do you think the raggedy man threw the frog at you?"

"Maybe." I look over my shoulder, half expecting to see the same frog darting after us. "The way the frog looked at me last night, it felt unnervingly perceptive, almost like . . ."

"It was a Lost One?"

I raise my brows, surprised that Axel is considering the same thing. "You don't think that's too far-fetched?"

"In light of the fact that your grandmother is an Anivoyante, no."

We start walking again, our eyes following six sets of footprints pressed into the mulch. "Maybe the frog is in league with the raggedy man."

"Maybe. Although that doesn't explain why you had a vision of him."

"No, it doesn't."

"There's one thing your visions have in common, though. Each time, you were in a heightened state of emotions."

That's true. When I had the vision of Axel, I was scared he was about to marry Ella. With my mother, I was clinging to my last moments with her. When I stole the double-reed pipe, I was running from a village mob. And when the frog struck me, I'd just heard the terrifying laughter of the raggedy man.

"I was afraid of something every time," I realize, coming to an abrupt stop. "Are you saying I'm going to have to work myself into a fright in order to have visions?"

He shrugs. "Another strong emotion might work as well."

This sounds more dreadful by the moment. "I thought my gift would be more like Grandmère's. She was never distressed or overwrought when she foretold someone's future."

"What if she was, but learned to control it over time?"

I think of the opaque black veil she wore when she read cards and the valerian tincture bottle she always kept nearby. Maybe they helped her bridle her ability. Or at least cope with it.

"Don't worry." Axel rubs my shoulders. "We'll figure this out. You'll find a way to trigger visions deliberately."

I do my best to return his reassuring smile, and we journey onward.

As the afternoon presses toward evening and shafts of light angle lower with the setting sun, we firm up our plan about the raggedy man and determine to capture him when he strikes again.

Twilight descends, and Axel pauses chopping firewood from a dead tree. "He's out there . . . I can feel it." He turns his ear to a screech of wind that kicks up a whirl of autumn leaves. "I bet he'll attack when it's fully dark out."

I'm wrapping the sheep cheese left over from our dinner when all the tension in the atmosphere seems to gather in my bones. There are no songs of night birds, scampering of small creatures, or humming of insects, only the creaking of towering tree branches in the wind.

When animals quiet like this, a predator is nearby.

I slowly reach for my crossbow, my skin buzzing with nervous energy.

A wolf howls in the distance. I know that sound, that particular timbre, pitch, and resonance. It belongs to the foremost predator of the forest. The Grimm wolf.

Axel's wide eyes lock on mine. "What are the chances your grandmother is well enough to shift into the Grimm wolf?"

"Next to nothing," I rasp.

"Then if the wolf attacks?"

My voice sharpens to a lethal edge. "We can't kill her."

"But what if she—?"

"We'll only injure her, same as with the raggedy man."

He works his jaw for a moment, but finally nods.

Once night falls fully, Axel and I sit back-to-back to better surveil our surroundings, our weapons positioned beside us. We're on edge, awaiting both the Grimm wolf and the raggedy man.

Skeletal branches cast flickering shadows past the encircling trees, dancing in time with the flames of our campfire. An hour passes. Then two.

My bag of tokens rests on my lap. I've been rotating through the tokens belonging to men, seeing if any spark a vision when I'm so full of fear. None have . . . but there is one more token to consider.

I reach for my pack and discreetly withdraw the diamond-patterned handkerchief, unfolding the key-wind pocket watch wrapped inside. I train my thoughts on Axel's uncle, Rudger, and open the latch of the engraved silver case. The gilt hands under the crystal dome are set for three o'clock. Strange. I've never wound the watch. I could have sworn both hands were resting at *XII* before.

I open my mouth to bring it up to Axel, but then press my tongue against the back of my teeth. I keep forgetting to tell him I snuck into his uncle's house and stole something that was meant for Ollie—a token I can use for Rudger . . . if Rudger is indeed Lost and not dead somewhere in his mines.

"Axel?" I don't speak loudly, but my voice still cuts through the crackling fire and hissing breeze.

"Mm?" I feel his head turn, resting against mine.

"I never told you how—"

The tree branches rattle with a burst of wind. But there was no wind . . .

I shove the watch and handkerchief inside my dress pocket. Grab my crossbow and lurch to my feet. Axel stands and scrambles for his hatchet. We keep our backs pressed together.

"Do you still have your scarf on?" I ask.

"Yes? And your cape?"

"Still wearing it."

"Then why is this happening?"

"It must be the raggedy man."

"Wonderful," Axel grumbles.

We know about Lost Ones who have gained control of some of the forest's magic, like Hansel and Gretel when they encaged us in tree roots, and my mother as Briar Rose when she sent a poisonous thorn to prick my finger as I touched the spindle of her spinning wheel.

Axel and I carefully revolve, back-to-back, as the trees writhe, their branches flailing like wild arms with hooked fingers.

A little creature hops into our clearing and latches its bulging eyes on me. I startle at the frog from last night with the V-shaped marking on its back.

Axel's back goes rigid. "He's here."

I think he means the frog, but then a cackle of freakish laughter hits my ears and strikes my nerves with icy needles.

Axel raises his hatchet. "Clara, turn. Very. Slowly."

CHAPTER 14

I start to pivot when the branches lash out for us. My crossbow is yanked away. Axel reacts quicker and hacks the limbs flying toward him.

I drop to the ground. Swipe for my knife. Before I reach it, a thin root coils around the hilt and snatches it from me.

I spin for Axel's knife. Grab it before another root snakes to catch it. I stay on my knees so Axel can keep swinging, and I pin my gaze on the raggedy man. Under the floppy brim of his hat, his eyes capture the firelight like two onyx gems. He's masked by his handkerchief, but I swear he's smiling at me.

Maim, don't kill. I throw my knife. It pinwheels for his leg, but a branch swoops and seizes it by the hilt.

The raggedy man laughs, a hideous sound made of corrosive screeches and heinous nightmares. Axel curses as his hatchet is wrenched away. The grating laughter grows louder, meaner, practically its own evil entity.

"Who are you?" I snarl, fighting to stoke my dwindling courage. "What do you want?" Lost Ones are always deranged for something they're missing, something they're desperate to gain back.

"She thinks I will tell her!" The raggedy man breaks into another round of violent laughter. "She thinks I will give up my fun so easily! But the riddler makes the rules." His dark eyes narrow into harsh slits. "And I will win what I am after."

Long strips of bark peel from the trees and collect on the ground. Spiderlike roots work to weave them together.

Axel finds my hand and grips it tightly. We try to escape, but the bark, tangling like rope, forms too wide a circle. We pull inward to the campfire until the flames lick our clothes.

The raggedy man stands at the circle's outer edge and taunts us with a rhyme:

"Little wolf, dressed in red
A babe in her belly, a hood on her head."

Axel shifts in front of me protectively. "If you lay a finger on her—!"

"I will win what I am after," the raggedy man seethes.

I sense something descending. Fearing a giant spider, I glance up. Several cords of bark spiral downward, almost touching us. "Axel!"

He tenses. "Run!"

We dash across the rope circle, hoping it's the lesser danger.

The raggedy man yanks another rope I haven't noticed, strung like a pulley from tall branches. It sets off a trap. Right when the ropes above touch the ground and knot into the circle, they spring back in the air—a newly formed net, with us caught in it.

My stomach plummets as we're launched high and rebound. We're left dangling thirty feet above the earth, our net spinning as the ropes overhead twist into a thick cord.

My pulse roars in my ears, momentarily drowning out the bone-chilling laughter of the raggedy man. He spouts the same rhyme from my vision and dances like a crazed man around the campfire:

"A curse is a riddle,
One that doesn't forgive.

Answer me this riddle,
And I'll let you to live.

"Are you ready to hear it?" he questions.

Entangled in the net, Axel and I have barely stopped twirling. A look of stubbornness passes between us. We won't deign to reply to the raggedy man.

Chuckling to himself, he rubs his hands and recites:

"Two names is the riddle,
Two words to pick apart,
One is my own name,
The other captured my heart."

His voice deepens to a crackling rasp. "What is your answer?"

"It's impossible," Axel whispers, struggling to tear the net apart. "Are we really going to be killed over such nonsense?"

I call to the raggedy man: "It isn't a fair riddle if you don't give us a hint!"

"A hint?" He snickers. "The little wolf doesn't know I already gave her one."

I swallow a bitter taste as I think of what he insinuated—that I would become pregnant, and he would win what he was after. "Axel, can you think of a man in the village who wanted a child? A man who became Lost?"

He scrubs his forehead, thinking.

"Tick tock, tick tock," the raggedy man chimes. "The first midnight is almost over."

The first midnight? What does he mean?

"Peter and Ellery Trager wanted a child!" Axel blurts to me.

I remember the young couple. Axel helped repair the roof of

their cottage when they were sick. They later went missing in the forest.

"Tick tock."

I squeeze my eyes shut, desperately hoping we'll guess right. "Your own name is Peter Trager," I call to the raggedy man. "And the name of the person who captured your heart is Ellery Trager."

He cups his hands over his nose and mouth against a surge of wild laughter that rakes against my ears and scorches through my veins. "Two more midnights! I can't wait to hear what you get wrong next!"

Axel whispers, "Does he mean we get two more tries?"

As if the raggedy man can hear him, he delivers another rhyme:

"Two more chances are yours
To guess right and survive,
Or the riddler steals the girl
And buries the boy alive."

He yanks down his handkerchief and imparts a menacing grin, his teeth cutting through his heavy beard and mustache. I strain my eyes but still can't make out his identity.

"Two more midnights!" he calls, and then whirls off into the darkness.

CHAPTER 15

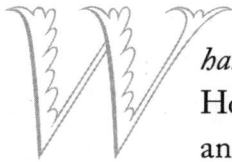

What happens twice will happen thrice. A Grimm's Hollow superstition. One I can't shake as Axel and I awaken the next morning, smashed together in the net still dangling thirty feet in the air. If we can't escape, we'll face the raggedy man again. And if we fail on this, our second midnight, and the superstition holds true, we're bound to fail on the third.

Stumped on the riddle, we focus on escaping. We have no weapons to cut the net with—as if to taunt us, the raggedy man left them below in sight—but we're determined to try.

We swing back and forth in the net, our momentum building, until we reach a high branch of an encircling tree. Axel grabs hold of it while I snap off several slimmer limbs. He lets go, and we rock back, hanging like a pendant over the little clearing beneath us.

We fasten the branches together with strips of bark. A frustrating endeavor, but hours later, we finally construct a long ramshackle pole with a clawed end.

We poke the ground with it, trying to retrieve our weapons, but only succeed in brushing a layer of mulch over them before our flimsy pole snaps apart. Axel growls and casts it aside.

We swing the net and break off a heftier branch, hoping its jagged end can saw the net apart, but the rope is too strong. As daylight dwindles, we resort to biting the rope, but it's no use.

When it's early evening, Axel drags his hand down his face and says, "Maybe we're better off trying to solve the riddle."

We give it another go, thinking through the men in the village who became Lost, and if any more other than Peter Trager wanted a child. We narrow down the list to five candidates. But five men is too many guesses for two more midnights, and no matter how we rack our brains, we can't shave down that number.

Parched for water and starved for food, I gaze drearily at our packs and waterskins below. Everything feels hopeless. My S-curve is in knots from being squashed in the net, and we're no closer to solving the raggedy man's riddle, or, for that matter, the murder that brought about the curse. "I don't want to be the lunar eclipse," I murmur.

"The lunar eclipse?" Axel twists toward me, and the net spins a little.

I promised myself I'd never tell him about the latest cards of my destiny. But that was because of Love Lost. I can leave that card out and share the others. "Grandmère had a moment of lucidity before I left Grimm's Hollow. She read my fortune."

Axel's brows dart up. "Clara—"

"I didn't ask her to. I didn't want it to happen. But it did."

The net casts crisscross shadows over his troubled face. "Do I want to know?"

"It can't hurt, I guess. The reading was ambiguous."

I tell him about the first card, the Midnight Forest, which he's familiar with, then the Dueling Rings, and how I accidentally knocked it askew before Grandmère could decipher its meaning based upon the direction it's drawn. "It either represents a solar eclipse for an epic beginning or a lunar eclipse for a dramatic ending. Grandmère said I will either break the curse or make it final."

Axel leans a fragment closer and takes my face in his hands.

"You're the solar eclipse, Clara." His thumb brushes along my jawline. "Never doubt it."

But I do. I can't help it. The Dueling Ring feels like it *is* me, divided between the Clara I was before I died and the Clara I am now, whoever she is. What if everything is backward, and the old me was my beginning and the new me is my ending—my rebirth leading to the tragedy of everyone I love?

How can I break a curse if I was never meant to live again?

I tuck into Axel and lay my head on his shoulder. We fall into a silence that stretches long and taut until the sun sinks, the moon towers above, and stars dot the sky past the weave of our net.

The more I pore over the riddle and the identity of the raggedy man, the more I'm stumped. I'm sure Axel is scraping his mind for answers too, but neither of us speaks. There's nothing to discuss when we haven't gleaned anything more about our captor.

It must be nearing midnight. I idly trace the lump of the silver-cased watch in my pocket. With my back to Axel, I pull it out and unfold the handkerchief it's wrapped in, popping the watch's clasp open to see its face.

The time has changed. It was set to three o'clock yesterday, but now it's set to two o'clock. I bring the watch to my ear to be sure it isn't ticking. I don't understand how the gilt hands are moving.

"I warned you to hurry away from this part of the forest."

At the sound of Ollie's voice, I nearly drop the watch.

"I told you the raggedy man likes tricks," he says. "But you let him catch you on purpose."

Seven feet away, Ollie perches on the end of a slender branch. If he were tangible and alive, that branch would snap. But he's only a weightless ghost, incapable of bending even the slimmest reed.

I wrap the pocket watch back up and stuff it between the

folds of my skirt. "We needed to meet the raggedy man again," I explain. "The whole reason we came here is to break the curse, Ollie."

Axel jerks around. "Ollie is here?"

Ollie's elfin eyes stab me with a pointed look. *"And?"*

It takes my overworked brain a moment to realize what he's prodding at. "And find your pennies, of course. But we can't do that—break the curse, I mean—until we figure out who triggered it in the first place."

He mashes his lips together. "That's why you asked me who murdered Zen Brimmer."

"Bren Zimmer. Yes. He was killed three years ago."

Axel wrestles closer to my side of the net. "Ask him if he knows who the raggedy man is."

Ollie crosses his arms over his chest. "The raggedy man is a good person. He just forgot that. He wasn't a murderer before."

I catch him saying "wasn't," and dread slinks up my spine. "Won't you tell us who he is, Ollie? You must know. You'll be saving us if you do."

Ollie looks down and pretends to pick at the branch, even though his ghostly fingernail can't scratch the bark.

"Or you can help us solve the riddle," I offer. Ollie has a gift for vanishing when I need him most.

"I don't know the answers," he finally replies. "No one has ever guessed the riddle right."

"What about the frog? Is it a Lost One helping the raggedy man?"

Ollie frowns at me like I'm soft in the head. "A frog is just a frog."

I exhale. Maybe he's right, but back to the point. "You said the raggedy man was good once. If you know that, you should remember what his name used to be."

Ollie lowers his eyes again. A gust whirls through the forest, swaying the branch he's on, but Ollie floats independent of it, his glossy brown curls untouched by the wind.

"What's going on?" Axel asks.

"Not much," I murmur. "Ollie's very protective of the raggedy man."

"Who is he to him?"

Then it strikes me like a hammer. "Rudger," I gasp.

Ollie squeaks, surprised.

"Rudger?" Axel's brows tug together. "What are you talking about?"

"The raggedy man is Ollie's father—your uncle Rudger." Guilt sweeps through me. "Oh, Axel, I've been meaning to tell you."

"Don't hurt my dad!" Ollie stomps off the branch and into the air, making no illusion of being upheld by anything anymore. "He doesn't mean to be a bad man. Just like your mother didn't mean to become a killer, Clara."

His words lance through my heart. I became a killer too. Her killer.

I whisper when I meet Axel's stricken eyes, "I—I went to Rudger's house looking for a clue about Ollie's pennies, and it was clear it had long been abandoned. I wondered if he'd become a Lost One without anyone knowing . . . and now I know he did. He's the raggedy man."

Axel shakes his head. "I would have recognized him, remembered his voice."

"He's Lost. He's become someone else."

Ollie glides closer. "Promise not to hurt my father, Clara!"

I laugh humorlessly. "We're the ones in the net!"

"Did you steal a token from Rudger's house?" Axel demands. He knows what it would mean, that I consider his uncle a murder suspect.

"Look, I know your relationship with him is complicated." I reach in the folds of my skirt for the pocket watch. It's time to show it to him. "But you never loved him like you loved your father."

"My father has nothing to do with this! My father—"

I brush the cool metal of the watch's silver case, and the bottom of the net falls out. My surroundings go pitch black. My ears abruptly silence.

I'm left suspended in nothingness—a terrifying void of my existence—and then everything rushes back. The net. My sight. The noises of the forest. Axel and Ollie arguing with me. Whatever our quarrel is about no longer feels important. I'm too captivated by the scene opening up before me, layered over reality and made of colors more vibrant, sounds more vivid.

I'm seeing a vision. Someone else's past.

But this time it's different.

I can't see the person. Because I'm *inside* them.

I'm riding in their skin.

I'm living their past with them.

I *am* them.

CHAPTER 16

I'm walking a narrow road between two craggy mountains, their steep slopes caked in powdery snow. Sunshine sparkles on the peaks. The snow is melting. I hurry faster.

Blackness comes. Then a burst of sunlight. Digging hands. Unfamiliar faces. A strange dialect.

More blackness. A narrow bed. A log cabin. Warmth from a fire. Numb fingers. Frozen toes. My head is splitting. I have double vision. Two spoons from two hands lift broth to my mouth.

I remain in bed as light outside the window changes rapidly. Gray and milky, golden and buttery, violet and rosy.

I finally rise, using a cane to venture outside. I stand in the middle of the road. Stare in each direction. Scratch my head.

I help a woman in the cabin butcher meat from gamey animals. I help a man mine precious stones from steep mountains. Their children tease me. I'm slow to understand their jokes.

Leaves change color. Snow falls. Wildflowers spring up. Waterfalls rush. I sleep in an addition built onto the cabin.

I grow steadier on my feet. I don't use the cane anymore. I laugh easier. I travel with the man to a village. We trade gemstones for food and supplies.

At the market, I'm drawn to a clockmaker's cart. I glimpse a silver-cased pocket watch.

Another autumn arrives. A carpet of golden beech and crimson maple leaves surround the log cabin. I stand in the road again and—

WAIT.

The scene I'm inhabiting staggers to a halt. I remember myself. Clara Thurn. Not whoever this person is or whose past I'm reliving.

The pocket watch is important, I think. *Show me more.*

As if my thought is a command, I'm taken back to the market cart. I hear myself asking the clockmaker a question, and my voice is a man's voice, a gentle baritone that stokes a flutter of familiarity.

"Can you engrave this pocket watch, sir?" I ask.

"Indeed, I can," the clockmaker replies. "What would you like the inscription to read?"

"Um . . ." I falter, unable to clear the fog clouding my mind. "I'll return when I remember the name."

Back at the cabin, I stand in the road again, looking back and forth. I find myself staring longer in the direction that leads downhill.

In the mines, I chisel at a stubborn chunk of ore. The mine shaft groans, the earth shifts. The block of ore falls and strikes my head.

Blackness returns.

I'm back in the narrow bed. Finally, my eyes open. And stay open. My mind opens too. I remember—

My eyesight flickers in and out. I'm swept into darkness and silence. Just as quickly, light and noise flood back in, less dynamic but more real. I'm grounded once more to the net and Axel's warm body beside me. The layer of the past has vanished.

The raggedy man's deep and crackling voice bellows upward:

> *"Shiny baubles, sparkling rings,*
> *Why do they need such pretty things?"*

"Leave those alone!" Axel shouts.

Blearily, I try to orient myself to what's happening. I scarcely understand the vision I had, let alone the raggedy man's sudden presence. When did he arrive?

He's bent over my bedroll, examining little objects that glint and sparkle beneath his lantern.

My mouth falls open. "My tokens!"

"It's your second midnight," Axel calls to the raggedy man. "Are you going to rifle through our belongings or ask us to answer your riddle? We're ready when you are."

"We are?" I whisper.

"Ollie just told us."

Did he?

I look where the ghost had been hovering, but he's gone. I try to remember our conversation, but my mind is fuzzy. Something about the raggedy man once being a good person.

"So anxious to meet your death, are we?" the raggedy man calls.

Axel scoffs, his jaw grinding.

The raggedy man removes his brimmed hat and waves it with a flourish, bowing low. "Very well, then. Answer me this riddle." He recites it again:

> *"Two names is the riddle,*
> *Two words to pick apart,*

One is my own name,
The other captured my heart."

He holds his hat to his chest and walks in a circle, his lantern swinging. "Tick tock, tick tock."

"The first name is Rudger Lorenz Furst," Axel declares. "The second name is Oliver Furst."

Clarity hits me square in the face. I remember everything Ollie revealed, and Axel's answers line up perfectly: Rudger's full name as well as the name of his son, his only child who died thirteen years ago from consumption. Lost Ones are always pining for something lost. No wonder, in his delirium, Rudger believes I can somehow give him back that lost child.

I hold my breath, waiting for his confirmation.

He buries his face in his hat and falls into a crouch, staying like that for several seconds.

I lean toward Axel. "Does this mean you guessed right?"

Rudger starts rocking back and forth, as if silently sobbing. Then he lifts his head and pulls his hat away. He releases a cackle so cruel and disturbing it raises the hair on my arms. "Wrong and wrong!"

My posture droops. Axel's nostrils flare, and a vein stands out on his forehead. Any Lost One can be infuriating, but dealing with his deranged uncle is pushing him over the edge.

Rudger rises and laughs harder, a jagged, grating sound of pure vitriol. He puts his hat on again, and his tone darkens into something even more freakish and caustic.

"One more midnight,
No chance to be saved,
And should you guess wrong,
Here's a glimpse of your grave."

He points at one of the encircling trees. A willow with weeping branches, its autumn leaves a putrid shade of yellow in the glow of his lantern.

I tighten my grip on the net, anticipating the worst but not knowing what it will be.

The quiet of the night grows so rife with tension that even the silence falls shrill on my ears.

At once, the weeping branches writhe to life, a nest of yellow vipers.

Axel and I jerk backward in the net. The willow whips for us. The branches lash around the net and drag us closer to its trunk.

Rudger's lantern light flickers against the ridges of the bark. Those ridges separate, pulling wider and stretching like they're suddenly made of wet, translucent skin.

A male face surfaces behind the strange window into the willow. It pushes against the skin holding it back. Protrudes like it's trying to break free. Its expression twists in agony.

It doesn't scream, but I feel it screaming. The horror curdles my blood and pounds like an echo through my skull.

The branches drag Axel and me forward until, past the cramped net, we're almost touching the tortured face. Axel cringes away. I flail and whimper. Willow branches rattle around us. Rudger cackles.

I'm too terrorized to breathe. My eyesight blackens at the edges.

Right when my dizziness peaks and my head bobs forward, the willow releases us. We swing backward in a jolt and crash into each other. I gasp for air. The agonized face shrinks back into the trunk. The ridges of the bark seal closed. The willow stills.

Rudger snatches my bag of tokens and madly dances away, his movements jerky, some rhyme on his lips incomprehensible past his demonic voice.

I recall the Grimm's Hollow superstition that's been in the back of my mind all day. . . .

What happens twice will happen thrice.

The second midnight will become the third.

And on the third, this game will be over.

CHAPTER 17

Morning birdsong flits into my awareness as I sit curled in a ball in the net, my cape folded tight around me, my hood drawn over my head and pulled low over my brow. My hands fist against my eyes, as if I can scrub away the horror of what I saw last night.

Axel touches my shoulder, and I flinch. I wasn't aware he was awake. "Did you sleep at all?" he asks.

"Between trying to solve this impossible riddle and worrying over you suffocating to death in that willow, not much." I pull back my hood and take him in. His eyes are heavy-lidded and a little bloodshot, and his golden hair is so mussed and mangy it's taken a life of its own. "Did *you* sleep at all?"

He gives a meager shrug. "Still processing that my uncle is the raggedy man."

"I'm sorry, Axel. I promise I meant to tell you sooner."

He dredges up a small, forgiving smile. "It doesn't help that he's trying to kill us."

"Kill *you*, you mean. If we fail, I only get stolen."

"And supposedly bear a child?" His jaw muscle ripples. "Rudger won't let you live when he realizes you're not pregnant."

I squirm, which only sends a sharp twinge through my S-curve.

Axel winces. "Sorry, I shouldn't have said that." He rubs my back. "Neither one of us is going to die, all right? I won't let my uncle bury me in a tree."

The willow looks perfectly amicable in the soft morning light, nothing like the garish monster it was under Rudger's influence. "I can't stop thinking about the agonized expression on that dead man's face, how it was screaming, writhing."

"Writhing?"

"Trying to burst free from that skin-like film that held him back."

"I saw a little sap. Is that what you mean? I had a hard time looking past his face, frozen in fear."

"It definitely wasn't frozen."

Axel's hand stills along my spine. "Are you sure you saw the same thing I did?"

"Of course."

"But the face wasn't moving."

"Yes, it was. It was freakish—absolutely terrifying." I swallow a rush of bile. "I don't want you to die like that."

Axel's forehead crinkles. "But how could that man be dead if he was moving?"

"Because . . ." Actually, I have no idea. "You think he was alive?"

"He couldn't be. And he *wasn't* moving. He looked like all the other dead faces we've seen in the trees of the forest. Only we couldn't see him until Rudger opened the willow."

I study Axel's face, waiting for a wink, a flicker at the corner of his mouth, anything to show he's teasing me. But his eyes are earnest. "Maybe you saw a vision," he says. "Something from the dead man's past."

It didn't feel like a vision, but that reminds me—"I *did* have a vision last night. When Rudger arrived."

Axel's brows launch to his hairline. "Why didn't you say you had a vision of him? It might have helped us guess the right answers to the riddle."

"I'm not sure it was Rudger. It was a man—I could hear his

voice—but I couldn't see him. It was like I *was* the man. Perhaps that's how Grandmère feels when she's in the skin of the Grimm wolf."

"What do you think triggered the vision?"

"I'm pretty sure it was this." I pull the handkerchief out of the folds of my skirt and unwrap the pocket watch. "I found it hidden in Rudger's house. The handkerchief has Ollie's initials, so I thought it would have sentimental value to your uncle."

Axel reaches for the handkerchief, his fingers shaking. "This wasn't Ollie's. It was my mother's." His thumb runs over the embroidered initials. "*O.F.* stands for Odette Furst. My father always kept it with him. Why did Rudger have this?"

Dread coalesces in my gut. I'm beginning to wonder—

"Clara, did you see . . . ?" Axel holds himself unnaturally still. I fear he's coming to the same conclusion. "Could the vision have been of my father?"

Perspiration flashes over my body. It had to be, and I want to kick myself for not realizing it sooner. I should have known from the beginning of the vision. Walking a narrow road between two steep mountains. Hurrying because of the melting snow. Being overcome by blackness, digging hands, unfamiliar faces.

It was the pass through the Ottenhorne Mountains, the avalanche that supposedly killed Axel's father, Kellen. That's why Kellen left him in the care of Rudger when Axel was twelve years old, to protect him from the dangers of the pass while he made his merchant travels.

"Clara?" Axel presses.

My tongue is slack. I can't simply say yes. I don't know how Kellen's story ended, and I don't want to give Axel false hope. He saved his one wish for his father, believing he died in that avalanche seven years ago. He asked *Sortes Fortunae* to bring the person he loved the most back to life. The book answered him, but Kellen never returned for Axel to enact its instructions about a red spindle. Instead, Axel later used that spindle on me.

Clearing my throat, I finally muster, "His voice reminded me of yours." That's why it sounded familiar. "So . . . it's possible."

It's more than possible. I feel its truth culminating in every fiber of my body. I *was* Axel's father in the vision, and although we never met, I know his son better than I know myself. I'm sure the person I was living inside was Kellen.

"What did you see?" Axel keeps his tone level, guarded. When it comes to his family, he's like a stained-glass window, carefully leaded at the seams, each piece delicately held together after years of painstaking work. "Was it his life before he came through Grimm's Hollow? Before he left me here and . . ." He rubs the monogrammed handkerchief. "How else could you have found this if he didn't leave it behind for me?"

"I'm not sure, but . . ."

"But what?" Axel's pensive stare bores into me.

I take his hand. I don't want to shatter him when he's already made of shattered pieces. "I only saw glimpses, all right? I don't know everything. So please don't jump to conclusions."

"Clara, just tell me."

I draw a steadying breath. "Your father survived the avalanche, but he was badly injured and his recovery was slow. I don't think he remembered who he was. A family in the high mountains took care of him. Time passed, he seemed to be doing better, and he wanted to buy this pocket watch. He hoped to get it engraved, but he couldn't remember the name. Then he was injured again and the vision ended. I don't know what became of him."

Axel holds himself rigid, his expression almost blank except for a tiny spasm cutting through his brow. Ever so slowly, he reaches for the pocket watch. Turns it over, like I did when I first found it. Searches for an inscription on the back cover. There is none. But he seems to know more about clockwork than I do. He opens the silver case by a latch affixed to the frame of the crystal dome cover. I glimpse the time the gilt hands are set to— one o'clock, changed again—before he pops out the watch face, attached by another hinge I hadn't noticed.

On the back of the watch face are partially exposed cogs and a wheel, but Axel isn't staring at any mechanism. His gaze fastens on the inside-back cover of the case, where words are engraved— the inscription I missed:

> *To my dear son*
> *AXEL*
> *Always loved. Never forgotten.*
> *From your loving father*

Axel's eyes gloss over with tears, which immediately trigger my own. "Why . . . ?" He rubs his hand down his jaw, but his chin won't stop quivering. "Why did my uncle have this? Why didn't my father give it to me himself if he—?" His voice cracks, and he chokes down a sob. "Is he alive, Clara? Is that what you're trying to tell me?"

My insides squeeze tight. What I would give to say yes. It would be like saying my mother survived the spindle I stabbed into her heart, that she ran away with me and my friends before her castle crumbled to pieces, that I never had to abandon her to be buried in the rubble, that she returned to Grimm's Hollow with me and Grandmère, who never became ill from wounds that didn't heal due to the heartache of a granddaughter who killed her beloved daughter.

"Yes" would be a fairy-tale ending.

"I hope so." I kiss his hand, tasting the salt of my tears on his knuckles. "I want this for you, more than anything. But I don't know. The only thing I can be sure of is he was alive for much longer than you believed."

"But . . . you could have another vision of him, right?"

"I'm . . . not sure. My visions still come unbidden and—"

"All you have to do is think about how you made it happen last night and do it again."

"I wish it was that simple."

"You said it was triggered by the pocket watch."

"Yes, but it was more than that. Ollie was angry with me. You were too. And then Rudger arrived. All those things could have contributed."

"I'm sure you can do it again." Unbearable hope fills his eyes. "I believe in you."

It's too much pressure. I may never find out what became of his dad. "Axel, I—"

A deep reverberating snarl startles me to silence.

A frog is in the clearing below, a blot of green in the thirty-foot distance, but familiarity prickles over me, and I'm sure it's the frog that's been following us.

It leaps away as a much larger creature stalks forward.

I gasp and clutch Axel's arm.

The Grimm wolf.

CHAPTER 18

alm yourself, Clara. Wolves can't climb trees.

The Grimm wolf lifts her large head and looks at us squarely. I squint, straining to see the color of her eyes. They have to be brown, not violet like Grandmère's. But then why has the wolf come? We heard her howl two days ago. Is she hunting us?

She prowls around the trees, sniffing. She locates a protruding root and starts gnawing on it.

Axel gapes. "That's your grandmother!"

"How do you know?"

"She's cutting us free."

He's right. The wolf isn't gnawing on a root. There's a rope tied around it, camouflaged with the trees. It leads to a high branch and the pulley system Rudger rigged to trap us. It's the rope holding us aloft.

"Quick, Clara." Axel moves his weight back and forth to swing the net. "We have to grab a branch to break our fall or the drop could kill us."

I help build momentum, and the net slowly swings higher.

The wolf rears back and yelps. The rope snaps, unraveling a bunch of strands. I brace myself, but we don't fall. Some of the rope still holds.

Axel and I swing harder. A branch comes within reach. I grab hold of it. The net volleys backward, and my arm yanks like it's being ripped from the socket.

Axel wriggles around me and catches the branch to help bear the weight.

Sweat drips from my temples. The wolf is watching us, waiting to bite the rope again. But the rope has a mind of its own.

Snap!

The last of it severs. The net falls limp. I cry out. Only our arms anchor us now.

The heavy net and excess rope drag at our bodies. The rough branch cuts into my palms. My arms are shaking. My grip is prying free. "Axel!"

He grunts, maneuvering us along the branch, hand over hand. "Keep moving! We have to reach that lower branch!"

Eight feet away, closer to the trunk, a branch veers upward—a branch we can rest our feet on. I wait until Axel's grip is secure before I let go with one hand, find new purchase, and repeat the careful process with the other hand.

We finally reach the lower branch and stand on it, relaxing a bit as it holds some of the net's weight. We still have to travel down the tree, lugging the net with us.

By the time we reach the ground, I'm practically crying from exertion. We haven't eaten in two days, and I've used every last bit of strength.

I collapse onto my knees, and Axel flops over beside me. The next thing I know, I'm getting nudged with the hilt of a knife. I glance up and meet a pair of vivid violet eyes.

"Oh, Grandmère." If I wasn't still tangled in rope, I'd fling my arms around her.

I take the knife from her teeth and start sawing the net. My hands are so weak, I keep dropping the blade. Axel picks it up and finishes, though his grip also slips twice. At last, he cuts a big enough hole for us to squeeze through.

We crawl out, and I uncurl my body to lie flat on the earth. My S-curve protests, but it's still wonderful to stretch my limbs and not be smashed anymore.

Grandmère's snout burrows into my neck, and I stroke her furry head. "Thank you," I say. "You gave us a fighting chance." The third midnight still awaits us, but at least we can defend ourselves when Rudger returns.

"Could you stay with us?" I ask, sitting up. "With you at our side, we might . . ." My voice fades as I take in the way she's panting, the haggard look in her eyes, her limply hanging tail. "You're still unwell. Grandmère, you shouldn't have come."

She whines the softest peal, and my heart wrenches. I wish I knew what she was trying to say, but I fear I already know. The last time we spoke, she said, *You will live. I will die to make it so.*

But I want *her* to live and all my family back together again. My father in the sheep pasture, my mother spinning yarn, and Grandmère reading us stories by the crackling fire.

The Grimm wolf rubs her cheek against mine, then she turns, head lowered, and wanders off into the forest the way she came.

Moisture gathers in my eyes. I don't know if I'll ever see her again, or how long she can keep holding on like this.

Axel comes beside me, and I curl into him, wanting to hide from the world and not face what lies ahead. A riddle that must be solved by midnight. Axel's madman uncle. The mystery of his father. A murder for which we have no clues. And time that's running short.

The time you have left
Is as a clock's gilt hands.
Measure it wisely
Lest the killer seize command.

"The pocket watch," I gasp. "The time has been changing ever since Rudger gave us the riddle. Three o'clock, then two o'clock, and today one o'clock. I think it's been counting down the three midnights."

Axel pulls the watch out and opens the clasp. It's still set to one o'clock. "You think my father obtained a magical watch?"

I've never heard of magic beyond these woods besides my grandmother's and the family of Anivoyantes she came from. "Either that or the forest's magic is working upon it."

Axel's thumb brushes the side of the watch where it can open to reveal the hidden inscription. "How does a countdown help if we already know when our time will run out?"

"Maybe it's a hint that the killer we're searching for is . . . well, your uncle."

He bristles. "That's a bit of a stretch, don't you think?"

"Aren't we looking for any kind of clues?"

Axel rises and stuffs the pocket watch away. "We should eat. It will help us think clearly."

I sigh. I doubt he can think clearly when it comes to his family.

We pull rations from our packs and try not to inhale them all at once. Our waterskins are running low, so we're careful to drink less. We need to find a creek or water hole soon . . . that is, if we survive the day.

"We should look for a large clearing." Axel kneels to pack up our gear. "Rudger's going to come after us, so the farther we are from trees he can weaponize, the better."

I grab my crossbow and the rest of my belongings, except my bag of tokens, which is missing. Rudger stole the most crucial thing I need to solve the murder.

I pivot to Axel. "What if we hunt down Rudger?"

"Hunt him?" he asks, as if he hasn't heard me correctly.

"He must have a place in this forest he calls home. We can

follow his tracks there and be the ones to surprise *him*. It's better than offering ourselves up as bait again."

"What about the Sommer girls? If we follow Rudger's trail, we'll lose theirs."

"Couldn't we retrace our steps back here?"

"Not if the trees move while we're away."

That stumps me until my gaze falls on a path of small, polished rocks in a tiny gulch. They remind me of the pebbles Hansel and Gretel used to find their way back home when they ventured out to lure Henni on our last journey.

"Axel, I have an idea."

CHAPTER 19

Considering how devious Rudger is, it's strange how easy his tracks are to spot. But I suppose we're the only people who have pursued him rather than fled. His clumsy, deep-footed imprints alternate with light and erratic ones, like he's either tromping or dancing his way through the woods.

I drop pebbles as we travel, hoping the trees won't knock them askew and we can find our way back to where we started. Assuming we live through tonight.

I tug my fur mantle tighter over my cape. Most of the Forest Grimm thrives with dense evergreens, fir, spruce, and pine, but we're in an area teeming with broadleaf trees. Beeches and scattered maples are dressed for the season in a parade of autumn colors. Under other circumstances, they might look beautiful, but today their yellows lean garish and deathly, and their reds glisten scarlet like spilled blood.

"Do you remember where your uncle was on the night Bren Zimmer was murdered?" I ask Axel, keeping my voice light. It has taken me an hour to pluck up the courage to broach this topic. It's better than insinuating directly that Rudger could be the murderer.

There's a hitch in his step, but he recovers and strides smoothly ahead. "Shouldn't we focus on solving Rudger's riddle?"

"That's what I'm doing." I lug my pack higher on my shoulders. No matter how I position it, my S-curve still twinges. "We're supposed to answer the riddle with two names: Rudger's own name and the one that captured his heart. His real name wasn't right, so his own name must be the name he's given himself as a Lost One. Maybe it has something to do with the murder—only if he's implicated, of course."

Axel hesitates, his hand brushing the feathery tips of dry wild grass. "I don't know where Rudger was that night," he confesses. "Not the full night, anyway."

Axel was sixteen years old and living with his uncle back then. "When did he come back home?"

"I didn't stick around to find out. Rudger left in a rage after supper. I knew it was better to steer clear of him when he was in one of his moods."

"What was he angry about?" I toss another pebble to mark our trail.

"Who knows? The slightest thing could set him off if he had enough to drink. And he usually did." On a deep inhale, Axel turns to face me. "I know what you're thinking."

"What?" I shuffle to a stop.

"Rudger is mean and violent, and I have little love for him, but he could never kill anyone."

If Axel doesn't realize how contradictory that statement is, I won't be the one to point it out. "Did he know Bren well?"

"Never saw them talk."

"Rudger never even asked him to forge a horseshoe?"

"We didn't stable any horses."

"Or repair a sickle?"

"Look, I'm sure they did some business, same as anyone in Grimm's Hollow. But I'd barely call them acquaintances."

I sigh, hitting the same wall I've come against from the start of investigating this murder: I don't know much about Bren, other than he was the prominent blacksmith in our village.

Nothing else was very remarkable about him. He had average looks—dusty brown hair, a soft and indistinctive nose, a slim build with muscular arms from his work at the forge—and an average personality to match. He didn't take part in petty feuds. He finished jobs on time. He never even had Grandmère read cards for him. A shame, since she could have warned him of his dire fate, like she'd warned me. . . .

The Midnight Forest. The Dueling Rings. Love Lost.

"We'll figure this out." The stubborn edge of Axel's voice is gone, replaced by his natural calm confidence. "The good news is we already know who captured my uncle's heart."

"We do?" We guessed wrong when we said Ollie.

"It must be my aunt, Ollie's mother. Her name was Lorelei." He starts walking again, following a meandering section of tracks. "It's hard to imagine, but I was always told Rudger was once kind and gentle. He doted on Lorelei and Ollie. They were his whole world. He was a better person when they were alive, a good farmer never indebted to anyone, and a faithful husband."

I study the slope of Axel's shoulders. "It's a pity he didn't save any of that goodness for you."

He kicks at a deep footprint. "He started drinking when Ollie and Lorelei died, and his love for the bottle eclipsed everything else."

I can't understand how someone who lost all his family could be so unwelcoming to Axel—Axel, who won the affection of so many villagers, always eager to help anyone in need, always ready with a smile to ease anyone's sorrows. "Maybe the person who captured Rudger's heart isn't as straightforward as we think. What if *you're* that person?"

Axel stiffens. Turns around. His brows climb toward his hairline. He falls into a fit of laughter rivaling one of Rudger's.

I fight a prick of defensiveness. "You could have grown on him over the years. And he *did* keep that pocket watch for you."

"Just to spite me," Axel quips. "Just to make sure I never felt my father's love again."

I bite my tongue against saying he can't be right—no one would be that cruel—but I haven't lived Axel's life. I was never beaten by a family member. I can only relate by knowing what my mother was like as Briar Rose, although that was only her Lost self. Before Rudger became Lost, he was already lost.

"About the pocket watch . . ." Axel's countenance brightens. "My father must have recovered enough to get it for me. And what if, while he was traveling back to Grimm's Hollow, he lost his memories again, but this time because of the curse? If he became a Lost One, it would explain why I haven't seen him."

"Possibly, but—"

"Then at some point Rudger bumped into him, got this watch and . . ." Axel shrugs. "There's bound to be an explanation for that part. But I really do feel that he's alive."

"I hope so." I paste on a grin, trying to match his optimism. "We don't know that yet, but—"

"We will soon. You'll have another vision and find out."

I struggle to hold my smile. My face feels as brittle as a sheet of glass beneath a sharp heel.

"I figured out what set off your vision too," Axel goes on, oblivious to the tension stirring within me. "We were arguing, and I got upset when you said I never loved Rudger like I loved my father. So you were thinking of my father when you touched the pocket watch."

I toss a pebble and remain silent.

"That means the vision wasn't totally unbidden. It was triggered by that token plus your thoughts of my father while your emotions were heightened. So all you have to do is repeat those things."

I doubt it's that simple. "I promise to do my best." My stomach tightens. I'm terrified of failing as much as succeeding. Either way, I could break Axel's heart.

"Is everything all right?" he asks.

A frog hops into my path, saving me from having to answer. I spot its V-shaped splotch and frown. "Look who's back."

Axel ambles closer. "What do you suppose he wants from us?"

"*He* could be a she. Maybe a spy for Rudger. Regardless of gender, it's still a Lost One up to no good."

"Should we try to capture her? Or him?" Axel whispers.

I nod slowly. The frog could serve as leverage against Rudger, someone valuable he wouldn't want kidnapped or hurt.

"Act casual," Axel says. Which is difficult when we're both already staring openly at the frog. It blinks, its translucent lower eyelid flickering up and down.

"I'm hungry," I announce, and remove my pack.

"Me too," Axel answers loudly. "What do you have in there?"

"Hollow bread, sheep cheese, a sack of—"

Axel dives for the frog. It croaks and leaps away before Axel's hands close over it.

I spring after it, but the frog bounds off into the thick underbrush.

Axel curses. I rake my hands through my hair. That went horribly wrong. Now the frog will probably find Rudger and signal we're coming.

Defeated for the moment, we allow ourselves a small break to eat and plot our next move. We agree we should still pursue Rudger. At the very least, we need to get my tokens back.

I'm surprised we haven't already found his home. The day is halfway over. How far did he travel each night to reach us?

Maybe we're walking in circles. It's hard to say. The forest has grown dark and shadowy, the sun hidden behind bruised-purple clouds.

It starts to rain. First a light sprinkle, then a steady pattering, then a downright deluge.

Rudger's tracks wash away.

I look behind me at the trail of pebbles I've been making all day. Even if they don't get buried in mud, if we follow them back, we'll face the same dilemma. The Sommer girls' tracks will be gone too.

Lightning strikes. I jump as a blinding flash zigzags down on a tree ahead. Axel grabs me, and we rush beneath a shorter tree.

Another bolt hits. We crouch, tuck our heads, and clap our hands over our ears against the deafening thunder.

Gradually, the lightning and thunder grow more distant.

"Now what?" Axel's breath fogs, his nose pink from the cold, and tendrils of hair slicked to the sharp planes of his face.

I have no idea. We could wait here until midnight, but for how dense the woods are with trees that Rudger could use against us, we may as well be offering ourselves up on a silver platter.

Six feet away, the frog with a V-shaped splotch crawls out from a hollowed log and fastens its bulging eyes on us.

I nudge Axel, and he scoffs under his breath. "Do you think it has a death wish?"

I remember my first encounter with the frog. It jumped on my face the moment I heard Rudger's cackle. "What if it's been trying to warn us? Help us?"

"What kind of Lost One would help us?"

"Maybe it isn't a Lost One. All we know is it's been sticking around for three days now and hasn't done us any harm."

Axel scratches the back of his neck. "What do you suggest we do?"

I purse my lips, thinking, then slowly approach the frog. "Don't worry. We don't want to capture you anymore." I kneel before it, noticing the pads on its thumbs, distinctive to males, and smile. "Hello, little fellow. I wish we knew your name—assuming you have a name and were once a person. How did you become a frog, I wonder?"

His throat bubbles, pulsing rapidly as he breathes.

"I know you can't speak, but if there's something you want to tell us, we'll do our best to understand."

The frog croaks and hops off into the rain.

I let out a heavy sigh. Ollie was right. Frogs are just frogs. There's nothing special about this one.

The frog lands on a stone and turns back, croaking louder.

I rise and Axel joins my side.

The frog leaps two more bounds, looks back at us, and croaks again.

"Axel, I think he wants us to follow him."

My wavering tone doesn't instill the greatest confidence, so it's no wonder Axel asks, "But we're not going to, right? Surely we'd be walking into another trap."

"If that trap is Rudger's dwelling place, that's what we're after, right? It's better than waiting around to be hunted."

Axel releases an exhale that puffs a steamy cloud into the damp and dreary woods. "I guess we'll find out."

He tightens his scarf. I double-knot the strings of my cape.

We follow the frog.

CHAPTER 20

As the rain falls with a vengeance, the frog leads us over flooded gulches, muddy paths, and slippery grass. The trees grow denser in tight, foggy thickets. We pick our way forward, eyes trained on the little green creature that has become our compass.

When night falls, dark clouds mask the moon and stars, and we're left to the mercy of our lantern light against the storm. The frog becomes harder to spot, but when we lose sight of him, it isn't long before he hops back and croaks at our feet again.

I lose track of the time, but I'm certain it isn't yet midnight. Rudger would be here, like an all-seeing apparition. Somehow, he would have found us.

"Any more ideas about your uncle's Lost name?" I turn to Axel, shouting to be heard above the downpour, even though he's only three feet behind me.

He shakes his head, drenched to the bone and utterly miserable. We've been tossing around ideas based on how other Lost Ones came up with their names.

Rapunzel was a literal name. "It's what I am," Fiora told us when we met her in her forest tower. "Rapunzel" meant "rampion," which her mother had eaten while pregnant, and it caused Fiora to be born with red-rampion-colored hair.

Then there's Ella, who the villagers started calling "Cinderella" when word spread that her wedding dress was covered in cinders as she was lured into the forest. Lost villagers who later encountered her must have still called her that name, which she adopted.

My mother introduced herself as Briar Rose in the fortress castle she'd claimed as her home. That name originated from her obsession with the color red. She'd forgotten she was searching for rampion, not roses, in her quest to find what she'd lost—me in a cape dyed with red rampion.

"If Rudger follows Fiora's and Ella's pattern, then 'Village Drunk' will be his new name." Axel wrings out his scarf, surrendering to the rain. "Our time has to be almost up, Clara. I don't think we're going to solve the riddle."

A pit of dread sinks in my stomach. "Then we'll find something to use as leverage against him."

If there is something. And if we ever arrive at Rudger's home.

I take another step. Something wriggles beneath my foot. I yelp and jerk back as the frog leaps away. I almost smashed him. "Sorry!"

He hops through a spread of trees so thick they may as well be a wall.

"Come back! I promise I'll watch where I'm going!"

He doesn't return.

I peer through the trees and grab two trunks, trying to squeeze through them, when to my surprise, they bend like tall reeds. Maybe they aren't trees, but some sort of freakish shrub.

I pass through them, and my lantern's glow floods my surroundings. My jaw unhinges. "Axel!"

He worms his way between the stalks and halts. "What in all the land, water, and sky . . . ? Is this what I think it is?"

I glimpse my bag of tokens a few yards ahead on a stone pillar in the center of this strange chamber. The frog leaps on top of the pillar and ribbits proudly.

"Yes," I reply. We've found Rudger's home.

It isn't so much of a chamber, actually. "Chamber" evokes something pleasant, like a spacious bedroom or reception hall. This is a predator's lair.

The area is roughly circular, thirty feet across, and surrounded by more stalky walls of pliable bark-like plants. They arch overhead and knit in a tangled roof that keeps out the rain.

In the center of the lair, more pillars cluster together in varying heights, some two feet tall, some six. They're like a shrine for a pirate's bounty, for upon each one is some kind of treasure. A dented flask. A violet ribbon. A lone leather shoe. A spyglass. A locket with a broken chain.

They're tokens like mine . . . except Rudger must have done more than steal to obtain them. Strands of hair are caught in the ribbon. The spyglass reveals bloody fingerprints.

They're *trophies*. Of people Rudger has killed.

I swallow a surge of nausea and turn my head into Axel's shoulder. I can't bear looking at them anymore.

"I tried to warn you away," says the voice of a little boy.

My head snaps up. I find Ollie sitting at the edge of a pile of leaves, mulch, and grass that Rudger must use for a bed. A rodent with a long tail burrows inside it, and I shiver.

"Oh, Ollie, this is terrible."

Axel shifts, hearing me speak to his cousin.

"I wish you never had to see your father become capable of—of this," I say, darting around the word "murder."

Ollie doesn't look at the trophies, but his eyes are large, almost swollen with grief. "This happens to everyone who stays too long in the forest. It isn't his fault."

"Still, you shouldn't have had to—"

"I told you he was a good man." Ollie sniffs. "He sang me songs every night. He tickled me to make me laugh. He plucked flowers for Mama's kitchen. Why can't you leave him alone?"

"You know why, Ollie," I answer softly.

"He didn't make the curse happen. If you hurt him, Clara, I'll never forgive you."

"Why would you think I'd hurt him?"

His somber mood flashes to anger. "Because you and your friends are the only ones who have survived this forest!" He rises, hovering an inch above the ground. "You even died, and then woke up again! That isn't fair! Why didn't *I* wake up again?"

His words pierce me. I blink back a rush of burning tears.

Axel jostles my arm. "Ask him if he's seen my father."

"I can't—"

To our left, the wall of stalks rustles. We drop our packs. Axel whips out his hatchet. I notch an arrow on my crossbow.

Ollie vanishes and reappears directly in front of me. I startle and nearly fire my arrow.

"If I tell you a secret about the riddle"—the ghostly edges of him streak and blur—"you have to promise not to hurt him."

Desperate for help, I nod rapidly.

"Ever since my father came to the forest, he's worn a special ring. He loves it more than all his treasures. It has a secret, and I think it can help you figure out the second name in the riddle."

"How?" Adrenaline courses through me. "Does it have an inscription?"

Ollie never says.

He fades to nothing, and then nine feet behind him, Rudger parts the stalks and enters his lair.

CHAPTER 21

Rudger isn't wearing the handkerchief over his mouth, and for the first time, I fully take in the Lost person he's become.

Dripping wet, his hair hangs to his shoulders, so filthy I wouldn't know it's naturally russet, like Ollie's. His brown eyes are beady and wild. The hollows beneath them sink deep, while his cheekbones protrude sharply, jutting above his thick, matted beard. He's thinner but wiry, emanating manic energy with twitchy movements and rapid blinking. He's like a rabid dog, crazed, violent, and vicious.

His eyes round to find us in his lair, but he can't be too surprised. He had to be following us to arrive so soon—and so close to what must be midnight.

"Little wolf and her feisty lover." Rudger's lip curls as he traipses toward his pillar shrine. "Are they ready to die?" he asks himself. "I will let her live until she bears the children."

I flinch. *Children? As in more than one?*

"But the boy will die tonight," he says. "They will never guess the names."

He steps onto a lower pillar and quickly scales the others, balancing on the toes of his tattered boots. He doesn't disturb the trophies, though I scan the lot for anything he could use against us. He snatches up a palm-sized object. It must be a tinderbox because he opens it and strikes something, then a spark catches kindling.

He drops it in the center of the pillars. *Whoosh*. A rush of flames blazes upward.

I startle, bumping into Axel. I didn't realize there was anything down there, but now I see what looks like a stone-lined well. Except instead of water, it's filled with roughly hewn coal and some kind of oil or resin. Perhaps it's a relic from ancient days, used by soldiers who fought in the great battle. The stalks woven overhead roll back a little, undulating to fan out the smoke and stave off the rain.

"You were foolish to come here." Rudger stands tall atop a six-foot pillar and stares down at us. Underlit by the fire, his face is a bony canvas for eerie shadows. "But I do like this hitch in our game." His beard splits as he grins, two teeth black with decay. "It will be a pleasure to use my hut against you."

"What's our plan?" Axel says under his breath.

We never stole anything for leverage, and only one trinket can help us now. "Ollie said Rudger wears a ring with a secret, and it will help us solve the second name," I whisper.

"What about Rudger's Lost name?"

"No idea. But we need that ring at all costs."

Axel nods gravely. "Good thing I sharpened my hatchet."

I hope he doesn't mean to cut off his uncle's finger. I promised Ollie not to harm him.

"What do they whisper?" Rudger muses. "They think they are clever"—he twitches—"but no one is cleverer than me."

"You're right." I lower my crossbow and lock my knees to keep them from quaking. "It took a great deal of effort to solve the answers to a riddle so impressive."

"What are you doing?" Axel hisses.

"Stalling," I murmur.

Rudger narrows one eye. I finally glimpse the ring on his left hand. It's caked in grime, but one untarnished spot catches the firelight.

He slinks down the pillars until he reaches the ground. "Tick tock, my friends. Tell me your answers, if you dare. I know you haven't solved them. No one ever guesses right."

I draw a shaky breath. "Shall I begin with your own name?"

Rudger snickers, a scathing laugh that spider-crawls over my skin. He bows with a flourish as if to say *Be my guest.*

I wrap my arms around myself. "Only it's such an interesting name that I feel shy saying it." *Please let me sound convincing.* "Would you mind if I whispered it in your ear?"

Axel tenses.

"She plays me for a fool." Rudger sneers. "She's up to something."

"Unless you're scared of me." I bat my eyelashes, feigning innocence. "Are little wolves so very fearsome?"

Rudger doesn't budge. Does he expect me to go to him? I set down my weapons and start to approach, shadowed by Axel.

Rudger wags a warning finger, and the stalks forming the walls hiss and creak as they rub together and strain at their roots.

I throw an arm out, blocking Axel. "I'll go alone," I murmur. Rudger is within ten feet now. Axel hesitates, but ultimately withdraws.

As I close the gap, it strikes me that I've seen Rudger like this before, backlit by a fire—in the vision I had when the frog struck my face. But my viewpoint was much lower then. The raggedy man had seemed like a giant.

I slow to a stop, four feet away.

Realization pins me rigid.

It was the frog who triggered my vision.

When I touched him, I saw the past from *his* perspective.

"Tick tock, little wolf." Rudger leers. I look past him to the frog on the pillar with my tokens. Could he help me have another vision? If he's seen more of Rudger's past, he may have witnessed this riddle play out and know the answer.

The stalks of the walls rustle louder.

Cold sweat breaks across my forehead. I walk the final distance. I've never succeeded in conjuring a vision on demand. I'll try for the ring instead.

"What a name you have for yourself," I say. "I hope I pronounce it correctly." I maneuver to Rudger's left side, lift on tiptoes to reach his ear, and grasp his left arm for balance. Beneath his long coat, his wiry arm hardens, but he doesn't tug away. I'm about to whisper, when I drop my head and gasp, "What a handsome ring!"

His head jerks sideways. His beady eyes survey me suspiciously. "She doesn't tell me her answer." The stalks hiss again, and my heart tumbles faster.

"Let me guess." I steady my voice. "You won this ring off someone by using your clever riddle. Of course you did! No one can match your wits. And what a beautiful prize you gained!"

I reach for his hand, like I want to admire the ring, but he yanks his arm back. The stalks slither forward three paces. Axel shifts for his hatchet, but I hold up a hand.

"Little wolf will whisper her answer," Rudger seethes, "or the game is over."

"Of course I will." *Think, Clara, think!* "But I'll give the second name first and answer with a riddle of my own. I'm sure you'll find it thrilling."

Rudger arches a grime-streaked brow.

I swiftly whisper in his ear, "When you look at your ring, you remember the second name."

He stumbles backward. "She cheats! She tricks me!"

The stalks lash closer. Panic grips me. I reach for Rudger. Snatch for his left hand.

He twists and slaps my face. My head whips sideways. Stars fleck my vision.

I'm so startled by the pain that my other senses dull. I don't notice how fast the stalks pick up speed, how shrilly they hiss, how quickly Axel charges for Rudger, or when the frog leaps from the pillars. It just feels as though, when I blink and refocus, mayhem reigns all around me.

Axel's hatchet swings for Rudger's left arm. The frog rebounds into Rudger's face. The tree-like stalks rage forward like monsters in seafaring stories, tentacles flailing.

Four stalks wrap around my waist. Hoist me in the air. I kick and flail, but can't break free.

"Axel!" I shout as two stalks whip for him.

He whirls and swings his blade again. The stalks sever in half.

He charges toward me, but more stalks attack him. He chops them down, but they keep coming.

"Call off your trees!" I yell at Rudger. "We're not cheating! I know your name!"

I turn to the frog. Open my hand. *Please trust me.* "Jump!"

He hesitates a split second. Then bounds toward me.

"I know what I'm doing," I rasp, more to myself than him. I found a way to channel my last vision. I directed it back to the clockmaker's stall and the pocket watch. "Let me in," I tell the frog as he leaps. "Teach me the answers I need."

He lands in my palm.

The lair flickers to black. Noise cuts in and out. Then all commotion silences.

The void closes over me, then disappears in a beat. My eyesight and hearing return. I'm back in the lair, but layered over it is the vibrant past.

The realm of visions.

CHAPTER 22

’m low on the ground and, strangely, can see in every direction. The frog's protruding eyes widen his field of vision. It's nighttime, and he's in the Forest Grimm.

The hazy figure of Rudger approaches and stumbles along a stream. He drinks from a flask, but he isn't deranged like the raggedy man.

I watch him sleep. Watch the forest play its tricks. He panics when he awakens, noticing the new placement of trees. Too scared to move, he stays there for another day and night.

Again, he sleeps. Again, the trees shift and he awakens. Only with less panic and more wonder. He traces the stream back to the village and repeats like a mantra, "The water didn't move."

Another night comes. Another moon. Rudger's beard has grown longer. He carries a pack and walking staff. His clothes are green, beige, and brown, same as before. Nothing is rampion red. How is he able to enter the forest?

He travels farther this time, never wandering from the waterways. But after a few days and nights—shown in rapid succession—he returns home again.

The pattern continues. Rudger journeys and comes back, each time more weatherworn and desperate, his eyes scouting all around him. What is he searching for?

He's becoming dirtier, twitchier. His clothes tear and fray. He twists the silver ring on his finger. "You can't hide forever," he babbles. "Why did you leave me?"

He never drops a name.

One day, he doesn't return home. He stops walking along a riverbank and screws up his brow. "Where did . . . ? What was . . . ?" He rubs the back of his neck the way Axel does and wanders off, leaving the water.

Whatever was protecting him from madness is no longer working.

In flashes, I glimpse him over the next months until he transforms into the person I met a few days ago, wild and ragged and dangerous.

He hunches over his reflection in the water, rocking back and forth and moaning. He speaks in cut-off phrases and strings of mean words. "Never love me . . . Ugly. Gaunt. Bony. Legs like stilts. Filthy. Frazzled. Tattered. Rumpled . . . rumpled on stilts . . . rumplestilts . . . rumpelstiltskin."

His moans hitch into sobs, which swiftly turn into maniacal laughter. "Love me now." He rolls onto his back and claws at his ring. "I'll make you!"

Blackness crowds my eyesight. The vision is ending. I've seen everything important about Rudger that the frog can show me, and I'm being pulled from his memories.

Wait! I grasp at his mind. I haven't formed any conclusive answers. I was focusing on the forest, but did the frog ever go to the village? Animals can cross the ash-lined border freely. It's how Grandmère comes and goes as the Grimm wolf.

Blackness swims over everything now, like I'm caught in a swarm of dark moths. I can't fight the pull. There's only time for one more glance at a memory.

Show me the last time you saw Rudger in Grimm's Hollow, I think desperately.

In a blink, I'm on a side street near the village square. It's dusk, and Rudger shuffles past me, walking into a tavern. By all appearances, he looks as he once did. He isn't Lost.

The swarm of blackness thickens.

That's all you saw of Rudger?

Then it strikes me that my vantage point is higher than the frog's other memories.

Turning, the frog catches his reflection in a shop window.

But it isn't the frog staring back at me. It's a boy. Teenaged. Sad eyes. Naturally peaked brows. That's all I can see of his face past the swarm, but it stokes familiarity.

Do I know you?

I'm sucked from the vision and slammed back into Rudger's lair.

My back is scalding. The frog croaks wildly in my grip. My eyesight blurs with rippling heat. *Oh no.*

I angle my head around. Peek below. Gasp to see I'm dangling over the blazing fire, only held up by the stalks coiled at my waist. But they're lowering, lowering . . .

I release the frog, and he jumps free.

"Clara!" Axel's voice is hoarse, like he's been shouting on end.

He isn't far from where I last saw him, so I couldn't have been in the vision for long. He's cut down several stalks, but they're still attacking. Rudger keeps sending more across the lair.

I'm lowered another inch, and the hem of my cape catches fire. I yank up the fabric and smother the flames. "Here is the first answer to your riddle!" I call to Rudger. "Your own name is"—I sift through the words he babbled—"Rumpelstiltskin!"

The stalks holding me freeze.

Rudger's eyes flare so wide the whites around his irises shine. "How does she know?"

Relief floods me. *I answered right.*

Axel takes advantage of Rudger's stupor and rushes up the

pillars to help me. He hacks away the stalks binding me and pulls me to safety.

Rudger's expression darkens to a withering scowl. "They think they have won, but they haven't finished answering the riddle. What is the second name?"

Any smugness I feel dies in the burning acid of my stomach. "We need the ring," I breathe to Axel.

"Sneak behind him," he murmurs, sweat dripping off his nose. "I'll distract him."

Hatchet raised, he takes a wide leap off the pillars. Rudger trips backward. Looks to the stalks for help. Three come flying for Axel.

I scramble down the back of the pillar shrine, haphazardly knocking trinkets and baubles out of my way. Ducking low, I race around the lair.

I'm within six feet of Rudger now. His back is turned, his focus on Axel.

Axel's hatchet is flying in every direction. Our surroundings are a storm of writhing stalks. I can't see past them to find my knife or crossbow.

The frog hops on my shoulder. Croaks loudly and jumps behind me. I turn and spy my knife.

I pluck it up. Whip off the sheath. Charge for Rudger. "Rumpelstiltskin!" I shout, knowing that name will draw his attention.

He whirls around, his coat parting. I swipe fast. Cut a shallow line across his stomach. Blood blooms through his shirt.

He staggers on his feet.

I slash at his left hand with all my strength. The blade slices deeper across Rudger's palm. He crashes to his knees. Cradles his hand.

A thick stalk lashes for me. I'm about to shout Axel's name, when his hatchet flies within inches of my head. It soars past my face and impales the stalk. He hurries to free his weapon.

I dive at Rudger. Grip his left hand. Squeeze the bloody wound. He wails. I hold my knife to his throat. "Give me the ring if you want to live," I growl. I've never heard myself sound so vicious.

He wrests it off. "She cheats! She tricks me!"

I feel the cool metal in my palm and close my fist around it. "Call off the trees!"

He sneers harder. I labor to steady my trembling hand. "She lies," he whispers to himself. "She will not kill me."

With unbridled venom, he shoves me back and lands a hard kick on my stomach. I skid across the ground, wheezing. I've dropped the ring.

I scramble for it at the same time Rudger does. Axel pulls his hatchet loose and swings at a fresh set of writhing stalks.

Rudger is closer to the ring. He reaches for it, fingers splayed. They're about to close over it when the frog leaps ahead of him. He scoops the ring into his mouth and bounds for me. Spits the ring in my palm.

I rub the grime away and search for an inscription. There is none. But there *is* a tiny hinge. The ring can open.

Rudger lunges for me. Axel brings his blade to the back of Rudger's neck. "You won't touch her again," he warns, panting. "And call off the damn trees."

Rudger stiffens. The stalks tangling overhead still at once.

I locate a slim lid that curves over half of the ring. I slip my fingernail under the end and pop it open. Inside is a lock of intricately plaited hair, wrapped like an inner ring at the silver ring's core. I gasp as I take in the hair's unmistakable shade: rampion red.

I raise my head and meet Rudger's crazed eyes. "The name of the person who captured your heart is Fiora Winther."

CHAPTER 23

Rudger releases a howl of rage that dissolves into a wail. "Now I cannot steal her babies! I'll never have my children."

I sneak a look at Axel to see if he's drawing the same conclusions I am. From the way he's staring openly at the lock of red hair and how wide his mouth hangs open, it's safe to say *yes*. As impossible as it is to fathom, Rudger and Fiora were once lovers, and Hansel and Gretel are the children who came from that union. Which means they're Axel's cousins.

I consider telling Rudger that they're no longer in the forest, but hold my tongue. When the twins were three years old, Fiora fled here with them for a purpose. I assumed it was to avoid scandal for bearing them out of wedlock—as they grew, they were harder to keep hidden—but for whatever reason, Fiora didn't marry Rudger. And since I don't know that reason, I feel obliged to protect her.

"We won your game, so you need to keep to your terms," I say. "You'll let us live."

Rudger's nostrils flare, but he reluctantly nods.

"Swear on this ring and Fiora's name that you'll never harm us again."

Rudger's eyes linger on the silver band. "She cheated. She didn't play fairly," he mutters. "She should give me back the ring."

"No." I close the lid over Fiora's hair. "*You* cheated. You tried to kill us before we had a chance to fully answer your riddle. I'll keep this ring to right that wrong."

"But how will I find what I've lost without it?" he whimpers.

I doubt Rudger ever realized what this ring once did for him—it must be how he entered the forest without consequence for a time. But I don't dare give it back. We haven't ruled out the possibility that he murdered Bren Zimmer. This can serve as my token for him.

"Swear on this ring and Fiora's name that you'll never harm us again," I repeat.

Axel presses his hatchet closer to his uncle's neck.

Rudger swipes tears from his eyes. "I swear on the ring and Fiora's name!"

I slip the ring on my pointer finger. "Let's tie him to a pillar," I tell Axel.

Axel pulls his blade away, but he can't stop staring at the back of his uncle's emaciated neck and the hollowing around his vertebrae. "Do you have food to eat?" he asks, emotionless, though the question betrays a sliver of affection.

"The boy doesn't know how well I survive here." Rudger straightens his coat. "Roots and berries fill my belly. Crickets and worms, mice and frogs." The frog with the V-shaped splotch hops two yards away. "I live like a king."

Jaw clenched, Axel gives him bread and cheese from our packs, and Rudger eats them greedily despite his claims of self-sustenance. We guide him to sit against a pillar and rope him to it.

"We have some riddles *you* need to answer," I say. "But they can wait until tomorrow." I'm sure it will be a long conversation, Lost as he is.

"I do have one riddle for tonight." Axel withdraws the pocket watch and dangles it from the chain. "A man named Kellen Furst may be in this forest. He looks like me. And he would have had this pocket watch at some point. Have you seen him?"

"If I did, I would have stolen that already."

"You did, actually."

"We don't know that," I interject.

"It was at his house."

"In *here*?" Rudger blinks.

"No, in the village," I say. "Before you were Lost."

"I lost myself?"

Axel rolls out his neck. "Forget about the pocket watch, all right? Have you seen a man who looks like me?"

Rudger's brow folds into a dozen furrows. "*You're* the man who looks like you."

Axel drags a hand down his face.

I touch his shoulder. "Let's get some rest. Any discussion with him is futile tonight."

I spot the frog on the shrine of pillars, perched on my drawstring bag of tokens like before. "Don't worry, I haven't forgotten about those."

"Hmm?" Axel says.

"I was just talking to the frog." I climb the shrine and retrieve my bag. "He helped me have a vision tonight. He's like a living token, Axel. When I held him, I saw Rudger's past through his eyes. It's how I learned Rudger's Lost name."

"I was wondering how you came up with that." Axel unstraps our bedrolls. "Keep having visions, Clara, and you'll be able to figure out where my father is in no time."

Anxiety needles my gut. He's talking like he's sure his father is alive, but if he isn't, I don't want to be the one to see it in a memory and have to break the horrible truth. That would be a death blow to Axel, a spindle that kills rather than saves.

"Did the time change on the pocket watch?" I ask, switching

subjects. "I'm betting the hands are at midnight now that the countdown is over."

Axel pops the silver case open. "Um, no. It's set to eight o'clock."

"Eight o'clock?" I walk over to see for myself. "For eight days, do you think? Eight days until what?"

"Maybe nothing." He shakes the watch. "Maybe something is faulty."

A niggling feeling says otherwise, but I'm too tired to puzzle over what it all means. Let it be another riddle for tomorrow.

I help Axel finish setting up our beds and lie down beside him. The last thing I want to do is sleep near Rudger's killing trophies, but it would be unwise to let him out of our sight, even if he is tied up and swore an oath not to harm us.

Twelve feet away, his beady eyes are fastened on me, his lips curled back to show his teeth. I shiver and tuck closer to Axel's warmth. "We haven't tied our ankles," I whisper.

"Don't worry." He wraps a strong arm around me and kisses my brow. "I won't let you go."

He holds the pocket watch, and I imagine its sound if it were ticking . . . perhaps like the slowing patter of rain against the last stalks woven into the ceiling.

Tick tock, pit pat, tick tock, pit pat.

Axel is the first to fall asleep to the lulling rhythm. Rudger's snoring soon follows, and I relax a little. The frog lopes nearer and settles beside me. My back faces the fire and casts the frog in shadow. I can only see the general shape of his body and the glossy sheen of his eyes.

I stroke the top of his head. "Is this okay?"

He croaks once, so soft it's almost like a purr.

"You saved our lives tonight. If you hadn't brought me the ring, we wouldn't have survived. I should also thank you for allowing me to have a vision of your past," I say, in case he doesn't realize what happened when he leapt into my hand. "That also saved us. I suppose there's a lot more you could help us with. Maybe you've seen other Lost Ones, for starters."

Croak.

"I look forward to visiting more of your memories . . . if you're willing."

Croak.

"It would be nice to learn who you are too."

Croak.

"Well, goodnight, then."

His croaking stops. He folds his limbs under his body and lowers his head. I stroke him for a few more minutes until I fall asleep.

Beautiful music drifts to my ears, a simple melody made lovelier by its haunting minor key. It's the sort of song that's always called to me, plaintive and soothing. How nice it is to hear it in a dream. It's as if my mind is helping me relax after a very stressful few days.

I find myself in the village square of Grimm's Hollow. It's market day. A woman at a cart is selling bouquets of violets, snowdrops, and irises. Spring flowers.

Spring.

I inhale the floral, budding fragrance. I haven't seen any signs of this season since before the curse.

I take another look around me and spy villagers with easier smiles, rounder cheeks, and unguarded demeanors. Among them are several Lost Ones. Ada Krause sells bottles of her signature cherry brandy, and Kasper von Weyler showcases a clever cuckoo clock to children who laugh and clap when the bird pops out, not only singing, but also flapping its wings.

One of those children is Henni. She's eleven or twelve and

simply adorable in her short-skirted green dress, high-kneed socks, and two braids with fat bows on the ends.

As the music continues to wash over me, I spot the source. On the west side of the square, under the shade of an awning, a teenaged boy leans back against a half-timbered shop, one of his legs bent as he plays a double-reed pipe.

I wander over to him. His pipe is among my tokens. I snatched it from Herr Oswald's bag at the autumn festival. This must be Harlan Oswald, Herr Oswald's son.

His walnut-brown hair hangs to his jawline, and his brows are peaked like slightly flattened *V*s turned upside down. His most dramatic feature is his dark eyes, and when I study their natural downward slope, giving him a somber countenance, my skin tingles. He was the boy whose reflection I glimpsed in my last vision. Which means . . .

This isn't a dream, but another vision.

A second vision brought on by touching the frog.

A frog who must be Harlan.

Or at least *was* him once.

I drift closer to him, unabashedly staring as I try to absorb everything. I've never had a vision while sleeping, or one so vivid. But in other ways, this vision feels more like the first two I had on my last journey, the ones of Axel and my mother. I don't feel as if I'm in the body of the person whose past I'm seeing—and this must be Harlan's past—instead, I'm an observer rooted in my own perspective.

I stop six feet away and listen to him play awhile. He doesn't have a cup set out to collect money; he seems content to perform for pleasure and the enjoyment it gives others.

Lila Sommer especially enjoys it. She makes a point to pass Harlan three times, twirling a spiral of her ebony hair, and all eleven of the other Sommer girls follow like ducklings, their hair ribbons flitting as if they've grown tail feathers.

Lila is the most striking with her large amber eyes, shimmering bronze skin, high cheekbones, and perfectly arched brows. Before Lila and Harlan went missing in the forest, they were sweethearts. This memory must have been before they became a couple, or else Lila wouldn't be acting so coquettish.

On the fourth pass, she stops in front of him, one brow lifted as if Harlan should do something more to impress her. One side of his mouth quirks up. He plays a sweeping trill of notes that demonstrates amazing breath control and deft fingers as they dance over the tone holes.

Lila flickers a smile, raises her chin, and prances away, her friends bustling in her wake. The younger ones glance back at Harlan and giggle.

He grins after them. His eyes don't look sad when he smiles; instead, they evoke a sort of sweet serenity. Harlan turns and spears me with a direct gaze. "You were very brave tonight."

A jolt rocks my heart. *He can't be looking at me.* I glance over my shoulder, but I'm the only one nearby. "How is this possible?"

He chuckles softly. "These visions are your gift, not mine, Clara. Whatever the reason, it's nice to finally speak with you."

"But . . ." My brain is like a clock with snagging, grinding gears. "This is *your* memory. You're in the past; I'm in the present. And what do you mean, I was brave tonight? How does your past self know what happened *tonight*?"

"Like I said, it's your magic." Dimples flash on his cheeks.

I step backward and cross my arms. "Are you an Anivoyante?" Maybe Grandmère didn't know about other shifter seers in the world.

Harlan unhitches himself from the wall. "I've heard you and

Axel use that word before. It's something to do with your grand-mother becoming a werewolf, right?"

I snort. "Werewolves are make-believe."

"If you say so." One of Harlan's peaked brows lifts higher. "I wouldn't question it after some of the strange things I've seen in the forest." He steps out from the shade of the awning and stretches his arms in the sunshine. "If she isn't trapped as an animal, like I am, I doubt we're the same thing."

"But how did this happen to you?" He's talking as if he's in the present, but the Harlan before me appears to be about sixteen years old. At this time in his life, he would have been looking forward to all that came with his coming of age. Such a pity that a year and a half from now, he would become one of many villagers who went missing during the first year of the curse. Unless . . . "You *are* a Lost One, aren't you?"

"Not exactly." He toys with his pipe. "Not in the sense that I've lost my sanity, like Rudger. That's what the curse did to the others I've seen in the forest. But I'm different. The curse turned me into a frog—my own brand of misery."

"Maybe being an animal preserved your wits."

He shrugs. "Maybe."

"In any case, I'm grateful you were able to help me solve Rudger's riddle."

"I'm glad my memories were useful."

I nibble on my lower lip. "Would you be willing to help me solve another mystery? It has to do with the curse and whoever is responsible."

Harlan cocks his head. "I've heard you and Axel talk about that too."

"If we could end the curse, you'd be human again, and the Lost Ones will be saved. They'll return to their former selves and find their way home."

"Those who are alive, anyway." His gaze cuts to Lila, and his eyes turn wistful.

She's at the cart of a haberdasher merchant. She and her friends are playing with a long turquoise ribbon, wrapping it around her waist as she twirls and laughs. "Is she still alive?" I ask delicately.

Harlan's gaze drops. He dawdles for a moment, pocketing his pipe and running a hand through his hair. "That's what you want me to tell you, isn't it? If any Lost Ones are still alive?"

"It would save a lot of time," I admit.

"I can't claim to know everything. Some people I've seen might have since died."

"Anything you can share will help."

"What if the person you're searching for *is* dead?"

"They can't be. It's a long story, but *Sortes Fortunae* gave clues. Basically, this person is also hiding the page that went missing from the book, which we need to break the curse, and if we don't hurry, they could seize command."

Harlan's brows rise. "Sounds complicated."

"And urgent." I'm pressuring him, but I've no other choice. I need his help.

He kicks at the cobblestones. "It's a lot of names to remember." He tosses me a teasing grin. "Too bad you couldn't have brought your notebook."

I tug the folds of my cape closer. "It's strange that you know about my notebook. *All* of this is strange. I hope you never watched me do anything embarrassing with those all-seeing frog eyes."

"I'm good at burrowing when I need to," he replies wryly. "I've tried my best not to be invasive."

"I suppose I'm one to talk when I've had three visions of you."

"I don't mind."

"You're too generous." I cough. There's a strange tickle in my throat. "Do you think you'll remember this?" From how the present is colliding with the past, it makes me believe anything is possible.

Harlan turns up his hands. "Ask me in the morning."

Something stings my neck. I swat at it. "Do you smell that?" My lungs strain for air, and I cough harder.

"Smell what?"

"I think something is burning."

I flinch as I'm stung a second time. An ember flashes by. Smoke clouds my eyes. I can't see anything past it. "Harlan?"

I'm thrown into blackness, silence. Then my eyes open. Sound roars. Heat blazes.

Rudger's lair is on fire.

CHAPTER 24

I cough and roll over, nearly retching from the cloying smoke. Someone hauls me to my feet. *Axel.* Past the haze, his blue eyes pierce mine. He wraps a corner of my cape over my nose and mouth and buries his own face in his scarf. Burning stalks drop around us as he rushes me outside Rudger's lair.

This living nightmare is surreal and singes at the edges of my sanity. I still have one foot in the realm of visions, the peaceful springtime of Grimm's Hollow. As I grapple with what's happening, I suddenly remember Rudger.

We tied him to a pillar!

I've barely choked in fresh air when I wheel around to run inside.

"Clara, no!" Axel yanks me back as a blazing row of stalks topples over.

"But your uncle!"

"He's gone."

"Gone? Gone as in . . ." I can't say it. I can't have any more death on my hands.

"He's alive. He escaped." Axel grimaces. "I'm sure he did this."

I gaze at the raging flames, like a giant-sized bonfire gone horribly wrong. Rudger's control over the trees is on a level I never anticipated. He must have commanded each stalk to run dry of rain, rendering them flammable.

"He promised not to harm us." I sound like a child who's just learned a pet snake will still bite.

"I wasn't holding out hope on that. Rudger was never good at keeping promises."

I jolt forward as I realize something else. "Our packs! My tokens!"

"I threw everything outside." Axel points to our ramshackle pile of belongings. One of the lantern's panes is shattered, and a corner of a bedroll is smoking. At least our packs and my bag of tokens aren't damaged.

I gasp, remembering more. "Harlan!"

"Harlan?"

"The frog!" I turn every which way. "I had another vision in the night. The frog is Harlan Oswald from the village and—" My voice catches. "Oh, Axel, what if he's dead? He wasn't even a Lost One, like the others. He was going to help us and—" I can't take in air.

The world rocks, and the blazing orange of the fire darkens to red. Red like the spindle with a piece of my cape fixed on the end. Red like the blood that rushed from my mother's heart when I stabbed that spindle inside it.

This wasn't supposed to happen! I'm not supposed to kill anyone else!

"Clara, you're not breathing." Axel bears me up. "Listen, you didn't kill anyone."

Did I say that aloud? "But I did!"

He takes my chin. Turns my face so I look at him. "You didn't set the fire. This is Rudger's doing. Whatever happened to the frog—to Harlan—it isn't your fault." He kisses my brow, strokes my cheek. "It isn't your fault, all right?"

I nod slowly, shaking, hiccupping for breath.

Ribbit.

I freeze. Cautiously turn.

The frog with the V-splotch peers up at us, alive, whole, throat bubbling as if he hasn't a care in the world.

I melt to my knees. Scoop him up, laughing even as my eyes leak and nose runs. "Harlan!"

His lower eyelid blinks upward.

"Axel, this is Harlan!"

"Um, hello," Axel manages, rubbing the back of his neck. "Clara, we should probably move farther away from the smoke."

I set down Harlan and help Axel gather our things, though I keep checking to make sure Harlan stays close, as if he'll suddenly vanish or burn if I look away too long.

We find a little creek and wash up, taking a few minutes to eat and recover from the shock of the fire. Behind us, the lair burns to the ground without catching more of the forest ablaze.

I huddle under my cloak and stare at the locket ring on my finger. "I'm surprised Rudger didn't try to steal this," I say to Axel.

"Maybe he meant to." He bends at the creek to refill our waterskins. "But the fire got out of hand too quickly."

"It's a shame we never figured out if he was the murderer before he got away."

Axel bristles, but swiftly disguises it by shaking ashes off his arms. The possibility that his uncle could be the killer still seems difficult for him to swallow. "You can still have a vision of him, and if it amounts to anything, then we'll figure out what to do."

I flip the locket's lid open and shut. I still doubt I can have a vision at the snap of a finger. The last two visions came easier, but they were brought on by touching Harlan. For some reason, I connect to him more effortlessly. "Perhaps I won't have to have so many visions. That's what Harlan said he could help with."

"Not having visions?"

"Yes, because he knows which ones are worth having—which Lost Ones are still alive." I reach for my pack and pull out my notebook and graphite stick.

Harlan crawls closer, and I tap the graphite against my lips.

"Do you remember the vision from last night? Croak once for yes and twice for no."

Croak.

"Brilliant." I flash a smile. "You can make sure I get this right."

"Wait." Axel scratches his head. "You spoke with Harlan—in his *past*. About Lost Ones *today*. And Harlan remembers this exchange?"

"I don't understand it either. I wish Grandmère taught me more about my ability. There's so much I still don't understand."

Axel scoots nearer. "Maybe this means you could talk to my father in *his* past about the present. Then we could find out where he is."

My grin falters. I force a little nod. "Well, we better get busy." I face Harlan. "Start croaking if I make a mistake."

I fill several pages with lists of Lost Ones who are dead, those who were last seen alive, and those who Harlan never saw at all, as well as other tidbits he's remembered of their last whereabouts.

I forget some of the details, but I check the names against another list I've kept of every Lost One and find the discrepancies. With our system of numbered croaks, Harlan lets me know if they're dead, presumed alive, or never seen. Occasionally, I write down something wrong, and he ribbits incessantly. I work with him to figure out the error and correct it.

When we're finished, I flip through the pages, my chest aching as I reread all the names of the dead. That list is the longest. There's Erma Faust, who used to make elderflower candies for market day. Lamar Stroman, the only one in Grimm's Hollow who could play the hummelchen bagpipe. Jorinda Frey, who annually touched up the paint on the Cuckoo House and its dancing figurines.

And there's my mother.

I don't write her name, as this is a list of suspects who are no longer suspects, but she's still written in my mind. She left me with etchings in other places too . . . my throat where she drank my blood, the scar where I scraped my elbow as a child and she coated it in salve and kissed it better.

I draw a breath to compose myself. "It's terrible that so many villagers have passed away, but at least our chances of figuring out who the murderer is are so much better. I'm glad we can save others before anyone else has to die."

"It's good news," Axel agrees. He pores over the names of those presumed alive or never seen before by Harlan.

Before today, I'd counted fifty-seven Lost Ones who could be murder suspects. Harlan confirmed thirty-six are dead—some killed by other Lost Ones and some who perished from starvation or other dangers in the forest. That leaves twenty-one people we need to account for. Twenty-one murder suspects.

I fetch my bag of tokens. I'd collected thirty-four before Axel and I left Grimm's Hollow. We remove the ones that are no longer necessary and bury them in a cloth. We mark the spot with stones and promise to return to bring them back to the village.

Among the tokens we keep are some belonging to the first seven Sommer girls, including a coral bead bracelet of Lila's— Harlan said she was alive last time he saw her—as well as Rudger's ring, Johann Schade's green marble, and Harlan's double-reed pipe.

"I hope you understand why I took this," I tell him. "It was nothing personal."

Croak.

"I'll give it back, of course." Not that he can do much with it as a frog.

Croak.

I place the drawstring bag in my pack, hating that our tokens now number an unlucky thirteen. But then again, there's one more token we should count among them, one more name that should be in my notebook, although I didn't have the courage to write it down.

Kellen Furst.

Assuming Kellen *did* return from the mountains, we don't know when that happened or if he became Lost along the way. But if he's alive, I have to consider him a suspect.

From everything Axel has said about his father, I can't imagine he's Bren's killer. But I have to be unbiased if I want to solve this mystery. I have to go by facts, not emotions—not how much I care about a person, or how much the person I love cares about that someone.

For Axel's sake, I will keep any suspicions about his father to myself.

"Where to now?" He straps his hatchet onto his pack.

I consider our options. It's raining again, which means Rudger's fresh tracks will soon wash away. It would be a waste of time to pursue him when we don't know which direction he's headed. Or we could stay here, where there's a water source, and I could focus on having visions instead of traveling aimlessly for missing Lost Ones.

But maybe it wouldn't be aimless to search out one group. They never stuck to one path, but their direction was straight, beelining through the forest no matter the obstacle. I don't know their destination, but with any luck—and perhaps a vision or two—we can reach them.

"Let's cut northwest and find the Sommer girls."

CHAPTER 25

wo days after we travel away from Rudger's lair, the trees spread wider, as if they can breathe easier the farther they are from his influence. My lungs open as well, no longer pinched from anxiety. I can absorb the scent of the forest now, musty-sweet with damp autumn leaves, and appreciate the cool, crisp air as I work up a light perspiration from walking for hours on end.

A pinch in my stomach warns we're not finished with Rudger, but for now, I smother it and set myself free from him.

I turn my focus to the Sommer girls, who have surely outdistanced us by now. Using the sun at dawn to anchor our coordinates, we travel as straight as we can northwest. But as the sun sets the first and second night, we discover we're off course. We correct our position and determine to start afresh each morning.

I wish we could use a compass. The clockmakers in Grimm's Hollow make fine ones, but ever since the curse fell, they've become unreliable. Their needles just spin and spin.

As we set out the third day, Harlan does what he's done the last two—he hops inside my hood as it falls open like a waiting pocket, his preferred mode of travel.

"Don't you think it's strange how close he likes to be to you?" Axel asks.

"Not really." I cut across a little meadow and retie one of my bodice laces. My S-curve is still acting up.

Axel follows behind me. "But if you think of him as a person, isn't it a little disturbing? Not only how he likes to slip inside your hood, but how he curls up beside you at night. You two were never friends in the village."

That's true. Harlan was—is—three years older and had a different set of friends. "Well, he *has* been a frog for over two years. I'm sure he's lonely."

"We don't know that he's been a frog that long. All he said in your vision was that the curse turned him into an animal. He could have been in the forest a long time before that happened."

"But then he would have become Lost, and he's not. He saved our lives by getting me the ring." A maple leaf twirls onto my hair, and I flick it away. "Besides, we can ask him directly when he became a frog, although I don't know why it matters." I wiggle my hood to catch Harlan's attention. "Did the curse turn you into a frog right after you entered the forest, or was it later? Croak once for 'right away' or twice for 'later.'"

Harlan crawls up higher. *Croak.*

"There you go." I look over my shoulder at Axel. "It happened right away."

The vertical lines between his brows stay creased.

"If it makes you feel any better, frogs are supposed to bring good luck."

"I've never heard that before."

"It's true. They're associated with water, and everyone needs water for survival. Frogs promise protection."

"We have red rampion for that."

"I'll take all the protection we can get."

Axel finally lets the topic slide, and we journey onward in peace for a couple of minutes until he brings up another triggering subject. "Are you feeling up to having another vision?"

I know visions are vital to solving the murder, and I've been mulling over ways to conjure more, but I'm still recovering from everything Rudger put us through. Conjuring visions back-to-back in the middle of all that has made my brain tired and my bones weary.

"Soon," I answer vaguely.

It isn't the idea of having any vision that's eating at me. It's the one Axel really wants me to have. The one that confirms his father is alive and reveals his location. The vision bound to destroy him if his father didn't survive.

I know he's trying not to pressure me, but the pressure is there. He's been going out of his way with small acts of kindness. He keeps our fire burning, prepares my meals, shakes off leaves and mulch from my bedroll, organizes and reorganizes my packs, brings me bouquets of wildflowers, arranges all the tokens on a log when we set up camp in case I'm ready to use them. But the pocket watch always rests in a prominent position at the center.

As if that token is currently on his mind, he says, "The time on the watch is set to four o'clock now, by the way."

I nod, unsurprised, as it's been counting down an hour each day since we left Rudger's lair. We just haven't figured out why.

"What if it has to do with my father?" he asks. "He was the one who bought the watch."

"If it does, what would the hours mean?"

"Maybe something will happen in four days that's pivotal to finding him."

"Maybe." I hope he's not counting on it being a vision.

Our pace slows as the ground becomes rockier and the terrain more uneven. Occasionally, a cluster of boulders obstructs our path, and we're forced to move around them and try to keep heading in the right direction. I hope we're not too off course. If the Sommer girls ever stopped to settle in one area, we might miss them altogether.

We make camp at nightfall, and the respite I've been feeling from my troubles starts to fade. The scraggly trees growing between rocks are like a woodland of skeletal hands and sharpened claws.

Click, clack, click, clack. I pop the hinge of the locket ring open and closed, my new nervous habit. I disregarded the pocket watch's time earlier, but now I can't stop thinking about it. The last countdown led to Rudger's third midnight. Will this countdown have a nefarious ending too?

> *The time you have left*
> *Is as a clock's gilt hands.*
> *Measure it wisely*
> *Lest the killer seize command.*

Click, clack, click . . . A tiny imprint on the ring catches my eye, right by the hinge underneath the lid concealing Fiora's hair. I supposed it was a scratch before, but now my lantern light snags on its complete minuscule design. . . .

A horseshoe with a Z etched in the middle. A stamped signature. A blacksmith's touchmark.

I sit up taller. I've seen this touchmark before.

"Axel, can you bring me your hatchet?"

He's just finished chopping more firewood. He passes it over.

I examine the side of the blade that had first belonged to my father. Sure enough, the same stamp is there, only larger. Bren Zimmer's touchmark. He forged this tool, like he must have forged the locket ring.

I show Axel both touchmarks. "Doesn't it feel significant that Bren made this ring?"

He looks a little lost. "He *was* a blacksmith."

"But this is Rudger's most valuable treasure. He loved Fiora.

Or once did. It's why he searched the forest—for her and their children. This ring ties Bren into all of that madness."

Axel rubs his neck beneath his scarf. "If you're looking for motive, Clara, this might be reaching." His gentle tone betrays a hint of exasperation. He's tired of considering Rudger as the murderer. "Bren made the ring, that's all."

I sigh. He's right. It doesn't add up. My head tells me that, and yet . . . "I just have a feeling there's something more here. What if being a Voyante of the Bygone means I can divine inklings of the past *without* visions?"

Axel searches my eyes, and his shoulders relax. "If there *is* a connection between Rudger and Bren, what's your next move?"

I twist the ring on my finger. "I need to do what I was planning on before Rudger escaped—have a vision to rule him out as the murderer."

Axel averts his gaze. I'm sure he'd prefer me to have a different vision right now, but he finally exhales and meets my eyes. "All right."

I press a grateful kiss to his lips. I don't need his permission, but we're a team. It's good to have his support.

I hurry away to find a quieter place to be alone with Rudger's ring, careful to stay within view of Axel. When Harlan hops to follow me, I shake my head. "Not this time, all right? My vision needs to come from Rudger's memories."

Once I'm alone, I try to draw upon the feeling of how easily I slipped into the last vision of Harlan, without any excess emotions. I was calm and about to fall asleep. I pace and dwell on the present. I drink in the scent of mist and pine and falling leaves. I listen to the crunch of brittle autumn grass. I rub my thumb against the ring. But my sight doesn't flicker. My hearing doesn't falter.

This isn't working.

Maybe visions of Harlan came easier because he helped us

find Rudger's lair and my tokens, and even saved our lives. I had compassion for him.

Having compassion for Rudger is much harder.

I try . . . but it doesn't transport me.

I groan and turn in a circle. There must be some key to unlocking him. Then it comes to me.

I return to the campsite and approach Axel as he removes a traveling kettle from the fire and sprinkles herbs in the boiling water. "Do you know if your uncle ever had my grandmother read his fortune?"

"Not that I remember." He watches as I withdraw the deck of cards from my pack. "Are you going to try using the cards to see his past?"

"Kind of. At least I hope they'll spark a vision." I pick at a seam of my cape. "There's one more possibility."

A lock of golden hair tumbles across his brow. "What's that?"

"I could try talking to Ollie again. He's usually nearby." Maybe he can help me develop more sympathy for Rudger. "But he'll want a favor—the same one he's always wanted."

I catch my lower lip between my teeth. "Would it be terrible if I just gave him *any* two pennies?" I think of the coins in the little purse I've brought on the journey. "It's Ollie's guilt that's trapped him in the forest. All he really needs is to give the money he promised to the poor man. I can do that when we return to the village." *If* we return. "Maybe if I show Ollie that I already have some pennies—"

"You think you can trick me?"

I yelp and stumble back when Ollie appears right in front of me.

CHAPTER 26

Ollie is sitting on the kettle like it's a convenient stool and not a scalding pot.

Axel stands. "What's the matter?"

I release a slow breath. "Ollie just surprised me, that's all." I spin to the ghost. "I wasn't trying to trick you. I simply wondered if my pennies could serve as your pennies."

"That's cheating!"

"But they add to the same value."

"Wrong. Only *my* pennies can save my soul."

His large elfin eyes have such a stubborn set that I won't attempt to persuade him otherwise. "I suppose you're happy your father got away unharmed," I say to redirect the conversation.

"Except he *was* harmed." Ollie glares. "You cut his stomach *and* his hand." He rises and turns on Axel. "And *he* kept swinging his hatchet like he wanted to chop him into bits."

"But he didn't. And I only gave Rudger a couple of scratches. We kept our promise."

Ollie purses his small mouth. "I guess."

"Anyway, I'm glad you came. I've been wanting to talk with you—about your father, actually."

"And *my* father," Axel interjects.

"Oh." Ollie meanders away and spots Harlan in a pile of leaves.

"Did you know you were the first person to tell me I had magic?" I drift after him. "You said I could see the past through ghosts and memories. Now I'm trying to see *your* father's memories."

"Why?" He pulls a face. "You figured out the riddle, and he doesn't know where my pennies are."

"He could be the reason Grimm's Hollow is cursed."

Ollie pounces on Harlan and traps him in ghostly hands. Clueless, unharmed, and not at all trapped, Harlan doesn't budge or make a noise.

"I hope your father isn't the reason," I forge on, wondering if Ollie is even listening anymore. "That's why I want to see his past, so no one blames him. You could help by explaining more about why you love him."

Ollie snorts. "Because he's my *dad*."

"Yes, but you said he sang you songs and tickled you. What other nice things has he done?"

"Just normal things dads do." Lying on his stomach, Ollie peers between his cupped hands to stare at Harlan.

This isn't getting me anywhere. Now that Rudger is beyond our reach, Ollie isn't concerned about persuading us of his father's goodness anymore. "Did you know my grandmother is a fortune-teller?"

His curls flop as he sits up, suddenly interested. "Did you ask her where I hid my pennies?"

"No, that's not . . . Her gift is to read the future. But in the past, maybe she learned about your *father's* future." Now I'm confusing myself. "Did he ever mention a card reading?"

"He played cards at the tavern."

"Right, but these would be fortune-telling cards. If I can figure out his cards, it could help me see his past."

"Because of the pennies? Those are in *my* past."

"This isn't about your pennies!" I burst out. Trying to make Ollie stay focused is like trying to catch a dragonfly by its wings.

He blinks rapidly as if he's going to cry. "You never want to talk about my pennies! So I'm done talking to *you*! Good luck seeing stupid memories!" He stomps off, though his feet don't make a noise.

"Oh, Ollie, don't go!" I rush after him, but he vanishes faster than ever.

Slump-shouldered, I turn back to Axel.

"I take it he didn't say anything helpful." He musters a sad smile. "About anyone."

"Sorry." I knead my brow. I've let Axel down, and all I ever do is upset Ollie. He has every right to be angry. He's helped *me* before, but I've never helped him. I doubt he'll visit again unless I really do find his pennies.

I drag myself back to our campsite and the deck of cards I left on a log. Striving to regain my composure, I sit on my bedroll and fan out the cards. Even if Grandmère never read cards for Rudger, divining them now might help me forge a connection.

Axel leaves me to the task and continues preparing dinner.

I massage my temples, where a headache is setting in. I'm so tired of Rudger. I'd rather see a vision of anyone else. And I wish I hadn't offended Ollie.

But if I'm truly a seer of the past, why couldn't I see Ollie's past?

I don't have a token for him, and the fortune-telling cards can't help. Ollie died as a child. He would have never asked Grandmère to read his fate before the age of seven. Still, I find myself idly flipping through the deck, wondering which cards might have been his.

My focus strays, and I lie down, lulled by the crackling campfire, the chirping crickets, the distant song of a nightingale. Even Harlan's rhythmic breathing beside me is like a tincture for sleep, and I struggle to keep my eyes open.

As my lashes start to bat closed, I glimpse two cards I must have pulled out, because I now hold them in a tight grip.

The Fanged Creature and Fortune's Cup, turned upside down.

An untimely death and a tragedy.

Likely one and the same.

They make sense for Ollie. They *were* his fate.

But they're also the cards Grandmère drew for herself.

My throat constricts. *Don't let this be Grandmère's destiny. For once, let her fortune-telling be wrong. Let her be innocent.*

My mind grows foggier, and my thoughts scramble. *Innocent?* Of course she is. Grandmère could never be a murderer, never have invoked the curse. Yet I can't shrug off the idea. Even as I drift off to sleep, it tethers deeper in my brain, and I fight to pull it free.

Let her be innocent. Let her be innocent. Let her be . . .

I'm creeping through the forest and spying on the meadow where Devotion Days are held in Grimm's Hollow. But this isn't Devotion Day. There are no offerings on the carved altar. There isn't even an altar. Even stranger, there isn't an ash-lined border separating the village from the forest.

All the land is thriving. The meadow grows abundant with starry columbine, nodding poppies, and feathery goldenrod. It's summertime—and before the onset of the curse.

I slink lower and slip forward, silent and stealthy through the wild grass. I'm on the village land now, the forest behind me, and the Clara I am within the visionary form I possess gradually realizes it's nighttime. My vision is so keen in the dark I hadn't noticed.

I glance down. All I see of myself are two massive, furry fore-paws. Shock radiates through me. I'm the Grimm wolf, and this vision is her perspective.

I sneak closer without any willpower of my own as Clara. I'm living out a memory of the wolf's. As I approach the meadow pavilion, my gaze slides between the four night watchmen posted at each corner. The guards of the Book of Fortunes.

Please don't attack and eat someone. I don't want to see that. I try to think of another memory I'd rather have her show me, but then again, maybe I should see this one through. I could be more than the wolf. I could be Grandmère, and this could be *her* memory.

My wolf eyes focus on the halberds each night watchman is holding. If I attack, they won't be defenseless. But the wolf is clever. In the darkness, she—I—pad forward and knock the first watchman's lantern over. Its candle extinguishes. I dart away before the man sees me clearly.

"Who's there?" he calls.

A second watchman joins him to relight the flame, but I lash forward and put out both of their candles, slipping back into the cover of night again.

The watchmen are spooked now. "I think that was a wolf," the second watchman hisses.

"Wolf?" The third holds his lantern high to see farther into the darkness. "Not the Grimm wolf?"

"It had to be. It was huge," the second answers. "And we haven't seen a bear in these parts for nearly a century."

I sneak around the pavilion and lunge for the fourth watchman. His lantern crashes. The candle flickers out. I grab his leg by my teeth, yank him on his back, and drag him away while he screams. He swings his halberd, but I lightly nip his arm, and he releases the weapon.

I was right. I am Grandmère in the wolf's skin. The Grimm wolf wouldn't take precaution to not kill a man.

I pull him a quarter mile away until I reach a gully with a thick cluster of brambles. I hurl him into it unceremoniously. He cries out, landing in the web of thorny branches he can't escape.

I race back to the pavilion, taking a wide arc to get there. In the meantime, two other watchmen have left their posts to rescue their friend. Which must be exactly what Grandmère hoped for.

One watchman remains, the man who seemed most frightened by the Grimm wolf. He stands beside *Sortes Fortunae* on its pedestal and trembles like a windup doll.

I pounce, a vicious growl in my throat, and he jumps, drops the halberd, and flees like a madman for the village.

My eyesight and vantage point change. The night grows dimmer. I sit up in the meadow, several yards from the pavilion. *What's happening?* I stand, smooth my skirt, and flip my braid over my shoulder.

My skirt . . . My braid . . .

I'm human. I look down to find wrinkled hands with age spots instead of forepaws with long, sharp claws. I'm Grandmère in her own body now.

I rush to the pavilion. The Grimm wolf is still there, an idle and unwitting guard of the Book of Fortunes. Her eyes don't have a violet cast like when Grandmère is in possession of her. They're brown, wary, dangerous.

"Good girl, Adiah," I say, Grandmère's voice my voice, and I sink my hand into her thick coat. She allows my touch. Grandmère and the wolf must maintain some kind of bond even when the wolf is wild.

I glance in all directions, as if to check if anyone else is nearby. None of the watchmen have returned. Quickly, I approach *Sortes Fortunae* and rest my hand on its closed cover.

Dread pools inside me, the Clara within Grandmère. *What is she doing?* She made her one wish long ago, when she was a young woman, when her skin was firm and unmarred, when her braided hair was near-black like mine and not silvery gray.

I hear her begin to speak. I see her hand opening the book. But her voice is quieter, and my viewpoint is retreating. I'm slipping away. Everything is blurring, fading.

Is this my doing? Is it because I don't want to see the rest of this memory? If Grandmère is making a forbidden second wish—possibly a murderous wish—I don't want it to be real.

Let her be innocent.

Everything streaks past me like I'm running. Maybe I am. Running from the horror of what might have happened and its implications. But it still closes around me, squeezing my rib cage and pinching my breath.

Why would Grandmère go to such trouble to be alone with *Sortes Fortunae*? What was she trying to do?

What *did* she do?

Some of the streaking subsides. A stream swims into focus. I stand at its banks, where a man lies facedown in the water. Red blooms around him, and the hilt of a knife juts out from his back.

Bren Zimmer.

No, no, no. Why am I seeing him? This is Grandmère's vision, her world of memories. But it's gone too far. I whirl to leave. I don't want to see this either. *Wake up, Clara!*

In the damp earth of the bank, two images capture my gaze.

A pocket watch.

Huge canine paw prints.

Wake up! Wake up!

"Clara, wake up!" *Axel.* His voice is muffled, gurgling.

My eyelids flash open. Everything is dark, murky. I'm thrashing but strangely weightless. I suck in a breath and choke. A rush of bubbles flies up in my face.

A terrible realization stabs me, dagger sharp.

I'm awake from my vision. But I'm underwater. I'm drowning.

CHAPTER 27

I kick and paddle my arms, but every direction is darkness. I can't tell which way is up. My hands brush slick algae and polished rocks. I've hit the bottom of the stream. I wheel around and push upward.

My lungs burn, desperate for air, waterlogged from what I must have gulped in. Blackness crowds the scant light surrounding me. It's like I'm slipping into another vision, but I fight the pull. I can't lose consciousness now. I'll die.

I beat my arms against the water, frantically trying to surface. But my cape, my dress, my boots are leaden. They suck me down.

I'm going to die.

Fate has finally come for me. My punishment for living when I should have died, for killing Mother, for how the repercussions are killing my grandmother.

Hands find me. Arms wrap around me. I'm tugged upward.

My head breaks the surface. I cough and sputter, raggedly breathing in cool night air. Axel's strong body bears me up. He swims us to shallow waters. The current isn't fast, but somehow I'd drifted to a deep spot. I don't even remember jumping in. I was asleep before I fell into a vision.

"How am I—?" I don't have enough air to finish. I gasp in another breath. "What happened?"

Axel tugs us onto the stream bank. I pant and roll onto my back. He curls closer, draping a leg and arm across my body. Harlan appears and hops all around me. I must have scared him too.

"I saw you'd fallen asleep," Axel finally replies. "So I let you rest while I ate supper. I was going to tie our ankles together soon enough, but the next thing I knew you were gone."

His heavy breaths warm the freezing skin of my neck. "I followed your tracks—they circled and doubled back and made no sense—and when I finally caught up to you, I could tell you were sleepwalking."

"Sleepwalking?" I pull back to see his face in the light of the lantern he left on the bank. "But I've never sleepwalked before."

"Your eyes were glazed over and you wouldn't listen to me. It was almost like you were in a trance."

"Like Ella and the Sommer girls when they were lured into the forest?"

"Kind of. They seemed more focused on their destination, though—a magical pull, not really sleepwalking. But you were wandering all over the place. And when I yelled after you, you growled at me." His fingers skim the fur mantle I'm wearing. "What if you're becoming more like your grandmother?"

I shiver with the weight of being the Grimm wolf again, her hulking size, four legs, and strong jaws. "I'm not an Anivoyante," I assure him. "I can't slip into wolves, and I only see visions of the past, not the future."

"Is that what happened?" He lifts to rest on one elbow. "Were you having a vision? You fell into the stream like you didn't even see it was there."

"I had a nightmare of the Grimm wolf. That's probably why I growled." The words tumble out with such ease I almost convince myself they're true. I should tell him what really happened—that I had a vision, not a nightmare—but my throat closes. I don't want to admit what Grandmère did. Or might have done.

"Clara, you're shaking." Axel pulls me up and rubs my arms. "We need to get you warm."

We return to the campfire. He throws on more logs, and we remove most of our wet clothes until I'm left in my chemise and cape, and he's only wearing his scarf and undergarments of cropped linen pants. We drag our bedrolls as close as we dare to the fire and lie down, holding each other close against the chilly autumn night.

He asks more questions about my nightmare, but I only give short answers. I don't want to think about Grandmère with the Book of Fortunes. Or the paw prints at Bren Zimmer's murder scene. Or anything that could implicate her.

What if she was a killer like my mother, but without the excuse of being Lost?

Is that what I am too? A killer?

My breaths quicken. I can't take in enough air. I feel as if I'm drowning all over again.

I can't think about this. So I won't think at all. I'll concentrate on this moment. What's real and solid. *Axel.* His body wrapped around mine, so much of his skin exposed and glowing golden from the campfire.

I slide up to his mouth and kiss him, my fingers threading into his hair, feeling the way the ends curl as they dry. I want all of him to take hold of me, to scorch through me like a fever. I need more, more. Of his strength holding me tighter. Of his scent, fresh with green wood and mountain pine.

My mouth moves ravenously against his mouth, my skin damp again, but now from vigor and the campfire's heat. It's scalding me. I don't care. Let it burn me to ashes. I want this new Clara gone. I want to be the old me again, unscathed, untarnished. Innocent. That was the girl Axel fell in love with. He can help me find her once again.

My hands drag up the sides of his thin trousers. They find his waistband, and my fingertips trace under it. He moans, sweating as much as I am.

"Clara, are you sure that . . . ?" His hands travel up my back. I'm not even self-conscious when they stroke over the crooked parts of my S-curve. "You've had a difficult night." He speaks slowly, staggeringly. "Maybe we shouldn't do this for the first time right now."

Yes, we should. My lips trail down his neck, and my teeth graze the long tendon there. He has to need this as much as I do.

I grasp one of the sleeves of my chemise. Start to tug my arm out. Axel clamps his hand over mine. His voice is firmer when he says, "No, Clara. Not tonight."

I freeze. Slowly pull up to sit where I'm straddling him. Beads of sweat roll down my temples, down my décolletage, and under the neckline of my chemise. I suddenly feel exposed and ridiculous. A flush burns up my neck and ears, scalding deeper than the heat. I lower my gaze and awkwardly slip off of him.

His brows pull inward as he sits up and caresses the side of my face. "I want this." He kisses my bare shoulder where my chemise has fallen loose. "I want this more than you know. But you mean everything to me, and so does your family. Your father was especially good to me. If he were still alive, I'd want him to know I always treated you with respect."

His words stir inside me, and I admit they resonate. We shouldn't be rash with intimacy. But another part of me doesn't care about propriety. I don't have most of my family anymore. I may not even have my grandmother much longer, and I don't know how dark the legacy is she's leaving me with. What I need now is Axel. His love and mine, forged in the deepest way possible. Why can't he understand that?

I stare at my hands, covered with scratches from the rocks in the stream. Axel is hurt much worse. A large purple bruise forms along his abdomen. He must have gotten it from saving me.

My shoulders fall. How can I say it was love I wanted tonight? I'd just wanted to lose myself in him. Or find what I've lost in myself. Do anything to escape what I don't want to face.

"It's too hot," I finally say, not the most delicate reply, but it's the best I can do.

Axel studies my face, as if trying to read my thoughts, but when I don't divulge more, he helps me to my feet. We move our bedrolls farther from the fire and settle down again, tying our ankles together. He presses a kiss to my brow, and I manage a small smile.

"I'm here for you," he says tenderly. "I hope you know that."

I nod. But I don't know that I'm really here for him. How can I be when I'm so divided inside? I want him. I love him. And I do want to give myself to him. But when that happens, I want to be truly committed.

And perhaps I'm not if I can't even tell him that Grandmère might be a murderer.

CHAPTER 28

I awake before Axel does and untie our ankles, still cloudy-headed from my vision. In a daze, I let my eyes wander over him. He's like a painting of a shipwrecked prince, beautiful and disheveled with his tawny skin bare, apart from his short linen pants, his golden hair mussed with wild waves, and his eyes closed with lines pinched between his brows, like he's the one suffering from tumultuous visions.

My first thought is to kiss him, to lie back down and slip into his arms, to comfort him and whisper loving words. But I retract the hand that reaches for his face. How can I pretend to be soothing when what's hidden inside me is a secret that could shatter him? My grandmother wasn't the only person implicated in my last vision. From the pocket watch I saw near the paw prints at the stream, either Rudger or Kellen was too.

I stand and gather my clothes and Axel's, as well as his pocket watch. I reflexively flip open the silver case, and the gilt hands jump out at me—two o'clock.

Two o'clock, for two days?

My stomach churns. I hope that's not all the time I have left to solve the murder. I'm growing closer, but nowhere near close enough.

I shut the case. Roll out my shoulders. We need to keep moving.

As we set off in our continued search for the Sommer girls, I consider turning back for Grimm's Hollow. But the thought of questioning my dying grandmother about whether she committed murder makes me sick inside.

I find myself making excuses for her. Yes, I saw large paw prints by the stream, but a wolf can't stab a person. Grandmère would have to be in her own body for that.

But maybe she was.

On the night Bren was murdered, I woke up late to find Grandmère missing. I didn't think much of it then. On a sheep farm, it isn't unusual to attend to an emergency at any odd hour. But now my gut folds into hard creases at the thought of her absence. It only implicates her further.

I retreat more and more into myself as the day continues, bogged down with worry and exhaustion. Axel asks me what's wrong more than once, but I only answer with shrugs and little shakes of my head.

"If you're angry about last night," he says in the late afternoon, when we've been trudging along the stream following our north-west direction, "I was only trying to treat you with—"

"I'm not upset about that."

He regards me. "Then what is it?"

I don't want the murderer to be Grandmère, but for your sake, I don't want it to be Rudger or your father either. "I'm not in the mood for talking. I don't have much energy, and I'm just trying to . . ."

"Concentrate?"

I frown at the hope sparking in his eyes, but I'm too weary to discern why it's there, so I nod, and he leaves me in peace. Not that my spiraling thoughts are peaceful, but maybe I've found a reprieve for Grandmère. Yes, she had the opportunity to commit murder and obtain the missing page, but there's one thing she didn't have. Motive.

I never saw her argue with Bren, and she never spoke about him unkindly. She never spoke about *anyone* unkindly. Grandmère has always been sympathetic, generous, and wise. How could she have triggered the curse?

Maybe it was Kellen.

He could have returned for Grimm's Hollow, but on the way, forgot who he was again, and in the confusion stumbled upon a certain stream, withdrawn a knife, plunged it into the back of Bren Zimmer . . .

He would have lost the pocket watch, of course. Perhaps the Grimm wolf appeared and frightened him off. Or perhaps the wolf left her paw prints for another reason.

What if Grandmère maneuvered deftly between the wolf and her own body, shifting quickly between forms like she did after she scared away the night watchmen? She could have been the one who stabbed Bren.

My heart palpitates. I rub the heels of my hands against my eyes.

"Are you trying to have a vision of my father?" Axel asks, trying to talk to me again after a dry spell of conversation that feels longer than the curse on Grimm's Hollow.

I startle at the mention of his father. "What? No! Why would you say that?"

"I saw you tuck away my pocket watch this morning. I thought you were keeping it to finally try to have another vision of him."

My jaw hardens as he says "finally try." I don't miss the flicker of exasperation in his voice. "I didn't realize I'd kept it," I say, removing it from my dress pocket and passing it over.

Axel shuffles back a step. "Maybe if you hold on to it longer—"

"I don't want to have another vision of your father!" I shove the watch at him. As soon as I explode, shame overwhelms me. Still, it takes all my strength not to combust altogether. I'm bristling with friction. All my emotions are suddenly colliding and igniting. Perhaps it's the toll of too many visions, too soon together.

After a stretched-out moment, I scrape up the energy to add, "Maybe I can't." I don't mean to sound severe. It's like I said *I never will.*

I brush past him, but I feel Axel's eyes boring into the back of my skull. His disappointment is as tangible as his frustration. His next words come out measured, but also clipped: "Why not, if all you do is have visions lately?"

I come to a stop, acid boiling in my veins. Without a backward glance, I reply stiffly, "Stop. Asking. Me."

I'm met with silence that crackles with hot energy. After what feels like another eternity, he roughly answers, "We'll camp here," before he clomps away, thunder in his footsteps.

As soon as he's gone, my belly knots and I'm filled with self-loathing. I want him back as much as I want to be alone. It will be a new moon tonight, and he shouldn't wander when the sky will be so dark. But maybe what I want most is to sleep for days, to wake and find this curse magically broken, to be back in my cottage with a grandmother who is well and was never murderous. I want a happily ever after . . . even if it is a lie.

Eventually, I make my way to the campsite Axel is preparing. We've traveled over a rocky hill and are now at the base of its other side. The stream cascades in intervals down stony ledges, a sort of gentle waterfall. I hope the rushing water can drown my dismal thoughts.

We sit around the campfire, and Axel withdraws food rations for himself, but doesn't offer me any. Although his anger is justified, I'm still annoyed. Just to spite him, I don't pull out any food for myself. I'll starve for the night.

It's a ridiculous brand of vengeance, and I've never been more petulant, but I can't muster enough remorse to be reasonable. I genuinely don't know what foul thing has gotten a hold of me, but whatever it is, I can't shake my dark mood.

Neither can Axel. As soon as he finishes eating, he pushes up and mutters, "I'm going for a walk."

"Take as long as you like," I quip before I can bite back the words.

Axel's glare is both shocked and furious. He storms away, and I bury my head in my hands. *What is the matter with me?*

Harlan, who has kept his distance, creeps forward.

"Go away," I snap. "I'm angry with you too." I have no reason to be, but I'll lash out at anything that has a face and a brain right now.

I stomp to my bedroll. Axel has already laid out his, but he didn't arrange mine beside it. Fine. I spread out my bedroll a good ten feet away. *Have fun tying our ankles together now.*

The sun is barely setting, but I'm going to sleep before my irrational fury catches more fuel and burns this forest to the ground.

I usually stay in my clothes at night, but they itch and squeeze. I feel cloistered by everything. I throw off my fur mantle, unlace my bodice, and yank off my blouse, skirt, and shoes. I'm left only wearing my chemise, cape, and stockings. I have half a mind to tear them off too, but I haven't completely lost my wits.

I lie on my side, and Harlan plops right in front of me. "Are you serious?" I glare at him. "If you don't give me space tonight, I'm liable to pound you into slime."

He croaks once, meaning "yes," whatever that is supposed to tell me right now.

"You should learn how to speak, so I don't have to meet you in visions."

Croak.

"Go away, I'm serious."

Croak.

I push him back a foot, but he still stays there, his bulging eyes locked on mine. "Did anyone ever tell you that you make a very annoying animal?"

Croak.

"Lila wouldn't be so attracted to you if she saw how insufferable you are as an amphibian."

Croak.

I clamor for a few more insults, but the gears of my mind are staggering to a halt. My bones feel heavy, my eyelids leaden. I just need to close them for a moment. I won't fall asleep. I really should tie my ankle to Axel's first. I'm only going to rest here a little until he returns.

I feel Harlan's four legs crawl into my palm.

"Stupid frog," I mumble, but I don't shove him away.

Darkness gathers, and I can't fight it anymore.

I drift into slumber.

CHAPTER 29

I'm standing on the Oswald farm in Grimm's Hollow. It's pig-slaughtering day. That much I gather from the A-frame scaffold, sledgehammer, carving tools, and tables outside. A few neighbors have come to help, wearing coats and hats. It must be on the cusp of winter. Animals are killed when the cold moves in so the meat is easier to preserve.

Harlan paces near the scaffold as a freshly killed pig is hoisted up by its hind legs. He won't look at the beast. He seems to be doing all he can to maintain a semblance of calm. He whistles softly, the same song I heard him playing on his pipe in my former vision of him.

A moment ago, I would have kicked and screamed to know I'd slip into another vision, but now all I feel is relief. My fatigue is gone, and with it, my fury. Which makes me never want to leave this memory, no matter what's happening.

Herr Oswald passes his son a knife, whispering something. Harlan lowers to one knee and slashes the pig's throat. He backs away as blood pours into a bucket and others rush in to take over.

He crosses to a table and leans both arms against the wood, exhaling slowly. I'm about to approach him when another girl walks through me. I flinch. It's the strangest thing seeing another person glide out from where I've just been standing.

Lila Sommer's ebony hair is drawn into a braid, and an apricot kerchief keeps back her stray curls. She strolls around the table, tracing its perimeter with a finger. "Why are you so sullen?

You haven't even said hello." It seems she and Harlan are now a couple.

He rests his weight on his knuckles. "You shouldn't have come."

"Why?"

"Because this is humiliating."

"You're a pig farmer." Her bronze skin shimmers above her scooped neckline. "Pig farmers slaughter pigs."

"Doesn't matter. You shouldn't have to see this."

She laughs, a trill both dainty and daring. "Do you believe a little blood could frighten me?" She furtively glances around, then drags her finger along the flat of the knife's blade, collecting blood. She paints a symbol on Harlan's face, a star above a horizontal crescent moon.

"What are you doing?" he murmurs, his eyes heavy-lidded, despite the morbidness of her actions.

"It's a symbol. It means I am yours, and you are mine."

Ice prickles up the back of my neck. It's like Lila is enacting some kind of witch's spell. But witches aren't real. The only kind of magic in this world is the forest's magic and the magic of my maternal bloodline.

Unless the women in Lila's family have magic too . . .

Her grandmother, Ekhoe, came from a land much farther away than Grandmère's. Who am I to say Ekhoe couldn't have learned a different sort of magic there?

"We won't allow anything to come between us," Lila says like an oath. "Especially blood that means nothing. Let's make it mean something." She smears a final streak of red onto his top and bottom lips. "This means we are bound."

She brings her mouth to his, sliding her tongue inside, not shy of tasting the blood. Under her influence, Harlan disregards it as well, kissing her back with fervent passion.

The other villagers are so busy preparing entrails that no one notices. I alone am the awkward onlooker, though I feel more like an intruder. I have no idea what unwittingly provoked me to enter Harlan's mind to see this, but I've overstayed my welcome.

I turn to leave when Harlan's voice pins me still. "Clara?"

I wish I could vanish. He must realize I've been spying on an intimate moment. But when I revolve, Lila is no longer there. None of the villagers are. All evidence of the slaughtering is gone, save for a few ruddy spots where blood soaked the earth, muted pink now by a light powdering of snow.

"I'm sorry." My cheeks burn. "I didn't mean to come here."

"Don't be sorry." One side of his mouth hitches up. "You're the only person I've had a real conversation with in over two years."

"I suppose that's true." It's also very sad. "Still, this vision was an accident."

He flashes a dimple. "It's all right. People learn best by making mistakes. I've made plenty."

I reach to fidget with my cape, but I'm not wearing it. Instead, my father's winter coat is wrapped around me. "Was falling in love with Lila a mistake?"

Lines pinch between Harlan's brows, but then he breaks into a warm laugh. "You're very bold, Clara."

"Sorry." I really have no excuse, except—"Being with you in visions doesn't feel real, I suppose. Not in the same way life does."

He ambles up to the covered porch and beckons me to follow. We sit on the steps together. The snow falls harder, but I only feel a glimmer of coolness.

"Falling in love with Lila wasn't my mistake," he says. "But because I wasn't brave enough to declare my feelings, there were consequences. Lila became Lost, and I became, well, a frog." He heaves a miserable sigh. "Have you ever done something bad like that before?"

"Oh, Harlan. I'm guilty of far worse."

"You? Even with warnings from a fortune-teller grand-mother?"

"Fortune-telling only complicates things." I pick at my finger-nails. "A few months ago, my grandmère drew a special card for me. The Red Card, but its true name is Changer of Fate. It made me reckless. I tried something dangerous to save Mother, and it went horribly awry."

I meet Harlan's gaze, expecting to find judgment there, but instead I discover pity. "What happened?"

"Um . . ." I don't know where to begin. "Red rampion is the seed of all magic. It's said to be the first thing to grow in this forest. And it's a protective magic." I tell him about the red ram-pion in my cape, Axel's scarf, and Fiora's hair wrapped inside Rudger's locket ring. "When my mother killed me—"

"Wait, your mother killed you? How is that—? How are you—?"

"Alive?" I take a breath. "Axel plunged a bit of my cape into my heart with a spindle, and it brought me back."

I wait for Harlan to say that's impossible, but he doesn't. "So you thought you could save your mother in the same way?"

A rush of grief renders me speechless for a few seconds. "I was foolish. She wasn't dead like I'd been." I duck my head a little. "I killed her."

Harlan watches the snow as it spins in eddies and twirls of the wind. His nose and the tips of his ears are pink. "I've never heard of anything more courageous."

Courageous? I don't know about that.

"Is that why you always stroke your cape?" He brushes his fin-gers near his heart to show me the spot. "Is that her bloodstain?"

"I didn't realize I touched it so much," I murmur.

His breath puffs a cloud between us. "What do you think your mother would say about how you tried to save her? Imagine you could see her one last time."

I trace my wrist where I once wore the rose-red strip of wool. "I don't know."

"Do you believe she would be understanding and forgiving, or harsh and rebuking?"

I squirm but finally answer, "Understanding and forgiving."

"There you go."

I'm unsure if I can relinquish my guilt so easily. "What about Lila? Would she be understanding and forgiving if you could speak to her again—the real her, not the Lost one?"

His smile falters. "I wish I could say yes."

Before I can ask why, the vision shifts in a dizzying swirl. Harlan disappears, and my vision flickers to black. An instant later, I'm standing farther away from the Oswald farmhouse. Dusk is falling. Time has passed. The farmland has withered, but the forest in the distance is lush and green. A wreath is hung on the door to welcome the autumn harvest, but it's made of thorny weeds instead of sheaves of grain. The curse has fallen.

Candlelight glows from the window in the front room, and I spy Harlan's silhouette. In a blink, I'm several yards closer, right outside the window. He isn't alone. Lila leans against the mantel and weeps into her folded arms. He reaches out to touch her, but she recoils and shouts words I can't hear over the tree branches rustling in the wind.

Harlan takes the lashing with an astonishing amount of stoicism. It's as if this isn't the first outburst she's had, but instead of growing frustrated, he's become skilled at handling her moods.

He reaches for her again and, at last, she melts into his arms.

He whispers something and smooths her hair, and she eventually lifts her head and lets him kiss her for a long spell.

Just when I think she's fine, she abruptly pushes back and slaps him hard across the face. She bursts into more tears and rushes outside, slamming the door.

Harlan holds himself stiff, and then drops his chin. It's clear how taxing their relationship has become. "Are you going to come inside, or should we talk through the windowpanes?"

"Sorry, I didn't mean to eavesdrop again." Suddenly I'm inside the house, rooted where Lila stood. "I don't know why I didn't wake up."

Harlan gives a lopsided grin. "Don't worry, Clara." There's a kettle hanging over the fire, and he pours its water over the herbs in two earthenware cups.

"Maybe I slipped into another vision because you wanted me here," I speculate. "Although I don't know if my magic can respond to someone's yearning like that."

"You think I was yearning?"

"No." Warmth dashes through my belly. "I don't know why I said that."

His smile warms. "Well, I was."

I flush, realizing how alone we are. We're always alone, I suppose. No one else notices me in these visions except him. But with no other people milling about, this cozy room feels all the more intimate. "What would you be yearning for?"

He blows steam off his tea, and the mist shrouds his heavy gaze. "As a frog, I'm desperate for one thing. A kiss."

I release a shaky exhale. "A kiss?"

He moves closer, and my eyes lower to his very human, very kissable lips, so different from the frog's wide, flat, and perpetually frowning mouth.

"Why would a frog want a kiss?"

"Because if I'm kissed as a frog, I'll no longer be a frog."

I want to laugh, but the sound lodges in my throat, where my pulse flutters. "If it's that simple, why are you still a frog after all this time?"

"*Is* it so simple?" He sets down his cup. "Would you have kissed me if you hadn't come to know me in your visions?"

"I might have kissed you on top of the head."

"This kiss needs be on the mouth."

"The *mouth*?"

"Imagine a Lost One wanting to kiss a frog on the mouth. You've been my greatest hope from the moment we met, Clara. You're not Lost. I can reason with you. And you're different. Special."

"How?" I'm scarcely breathing again, uncomfortable yet too comfortable by the nearness of him.

Harlan sounds like he's reciting one of Rudger's riddles when he answers,

"White for a pure heart,
Red for rampion-stained lips.

"You're that pure heart, Clara."

I shrink back a step. "Pure heart? But you saw how awful I was today."

"That doesn't diminish who you are."

I place a hand on my stomach, where either butterflies have taken flight or I'm about to be sick. I feel as if I'm balancing on the point of a dagger, and if I slip in one direction or another, I'll cut away something precious, and nothing on this journey will be the same.

"What's all this about, Harlan? I can't kiss you. It would be a betrayal to Axel."

"I'm sorry." He scrubs his brow with his knuckles. "With the new moon here, I'm becoming overanxious."

"The new moon? What does that have to do with anything?"

"I need to explain better." He gestures for me to take a seat in an armchair, and I gladly do so. "Perhaps you were wondering why Lila was so upset in this last memory."

"I was," I confess.

"The longer our relationship continued, the more she grew paranoid that I didn't love her in return. Anytime I spoke to other girls, she became irrationally jealous." He paces in front of the flickering fire, his body casting long shadows across the floorboards. "I didn't know that, for many months, she had been working to solve the riddle the Book of Fortunes gave her after she made her one wish."

I know from the register of wishes in Grimm's Hollow that Lila made her one wish two months before the curse fell. "Did you ever glean what it was?"

He scratches his cheek as if he's embarrassed. "I believe she wished for me to love only her."

The pig's blood she painted on his face amounted to the same desire: *This means we are bound.* If that act held some mysterious Sommer family magic, she must have been truly obsessed to use her one wish for the same thing.

Harlan sighs, combing his fingers through his hair. "She didn't know I was going to propose. I'd wanted to for a long time, but I didn't think I could provide the life she deserved. I was a fool. I'm to blame for what she did."

"What was that?"

He hesitates to answer for a moment. "I should tell you Lila's riddle first:

"White for a pure heart,
Red for rampion-stained lips,
Black for a faceless night,
A kiss to seal your wish.

Beware enacting your wish,
Lest you err or do worse,
And mind turns to madness
And love becomes cursed."

I puzzle over the words. "A full moon appears to have a face, so the faceless night must have meant a new moon, like tonight."

He raises his eyebrows. "That took Lila much longer to figure out."

"And she needed to kiss you on a new moon for her wish to become true," I say. "Were the rampion-stained lips literal?"

"I think so. Crushed scarlet flowers were scattered nearby, so I later drew that conclusion. Lila's only failing was not having a pure heart when she kissed me. Her wish was selfish to begin with."

"So her love for you became cursed. *You* became cursed. You became a frog."

"And Lila immediately fell into madness. She ran off into the forest and became Lost before she ever set foot there."

"I'm so sorry, Harlan." I don't know what else to say.

He looks down and exhales slowly, but when his gaze lifts to capture mine, his countenance shines with hope again, and I know I am that hope for him.

"There was one last part of the riddle," he says.

"But do not despair,
For the tasks done right by another
Will undo the enchantment
And reverse the spell."

Goose bumps prickle over me as I piece together the meaning: "The tasks are the first part of the riddle. And if done correctly, the spell over you will break."

"I'll be human again." His smile reaches his eyes.

I mull over what needs to happen for that to come true:

White for a pure heart,
Red for rampion-stained lips,
Black for a faceless night,
A kiss to seal your wish.

Harlan believes I'm pure-hearted, and tonight *is* a new moon. But—"My kiss won't work without red rampion. A rampion-dyed cape isn't the same as rampion-stained lips."

"What if I told you I found red rampion growing nearby?"

"I'd say that's the greatest coincidence."

"Or fate. You believe in fate, Clara. And you believe in changing fates. You could change mine. Tonight."

I'm teetering on a dagger's point again. I should release Harlan from the prison he's been in for two and a half years. Any decent person would. So why does it feel so treacherous?

I hold the acorn pendant tightly at my neck. I wish I could ask Axel what he thinks. But who knows if he'll even return tonight? If he doesn't, the new moon will have passed, and it would be cruel to make Harlan wait for the stars of his destiny to line up like this again.

"Be my Changer of Fate, Clara." Harlan walks over to me and extends a hand. "I've already told you how. A simple kiss."

It *is* simple. Very simple. Axel wouldn't begrudge me saving Harlan with a kiss that means nothing more than his freedom.

I set my hand in Harlan's and let him pull me to my feet.

The instant I rise, the vision breaks, and I realize I must have sleepwalked again, for a clutch of crushed red rampion flowers are in my fist, and I'm standing three inches in front of a low-hanging branch. As a frog, Harlan is already perched there and level with my face. My lips are ready and moist. I must have already wet them with the juice of the flowers.

All that's left for me to do is lean in and press my mouth to the mouth of a frog who has become my trusted friend.

It is simple. Very simple.

I'm helping someone I care about. That's who I am—a person who helps people, one curse at a time. That's who I want to be, at least, a Clara Thurn who doesn't have to kill to save, like how I killed my mother. Now I can save in a new way.

I meet the frog's round eyes, drift forward, and give him a kiss.

CHAPTER 30

The mouth that is cool and slimy turns warm and soft, the lips growing full and supple as they transform and meld perfectly with mine.

Eyes closed, I don't see the changes happening to Harlan, but I feel them. A body taking shape before me, a chest against my chest, a nose brushing my nose, hands that anchor to my arms, then slide down to my hands and back up to my waist, feeling what human hands haven't felt in such a long time.

As the kiss lingers, his mouth explores mine, and I don't have the heart to pull away. I know what it's like to come back from the dead, and although Harlan wasn't dead, he was close, absent from his real body for two and a half years.

And maybe *I* don't want to pull away. I'm in that slippery state between realities, somewhere in the middle of the past and the present, and Harlan is anchoring me too. I've only been with him as a human in his memories, and while they were vivid, they don't match this level of tangibility. He's realer than ever now, which also makes him surreal, and I'm dizzy absorbing it all.

Snap. A twig cracking under a footstep. At once, I'm pulled to the present.

I draw away, gasping. I shouldn't have been kissing Harlan that long.

I startle to see his face, stark with the crispness of the present, and older than what I'm accustomed to in my visions. He looks the age he is now, twenty. His jawline is more pronounced, his cheekbones more defined, his eyes wiser in how they tug down at the corners. He wears simple trousers and an unbuttoned home-spun shirt, like he was in the middle of getting dressed when he turned into a frog.

He holds up his hands, staring at them in wonder. He feels his face—his ears, nose, and hair. He swings his arms, wiggles his feet. He laughs, leaning forward like he's going to kiss me again. I shift back.

Another twig snaps, but softer. I turn and my stomach drops. A few feet away, Axel is staring at me like he doesn't know me, hurt and shock written plainly across his face.

I take a faltering step toward him. "This isn't what you think."

"I asked her to break the spell over me," Harlan quickly sup-plies.

"It required a kiss," I add.

A mirthless laugh escapes Axel. "*That* kind of a kiss?"

I struggle for words and find none. Axel flexes his jaw muscle and revolves to leave.

"Wait!" I rush after him. "Don't go. We need to stay together!" *Love Lost.* Grandmère warned me about this. "Please, Axel!"

He calls over his shoulder, "I can't—"

Whatever he was going to say is cut off by a great shudder in the earth. The three of us keel over to the ground. Trees sway violently around us. A giant oak tears up from its roots and topples toward me. I scramble to safety—to Axel—just before it slams down.

Two more trees fall from the quaking. He and I dodge them, grabbing for each other, crawling in a rush to safer places. As the ground rolls, we cocoon our bodies together. I clutch him with all my strength, my heart in my throat. I wait for the quaking to stop, and when it doesn't, I realize why. This is about Harlan. The forest is rejecting him because he's human again. He isn't protected with red rampion.

I try to pull away from Axel, but he holds me tight. "I have to give Rudger's ring to Harlan!" I shout to be heard above the commotion. Fiora's hair hidden inside it will protect him. At least for a time until it loses effect, like it did with Rudger.

Axel understands and lets me go.

I stumble toward Harlan, past the other side of the fallen oak. I'm wearing the locket ring on my pointer finger, where I've kept it on for days, hoping to have another vision of Rudger.

"Harlan!" I call. His head pops up, guarded by his arms. I tug off the ring and hold it up. We slowly work our way toward each other.

Fissures open beneath us. Branches snap free and drop. The earth shudders relentlessly. Axel stays close, helping me find a clear path, steadying me, steering me away from danger.

Finally, I make it to the fallen oak. Harlan is on its other side. I reach to give him the ring. He reaches back. The trunk is too wide. We climb it.

A thick branch cracks off another tree. Axel catches it before it strikes my head.

My fingers brush Harlan's. With all the shaking, it takes him a moment to grasp the ring. Once he slips it on, the earth abruptly stills.

I sag against the oak's trunk. Harlan rolls onto his back and clutches his ring finger to his chest. Axel labors to steady his breath.

Something stirs at my feet. Did I trample some poor woodland creature? I look down, but it's only a pile of autumn leaves—leaves that are moving. They rustle like they're rousing from a slumber, and then flutter upward as if falling again, except falling upside down.

I watch in wonder, unsure if this is real and the world has gone topsy-turvy or if I'm hallucinating. It's as if I've consumed poisonous mushrooms and I'm back in Ella's mystical forest ball-room again.

Around us, more leaves rise and spiral upward in reverse breezes. Even stranger, they reattach to trees. A great maple's brilliant red leaves fasten back onto its branches and turn summer green.

Am I having a vision? Is this some kind of sped-up reverse glimpse of the past?

Axel's eyes are round, his mouth parted in awe. He's seeing this too. One glance at Harlan tells me he's also in the present with me, although his expression is wary and suspicious.

The bizarre reversal continues. Even dried pine needles float up and become evergreen on trees again.

Beneath me, the fallen oak groans like we're about to experience another earthquake. Harlan and I scramble back to opposite sides. But the ground doesn't shudder. The oak lifts and rights itself as if it never toppled. The other fallen trees do the same.

Finally, the reversal ends, and the forest is restored, but not only to the state it was in before the earthquake, but also before the partial lifting of the curse. It's back like it was for three years until the recent autumn—enchanted in an endless summer. An enchantment that drained Grimm's Hollow of its resources, water, and rich soil.

Harlan, Axel, and I exchange bewildered glances. What does this mean?

Has the curse returned in full force?

CHAPTER 31

It must be nearing midnight, but Harlan, Axel, and I haven't tried to sleep. We're too shaken by what happened to the forest, although we haven't spoken about it. We sit around our campfire as Harlan plays his double-reed pipe. I gave it back, like I promised when he was a frog.

Now that he's human again, our group of three is large and awkward. None of us sits close. The spaces between us might as well be great fissures for how distant they feel—the space between me and Axel the hardest to close . . . to heal.

I ask if he'll walk with me, but when he doesn't reply, Harlan says he'll leave us alone. As he strolls away, I turn to Axel. I ache to touch him, to show him nothing has changed between us. But I fear he'll shove me away if I move an inch nearer.

"I'm sorry about the kiss," I say. "I shouldn't have let it go on for so long. I was lost in the moment."

"Clearly." His response stings, but at least he's speaking to me.

"I meant 'lost' as in 'lost between the vision I'd had and the present.' The kiss didn't mean anything."

"But it did." He finally meets my gaze. Embers reflect in his eyes, flickers of orange overbright against his piercing blue irises. "It transformed him. Harlan isn't a harmless frog anymore."

"He isn't *harmful*. He helped me discover Rudger's Lost name. He helped me get the ring. He saved our lives."

"Have you ever considered Harlan might have an ulterior motive?"

I sit back. This is Axel's jealousy speaking, nothing more. "I don't have any special feelings for Harlan. He's in love with Lila Sommer. I swear, the kiss meant nothing."

Axel laughs once, a small sound of mourning that rends my heart to shreds. "The fact that you keep saying that means it did."

"Axel . . ."

"Remember the promise we made when we set out on this journey? We said we'd trust no one but each other."

"We were talking about Lost Ones. Harlan isn't Lost. He wants to help us break the curse."

"Yet the curse has only grown stronger. Did you know the time on the pocket watch hit twelve o'clock today?"

"That has nothing to do with him."

"Maybe not. But it might have to do with you tampering with the forest's magic—magic that must have turned him into a frog in the first place."

"I was only reversing—"

Harlan returns, pausing to take in the tension still rippling between us. "Bad timing?"

"It's fine." Axel pushes up. "I was just going to bed."

I sigh. "We should do the same," I tell Harlan, then realize the three of us are going to have to sleep together from now on. I suddenly miss Henni.

We stumble around until we awkwardly settle on me being in the middle. Lying crosswise on the two bedrolls, we tie our ankles together, one of mine to each boy. I feel like the strings of a fiddle, strung too tight and ready to snap if I turn one way or the other.

I toy with my acorn pendant and gaze into the moonless night.

The forest canopy teems with summer leaves, only allowing a few freckles of stars to shine through.

The curse *must* have returned in full force. There's no other explanation. Whatever provoked it, the partial lifting is gone.

I wonder how this is affecting my friends back in Grimm's Hollow. How it's affecting Grandmère.

My chest squeezes. *Please be alive.*

There's no fog in the forest, yet I feel one crowding over my mind, pulling me under to a place that's near sleep but isn't sleep. I'm too exhausted to be wary of it. My thoughts are tied up with the people I love back home.

Be kind to them. I imagine I'm speaking to the magic of the forest, the magic that either blesses or curses Grimm's Hollow. *Protect them.*

Unfortunately, I don't possess any magic beyond seeing the past.

Then let me see it.

Show me what happened today.

As soon as the thoughts trip over my mind, I'm swept away into a vision.

This one is different, more like flickers of time, glimpses that blink away as soon as I capture them.

Grimm's Hollow is shaking. Somehow, I see it all at once. In the village square, the Cuckoo House rocks on its foundations. The bird pops out at the wrong time and cuckoos out of sync with its mechanical beak.

Then I'm at the meadow with the pavilion housing *Sortes Fortunae*. Six night watchmen surround it, rather than the customary four. They clamor to protect it as the pedestal teeters. On the fringes of the meadow, the ash-lined border of the forest rolls several yards closer.

Now I'm on Rudger's farm. The earthquake has stopped. Fiora and Ella, discreet in dark cloaks, approach the ramshackle house with baskets of supplies and food.

Henni walks out on the porch, shoulders hitched up as if she fears the earthquake isn't over. Ella tries shooing her back inside, but then startles as the autumn trees rustle.

The three friends freeze, mesmerized by what happens all around them—autumn turning back into summer. Except this summer isn't lush and green, like the forest became after the reversal; it's parched and dismal. Hot, cursed.

At once, the leaves drop from branches and disintegrate into dirt. Puddles suck away into dry cracks of thirsty land.

Before I can see more, I'm taken to my sheep farm. Conrad is drawing water from the well, but his bucket comes up empty. Now I'm inside the cottage, Grandmère's bedroom. The earthquake has disturbed her furniture. Dresser drawers hang open. A vase is shattered on the ground. None of it has awoken her. She remains asleep under her quilt.

Relief overwhelms me. She's alive. But as I observe her closer, I find her cheeks have sunken in, the sockets around her eyes look hollower, and her skin is a sickly shade of gray. Her breaths rattle, and from the strained lines on her brow, each gasp is painful.

Tears prick my eyes. If I wasn't sure she was dying before, I am now. She spent too much strength shifting into Adiah to free me and Axel from the net.

My throat tightens to hold back a sob. How can I finish this journey now? How can I let her die without family beside her?

Her mouth struggles to form a word, like she's about to talk in her sleep. I lean closer. "C-Clara," she wheezes.

My pulse quickens. Can she sense me in this memory, like Harlan did? "I'm here."

Her next words are threadbare, choked from lack of breath: "The Dueling Rings. An eclipse. Solar or lunar. A beginning or an ending. You will either break the curse or—"

She falls into a coughing fit, so I say the rest. "—make it final. Yes, you've told me. Save your breath."

Eyes closed, she shakes her head slightly, stubbornness thinning her lips. "Be the solar eclipse. Break the curse. Be the beginning." She coughs. "Let me be the end."

"Don't say that. I'm not letting you—"

My words cut off as Harlan's pipe music floods my surroundings. His signature song.

I feel the pull of being sucked away to another time, another memory.

"Grandmère, let me stay!" I beg, as if she has any control here.

As her violet eyes flicker open, I'm taken to Harlan's farmhouse, but he isn't inside. It's his father, Herr Oswald, who sits in the armchair I sat in during my last visit to Harlan's memories.

He's playing a pipe, but not the double-reed pipe I stole. It's his own willow pipe, though it doesn't sound as bright as it did during the autumn festival. The signature song resonating from it draws a deeper, richer tone.

From the crooked paintings on the wall and the toppled figurines on the mantel, I note the timeline of my vision hasn't changed. He's just experienced the earthquake too.

Once the song finishes, he sets down his pipe, walks to the window, and stares at the encroaching forest. His shoulders sag, and he pinches his eyes closed.

Abruptly, I'm swept to the forest, where the seasons reverse so quickly I don't know *when* I am anymore. Not until I see Bren Zimmer's dead body in the stream. Then in another flash of a reversal, Bren is alive and beside the stream. Suddenly, my perspective shifts again, and I've become Bren. I see from his eyes, his vantage point.

A man charges at me and snatches a knife from the ground. Something shiny falls from his jacket. The pocket watch. Right when it hits the bank, the man's face peels from the shadows.

I'm sucked away before I witness what happens next, but my nerves jangle.

That was Kellen! He's alive!

Or at least he was on the night Bren was murdered. And from how he was holding the murder weapon, he likely killed Bren himself.

My heart plummets. *How will I tell Axel?*

The vision flashes. Now Kellen is following a woman with long spirals of ebony hair. They walk through a corridor with rough-hewn stone walls lit by an eerie turquoise glow. Reaching a bend, the woman faces Kellen. I inhale in a sharp breath. Lila Sommer.

She looks older than the Lila from Harlan's memories. Wilder too. Her amber eyes are feral yet more beautiful, though recklessly so. Dirt bronzes her cheeks, and something red glosses her lips. I fear it's blood. She wears a crown of thin roots, moss, and ferns.

She's Lost.

Meaning she and Kellen are somewhere in the forest.

She opens her hand, arches a black brow, and Kellen passes her something—a page with a torn edge. My adrenaline spikes. The missing page from the Book of Fortunes.

Lila's bloodred lips curve upward, and she saunters around the corner.

The vision starts to break. Blackness crowds around me, and all sound suctions from my ears.

Then I sense nothing. I'm in the void of all feeling. As quickly as I was drawn here, I'm ushered out, jerking wide awake and gasping.

Sweat rolls down my temples.

I know who murdered Bren.

And I've seen the missing page.

CHAPTER 32

shake Axel and Harlan awake and hurriedly untie our ankles. "I had another vision! We have to find Lila. She has the missing page!"

"Wait, slow down." Axel rubs sleep from his eyes. "You had a vision of Lila?"

"Partly. In a way."

Harlan sits up. "Did you say *Lila* has the missing page?"

I rush to grab my blouse and skirt from where I've hung them over a tree branch. "Yes, but the vision wasn't from her perspective."

"What token were you holding to channel the vision?" Axel asks.

"I wasn't holding any tokens."

"Then are you sure it was a vision and not a dream?"

"I know the difference." I grab my bodice and sweep my cape to my side, preparing to dress around it, as I can never take it off.

Harlan's eyes linger on my chemise, which must be transparent with the rays of morning sunlight glowing behind me. Heat sweeps my cheeks. I'm not used to the realities of traveling with another boy besides Axel. It felt different when Harlan was a frog. I move behind a tall blackberry bush for privacy.

"What makes you think Lila has the missing page?" Harlan kneels to tie up a bedroll. "What did you see?"

I sneak a glance over the bush at Axel. In my anticipation to set us on the correct path, I didn't think through what I'd have to explain about his father. "She was holding the page while walking down a stone corridor."

Harlan's hands start shaking, and the bedroll comes undone. "You didn't see how she got the page in the first place, did you? You don't think she was involved in Bren's murder?"

"I'm not sure." I slip on my skirt. "I only saw a few glimpses from the murder scene." Again, I forgo any mention of Kellen. "But Lila might be an accomplice if she ended up with the page."

Axel tucks his shirt in. "Wait, if you didn't see the vision from Lila's perspective, then whose was it?"

"Um . . . many people's."

"Has that happened before?"

"Not exactly." I wriggle my blouse on, carefully untying and retying my cape. "I saw two memories when I had my last vision of Harlan, but they were both his."

There's a hitch in Axel's movements, but he rolls out his shoulders and starts pacing. "So you think you saw many different perspectives last night?"

The answer is yes, but I say, "Possibly," hoping he'll drop it.

"Whose perspective were you in when you saw Lila with the page?"

"Can't remember." I trap all my attention on tightening the laces of my bodice.

"Strange."

"Mm-hmm."

Axel ambles around the blackberry bush as I finish dressing. "Is everything all right, Clara?"

I nod one too many times. "Just eager to get traveling. Harlan must know where Lila is."

"Why won't you look at me?"

I grab my shoes and force a glance his way. "What do you mean?"

"I know you. Something's off."

I sit on a large stone, slipping on my right shoe as I desperately try to think. *Do I tell Axel the truth?*

"Clara?" He crouches so we're eye to eye.

I slip on my left shoe. The wedge-lift doesn't sit right beneath my heel.

"Were you in Rudger's perspective when you saw Lila?" he asks softly.

Oh, how I wish. Axel would hate it, but it would be so much easier to accept. I shake my head, my eyes still lowered. He has to know who it was now. He's too smart, and he *does* know me too well.

There's no more delaying. I have to tell him everything.

I twist my hands in my lap. Axel already looks sick from what I'm about to divulge. "On the night Bren was killed, your father was alive," I begin, though my voice is raspy, fighting my efforts to spit out the words. "I know because I saw him at the stream in the forest . . . and I was in Bren's perspective."

Axel stiffens with invisible armor, but past it, his eyes penetrate mine, worried, yearning, and afraid.

"Your father picked up a knife . . . and he ran to attack Bren." I want to shrivel up and hide in my untied shoes. "I'm so sorry, Axel."

He falls silent for a long moment. I watch every movement of his face. His lips as they twitch and tremble. His eyes as they blink against a surge of moisture. His jaw muscle as it ripples from flexing.

He shakes his head, just the tiniest motion, but then it grows more pronounced, more determined, more stubborn. "No."

"No?"

He inhales, nostrils flaring. "Did you see my father actually kill Bren?"

"No, but—"

"Then he didn't do it. He would have never killed another person."

"But I saw—"

"You saw him rush at Bren with a knife. He could have been trying to help him, give him the knife so he could defend himself."

I seriously doubt it. The look on Kellen's face was pure fury. "Your father was also the person who gave Lila the missing page. He was with her in the corridor."

A crease mars Axel's forehead, but he swiftly irons it away. "That doesn't implicate him in the murder."

"Axel . . ." I reach to touch him, to soften the blow. "You know it does."

He flinches and stands. "Did you see my father make a murderous wish and tear out the page?"

"No, that was—" I bite my tongue too late.

"That was who?" he presses.

Now I'm the one rising and retreating. I trip and catch a branch to steady myself.

Harlan comes around the other side of the bush, and I'm cornered by both boys. "Are you two all right?" he asks.

Axel ignores him. "That was *who*, Clara?"

My chest collapses on itself. "My grandmother," I murmur, almost incoherently.

Axel's brows spring toward his hairline. "Your *grandmother*?"

"She didn't make a murderous wish." I cross my arms tightly around myself. "I didn't hear what she said. And I never saw her tear out the page."

In a rush of words, I explain how she scared away the night watchmen while in the body of the Grimm wolf, then spoke to the book alone when she'd returned to her human form. I also share how I saw huge paw prints near the stream where Bren was lying dead. "But she couldn't be the murderer."

"And how is that?" Axel scoffs.

"She doesn't have motive."

He throws up his hands. "Neither does my father!"

"But he was holding the murder weapon."

"And she was making a murderous wish!"

"We don't know that!"

"Just like we don't know my father stabbed Bren!"

Harlan moves between us, hands raised. "All right. Both of you need to stop and breathe for a moment."

Axel and I spear him with withering glares that could leech all the green from this forest.

"Let's talk about Lila." Harlan pivots. "She's a safe topic. At least for you two." A tic runs through his brow. "Clara, you mentioned Lila had the missing page while walking down a stone corridor. Is there anything else about the place that you remember?"

I breathe in deeply, still infuriated with him, then realize breathing deeply is exactly what he instructed, so I try not to breathe at all. "It was glowing with turquoise—not the gemstone, the color."

Harlan clucks his tongue. "She's in her kingdom."

"Her what?"

"Back in the village, Lila used to fantasize about a mystical kingdom where she could rule as queen. When she fell into madness, that dream twisted. In the forest, she's claimed an underground dwelling place that she believes is her kingdom."

"Where is it?" Axel asks.

"That's the problem." Harlan sits on the stone where I sat to tie my shoes. "I know the general location, but as a frog, I couldn't always find the place. For one thing, it doesn't have an entrance."

I step closer. "Then how did you get inside?"

"I waited for a certain Lost One to open a way in. He has power over that part of the forest. You might remember him from the village. Johann Schade?"

I nod, picturing the green marble in my collection. My token for Johann. I was never able to have a vision of him, but I haven't tried since the night before the autumn festival.

"Lila works with him to come and go from her kingdom when she needs to gather food or supplies. But her patterns are erratic. I've been left waiting for an entrance to open for several weeks before."

"We don't have several weeks." Not when the worsened curse is affecting people I love.

Harlan nods. "Fortunately, I'm not a frog anymore, so I can speak with Johann and request an entrance myself. If he won't listen to me, I'm sure he'll listen to you."

I laugh. "Why?"

One side of Harlan's mouth curves up. "Because you're the Changer of Fate."

I roll my eyes, but don't dispute it. In all honesty, I desperately hope it's still true.

"How exactly does Johann open an entrance?" Axel asks.

"He tunnels a great beanstalk into the earth," Harlan replies. "Lila calls him Jack."

CHAPTER 33

The place above Lila's underground kingdom is an area of the forest Harlan has named Soldiers' Vale because of the giant stones surrounding it that resemble people, and the great battle that took place there long ago.

From his description of how to get there, it's in the general region of the cavern where I found *Sortes Fortunae* on my last journey, which will take several days to reach.

As we begin traveling, the adrenaline I'd felt after seeing the missing page in a vision wears off, replaced by overwhelming exhaustion, my toll for having visions.

I start to wonder if I've learned how to sleep while walking—different from sleepwalking. It's a mad-hatched thought, but perhaps it explains some of the strange things I find myself doing.

One day I'm tightly pacing within a copse of trees, when Harlan jostles my shoulder. "Let's keep moving, Clara. These aren't the Sommer girls."

"Yes, they—" I waver on my feet. "Sommer girls? What do you mean?"

"You were talking to the trees. You said the girls' names."

"I did?"

"But these trees don't even have faces," he says.

He's right. I'm surrounded by spotted trunks of aspens, no warped faces among them.

Another day, I'm kneeling to get a drink from the river we're now following. The water is glass-like. We're close to a beaver's dam. As I cup a handful of water to my mouth, a baritone voice breaks into my awareness: "Clara?"

I catch myself staring at my watery reflection, my position different from a moment ago. The green eyes gazing back at me look briefly vacant. I turn around and see a handsome boy with tousled golden waves and eyes as blue as the shallows of the river. My skin warms, and I shyly tuck a lock of hair behind my ear.

"Hello . . ." It takes me a moment to place his name. "Axel." I clutch my acorn pendant, a little shaken by my lapse of memory.

Two worry lines carve between his brows. "Who were you speaking with?"

"You?"

"Before that."

"Oh . . ." I look back at my reflection. "Myself?" I ask, although I don't remember.

"You said, 'Are you a ghost?'"

Did I? I try to laugh, but my amusement fades, swallowed by the pit of dread gaping wide in my stomach. "I think I need to sleep," I confess. "Except I don't want to have another vision. I've had too many lately. My mind is strained."

His worry lines burrow deeper. "Do you know how to keep them from happening?"

"By staying awake? Or thinking of nothing before falling asleep?" I've been trying both, but staying awake only makes me groggier, and thinking of nothing is nearly as exhausting.

So far, I haven't had another vision since the one with Kellen and Lila. But each night, I fear I'll have one that gives enough proof, even for Axel, that his father murdered Bren, or that Grandmère really made a murderous wish.

Axel helps me to my feet and calls for Harlan to stop walking. We're done traveling for the day. He guides me to a place to make camp. I feel his hand brush the small of my back to steady me, but he never maintains touch for long. He's still struggling to forgive me.

I lie down midday and sleep through the afternoon, that night, and well into the next day's afternoon. I manage to hold back more visions. All the glimpses I see now are when my eyelids flicker open and I catch Axel keeping guard, never leaving me out of sight.

Never leaving me alone with Harlan.

I wonder if Axel really distrusts him so much, or if it's Harlan's connection to me he dislikes—the pity I had for him that compelled me to kiss him longer, the bond we somehow share that allowed us to speak in his memories.

The only time Axel eases up is when he sleeps at night, our ankles firmly tied together, even if my other ankle is also tied to Harlan's.

The day comes that our food rations run dry. All that's left is a hunk of moldy Hollow bread. It's time to hunt for food. We fish in the river and use my crossbow to shoot small birds. The forest hides larger prey from us, but we manage.

As we press onward, the landscape grows rockier than any we've crossed so far. Harlan says we're getting closer to Soldiers' Vale, and Axel's pocket watch suddenly shifts to a new time. Four o'clock. Four days. I wish I knew what dire event the countdown led to.

All I know is we need to complete this journey as quickly as possible. I want to embrace my grandmother before she stops breathing. I need to tell her I did what she asked me to do.

Near sunset, Axel suggests we make camp at the base of a rocky ridge. Harlan says once we climb to the other side tomorrow, we'll arrive at Soldiers' Vale. I'm too anxious to wait any longer. I persuade the boys to finish the journey tonight.

We travel up the switchbacks of the ridge, over the crest, and down the slopes into the valley. Even under the moonlight, the massive stones encircling Soldiers' Vale are impressive—great pillars of eroded limestone that give the impression of giants. Smaller pillars dot the valley, which is cloaked by a vast meadow, its wildflowers silvery and swaying.

Harlan guides us to a tree at the valley's western edge. An apple tree, and one that's bearing fruit, as if it alone is still caught under the spell of autumn. According to Harlan, Jack frequently visits this tree—it's the closest thing he has to a home—so it's best to stay here until he shows up.

Resigned to sleep for the rest of the night, we make camp and pick three apples from the tree, hoping Jack won't mind. Strangely, different varieties of apples hang from the branches. Axel and Harlan choose green ones, and I select one as vividly red as my cape. We eat them to the core.

"What happened to the beanstalks Jack already tunneled for Lila?" I ask Harlan as the three of us settle down on the bedrolls and tie our ankles together. "Can't we use one of them?"

"They're gone." Harlan yawns widely. "Once Lila's finished with them, Jack buries the beanstalks even deeper than her lair. The next time she needs to come aboveground, he grows a new one and does it all over again."

I think of Jack's marble, a clear globe with a ribbon swirl of green in its center. Is it mad to think that's why his control of the forest bent toward beanstalks? Was it some kind of strange memorial of who he was in his former life—an apprentice glassblower named Johann with a unique marble as his prized possession?

"How dangerous is Jack as far as Lost Ones go?" I ask Harlan, but he only answers with a heavy snore. I turn to Axel on my other side. "What do you think? Should we be worried about . . . ?" I trail off, seeing he's also out cold. They're both impressive sleepers, but they've outdone themselves. Our night-time trek must have worn them through.

Unsurprisingly, I have more trouble falling asleep. I squirm and wriggle, wedged between them.

An hour passes. Then two. I need to relieve myself.

I quietly untie my ankles and slip away to a cluster of nearby trees. Once my business is finished, I amble back to the campsite, a little wobbly from fatigue.

A sudden wind kicks up, whipping through the trees like the wails of dying men. Branches snap against each other and the sound falls strangely metallic on my ears, like clashing swords. It's easy to imagine the great battle of old happening all over again.

I scoff at myself. I'm imagining things, already drifting into dreams while still upright on my feet. I'm sleepwalking. No, walking in sleep. Almost sleeping. Whatever.

As I approach the apple tree on the opposite side from where the boys are lying, I stagger to a halt and take in the frozen face in the trunk. It must be freshly absorbed. Its features are distinct and only covered by a thin layer of bark. "Johann," I gasp.

Johann as in Jack. And Jack is dead.

CHAPTER 34

Tears gather in my eyes. "I'm so sorry," I tell the trapped corpse of Johann. Maybe I should be more worried about how I'll find a way down to Lila without him, but all I feel is grief for failing another Lost One before he died.

I touch his scaly face. I wish I'd gotten to know Johann before he became Lost as Jack. He kept to himself, except for working with his master glassblower. He only came out for some festivals, his hair combed flat to his head and his clothes patched and pressed. He never danced, but he'd sit on the edge of his seat, like he was trying to drum up the courage to approach the girls.

I don't know how to mourn him properly. If this were a grave, I could lay down flowers. Although, I might have something better. I walk around the tree and find my bag of tokens. I rummage inside it until my fingers brush a small, hard globe: Johann's green marble.

I return to him—what's left of him—and place the marble in a knothole where the hollow of this throat would have been. "If it still means anything to you," I say, in lieu of a eulogy, "I *am* doing my best to break the curse. I hope it will give your soul peace."

As I gaze at the scaly wood growing over his somber eyes, my predicament finally steals over me. "It's a shame we couldn't have met sooner. Lila has something I need to break the curse. I could have used one of your beanstalks." I sniff. "Anyway that was a beautiful marble you made. Goodbye, Johann . . . Jack—whatever you prefer being called now."

As I back away and weave around the tree, I startle as the air ripples with a hint of illumination. A bodiless voice replies, "I prefer Jack."

My breath catches as the illumination brightens, undulating until it steadies into the ghost of a young man—Johann Schade from Grimm's Hollow, Johann who died as Jack and must still be Lost as Jack.

His lanky frame and oblong face are almost the same as I remember, although he's grown thinner and appears older, having gone Lost in the second year of the curse.

My knees rattle. I've never seen another ghost besides Ollie. "H-hello, Jack."

He averts his gaze like he's shy of me. "You were talking about breaking the curse," he mumbles. "I don't want it broken if it means I'll have to leave the eldest princess. I'm duty-bound to her."

I tamp down my shock. The princess must be Lila, and if she's the eldest, there must be others. "But if the curse is broken, the eldest princess would be free, and she'd want to free those who serve her," I reply, hoping it's true.

"The eldest princess never frees anyone. Besides, I don't like sending princesses below anymore, not unless the eldest invites them first."

"I'm not a princess."

"You're all princesses in the end."

"Wait . . ." What he said a moment ago finally strikes me. "Are you still able to open an entrance to Lila's kingdom?" His phrasing made it sound possible.

He doesn't answer, but his shoulders curl inward like it's true and he's hesitant to give me access.

"Do you recognize the marble I placed in your tree?" I ask.

He shakes his head.

"I brought it from Grimm's Hollow. Did you know all the people in this forest have lost something, though most can't remember what exactly? Imagine you started growing beanstalks because they reminded you of what *you* had lost? What if you once wanted to become a glassblower and make green marbles such as this?"

I fetch the marble from the knothole. "What if you could still make beautiful glass creations to show others what you had to offer? Imagine how impressed the eldest princess would be if you gave her this marble?" I hope I'm striking at the core of who Johann was, a timid man who never had the courage to ask anyone to dance. If so, I'm sure he was—and still is—besotted with Lila.

He nibbles on his lower lip. "I can't give her something that I can't hold."

"But *I* can." I smile warmly. "I can tell the eldest princess this is a gift from you. All you have to do is open an entrance for me."

"What about the curse? What if she doesn't want it to be broken either?"

"Then I'll try to strike a bargain with her. She must have lost something too."

"Yes." Jack's somber eyes roam over me. "White, red, and black."

"Come again?"

"You'll do well, actually."

I don't understand, but I'm not going to ask too many questions now that he's being cooperative. "Good."

He stands a fragment taller and nods, then turns to walk away.

"Where are you going?"

"To grow a beanstalk." He looks over his shoulder. "Are you coming?"

"Oh, I didn't realize . . ." I tug on my cape. It's all I'm wearing over my chemise. "I just need to get dressed, get the boys, and—"

"They're not going to wake up for a few days."

My heart pounds. *What?* I race back to where Axel and Harlan are sleeping. I jostle them vigorously, but they don't stir. "What did you do to them?"

Jack peeks around the tree. "They did it to themselves. They ate the green apples."

"You could have warned us!" I shake Axel harder. Shout his name. Pluck a red apple and try to feed it to him.

"Nothing you can do will break the spell," Jack says. "They'll have to wait it out. But if you want me to open an entrance, I need to do that now."

My blood burns as I scrutinize him, under no illusions anymore that he's still shy. He's just a crafty and manipulative Lost One. "Why now?"

"I'm a ghost." He shrugs. "I can only grow a beanstalk by using a loop."

"A loop?"

"A repetition of something I did when alive. Loops have to be identical, though. I *can* grow another beanstalk, but only if it's grown exactly as it was before. About a year ago, I tunneled one nearby, at this same time of night. The window for that loop is closing, though. If we miss it, you'll have to wait five more weeks until I can trigger another one."

I hold my muscles tense. I can't trust Jack, and all of this feels too contrived, but what if he's right? I can't wait five more weeks, not when the pocket watch will shift to three o'clock soon and Grandmère is on her deathbed. "I at least need my bodice and shoes. They help my . . ." Jack spins away, his illumination fading. My pulse jumps. "Wait, I'm coming!"

I dash after him, my chest squeezed tight from having to

leave the boys behind. If they don't wake up again, I'll never forgive myself.

Jack leads me to a clearing free of boulders and trees, and he scouts around until whatever he sees among the rocks and wild grass confirms we've arrived at the right spot. "You'll need a name that will please the eldest princess," he says.

"I already have one. Clara Thurn."

"That won't do."

I grind my teeth. "Then what do you suggest?"

He tilts his head at me. "I was thinking Snow White."

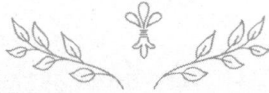

CHAPTER 35

A flick of a wrist. A burst of green like a giant fountain. Jack's beanstalk. It surges up and makes a sharp twist downward, piercing the earth as if its tip were forged steel. The beanstalk whips as it tunnels, slightly widening the hole, the path I'll have to follow.

I stand back with Jack as we wait for the beanstalk to finish growing, sinking. The moment it stills, faint light tinges the sky and fades the stars. Dawn is coming. I hope against hope that Axel and Harlan will wake up soon and follow, that the beanstalk will remain in place and keep the entrance open. But if they're really spelled to sleep for a few days, I'm likely on my own.

I step up to the beanstalk, its many vines twisted together, forming a girth of fifteen inches. I peer into the hole that surrounds it. I wish I had a lantern. It's pure darkness down there.

I don't have any pockets, so I tear a few stitches open at the hem of my cape and stuff the green marble inside. I grasp the beanstalk, step onto its leaves, my footholds, and give a parting glance to Jack. He offers no words of encouragement, only stares with an expression teetering between guilt and desire.

I steel my nerves. *Don't think, Clara. Just move.*

I enter the freshly churned tunnel and descend the stalk.

Darkness enshrouds me. The scent of rich soil fills my nostrils. My back brushes earth as I grope downward, leaf by leaf, vine by vine. Tiny legs skitter across my shoulders. Slimy things wriggle over my limbs. I try not to picture centipedes, beetles, worms.

Just keep moving.

The descent is longer than I imagined. Each second feels like a hundred. It's like I'm in the transition of a vision, the in-between of the past and the present, a timeless hell where I'm alone and at the mercy of magic I don't fully comprehend.

Terrifying thoughts plague my mind. What if Jack's beanstalk never grew to the depth of Lila's caverns? What if he closes off the hole, and I'm trapped in the middle of an underworld I can't escape?

My chest constricts. My breath comes in shallow gasps. I'm suffocating just from thoughts of suffocation.

Stop thinking, stop worrying, keep moving, keep breathing.

The tunnel starts to widen. The earth hardens to limestone. Mineral-rich air wafts over me, thick and warm with humidity. Utter blackness gives way to a soft turquoise glow. I discover the source of the illumination: glowworms. They hang in abundant ropes like blue-green seed beads.

They swarm the cavern I emerge into, filled with icicle-like stalactites and little towers of stalagmites. Less than thirty feet below, I spy the bottom of the beanstalk, or rather its tip, since it grew upside down. It creeps into a steaming fissure of limestone and stops tunneling.

No one else is in the cavern. Lila and the other "princesses" must be in some other connecting place, however vast this "kingdom" may be. What if Kellen is down here too? I forgot to ask Jack about him.

The closer I descend to the floor, the stronger I smell the vapors from the fissure. They're sweet like cherry brandy and buzz through my head like I've drunk a full bottle.

My movements grow clumsy. My grip weakens, legs wobble.

As much as I love the blissfulness washing over me, I need to hurry away from the vapors before I become lost in the euphoria.

I've almost reached the bottom. Ten more feet. I lower to another leaf, and its stem snaps. I shriek and plummet feet first so I won't roll into a stalagmite.

Pain shudders through me. My hip and S-curve take the brunt. I grab a stalagmite to stick my landing, but the cave floor is slick. I slip on my back. My head whiplashes against the limestone. Stars burst in my vision.

I groan and curl into a fetal position.

I'm right beside a fissure. Vapors rush into my lungs. My pain eases. My mind calms . . .

. . . and it's wonderful.

I'm approaching oblivion.

You shouldn't stay here, a tiny corner of my brain warns. But I can't heed it. My head pounds from my wound. My eyelids flutter closed, and blackness crowds over me.

For the second time, I feel as if I'm slipping into a vision. But I don't want one.

I stretch out my limbs. Struggle to crawl away. But my body is too heavy, and my head feels too light. It's filling with clouds and pops of starlight, fumes and dizzying smells.

I strain to move, but I can't even claw an inch forward.

Suddenly, my muscles go lax.

No . . .

Sleep rolls over me with tidal strength. I can't fight the spell.

No visions is my last wish. *Let this be a dreamless sleep.*

And I do sleep dreamlessly.

But when I wake up, I can't remember anything that happened while my eyes were closed.

I can't even remember where I am or the reason I came.

I feel . . . lost.

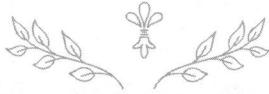

CHAPTER 36

My eyes open to streaks of glowing turquoise and a towering green vine that plunges into the high ceiling of a cavern. Strangely familiar. I sit up gingerly. My back and head throb, but I don't mind. I'm too drunk on the surrounding mist of fumes.

The ground is slippery, so I crawl toward a branching tunnel. Gemstones sparkle from its walls. Maybe down that tunnel I'll find the reason why I've come.

Within it, the ground is drier, aside from a trickle of silty water running through. I step around it and walk farther. Ropes of pearly blue-green beads light my way.

A pattering of feet echoes toward me, rhythmic and alluring. Past the bend of the tunnel, there must be people. Perhaps they're why I'm here.

A little tipsy, I grope the cave walls and turn around the bend. The tunnel continues another several yards, but beyond it, I spy a breathtaking cavern, even more mystical than the last and overflowing with beaded ropes. I try to reach that place, but everything rocks and sways. My head still buzzes from the vapors.

As I inch forward, I notice many people in the cavern. Their slippered feet slap the limestone as they move in a circle—a dance, I realize, watching them step inward and outward, holding hands.

They're . . . girls. Twelve of them.

Each one is dressed in a fraying, filthy gown, their hair wild, half matted and half frizzy. On their heads, they wear wreaths of various kinds, made from long-stemmed mushrooms, tangled moss, and stringy roots.

I don't hear any music, but the girls must, for a secret song keeps them dancing in unison. They abandon themselves to it, closing their eyes and letting their heads fall back and roll side to side.

My chest pangs with longing. I want to feel that same passion and freedom. That must be why I've come, so they can teach me.

I creep forward like some graceless creature of the underworld. It doesn't matter that the girls are clothed in grime or that their slippers are worn with holes. I'll fit right in with my dirt-streaked chemise, bare feet, and . . . red cape?

I pause, wobbling, and examine it closer, my fingers brushing a stain that almost spurs a memory.

Suddenly, my stomach twists with a bout of nausea. Everything moves, tilts, and turns upside down. Now the girls are dancing on the ceiling, their skirts swaying, their circle ever rotating. Stepping inward and outward, they look like flowers shriveling and blossoming, changing season by season.

I stumble as a great empty picture frame appears before me in the tunnel. Sparkling gemstones encrust the wood, and the frame is so large I could step right through without ducking my head.

As I approach it, one of the girls on the dance floor steps away and joins me on the other side of the frame. She's my age and also small in stature with ratted sable hair, emerald eyes, and milky white skin . . . no, snow white.

I take in her filthy chemise, bare feet, and red cape, and the eyes gazing back at me widen. "You're *me*," I say to my reflection. This isn't an empty frame. It's a—"Mirror." "Mirror," my voice echoes down the tunnel.

My reflection stares at me expectantly, as if waiting for me to say more. But all I want to do is dance with the girls.

I move to the left and the right, searching for a gap to slip through, but the mirror fills the tunnel edge to edge. "How do I get past you?"

"Ask the deepest question of your heart," my reflection says, "and I will give you a true answer. For mirrors never lie."

The deepest question of my heart? That is hard to pin when I can't even remember my own name. "Mirror?" "Mirror," my voice echoes. "Who am I?"

"Is *that* the question of your heart?" mirror-me asks.

"Yes." Nothing can be more important.

My reflection changes, growing taller and maturing into someone old enough to be my mother. She wears a cornflower-blue dress, and roses bloom all around her.

I don't understand. "Is this who I will become?"

"Is it?" the woman in the mirror asks.

"I thought you had the answer."

"Answers do not come without first asking many questions."

"I asked one already: 'Who am I?'"

My reflection alters again, her hair graying and skin wrinkling. Her eyes transform from ivy green to vivid violet.

"This woman is old enough to be my grandmother," I tell the mirror. "How is *she* who I am?"

"You have already asked a question," the old woman says.

"You said I should ask many."

"Indeed. But I will only answer one: the question of your heart."

My fists clench. I'm trying. "Mirror?" "Mirror," comes my echo. "Who am I?"

The old woman grows pointed ears, a snout, fur, and fangs.

A huge wolf stares back at me, its eyes remaining violet. "Is this what you wanted to see?" the wolf asks with the same voice as the old woman's.

"I don't know." I shiver from the wolf's gaze, yet yearn to stroke her fur. "Why are *you* asking me questions?"

"Because I am your reflection, and you have always shown abundant curiosity."

I don't like this looking glass. "Enough of your riddles, Mirror." "Mirror," the wolf repeats, grinning. "Who. Am. I?"

The reflection morphs into the woman in the cornflower dress. She tips her head back and drinks in the moonlight shining in her world. Then her dress shifts into a gown woven with red flowers, and she grows fangs. A spindle pierces her heart, and she crumples, only to rapidly stand again. Now she's the old woman, but she wears a cloak of fortune-telling cards and torn-out pages. The pages fill with words written in magic green ink:

Secret bearer
Seer
Matriarch
Wolf
Murderer
Curse bringer

The reflection reforms into the girl wearing the dirty chemise and red cape. In one hand, she holds a knife and a spindle, both dripping blood. In the other hand, she clutches a long stem of red flowers that tip downward like bells. *Red rampion.* Above her shine the moon and the sun, though both are vanishing in a double eclipse.

"You choose who you are," mirror-me says.

But I still can't decide who that is.

My reflection drops what she holds and offers her hand. I take it, and she pulls me through the mirror.

Once I'm on the other side, the mirror disappears and the tunnel rotates. The twelve girls turn right-side up, and the dance floor rests on the bottom of the cavern once more. I drift closer, and some of the girls sharpen into focus, though six remain blurry. *Six are ghosts.*

My heartbeat quickens, a warning *thump-thump-thump* in my chest.

If I dance with them, is that what I'm destined to become?

One girl notices me and breaks away from the circle, gliding toward me at the rim of the dance floor. She isn't the youngest or the eldest, but somewhere in between. I breathe easier seeing she's alive, her black curls and russet eyes crisp-edged.

"Have you come to help us?" she asks somberly.

"I'm . . . not sure."

"We're two groups of unlucky numbers without you."

I think I understand. Although they dance as twelve, six are living and six are dead, so no group makes seven.

"If we dance beautifully enough, perhaps we'll find what we've lost," the girl goes on.

I have the strangest feeling we've met before and had this very conversation.

"You'll help us, won't you?"

"I never learned the circle dances," I confess.

The girl smiles. "We'll teach you. But to become a princess, you first need dancing slippers. You may borrow mine." She removes her worn-soled pair.

"Thank you." I slide them on my feet and tie the fraying ribbons around my ankles.

"You have come just in time."

"For what?"

"The enchanted dance. It occurs when the princes come at midnight."

Midnight? How long was I asleep and breathing in the vapors? Wasn't it almost morning before I . . . ? I lose the thought before it fully forms.

"Do you feel that rushing in your head?" the girl asks. "Like a drone of bees or a crashing waterfall?"

I nod. Did she breathe in the vapors too?

"That's the music, the magic. Listen to it. Succumb to it. That's how you become one of us."

I close my eyes, open my ears. I don't want to die by dancing, but I *do* want to join this sisterhood. If I make six become seven, I would be among the seven living. We would form a lucky number.

The buzzing in my skull finds a rhythm, a song. It sweeps into a mesmerizing melody, filled with strings of unseen instruments. "I hear it."

The girl takes my hand. "Now you are ready. Open your eyes and join us in the mystic kingdom."

I open my eyes, and I enter.

CHAPTER 37

I walk onto a dance floor that's solid underfoot but glimmers like water, bouncing back the light of turquoise glowworms, golden fireflies, and luminous purple mushrooms. Pillars of twisted roots surround it like marble columns in a castle. Giant crystals hang from the limestone ceiling, and gemstones stud the walls, their sparkling facets also reflecting light.

I'm no longer in my filthy clothes, but dressed in a white gown of fluttering moth wings and dandelion puffs. My red-hooded cape ripples to lie behind my shoulders, shining like silk and lengthening into a train. Gentle pressure settles on my head, and I reach up, feeling a crown. Unlike the other princesses' crowns of twigs, moss, and ivy, mine is made of hard things with pointed ends. Teeth, I realize. Wolf fangs.

If I frighten the others, they don't show it. They make space for me in their circle, and I move between a living girl and the ghost of one. Each princess holds her right hand aloft, pointed toward the center. I do the same. The tips of our fingers brush as we dance, round and round.

The twelve princesses wear their own beautiful dresses, their rags replaced by gowns of beetle wings, silver fish scales, moss patches, and mushroom caps.

The most striking princess, by far, is the one who looks to be the eldest. Embedded in her large crown of thin roots, moss, and ferns are clusters of sparkling rubies. Her dress is leathery and black, crafted from bat wings, and hugs the curves of her voluptuous body. Wild curls of ebony hair hang in spirals down her back.

Her amber eyes find mine across the circle, and her brows draw together. She hasn't noticed me until now. I'm about to introduce myself, but my mind grinds and sticks. I still can't remember my name.

The root pillars surrounding the dance floor writhe. I startle, and the eldest princess's bloodred lips curve upward at my skittishness. "What's the matter?" she asks as our circle changes direction, rotating the other way. "Are you afraid of our princes? They may be dead, but they make wonderful dancing partners."

Twisted among the roots, each pillar has a face I didn't see before—a dead face like those in the trees aboveground. Other memories flit about my mind, but fade before I can catch them.

The roots unravel to reveal the ghosts of princes. Stepping out, they look like soldiers of various ranks with differing armor of chain mail, padded vests, studded leather, and breastplates. Each holds a weapon in both hands, as if in the manner they were buried: swords, daggers, maces, and battle axes.

They stow their ghostly weapons in the roots and stride onto the dance floor, deftly taking the arm of a princess and spinning her away to the music.

I look for a partner, but there are only twelve princes and I make a thirteenth princess. The eldest princess throws me another mocking smile. She lifts her hand and curls a beckoning finger at the cavern ceiling.

At the edge of the hanging crystals, a tangle of roots comes alive like a nest of vipers. It wriggles down from the ceiling and twists to make a thirteenth pillar, from which emerges the ghost of a thirteenth prince.

He sets aside his crossbow, removes his plumed helmet, and whisks me away in his arms. At least I imagine it's his arms bearing me up, but since they are ghost arms, I cannot lean into them. Nevertheless, we find our rhythm.

I move when I sense he wants me to move. I twirl when I should twirl. I become one of thirteen blurring couples, dancing on and on and on.

At some hour, the night must meld into day, because eventually the princes disappear and I'm back in the circle of princesses, ever moving, never stopping, constantly drowning in the delirium.

My lower spine hurts, escalating from a twinge to a horrible throbbing. I can't stop dancing to find relief. Stopping is forbidden, I've gleaned. No one does it. Perhaps when you do, you die. And I'm only just alive again.

A hitch mars my movements. *Alive again?* How could that be possible? That would mean I was once dead, which makes no sense.

I stumble to the center of the circle, breaking away from the girls. I try to keep dancing, but I can't stay in cadence. My back is on fire, and my thoughts burn with a deeper blaze. I can almost remember who I am . . . why I came here.

The eldest princess's amber eyes follow my every movement. I twirl and twirl, each revolution bringing me back to those eyes, heavy lashed and cunning. I've seen them before, perhaps in a dream. She's important. Dangerous. Beloved by someone. She has something I need.

I twirl again, and my back pulls sharply. I buckle; the eldest princess races to usher me off the dance floor. At the mouth of the tunnel, she seats me on a protrusion of limestone that serves as a bench.

Cave water trickles in a pool near our slippered feet, and she scoops it into a cupped fern leaf and tips it in my mouth. "More," I croak, realizing how parched I am. I lose count of how many more drinks she serves me. I just choke them down, silt and all, until I'm quenched.

"Thank you." I dry my mouth with my sleeve.

She laces her hands in her lap, her fingernails long, sharp, and stained black. "If you are here," she says, her voice purring in a deep octave, "then Jack disobeyed me."

"Jack?" I picture a green marble, but I can't recall its significance.

"He is only permitted to admit princesses at my invitation. But I can forgive him, for you are a girl of white, red, and black." Her ravenous gaze sweeps the length of me. "All my princesses must embody one of the colors. Look." She points to the girl who gave me her slippers. "There is Raven's Wings, named for her lustrous dark hair, and the princess beside her is Moon Milk, for the shining whites of her eyes, and there is Red Poppy, for she is always drowsy. If I had found you, rather than you finding me, I would have given you a name before you entered."

"I already have a name."

"Do you?" One of her elegantly sculpted brows arches.

"It's—" Fog rolls over my mind, and I inwardly curse. I think through the three colors, trying to spark my memory. Then it comes: "My name is Snow White."

Her eyes narrow to sparks of amber. "Yes, that is fitting, for you are fair." She strokes my face with icy fingers. "Though I could have named you Scarlet Rose for your lips or Starless Night for your black mane." Her fingers float over my mouth and a lock of my waves. "You are a marvel, being all three of the colors. Perhaps you are who I've been looking for, the one who can find what I've lost."

I want to scoot back. She's leaning too close, but I fear offending her. "What did you lose?"

"White, red, and black. Why do you think I seek them?"

I have no idea.

"Would you like to see what else bears the colors?" She saunters across the tunnel, her dress glistening like black water. The eleven princesses continue dancing behind her. From a large crevice in the limestone, she reaches for something. I picture a single loose page with a serrated edge, as if it was torn from a book. But all she withdraws is an apple.

She strikes it against a hard edge, and it splits in half. "I gather these apples when I leave my kingdom. They grow on a special tree just to please me."

She gives me one half, sitting stiflingly close again, her breath sickly sweet and metallic. "Do you see the white flesh, the red skin, the black seeds?" I nod, and she smiles, satisfied. "All three colors."

A riddle dances across my brain:

White for a pure heart,
Red for rampion-stained lips,
Black for a faceless night,
A kiss to seal your wish.

I can't place where I learned it, but the riddle feels critical. "Perhaps what you've lost—what you need—is a kiss."

"A kiss?" She sneers. "I prefer to dance. Kisses bring curses."

"Or they break them."

She tilts her head, her ebony spirals tumbling like snakes over her shoulder. "How so?"

"I . . . don't remember."

She bites into her half of the apple, her eyes probing mine. "Have you ever been kissed?"

The scent of dry grass hits me, and I picture a cozy mote-filled hayloft. I catch the briefest glimpse of a beautiful golden-haired boy with soul-searching blue eyes, and I feel his warm lips light upon mine. But I can't tell the eldest princess about him. He's a secret I want to protect. "A frog once kissed me," I answer. "Or maybe I kissed him."

I expect the eldest princess to burst into laughter, but she grows limestone still, apart from the flare of her nostrils and a twitch of her brow. "If a kiss doesn't bring a curse, it should at least promise limitless magic." Tension ripples off her. "Did yours?"

There *was* something magical about the kiss, something transformative, but I can't remember what. "I think so."

She sets her apple aside and slips even closer. The hair on my arms stands on end. "Did you journey alone in the forest? The last princesses who came traveled in a group following the music."

I think of the music the princess called Raven's Wings helped me hear. Is that what the eldest princess means? "I came with . . . boys," I say, piecing bits of my past together. "Before I met Jack, there were two others."

"Mortal boys?"

I concentrate harder, pressured to give a satisfactory answer. The frog probably doesn't count. "There *was* one boy." The beautiful boy, though I won't mention his hayloft kiss.

"Was he a real prince, then? An alive one?"

Another memory stirs . . . how I danced with him in another place, also a ballroom in the forest. I was wearing a magical blue dress, and we'd both sprouted swan feathers. "He *must* be a real prince." I'd felt his arms around me—real arms, warm and strong.

A sigh trembles through her body. She's rife with desire and obsessiveness, and I feel the urge to protect the beautiful boy again. "Did he promise you limitless magic?"

"I suppose." The dance we shared had felt endlessly enchanted.

She takes my half of the apple, tosses it away, and grabs my hands. "You should find this prince and bring him back to me."

"Back to you?"

"Back here," she amends.

My mouth runs dry. If I leave, I could escape. But I shouldn't. I was supposed to do something first . . . get something . . . or maybe give something. "Am I supposed to return a bracelet to you?" I picture a small circle of coral beads.

"A bracelet?"

"A token."

"For what?"

I shrug, fighting another wave of fog.

"A bracelet *would* be helpful to cover my scars."

"You have scars too?" I almost remember mine.

She pushes back her sleeve to reveal the striated band of skin around her wrist. "A rope burn from a fishing net."

A horrifying image springs to mind. I can't see it clearly—it's too dark and flickering—but it makes me feel as though someone I love has died.

I stand abruptly. "I should go."

The eldest princess's eyelids slit. "What about my bracelet?"

"I-I'll try to find it. That's why I have to leave."

Her smile thins. "I don't really care about the bracelet, Snow White. Just your prince."

"He's gone. He went back home."

She scoffs and rises, looking down at me. "Nobody in this forest returns home."

"Then I better go find him." I turn for the tunnel, but she seizes my arm. Her long fingernails dig into my skin and draw blood.

"I'm sure he will be the one to find you, like any true prince would. I'll make sure Jack holds the entrance open. I've changed my mind about you leaving. *You will stay.*" A tremor of madness sparks in her eyes.

I'm gripped by a chill, dead center in the chest. I understand what she means: if I don't oblige, she'll kill me.

I could try to yank free and run for the beanstalk. But even as the other princesses dance, they spear me with looks of equal hostility.

I can't outrun them all, not with my throbbing back.

"It's time to hear the music again, Snow White," the eldest princess says. "You have rested long enough. Those who stop dancing here die. You wouldn't want that to be your fate."

I wonder if it isn't exhaustion that kills them, but her.

Reluctantly, I allow her to guide me back to the dance floor under the crystals, glowworms, and fireflies. I struggle to block out the music, but it floods my skull relentlessly, causing my arms to raise and my feet to glide.

I join the circle, and I dance and dance and dance.

CHAPTER 38

My head is whirling. It feels as if I've been dancing for days. Even if I could stop, I'm scared my mind would keep spinning, forever caught in the turning circle of princesses. I'm losing who I am, step by step, twirl by twirl.

Mostly, I'm sure I'm Snow White. The eldest princess keeps calling me that. But fragmented thoughts make me doubt, glimpses of a past that doesn't feel limited to only white, red, and black.

I remember sitting beside a rosy-cheeked girl named Henni who wears her hair in braids and paints orange marigolds on teacups. Then I'm tucking a patchwork quilt of blue forget-me-nots around an old woman. Grandmère, I call her. Now I'm walking beside a boy who chews on a long piece of straw as golden as his hair. He teases me as I tend to a flock of sheep. He follows me everywhere.

He must be the prince who kissed me in the hayloft. Will he really come for me, like the eldest princess believes? As much as I want that, I need him to stay away. She desires him for herself, and what she wants, she destroys.

I'm sure of it when the youngest of the living princesses, Little Dove, collapses one day, breaking the fluidity of our circle. The eldest princess kneels and shakes the girl's shoulders, and when she doesn't revive, she drags her to one of the root pillars and commands the dead face, "Get rid of her."

The roots cocoon Little Dove and pull her up through a gap in the ceiling, where I imagine she's dragged to the forest for another tree to absorb.

Whatever happens, it isn't long before her ghost returns and joins our circle once more. Even death doesn't free us from this ring of dark enchantment.

"Why do you keep us here?" I ask the eldest princess when I'm too weary to think better of provoking her, when my feet bleed past the illusion of lovely slippers on my feet, when my back throbs past endurance, when tears of pain streak down my cheeks and chafe my skin. "What's our purpose?"

She meets my narrowed gaze across the circle and smiles serenely, though her eyes tighten at the edges. "I have told you: white, black, and red. One of you will bring him to me. I'm counting on you, Snow White—you who kissed a frog and traveled through the forest with a prince."

"But why must we keep dancing?"

Raven's Wings answers, "If we dance beautifully enough, perhaps we'll find what we've lost." It's what she told me when we met, as if she's already dead and playing out the same loop over and over.

"What good are we to you if we all die?" I ask the eldest princess.

She raises her chin. Under the turquoise glowworms, her bronze skin gleams with an otherworldly, deathly cast. "A true prince will seek out his princess, no matter the obstacle. It doesn't matter whether you're alive; you will draw him here."

I trip on my blistered feet. *Don't die, Snow White. Keep dancing.*

I don't have to ask how she means to stay alive herself. She's the only one with the power to leave this dance floor when she pleases. She can drink water and eat apples and even wander above while the rest of us wither.

Sometimes she favors one princess over another and gives her rest, briefly allowing a bite of food or a few sips of water, but by and large, she only looks after herself.

"And what will you do with this true prince?" I try to soften my scathing tone so she doesn't starve me prematurely. But she is too clever, and I am too belligerent.

She answers in her low, unnerving voice, "He will join me in my kingdom and share in my limitless magic."

"What magic? Dancing with you until he dies?"

"One wish has more power than that."

One wish? I stagger to a halt. The girls press against me to keep revolving, but I dig in my feet.

The eldest princess's eyes flash dangerously. "What are you doing?"

"I remember one wishes. I made one once."

"A wish to stop dancing?"

I shake my head as my mind expands. I made a one wish to break the curse on Grimm's Hollow, but in my heart, I wished to live and not die an untimely death, the fate that had followed me since I was a child. It was also my mother's fate, foretold by my grandmother.

"I saw them in the mirror," I murmur.

"What mirror?" the eldest asks.

I keep fighting the press of bodies, the yearning to dance with them. "The one in your tunnel."

"I have no mirror."

Then it was my own hallucination, brought on by the vapors, or possibly myself.

I'm someone who has visions. It's in my blood.

I gasp. I'm the granddaughter of Marlène Thurn, an Anivoyante who can possess the Grimm wolf. I'm the daughter of Rosamund Thurn, who became Lost as Briar Rose.

I won't be Lost like her.

"I'm not Snow White. I'm Clara Thurn. And I choose my own fate."

The illusion of grandeur vanishes. The girls' fine dresses, crowns, and slippers disappear, replaced by torn and filthy raiment. The glowworms, mushrooms, and crystals no longer multiply and glimmer with enchantment. This place isn't a mystical ballroom, only a dreary cavern, a tomb for the dead and the dying.

I yank my hands away from the girls and step into the middle of the circle to confront Lila. That is who she is, not the eldest princess, just the eldest Sommer girl, trapped in a delusion—trapped with all the Sommer girls, who the forest lured here. "You're hiding something I need."

She laughs once, derisive and cutting. "As are you."

"A page torn from the Book of Fortunes. Give it to me."

"Give me your prince," she counters.

"You already have the ghosts of thirteen."

"Yet none are my true prince." The root pillars untwist. "But they *are* loyal and dependable, always ready for our enchanted midnight dance."

Two thin roots snake out and tether to my wrists. The ghost of the soldier with the plumed helmet emerges from the pillar. "Dance with me," he says.

"Go to hell." I sneer.

He removes his helmet and grins. "Seems I'm already here."

"Clara!" A baritone voice echoes toward me.

My heart surges. "Axel!" I remember his name, the golden-haired boy from the sheep pasture, the hayloft, and a rush of a hundred other memories.

Lila shoves away another ghost soldier beckoning her to dance. "Is that your prince?" she asks.

I ignore her. "Be careful, Axel! There are ghosts here! They have power!"

"We're ready." He springs out from the tunnel, hatchet in hand. Harlan is right behind him with a broadsword he must have robbed from a soldier's grave.

The nearest pillars unwind and lash for them. Axel and Harlan chop and slice at the roots, but more pillars attack.

This isn't a loop brought on by the ghost soldiers. They haven't done this in their past lives to re-create it. This is Lila's doing. She has the greatest power here.

She thrusts her shoulders back and steps off the dance floor, sauntering toward the boys and dividing a hungry look between them. They're swiftly coiled in roots, despite all their heroics. "Which of you is the prince who has come for what is white as a pure heart, red as blood, and black as a faceless night?"

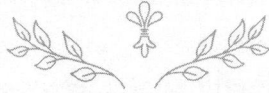

CHAPTER 39

"It's me, Lila." Harlan's voice is gentle but strained. "Don't you remember? Your Harlan."

Lila stiffens, holding herself proud as if she still wore a menacing gown of bat wings rather than a fraying apricot dress coated in grimy gray and black.

"I don't blame you for forgetting," Harlan says. "When I was cursed, so were you. You didn't mean for this to happen."

She circles him, hunting for some trick he's playing. With her attention so riveted, her power so diverted, the roots binding my wrists slacken, and I slip them off.

The other princesses and ghosts keep dancing, their focus on Lila. My soldier has also left me to dance on his own, as if even he can't resist the spell.

"But you couldn't have forgotten me completely," Harlan goes on. "Not if you made a place like this your home. It's just like the kingdom you daydreamed about, where you imagined us living as a prince and a princess who would one day rule as king and queen."

Lila sweeps close to him and searches his eyes ravenously. "Then you know how to share in my limitless magic? You know how to free it?"

Harlan smiles his dimpled smile, and I have to give him credit for how convincing he is when he answers, "I do."

Axel catches my eye and nods at the dagger Harlan has

sheathed on his hip. Their other weapons were wrested away, wrapped high above in the roots.

"I've missed you," Harlan tells Lila. "I've dreamed of this moment." As she becomes more mesmerized, I realize I won't have a better opportunity than now.

I brace myself for pain. Running will torture my back and bleeding feet. But it can't be much worse than what I've been enduring.

1 . . . 2 . . . 3.

I launch for Harlan.

The other princesses shout warnings to Lila. Harlan surges forward and kisses her. It stuns her still. I race faster, using my last reserves of strength.

Lila stumbles back from Harlan and whirls on me. I've almost reached her. She thrusts her arms out, and the roots whip. I duck and slide on the limestone. Skid past her. Grab Harlan's dagger.

Lila rushes at me. I turn on my knees. She takes hold of my throat. I reach around her leg and slice the back of her calf. Only a shallow cut, but it shocks her. She hisses and lets go.

I lurch up and bring the dagger to her neck. "Attack me again, and I'll kill you," I warn.

The roots lashing for me freeze. I wouldn't really kill Lila, I tell myself, trying to blink away the image of my reflection holding a bloody knife and spindle. But as I consider all the misery she's put me through, my dagger trembles at the base of her throat.

Lila isn't herself, Clara. Show her mercy.

I will. Later. Once my friends are out of danger.

"Release Axel and Harlan. The *living* princes," I clarify, when she looks confused.

The roots fall lax, and the boys drop free.

"Where is the page you're hiding?" I demand.

"What page?"

"You know the one," I seethe. She may not remember its significance, but she knows it's important or she wouldn't have taken it from Kellen.

Harlan races over and steadies my hand on the hilt. "It's all right, Clara. I've got this."

I realize I've drawn a drop of blood from Lila's neck. Shakily, I let go, and he takes over.

"You are no prince," she spits at him, teeth bared.

"And you are no princess." He scrapes his dagger against her tendon. "Take me to the page."

Jaw clenched, she guides him down another branching tunnel.

Axel runs to me. "Are you all right?"

I nod, and he helps me sit on the limestone bench.

He slides off his pack and hands me my shoes from inside. I almost cry with relief.

The eleven princesses and ghost soldiers watch our exchange with rapt attention. Some are enraged. Others curious. None can break free from the dance, though. They keep revolving with their partners as Axel removes my ruined slippers and washes my feet in the pool of groundwater.

"I've brought your clothes too," he says.

"My bodice . . ."

He doesn't need any more explanation. He hurriedly pulls it out and helps me lace up the front. His warm hands are a balm. A long exhale escapes me, and I sink against him.

"I'm sorry we couldn't come sooner," he says. "The green apples must have been poisoned. We slept until the pocket watch reached twelve o'clock."

I do a little math and draw back. "It's only been three days? It feels like weeks. I couldn't stop dancing."

He glances at the princesses, who must appear to be only four in number because he can't see the dead ones. "I gathered as much." He bites his lip like he's nervous to say something.

"What is it?"

"My father . . ." He releases a tremulous breath. "Have you seen him?"

My chest sinks, and I shake my head. "I'm sorry."

"No, I'm glad." He musters a fleeting smile. "If he were here, it might mean what you saw in your vision really happened."

"But it *did* happen."

He nods half-heartedly.

Is he still entertaining the idea that my vision was only a bad dream? "Axel—"

Harlan and Lila return. He still has her by dagger point.

Axel stands. "Do you have it?"

"In my pack," Harlan answers.

Axel must still be distrusting of him, because he checks the pack for himself. "It's there," he says.

"Is there any writing on it?" Perhaps we'll be lucky and find the answer to Henni's one wish already spelled out for us.

"It's blank," Axel says.

Lila cackles.

Harlan rounds on her. "Is something funny?"

"All of you are." She leans her head back against his shoulder. "Limitless magic indeed."

I grit my teeth. "Limitless magic is her delusion."

"Yes, she wouldn't stop prattling about it." Harlan blows one of Lila's curls away from his mouth. "Unfortunately, we'll have to hear more. She needs to come with us."

Axel frowns. "Wait, what?"

"Harlan's right," I say. "Lila needs to face justice in Grimm's Hollow. That may be part of breaking the curse. The Book of

Fortunes made it sound like the missing page would be with the murderer, and Lila *had* the missing page."

I recall what the book wrote for me at Henni's wish ceremony:

Only one page holds the secret to finally restoring peace.
Only one person is to blame for breaking it.
Both must be found, for one has the other,
And together they hide in the Forest Grimm.

"We can't risk the chance of losing her if we need her."

Axel groans a sound of surrender.

"We better get going," Harlan says.

"Wait." I rise, wincing as my back strains. "We have to bring the other girls."

Lila scoffs. "They can't stop dancing."

"Then tell them to stop."

"This place has too great a hold on them."

"But not for you?"

"It was my place to begin with."

"You have to at least *try*. Tell them to stop." She lifts her nose in the air. "Tell them!"

Sighing, she turns to the four living Sommer girls. "Stop dancing."

They aren't affected.

"Louder, and mean it," I say.

Lila's nostrils flare. "Stop dancing!"

Her sisters, Nixie and Geneva, and her cousins, Viveka and Sibilla, continue to twirl, their eyes wide and panicked.

I step onto the dance floor and tug Geneva's arm. She's the princess called Raven's Wings who gave me her slippers. She's been barefoot since, her feet far bloodier than mine. I pull and pull, but her muscles stay rigid. I try with the other girls, but they're also trapped in the dance.

"It's no use," Lila says airily. "Even if you could drag them away, at the first opportunity, they'll run back here and continue dancing."

Harlan lowers his head. "We have to let them go, Clara. The only way to free them is to break the curse."

I squeeze my hands against my temples. I hate this. I've never abandoned a Lost One who wasn't murderous. I have to do *something* to help them.

I rush to the crevice in the wall and find more red apples. Axel helps me stow them in the center of the dance floor.

"Tell the girls they can stop whenever they need to eat or drink," I tell Lila. "I know your power can allow them that much."

Her eyes flash, but she does as I say. At once, the girls break free from their partners and start gobbling the apples.

"Take care to ration those if you want to live long," Lila warns.

Harlan turns her away, and they exit down the tunnel.

Axel waits for me. My heart thumps heavily. I feel like it's the autumn festival, and I'm watching the Sommer girls cross the line of ashes all over again. I finally force myself to leave with him. We pass through the tunnel, now mirrorless, and enter the second cavern with Jack's downward-growing beanstalk.

As we climb it painstakingly, me with my battered feet and aching back, and Harlan as he struggles to keep Lila under his dagger, I can't stop thinking about my last glance at the eleven princesses, the four who are living and the seven who are ghosts. The soldiers disappeared, and the girls re-formed their circle, spinning round and round, even as they wept.

CHAPTER 40

J ack is waiting when we climb out of the hole surrounding the beanstalk. It's still nighttime, and his ghostly form is lit against the darkness, his gaze fastened on Lila.

He rushes over as soon as she emerges. Harlan stays close behind her. I warned him ahead of time that Jack wouldn't like us taking Lila away, and we'd need her to persuade him to let her go.

During the long climb, Harlan and Lila must have struck some kind of deal. I didn't hear all the words that passed between them, but I did catch some from Harlan. They were heavy with adoration and promised wonderful memories they would make together.

He's doing a good job of embodying everything she's been searching for, a living prince who will share in her "limitless magic." He no longer has to hold her by dagger point, but that only makes me itch for a weapon. Lila can never be trusted.

She takes Jack aside, and they have a hushed conversation, which must break Jack's heart because he's openly sobbing by the end.

"There, there," she says, and presses a kiss to his cheek. Jack has no way of feeling her touch, but the gesture must still console him, for his crying ebbs.

I hold my myself rigid, watching her. Seeing this softer side of Lila is hard to reconcile with who I fear she is: the murderer of Bren Zimmer and the person who killed my father.

I'm finally lucid enough to puzzle out the significance of her rope burn from a fishing net. My father died tangled in a fishing net. Maybe it's just coincidence, but I'm determined to have a vision of Lila to discover the truth.

Jack finally vanishes, and the rest of us leave Soldiers' Vale. We travel through the night and don't stop until late morning.

Harlan never lets go of Lila's hand. At first I think it's his way to keep her biddable, but when they walk to the bank of the river we're following and kneel for a drink, and Harlan *still* keeps hold of her hand, I wonder if he's worried she might try to run away.

Catching my quizzical stare, he says, "I'm trying to protect her. She isn't wearing anything with red rampion. I don't suppose you could cut off a bit of your cape?"

"White, black, and red," Lila says, coolly smiling at me, though her eyes are dark and vicious. "And you are ripe with red."

I bristle. I hate having to give her anything. "You know it won't restore her to her true self," I tell Harlan. "Ella and Fiora remained Lost until I partially broke the curse. Now that it's back in full force, Lila won't recover until it's broken for good."

"Like I said, I only want to protect her."

"But Lost Ones don't need red rampion. The forest doesn't try to expel them."

"It can't hurt, can it?" His brows pull inward. "Please, Clara. I'd feel a lot easier."

Guilt wriggles inside me. "Fine."

Lila's smirk thins to a sneer. "A kiss to seal your wish," she says, reciting a line from her riddle, like it's the most scathing retort.

I stifle my anger and tear a scrap of wool off the hem of my cape. As I do, the green marble drops out. I'd forgotten I'd stuffed it inside. I hand it to Lila along with the wool, speaking kindly for the sake of the ghost who loves her: "Jack wanted me to give this to you. He made it in a glassblower's workshop. It was his most valuable possession."

She turns it over, wrinkling her nose. "Jack was a disappointment. He never had limitless magic." She throws the marble into the river.

I turn shocked eyes on her. She presses the scrap to her lips and blows me a kiss.

That night, I decide, I will have my vision.

Thankfully, Axel doesn't trust Lila near as much as Harlan. He insists she sleep between them so her ankles and wrists are bound on each side. It's a good plan, although I wish Axel had an extra arm to hold me, not that we've gotten back to the place of open affection.

I wait until my traveling companions are deep asleep—which takes time as Lila keeps shifting between the boys, finally nuzzling her head against Axel's shoulder—and then I slip my hand into my skirt pocket, where I've stowed her coral bracelet. Using it as my token, I think about Lila and my father and fishing nets and drownings.

I think and think and think . . . and I have no vision.

The next day, I wake up grumpy, having wasted half the night concentrating on a girl I dislike more than anyone. I blame her for the blisters on my feet, the angry pain in my S-curve, the tear at the bottom of my cape, the curse on Grimm's Hollow, the death of my father.

I blame her for all my misfortunes.

We continue traveling, barely pausing to rest or eat. We forage for berries and hunt for game, all the while journeying for as long as possible each day.

"We *can* stop from time to time, you know," Axel says, walking beside me after catching me hobble when I thought no one was paying attention. "The pocket watch doesn't have a new countdown. It's stayed at twelve o'clock since we left Lila's caverns."

It doesn't matter. I won't relax while Grandmère is dying and all of Grimm's Hollow is suffering. "I'm fine. Just getting my strength back."

"Do you need me to carry you for a bit?" he asks. He did that here and there on the last leg of our former journey. I needed his help, but it had also felt romantic to be cradle-held. I can't allow that now. I don't want to force him so close to me when he won't even kiss me. At least he hasn't since I kissed Harlan to break his frog spell.

"That's all right. All I need to do is adjust my bodice." I fiddle with the laces. "There. Much better."

Axel nods, shuffling past me, his head bent forward.

I know I'm not the only one eager to get home. All of us want this journey over with. We have the missing page now. We probably have the murderer too, and if it isn't Lila, then maybe it doesn't matter. Maybe no one needs to be brought to justice to break the curse. The Book of Fortunes never stipulated that, not in so many words. Maybe deducing the murderer was merely a clue to help us find the page.

What *does* need to happen is for the book to be restored so Henni's one wish can finally break the curse.

When I'm not pretending I'm free of pain or wishing we had caught more than small fish and tiny birds to satiate our hunger, I can't help but notice I'm being watched. I'm used to the feeling; I sensed it when the Grimm wolf hunted me on my last journey, back when I didn't know it was Grandmère looking after me. But this is different. Stranger. Eerier.

It's ghosts who are stalking me, even anticipating me.

They stare openly as I pass by them in meadows or alongside boulders. They're at the edges of my path, as if waiting for me.

Some are soldiers. Some resemble villagers, ones I never knew and dressed in clothes from a bygone time. Some are villagers I *do* know, Lost Ones from Grimm's Hollow who perished in the forest:

Len Goldschmidt, Maritza Hafner, Orland Luft, Amalda Strauss, Daniel Trommler.

None of them speak to me. None smile. None return my subtle waves of hello.

If they're anything like Johann Schade, who became Jack, they don't remember their true selves. They're still Lost as ghosts. Trapped in the forest, even in death. They need me to free their souls. If I fail, I worry they'll be able to enact their own dangerous loops of the past.

"Can I see the missing page?" I ask Harlan one evening when Lila is under Axel's watch. She prowls along the riverbank as he tries to fish. Her shadow is sure to scare away anything under the surface.

"Haven't I shown you already?" he says.

"Kind of. I've seen it among your things." Axel and I gave Harlan our third pack to carry. "But I haven't examined it myself. I want to see if it will answer me."

Harlan fetches his pack. "You can try."

"You say that as if you *have* tried."

"Of course. I asked it what I'm sure you will."

"Which is?"

"What's the answer to Henni's one wish?" he says. "Wouldn't it be nice if we could do whatever the tasks are, without having to go all the way back to Grimm's Hollow? The faster the curse breaks, the better." He pulls out the page, folded in fourths, and passes it over.

I unfold it. Such an ordinary thing. Beyond the extra pulp in the parchment, it looks as if it could be a blank page torn from any notebook. It's hard to believe it's the key to breaking the curse. "Did the page write anything in reply?"

Harlan flashes a dimple. "See for yourself."

I take a step back. "Are you going to watch me?"

"Why not? It's not really a second wish, right?"

I'm still unsure about that.

I clear my throat and improvise an incantation, since the wish-making one might not apply: "*Sortes Fortunae,* hear my voice. My name is Clara Thurn, and I have a question." I inhale a deep breath. "What is the answer to the last one wish made on the Book of Fortunes?"

No green-inked words appear.

I change my phrasing: "What is the answer to Henni Dantzer's one wish?"

Nothing.

I scratch my head. "Harlan, I don't think you can be looking or listening."

He gives a teasing eye roll before he closes them and stuffs his fingers in his ears.

I whisper the incantation, the real one used for real wishes: "*Sortes Fortunae,* hear my voice. Understand my heart and its deepest desire. My name is Clara Thurn, and this is my third wish. I wish to know the answer to Henni Dantzer's one wish."

Magic green scrawl bleeds across the page, letter by letter, word by word. All my nerves, hopes, and emotions coalesce. I wait, heart pounding, for the full reply:

That answer is for Henni's eyes alone.

I stare at the sentence. Its brevity is an insult. "That's it?"

Harlan opens his eyes as the magicked words start fading. "You did it!"

"Well, it wasn't helpful."

"But the book responded to you!"

"It didn't respond to you?"

His cheeks redden. "I clearly don't have your gift, Changer of Fate."

Now I'm the one flushing. "If that's true, it didn't help me learn the answer I was after."

"Maybe because you were asking about *Henni's* wish." Harlan takes one of my hands and kisses my palm. I try to cage the butterflies in my belly, because he can't mean anything by it. All he's been doing for days is murmuring words of affection to Lila.

She's sharing Axel's sapling pole now, her hands over his hands. She isn't looking back at us, but Axel is. It seems he has been for some time.

I shuffle away from Harlan. "All right, I'll try that. Alone."

I head for the nearest trees, then seeing a handful of ghosts there, I wheel around and find a more secluded spot. I sit on the grass and speak the incantation again, this time followed by, "I wish for you to break the curse on Grimm's Hollow."

Green words come, but they're not any kinder:

That is Henni's one wish, and this is the page intended for it.
Save it for her.

A few minutes later, Harlan sits beside me, seeing I've folded the page and am hunched over, ripping up blades of grass. I don't know why I'm so upset. It's not as if I've been pining to break the curse directly. "I don't think I'm the Changer of Fate anymore," I admit, and tell him what happened.

"I wouldn't give up on yourself so easily, Clara. You escaped Lila's caverns. No other girl has done that before."

"You and Axel helped."

"You're the one who had a vision of Lila with the page. And don't forget what you did for me. Look at all these human fingers that belong to me now. Look what they can do." He slides his hand across the grass and weaves it into mine. His grin is teasing, but his skin on my skin is warm, and that heat makes its way to his eyes.

Again, butterflies swarm my stomach. Again, I don't know—can't trust—what Harlan is doing. Why is he playing with my feelings when his heart belongs to another girl?

"Do you still love her," I ask quietly, "knowing what she's probably done?"

I wouldn't be jealous if he did. I just wouldn't understand, and I need to. I keep trying and failing to have visions of Lila. I'm sure it's because I have no sympathy for her. If she killed my father, then I hate her. But that hatred also prevents me from entering her mind to visit the past.

Harlan looks down at our joined hands and brushes his thumb over a little scratch on my knuckle. "True love is unconditional, so I should say yes."

But he doesn't, so I'm left with more questions than answers, more frustration than pity, and more judgment than forgiveness for Lila Sommers.

CHAPTER 41

A few days later, I finally have a bit of luck and kill a larger bird with my crossbow: a wood grouse with a great fan of tail feathers. It will make a wonderful meal. I also find three stems of red rampion, amazed to have come across them for a second time on this journey. They feel like a sign of hope. I stuff them in my pocket to keep as a talisman.

Perhaps my luck has taken a turn for the better. Maybe I *will* have a vision of Lila.

I finish plucking the feathers from the bird and set it on the stream bank we're now following. I wash my hands and pull out Grandmère's deck of fortune-telling cards.

Harlan comes over and kneels, withdrawing his knife. He starts cutting off the grouse's head, feet, and wings, all the while grimacing.

I smirk. "Someone else can do that, you know."

"Axel's building the fire, and you've already done your part. I need to pull my weight."

"At least it's better than slaughtering a pig, right?"

"Debatable." He makes an incision below the grouse's breastbone to remove its organs. "My ancestors never had to do any of this."

"But the Oswalds have lived in Grimm's Hollow for generations. Haven't they always been subjected to village chores?"

"Not my mother's side of the family."

Harlan's mother passed away when he was young, so I never knew her. "Are you saying she was of noble blood?"

His eyes sparkle, seeing I've caught on. "She told me her great-grandfather could have been a king if his forebears hadn't been conquered in the old wars."

"A king?" My mouth falls open. I've never met anyone related to nobility. We're so far removed from all of that grandeur in the mountains. "In a way, you could be a prince, then."

One side of Harlan's mouth curves up wistfully. "My mom used to tell me that."

"Did she die in the consumption epidemic?" I ask, hoping I'm not being insensitive.

He stares at his knife as it drips blood. "No, in a farming accident. We had a tall granary. One day she fell into the seed. It sucked her under . . . and she suffocated."

"I'm so sorry." I feel terrible for bringing it up.

He waves a hand like it's all right. "It was a long time ago."

He returns to his task, and I flip through the deck of cards, unsure what to say for a minute. "Is that why Lila fantasized about ruling a mystical kingdom with you? Because she learned you're related to an almost-king?"

He breaks into a laugh. "I should have never told her. Or you. Promise you won't tease me about it."

"I wouldn't dream of it."

He watches me fussing with the deck. "What are you doing?"

"Hoping to have a vision of Lila." I shuffle the cards again. "I've been trying for days. I thought the cards would help. Do you know if she ever had her fortune read by my grandmother?"

He casts a glance at Lila, who is twirling around a ring of stones Axel arranged for the fire. Her hair is no longer caked with grime—Harlan coaxed her to wash it in the stream—but it dried wild and frizzy in the wind, making her appear doubly feral.

She's been growing more attached to Axel, often favoring his company over Harlan's. She's still Lost, still addled in the head, and she frequently forgets which boy is supposed to be her living prince.

"Um, yes," Harlan replies. "Back when she was trying to solve the riddle that the Book of Fortunes gave her after she made her one wish."

"Did she ever tell you which cards Grandmère drew for her?"

"Yes, but I can't remember their names. Maybe I can help you figure them out."

He gives me their meanings, to his best recollection, and I match them to the right cards:

The Lady with the Lily for beauty.

The Silver Moth for a negative change, which we surmise had to do with how she transformed Harlan into a frog and went mad.

Love Lost for how she and Harlan were tragically separated at the same time.

The Crownless Queen for someone who will either be stripped of power, come into power, or lust after power—and for Lila, with all her ramblings about limitless magic, it must mean lusting after power.

"I thought there were five cards." Harlan nibbles on his lower lip. "But I can't remember what the last one was about."

I skim through the deck and pause on Water Wild. Like Love Lost, it was a card in my father's last reading. Water Wild symbolizes a significant event in or around a moving body of water.

I place Water Wild in the spread with the others.

"Why did you choose that?" Harlan asks.

I play with the strings of my cape, wondering how much I

should tell him. "I know you care for Lila. But I'm starting to suspect she killed my father."

Harlan frowns like he didn't hear me right. "What?"

"Is that surprising, considering she likely killed Bren?"

He looks down at the bloody grouse. "I was still hoping she might be innocent. Maybe Axel's father killed Bren, and then asked Lila to hide the missing page."

I can't deny that Kellen is still a strong suspect—I *did* see him charging after Bren with a knife—but I can't shake the ominous feeling I have about Lila. "She showed me scars on her wrist when we were in her cavern. She said they came from a fishing net."

"She *did* live by a mill pond. I'm sure she fished there."

"Maybe." But Lila's family was wealthy enough to hire help for menial tasks like that. "You said it took her months to figure out her riddle. She could have thought that obtaining your love required a sacrifice."

Harlan chuckles nervously. "I don't know, Clara."

"Think about what the book wrote her:

White for a pure heart,
Red for rampion-stained lips,
Black for a faceless night,
A kiss to seal your wish."

He lifts his brows. "You have a good memory."

"What if 'a pure heart' meant a pure-hearted person, and that's why Lila chose to sacrifice my father? Maybe she started the riddle's tasks by killing him, and then worked to solve the others until she finally kissed you and everything went wrong."

"No." Harlan sets his jaw. "I can't imagine Lila doing something like that." Averting his gaze, he washes his bloody hands in the stream. "I better start cooking our dinner," he says, and takes the cleaned grouse to the fire.

I'm left alone at the water's edge, though I'm never really alone anymore. On the other side of the stream, four ghosts sit on the bank, where they've been staring at me all this time.

Three more ghosts join me later that evening, when the sun has fallen and the air smells of dark grouse meat and burning pine cones. They sit in a wide perimeter around our camp, but stay in sight. I have half a mind to tell them to leave me be—I promise I won't forget about freeing their souls—but I fear the repercussions, the loops they could set in motion if I anger them.

Having finished her meal, Lila takes up dancing around the fire. I thought being satiated would have calmed her, but it's given her energy, and with it, she's agitated. She smiles with too many teeth, and her eyes gleam feverishly.

"Dance with me!" She beckons to Axel and Harlan, curling a sharp-nailed finger.

"I'm too tired," Axel says, though his tone remains polite.

"I enjoy watching *you* dance too much," Harlan adds, winking.

I don't blame them for denying her. No one in their right mind would want to dance with the girl who cursed eleven other girls to dance on end, and for seven, it *was* the end.

Lila sulks. "Neither of you can be my true prince, then." She looks beyond them to the wide circle of ghosts. "You." She points to the handsome ghost of a young man and thrusts her chin up. "Come and dance with me."

He doesn't budge. She rakes her gaze over the others. "Won't any of you dance?"

"Who is she talking to?" Axel whispers.

"Ghosts," I reply.

He stiffens. "How many are here?"

Since I last counted, two more have come. "Nine."

He suppresses a squirm. "What do they want?"

"To make sure I break the curse. Ghosts have been appearing to me since we left Soldiers' Vale. They don't speak; they just watch me."

His brow creases. "Why didn't you tell me?"

I shrug a little. "They don't hurt me." I would have told him sooner if our relationship wasn't so strained. I used to tell him everything. But maybe that's not true. Maybe I've always been guilty of keeping secrets, just like Grandmère. I have a tendency to hide the darker parts of me.

Lila glares at the ghosts. "Stay cursed, then! If you won't dance with the eldest princess of the mystic kingdom, you aren't worth the wood growing over your bones."

I wince, turning to Harlan. "You should do something to soothe her before she says anything more to upset them." When he looks at me blankly, I suggest, "How about playing your pipe? Lila always loved listening to your music." At least the village version of her did.

"I'll give it a try." He pulls out his instrument, wets the double reed, and begins playing a plaintive song that suits the pipe's rich and mellow tone.

Lila releases a slow breath. Her agitated movements settle into serene elegance as she lifts her arms and raises one leg, balancing on the other. She's an exceptionally skilled dancer, and having real music to dance to instead of imagined songs, she displays the best of her ability.

As graceful as she is, though, the dance is tainted by her expression. The back of my neck prickles as I absorb her eerie half-lidded gaze and wry smile. It's as if she's saying *Don't forget that beyond my beauty I am venomous, devious, murderous.*

Later that night, when we're all lying side by side and Axel's eyes are still open, peering out into the surrounding darkness—the darkness he doesn't know is now inhabited by thirteen ghosts—all I want to do is to fold myself into him, hide from the world, and hear his comforting words.

I miss my best friend.

"Axel?" I whisper, trying not to awaken Harlan or Lila.

He turns his head. He isn't used to me starting midnight conversations lately. "Yes?"

"Do you think my mother is a ghost?"

His expression softens, and he angles his body toward mine, a tricky endeavor since he's tied to Lila. "I believe her soul still exists, if that's what you mean."

"But do you think her soul is trapped in this forest like the others?"

"You think her body was absorbed by a tree?"

"Maybe." I hadn't considered that possibility when the fortress castle collapsed around her a few months ago. "I thought I'd saved her, but—" My voice gives out. "What if I didn't save her at all?"

"But you *did*." He reaches up and tentatively brushes my cheek and the wetness gathering in the corners of my eyes. "The moment before she died, she recognized you. And she remembered herself as Rosamund."

"What if she's still stuck in the forest and unable to join my father in death?" My shoulders quake as I hold back more tears. "It would be like she was still cursed."

He searches my face for a long moment, and the wind whistles, sounding like the old hauntings of my mother, how I imagined her calling to me when she was Lost and I didn't know how to cross the ash-lined border to save her.

"I drove a spindle into your heart," Axel says, his fingers trailing down my neck to gently tap against my breastbone. "Between that spindle and your heart was your cape. The red rampion saved you in the end. So when you tried the same thing with your mother, I have to believe it also saved her, even though it didn't save her life. I truly believe she's free, Clara. She isn't in this forest anymore. You *did* save her soul."

I consider his words and the saving power of red rampion, remembering the three stems in my pocket. When I killed my mother, I partially broke the curse, and in turn, I broke the curse over Fiora, Ella, Hansel, and Gretel. They were no longer Lost Ones, because they had the protection of red rampion, even if it had faded for a time.

My mother's soul is free. She's with my father.

I tuck closer to Axel. "Thank you," I whisper.

I try to capture inside me the hope and peace that he offers, but it doesn't take hold. My scarred heart won't make room for it. It's a comfort that my parents' souls aren't trapped in the forest, but *I'm* still not at rest. Whoever wrought the curse that turned my mother into Briar Rose and whoever killed my father must still be brought to justice, even if that justice isn't necessary to break the curse. It's the least my parents deserve.

I slip my hand into my other pocket and feel the coral beads of Lila's bracelet. I think through her fortune-telling cards: the Lady with the Lily, the Silver Moth, Love Lost, the Crownless Queen, and Water Wild.

In Grimm's Hollow, I never really knew Lila. I've only come to know her through Harlan's eyes and as the eldest princess of the twelve who danced in her mystic kingdom.

It's time I learn about Lila through her own memories.

My eyelids bat closed, and the transition into a vision comes smoother than ever, no void of black or beat of silence, just a beautiful song. Harlan's signature song. But Lila is singing it.

CHAPTER 42

ila's voice is a rich blend of light and dark tones, so beautiful that my skin pebbles with gooseflesh. I'm in my own body in this vision, but I follow Lila's every movement, almost like her shadow.

She's sitting at a bedroom table with a mirror, singing to her reflection as she weaves her ebony hair into a complicated crown braid. I listen to the words she sings; I've never heard any accompanying to Harlan's song before:

"Come, my darlings,
Be you blackbirds or starlings,
Come, leave your nest for the night.
The primrose is blooming,
The evening is looming,
Come, take a wondrous flight."

She traces her finger around a miniature portrait of Harlan. "Come, my darling. Our kingdom awaits."

The scene flashes to the meadow pavilion in Grimm's Hollow. It's springtime, and the meadow is bursting with daffodils, tulips, and daisies. Lila greets villagers who take turns pinching her arms to remind her to use this opportunity wisely.

This is Lila's wish ceremony.

When it's Harlan's turn, he kisses her palm, like he kissed mine. "You're astonishing." His gaze travels over her white dress and the oak leaves wreathed in her hair.

She beams and plants her mouth on his, which sends a few villagers gasping. It's a bold move for a girl who hasn't been promised in marriage. She whispers in Harlan's ear, "My daydream won't be a fantasy any longer."

"What do you mean?"

"You'll see."

Now she's alone behind the pavilion curtain. She speaks the incantation to the Book of Fortunes: "*Sortes Fortunae*, hear my voice. Understand my heart and its deepest desire. My name is Lila Sommer, and this is my one wish." She exhales, inhales. Stands taller. "I wish for the limitless magic of the Forest Grimm."

Now *I'm* gasping. I thought Lila's talk of limitless magic was a reflection of her Lostness. I'd have never guessed it was her literal one wish.

I'm as close as a ghost looking over her shoulder when the book replies in leaf-green ink:

> *White for a pure heart,*
> *Red for a blooding,*
> *Black for a faceless night,*
> *A kiss for a sacrifice.*

A chill shudders through me. Parts of that stanza are different from what Harlan relayed, which means Lila lied to him. Red was supposed to represent rampion-stained lips, and the kiss was supposed to "seal your wish."

The book continues:

Beware enacting your wish more than twice,
Lest your efforts tempt fate,
And mind turns to madness
And love becomes cursed.

But do not despair,
For the tasks done right by another
Will undo the enchantment
And reverse the spell.

Except for "enacting your wish more than twice" and the bit about tempting fate, the last two stanzas haven't changed. Which makes sense. In the end, Harlan was still cursed to be a frog, Lila went mad, and I reversed the spell, transforming him back into a human.

Lila pores over the riddle and repeats the first stanza in a hush, simplifying it to "pure heart, blooding, faceless night, sacrifice."

My vision flashes to another day. She's in a basement kitchen, crushing poppies, roses, and red rampion with a mortar and pestle. She spits into the bowl three times, repeats the riddle's first stanza, and mixes her concoction into a pewter cup filled with what looks like dark brandy. Is it some sort of witch's potion? Drinking it down, she murmurs, "A kiss for a sacrifice."

The vision flickers across several brief scenes. All include kisses. Lila's lips press to Harlan's, Kellen's, Bren's . . . and my father's.

My vantage point rocks, thrown off kilter. *Lila kissed my father?* I want to run. Get far away. Give back what I saw and never see it again. But it tunnels into my mind like one of Jack's beanstalks.

I don't want to know more, but I have to, so I descend deeper.

I need to know why Lila had to kiss so many men to enact her one wish.

Another memory opens. Lila is kneeling over a deer shot down by an arrow. She paints its blood on her forehead, a vertical line cut through with horizontal ones. "For bravery," she murmurs to herself.

Now my father is walking along a bank, his eyes glazed over, his steps wooden. This isn't the stream where Bren Zimmer drowned; it's Mondfluss River in Grimm's Hollow. I recognize the dock stretching over the water, where fishermen tie up boats.

Lila stands at the dock's end. It's nighttime, and she's wearing a painted mask decorated with swirls of white, red, and black. It leaves her lips exposed and some of her forehead, where I spy the deer blood.

"Who are you?" My father squints. A lantern glows from a dock post, but its glass panes are dirty.

Lila imparts a bewitching smile. "Your loving Rosamund, of course."

Confused, my father drifts closer. He's clearly under some kind of spell, although it was Lila who drank the potion. Does it give her the ability to bewitch others? If so, it seems to be wearing off, because Lila isn't fooling my father. He touches one of her ebony curls and shakes his head. "Why are you pretending to be my wife?"

Her confident smile wavers as he turns to leave, but she catches him by the front of his shirt. She kisses him—the same kiss I glimpsed a moment ago. But I never saw what came after. Now it plays out before me.

My father yanks away. His boot heel snags on a warped board. He pitches backward. Smacks his head on a post. Fumbles to grab the post and steady himself, but his eyes lose focus. His head slumps forward. He slips unconscious.

He careens over the dock and plunges into the water, five feet below.

Lila gasps and hurries to the dock's edge. My father is floating away on the current. She throws off her mask, kicks off her shoes, and jumps in after him.

"Hurry!" I shout, even though I can't change the past.

By the time she reaches him, he's stopped breathing.

My chest feels like it's cut wide open. "Father!"

Lila tugs his body back to the dock. She clutches one of the posts and takes a breath like she's going to yell for help, but then she notices the fishing net hanging from the post's hook, and her jaws clamp shut.

Changing tack, she swiftly wraps the net around my father, struggling as some of the rope tangles around her wrist as the current pulls against him. She finally breaks free, her wrist soaked in blood, and releases my father, allowing the river to carry him where it will.

I yearn to follow him, but I need to stay with Lila. The vision jumps to another scene.

"My wish didn't work," she says to Harlan. They're sitting near her family's gristmill, and Lila watches the waterwheel whir with a drained expression.

Harlan takes her hand. "You never told me about your wish."

"Because I can't."

"I mean, the tasks that the Book of Fortunes laid out for you."

"White, black, and red," she murmurs hollowly.

"Hmm?"

Lila shakes her head, rising. "I want to be alone."

Now it's nighttime. She strolls to the meadow pavilion. She's wearing a beautiful coral dress that matches her bracelet, and wrapped over it is a deep blue cloak. A basket covered with a tea cloth hangs on her elbow, and she carries a bottle of wine.

"Good evening, gentlemen," she tells the four night watchmen, flashing her most disarming smile. "I've brought some refreshments, compliments of the Sommer family. We love to reward our most dutiful citizens."

The men amble over as Lila removes the tea cloth, revealing a mouth-watering assortment of glazed tarts and hand pies. I note how she's positioned near the pedestal with the Book of Fortunes.

"My mother also wanted you to have this mulled wine, our family's secret recipe." With both hands, she offers the bottle, but the tea cloth makes her grip slippery. The bottle drops and shatters. "Oh dear!"

As the four men crouch and tend to the mess, Lila tears out a page from the Book of Fortunes and tucks it under her cloak. "I'm so sorry. I'll fetch a broom."

The watchmen assure her that's not necessary, so she compromises by staying with them until the mess is cleaned and they have enjoyed the tarts and her conversation. Once they return to their posts, she bids them farewell and wanders back through the meadow toward the village.

At a rustling in the grass, she startles. A few yards away, a large bushy tail flicks above the grass and slinks out of sight. Lila hurries away.

Now she's walking along the village's main thoroughfare. She pulls out the page she's torn, squints at it, and glances above at the crescent moon. It must not be enough to see by, because she strides to a street lantern, finds the tinderbox, and lights the candle.

She speaks the incantation, asking the page, "What went

wrong with Finn Thurn? Why didn't you grant me my one wish?"

In green ink, words appear:

White for a pure heart,
And a kiss for a sacrifice,
Those you did offer,
But a blooding of red
You forgot from the slaughter.

"But I slaughtered a deer. I became blooded by it." She shakes the page. "What did I do wrong?"

The page only repeats a stanza from the original riddle:

Beware enacting your wish more than twice,
Lest your efforts tempt fate,
And mind turns to madness
And love becomes cursed.

She releases a cry of frustration and throws the page. She paces for a minute, then her eyes widen. "Finn Thurn didn't bleed," she murmurs. "I need to kill the man I kiss—on purpose—and blood myself with his blood."

The vision shifts to another scene. It must be the same night; Lila is still wearing the coral dress and bracelet. She drinks another potion of crushed flowers in brandy and returns to the thoroughfare.

A man walks in her direction, keeping to one side of the road, as if to pass her. But when he comes closer, his gait stiffens, and he pivots to Lila. He removes his hat, and I recognize his golden hair and blue eyes, though his pupils are dilated. *Kellen.*

"You look familiar." Lila's gaze roams over him. "But how do I know you have a white heart?"

"I've come for . . . my son." He frowns like he can't remember who that is. It's almost like he's Lost, but he can't be. The curse hasn't fallen yet. His behavior is stemming from Lila's bewitchment.

She purses her lips. "You must be Axel Furst's father. Which means you're Rudger's brother. *He* certainly doesn't have a white heart. Though that may serve me well. Someone will need to take the blame."

Kellen nods, bewildered and mesmerized.

"If I give you a kiss, will you help me?"

"Y-yes."

She wraps her arms around his neck and brings her mouth to his. The kiss is long and, on her part, fervent. I don't know whether it's for her enjoyment or to ensure Kellen's allegiance. Perhaps both. He is a handsome man.

She draws back, stroking his face. "Bring me something that can implicate your brother in another man's death. Preferably a weapon that can draw blood."

"I will see it done," Kellen says haltingly.

"And make sure no one sees you." She explains where he should find her, in the forest where the stream at Solace Trail meets a linden tree. "Do this and I will grant you a second kiss."

The vision flashes to that spot later on. Kellen offers Rudger's knife to Lila, and she kisses him as promised. His eyes look even more vacant. I wonder if her kisses enhance the spell's power.

Handing him the page from *Sortes Fortunae*, Lila says, "I will give you a third kiss if you hide nearby until I call you."

More time passes. The spot near the stream is now isolated. Kellen is gone, and so is Lila. But a few moments later, she returns, followed by Bren Zimmer, who looks unabashedly lovesick. Lila is wearing her painted mask. She's ready to make her sacrifice.

She walks near a large stone. I glimpse Rudger's knife hidden behind it. Her hands tremble. Killing my father was an accident. This time she means to commit murder.

She draws a measured breath and grabs Bren by his shoulders. She kisses him forcefully but hastily, then pushes back, shaking harder. "Don't look at me."

He lowers his eyes, confused. She bends to retrieve the knife. It quivers in her grip like she's been struck with the palsy. "Turn around." He obeys. She lifts the blade, but starts to whimper. "I can't—" She hurls it away.

Bren sluggishly revolves to face her. "Lila Sommer?" He glances around. "What am I doing here?"

She curses. Whatever spell she's wrought is ending. Strangely, the kiss didn't enhance it this time. "Kellen!" she shouts into the woods. "I need you at once! Bring the knife!"

He bursts out from the underbrush, grabs the fallen knife, and charges toward her—toward Bren. Bren bolts away. "Catch him!" Lila yells as she takes the weapon.

In a mad scuffle, Kellen seizes Bren and drags him back to the stream. Lila races over, coming at him from behind. She cries out and slams Rudger's knife into his back.

Bren's eyes bulge wide. He crumples to his knees and crashes forward to the ground.

Lila holds her stomach as if she's sick, but the moment passes. She kneels and presses her hand on the blood blooming on Bren's back. She smears a handprint across her face. Red drips from her chin and down the front of her dress. She's blooded herself with the man she kissed and sacrificed.

Rising slowly, she commands Kellen, "Drag him into the stream and leave the knife in his body."

Kellen obeys. Perhaps Lila's spell works longer on him because his mind is weakened from past injuries.

The vision flashes again, bouncing across several memories. The beautiful Sommer estate, which had always been lush, is withering, its grasses and flowers dying around the mill pond. Across the village, farmers' grain stores spoil or become eaten by rodents. Crop fields perish in the relentless drought.

The curse has fallen on Grimm's Hollow.

Alone in the woods on her estate, Lila screams at the page she tore from *Sortes Fortunae*. "Why won't you give me my one wish? I could save Grimm's Hollow! You shouldn't punish everyone because I did what you asked."

The page only answers with the same warning stanza:

Beware enacting your wish more than twice,
Lest your efforts tempt fate,
And mind turns to madness
And love becomes cursed.

She rages again, and when her fit is over—when she's sitting with her back against a dead walnut tree, her energy spent—she murmurs in a voice laced with dread, "The sacrifice must have to be personal. The pure heart needs to belong to someone I love."

I reel, shocked by the extremes she's willing to go to. Does she want limitless magic so badly that she would sacrifice Harlan? I thought everything she was working toward was meant to be shared with him, a magical kingdom they could reign over together.

Now it's an autumn night on the Oswald farm. A wreath woven from thorny weeds hangs on the front door. Lila, in her coral dress and deep blue cloak, steps onto the porch and knocks.

Harlan opens the door, his brow wrinkling as he takes in her painted mask and glossy red lips. He's fully cognizant, which means Lila hasn't drunk any potion. I suppose, with him, she wouldn't need to.

"Would you like to play a game?" she asks coyly.

He leans against the doorjamb. "Does this mean you're not mad at me anymore?"

"I was never mad, Harlan. Not really."

He cocks a brow like he doesn't believe her, but relents and takes her outstretched hand. The night is moonless, so she carries a lantern and leads him past the edge of the Oswald property, across the thoroughfare, and into a thicket of scrub oak near the ash-lined border of the forest.

"What is this game all about?" Harlan peers around like he's waiting to discover a blanket spread for an eventide picnic.

Lila sets down her lantern. "I want you to pretend this is our kingdom." She circles around him. "You're a knight who must pass a test of fealty to prove his devotion to his queen."

"Knight?" Harlan chuckles. "I thought I was supposed to be king."

"You must first win the queen's heart." Lila smiles demurely and withdraws a paring knife from her cloak.

Harlan broadens his chest. "Is this to be my dagger or my sword? Where is the dragon I must slay?"

Lila's grin spreads wide below her mask. "To win my heart, you must let me cut *your* heart. Just a scratch," she promises, pointing to his chest. "Here."

Harlan smirks. "Very well." He unbuttons his homespun shirt. "Make your cut, Your Majesty. You will find my devotion unswerving."

Lila swallows hard and slips closer, raising the quivering blade to his chest.

"Wait." Harlan takes her wrist. "I know why you're doing this, and I know why you've been so angry lately. I do love you, Lila. I'm sorry for all the times I haven't said it. I'm devoted to you. If you have to draw my blood to prove it, then do it. What is mine is yours. Always."

He lets go of her, and her eyes shine with tears. She drops the knife and yanks off her mask. "I love you too, Harlan."

She kisses him.

I brace myself for what will follow, and it transpires like I expected.

He turns into a frog.

She falls into madness.

With an agonizing wail, she races across the ash-lined border.

A great howl shudders immediately afterward. The Grimm wolf. She's chasing Lila. Lila bolts faster.

In a strange shift of the vision, I become Lila. My eyes are her eyes.

But why am I wearing my red cape?

I can't be Lila. I'm Clara. And I've awoken from my vision.

It's me who is running through the forest . . .

. . . me who is being hunted.

CHAPTER 43

Pain rips through my ankle. I cry out. The Grimm wolf has my foot in her jaws. I whirl and slam my fists against her body. "Let go!"

She grips me by the shoulders. Her hands are strong, her deep voice firm and filled with worry. "Clara, wake up!"

"I am awake." I thrash and kick.

"Look at me. Focus on my eyes. You're sleepwalking."

Axel.

It's his hands holding me, his baritone voice, his blue eyes a deep cobalt, like the sky of a summer storm.

I stop fighting and blink in bewilderment. Dusty gold light enfolds us. The sun is rising. We're standing near the bedrolls with our ankles bound. He's also tied to Lila, who is likewise tied to Harlan. They've been forced to stand, and Harlan struggles to keep Lila steady. She's ready to fall over from all my lurching about.

My gaze drops to my ankle. It's bleeding from the rope. So is Axel's. I gasp. "I'm sorry!"

"It's fine, Clara."

"This is how one gains scars." Lila tosses me a knowing look, her lip half-curled.

I sneer at her. All my fogginess vanishes. "Murderer!"

"Careful," Axel warns. "You don't know that."

"I *do*!" I jerk toward her, dragging Axel with me. She shrinks back, but can't defend herself. I grab the front of her dress and scour it for proof. It's the coral dress, though I didn't recognize it earlier with how dirty it's become.

"There!" I jab my finger below her neckline. "That's a blood-stain from killing Bren. I saw it happen. And these scars on her wrist . . ." I yank out her left hand. "They're from killing my father."

Harlan's face pales. "Lila couldn't have killed two men, let alone one."

"You desire blood?" Lila asks, raking her fingernails across my hand.

I hiss and let go of her. "She *did*, Harlan. She's responsible for everything!"

She spits in my face. I grab her throat. Harlan and Axel struggle to pull me back. "Stop, Clara!" Axel says. "I promise we'll hear everything you have to say. But if you want justice, this isn't it."

It takes all my restraint to release Lila's neck and step away. As I work to collect myself, Axel unties our ankles and the ropes binding him to Lila. Harlan does the same, but then ties her wrists together. "I'm sorry," he says, sitting beside her. "This is just until we hear Clara out. I'm sure she must be mistaken."

Lila whimpers softly, masking the demon that she is. "You don't love me."

"Shhh." He smooths her hair.

Axel offers me his waterskin, and I take a long drink. He guides me to sit on a grassy knoll and stands back, giving me space. "Tell us about your vision."

"It was a vision of Lila. Her memories." My body flushes as I fight to stay calm. Several feet away, Lila glares at me, sullen and viperish but also a little vacant. Only seldom does she recognize herself as a girl named Lila.

The ghosts who follow me creep nearer as I share the vision, starting with how Lila sang words to the special tune Harlan plays on his pipe.

"She wrote lyrics to it," Harlan explains. "It was her favorite song."

I tell him how she never wished for him to love her like he believed. "She wished for the limitless magic of the Forest Grimm. The book's reply was also different." I recite the tasks and the book's warning.

Harlan's posture sinks. He leans farther away from Lila. "A blooding and a sacrifice?" he asks her. "I thought you were trying to win my love."

"For that I must dance," she replies, only partly following the conversation.

I describe the three attempts she made to enact the tasks, including the one that resulted in my father's death. Teeth clenched, I blink back scalding tears. I won't let her see me cry.

I also share how she tore the page from the Book of Fortunes, and how the page wrote a clarification: the blooding needed to be from the man she kissed and sacrificed.

Nervously, I bring up Kellen's appearance on the thoroughfare in Grimm's Hollow and the strange spell that Lila put him under, like she did with my father.

Harlan rubs his jaw. "Lila's grandmother, Ekhoe, taught the girls a bit of what she considered magic. They drew symbols and made little potions. Simple and harmless things. Mostly ways to manifest what they *hoped* would happen. None of it was true power."

"*This* potion had power. Maybe because Lila added red rampion. It gave her the ability to bewitch people, although it worked better on some men than others." I explain how it wore off early with my father, but held fast on Kellen.

Whenever I mention Kellen, Axel averts his gaze. Soon he's only staring at the ground, his lips pressed in a hard line.

Reluctantly, I share how, at Lila's command, Kellen obtained

Rudger's knife and helped her ultimately kill Bren. "His will wasn't his own, though," I add, hoping that's a comfort, but Axel still won't speak.

"Then the curse fell," I go on, relaying how Lila still hadn't received her one wish, so in desperation, she planned to sacrifice Harlan. "She decided against it," I add, watching Harlan massaging the bridge of his nose. "She didn't mean for what happened when she kissed you, but it *was* on a new moon. That part of the riddle she never figured out."

"So I was sacrificed all the same." Harlan grins weakly. "Sacrificed to be a pathetic frog for two and a half years."

Lila merely shrugs. "You should have danced."

He shoves to his feet and distances himself from her. "None of this makes sense. If the Book of Fortunes really told Lila to fulfill different tasks, then how did you break the frog spell, Clara? You would have had to perform the same tasks she did."

I think through them:

White for a pure heart,
Red for a blooding,
Black for a faceless night,
A kiss for a sacrifice.

The parts of the riddle that changed were "red for a blooding" and "a kiss for a sacrifice."

"My mother had a pure heart," I answer. "She couldn't help what she became in the forest. And I killed her. I blooded myself with her blood. I still carry the stain on my cape. You know how the rest happened. You needed a kiss on a new moon . . . but I suppose my lips never needed to be stained with red rampion."

Harlan doesn't say anything, and I pluck up grass on the knoll, thinking harder. Some of the ghosts come to sit at my feet, and I try my best to ignore them. "The only thing is, I don't know *what* I sacrificed by kissing you." Though as soon as I say it, I realize I *did* sacrifice something—Axel's trust in me. Our eyes briefly lock, and I glimpse the heartbreak still trapped within him.

"I think you're right." Harlan's brows tug together. "The tasks had to be done in order—with you, and with Lila. She fulfilled the first two tasks when she killed Bren . . . and then the last two tasks when she kissed me on the new moon." He rubs his forehead. "Did I really just say 'when she killed Bren'?"

"I saw it happen, Harlan. I'm sorry."

But I'm not sorry that I know who's responsible for all the suffering that's come from the curse. Lila will have a lot to answer for when she faces the village council.

Axel finally meets my gaze. "I'm not convinced Lila is guilty."

I rear back. Is he joking? "I showed you the bloodstain."

"Lila could have bled in the last two and a half years."

"But in my vision—"

"There's something off about your visions, Clara."

My mouth drops open.

"I *do* believe in your gift." He holds up his hands. "But what you see isn't always accurate."

"How can *you* know?" He's not the one having them.

"Take red rampion, for example. How could red rampion make a love potion powerful? It only offers protective and saving magic. When have we ever seen it manipulate someone?"

"All I can tell you is that the love potion somehow gave Lila the ability to bewitch men." If it wasn't the red rampion, maybe it was the spellwork she learned from her maternal family. Maybe it does have power.

"But why was her bewitchment so inconsistent? Why did it hold fast on my father when it wore off on Bren and your father in minutes?"

"I don't have an explanation, except maybe it was due to your father's previous injuries."

"But some things *must* be explained—not guessed at—to be trusted." Axel strides over to me. "Things like my father remaining loyal to Lila for days, maybe months, when they supposedly traveled together to Soldiers' Vale to hide the missing page. How could Lila have pulled that off? Do you really think she drank love potion multiple times a day to keep my father under her spell? How would she have continued making it?"

"She wouldn't have needed to." My voice rises. "The curse fell after Bren died, so your father could have easily become Lost."

Axel mutters under his breath.

"What? It would explain why he never returned for you." I stand, my frustration reaching a boiling point. "Why do you have such a hard time believing me?"

He stalks away three steps, but then circles right around again. "Why would Lila want to frame my uncle?"

I throw up my hands.

"Think about when Lila first met my father," he continues. "Why wouldn't she have killed him? Why would she bother to frame anyone if she thought she'd have 'limitless magic' after completing her tasks?"

"Obviously because she didn't succeed the first time," I snap.

Axel storms away again but doesn't wander far. I sense him trying to come up with fresh reasons to argue, though at the moment all he does is grumble and run his hands through his hair.

"I'm sorry I don't have all the answers for you," I call. Softening my voice, I add, "I don't know why your father didn't return home."

Axel laughs bitterly, his eyes wet. "I wish you'd try." He says it so quietly I almost miss it, but when it reaches my ears, it may as well gut me.

I *have* tried. Or I've tried to try. But how can I *want* to try when this is what results from talking about his father? How will Axel face the truth? Whatever has become of Kellen, I have a dread and growing surety it's something terrible.

He exhales a great breath. "Look, I didn't mean to . . ." He rubs the back of his neck. "All I really wanted to say is that you shouldn't rush to name Lila as the murderer just because you don't want it to be someone else."

What does he mean by that?

"Do you think I'm making up these visions?"

"I never said that."

Lila stretches her tied wrists above her head. "We all have kingdoms in our minds."

Her words give us pause, and doubt creeps inside me.

I may not be going mad as Snow White anymore, but what if I'm going mad as a Voyante of the Bygone? What if I *am* making up some of what I see?

Axel grabs my crossbow and marches away. "I'm going to find us some food."

Harlan drifts back to Lila and unties her wrists. She smiles, cooing, "My prince," and he summons a grin for her, but it strains as his eyes lower to her bracelet of scars.

Some of the ghosts lose interest in me and retreat a few yards, but of course, they never leave.

I rake through all the visions I've had, searching for any more discrepancies or instances of wishful thinking.

From far away, a deep howl falls faintly on my ears. The Grimm wolf. I don't know whether she's violet-eyed or brown-eyed, desiring to save me or to kill me.

Unless there is no Grimm wolf on the prowl.

Maybe I imagined her too.

CHAPTER 44

'm going to have a vision of Kellen. Tonight. I mean it this
time. But I don't tell anyone. Axel might not believe me,
and Harlan is too preoccupied with keeping Lila calm. She
falls into hysterics every time I come near. An act meant to gain
more pity, no doubt. She claims I'll try to strangle her again. The
only thing that prevents me is the worry planted in my mind that
some parts of my visions may be wrong.

I'm determined the one I have tonight won't be.

This time I'll stay awake as I fall into the vision. There will
be no risk of blending dreams with the truth. But I need to be
certain I'm grounded in myself. Not Lost in any way.

*I'm the granddaughter of Marlène Thurn, an Anivoyante who
can possess the Grimm wolf. I'm the daughter of Rosamund and Finn
Thurn, sheep farmers from Grimm's Hollow. I'm a Voyante of the Bygone. I see the past, but I can't change it. I only learn from it. I want
to save people, not lose them.*

I don't want to lose Axel.

I *will* have this vision.

Axel, Lila, and Harlan lie down to sleep before I do. I tell
them I need to sharpen my knife, a good excuse since the blade
is dull. I scrape it against my whetstone by the light of the dying
pine cone fire until I'm sure everyone is sleeping.

I grab Grandmère's fortune-telling deck and find the Hour
After Midnight, the Famished Mice, and the Fanged Creature.
Rudger's cards. Through Rudger's perspective, I'll be able to see

Kellen. Rudger must have had some interaction with his brother in the forest, otherwise he wouldn't have snuck back to the stream where Bren died to collect the abandoned pocket watch.

Unfortunately, I never found a moment to borrow Rudger's locket ring from Harlan. I was going to offer a scrap of my cape in exchange, but every time I approached him, Lila fell into another fit, flashing me wicked smiles when he wasn't looking. The pocket watch will have to make do as my connection to Rudger.

I tiptoe to Axel, sit beside him, and carefully reach for the chain spilling out from his pocket. I wrap my fingers around it. Start to tug it out.

Axel flinches and grabs my wrist. I freeze. Slowly, his body relaxes and his fingers slacken. I wait a couple of minutes before I drag my hand away with the watch.

Out of habit, I open the silver case. The hands are still set to twelve o'clock, with no new countdown. But I don't trust the illusion of endless time. There's too much at stake.

I hold the watch in my other hand and lay my fingers over Axel's. I need to keep contact with him, another way to draw out a vision of his uncle through their shared blood. It should help me focus on Kellen too.

Axel adjusts his position and turns his palm up so our hands fit together better. My heart flits. Some buried part of him still welcomes my touch.

I remain sitting so I don't fall asleep. Without sleep, there is no sleepwalking, no reason to tie my ankle to Axel's.

I lay out Rudger's cards, and my thoughts stray to Grand-mère, who painted them, who must be missing them and missing me, like I'm missing her.

She's alive. I will her to be.

I close my eyes and strain to focus. This vision is about Rudger, not Grandmère. Actually, it's about Kellen.

Concentrate, Clara.

I feel the cool metal of the pocket watch in one hand and Axel's warm skin in the other.

I wait. I think of Rudger and his memories of Kellen. I try not to think of Grandmère.

I suddenly go weightless. Black encompasses me. Silence consumes me.

I settle into the void. Welcome it. There is no past, future, or present here. I don't have to solve anything or feel anything. I can't hurt anyone or break anyone's heart. The ignorance may be more protective than red rampion.

No, Clara. You can't stay here. Staying here is to be Lost.

I let go of the black and the silence and feel the ground beneath me again. I see the forest, hear the night birds, the humming insects. Layered over them is another view of the forest, another realm of sound. I focus on that plane and let myself fall deep into the vision.

I'm walking through the forest at night. The air is warm. The leaves are green. It's summertime, before the curse. I know because the forest isn't unnaturally alive. The pine trees grow their needles unevenly, and some of the cornflowers have wilted heads.

I look down at myself. It's hard to see by the light of the crescent moon, but I recognize these age-spotted hands, as well as the birds and flowers embroidered on my skirt. I'm in Grandmère's body, seeing through her eyes.

A scarf is wrapped over my head like a hood. I pull it tighter and continue down the path. Solace Trail, I realize, having seen it in many visions. A little outside of Grimm's Hollow, it follows a stream into the forest, the same stream where Bren died. I haven't arrived at that spot yet. I don't see the linden tree.

I approach a figure in the darkness. Bren Zimmer. Very much

alive. His clothes are wet, his hair disheveled, his shirt untucked and torn. The corner of his lip is bleeding.

I wait for my kind grandmother to ask if he's all right, if she can do anything. So it jars me to hear her ruthlessness pour from my mouth: "What have you done with my son-in-law?"

"Finn?" Bren replies wearily, in no mood for this conversation. "I heard he went missing, but I have no idea where."

"Do you expect me to believe that after I saw what you did tonight?"

Bren's eyebrow twitches. "I swear I don't know what happened to Finn."

"Don't lie when you've threatened me before!"

"*You*, Marlène. I threatened *you*. I wouldn't harm your family. That's your way of doing things." He tries to shove past me, but I catch his arm.

"I've told you, I'm not always in control of the wolf. If she had succeeded in harming those children, that's her instinct as a wild animal. I would have never—"

"I don't want to hear your excuses!" Bren wrests his arm from my grip. "Keep the wolf away from the Winther orchards. If I see it there again, maybe I *will* come after you Thurns."

He storms off, and my heart thunders. "A pact for your silence, then?" I call after him. "I will promise not to tell anyone that Fiora has children if you vow not to reveal I can shift into the Grimm wolf. You're the only one who has discovered that secret, and I must keep it safe."

Bren turns around haggardly and spits blood. "Ask me another night, Marlène. I've had enough of this one."

Before I can process what just happened, the vision flashes to another scene, one where I'm no longer within Grandmère's body. It's still nighttime in the forest, but I'm in a different place on Solace Trail and walking in a different direction, although I can't see the linden tree yet.

I'm in a man's body, but nothing indicates which man. He pulls out something from his jacket. A pocket watch. I scan his hands and find no locket ring. This isn't Rudger. I must be Kellen.

I whistle a happy tune and toss the pocket watch in the air, deftly catching it as I stroll down the trail. I toss it again, but nearly drop it as something peculiar appears in the sky. A blazing trail of light. A comet.

I feel Kellen's stomach roil and his fingers go cold. I know what he must be thinking. A comet is an omen of something terrible. I tuck the pocket watch away and slow my stride to a cautious tread.

The vision flashes. I'm by the linden tree now. Once again, I see the night through a different pair of eyes. The ground rocks beneath my feet, or maybe it's only the dizzy buzz in my head. The legs I'm standing on steady themselves, and I sneak a glimpse of the locket ring I'm wearing. I'm Rudger.

"Give her up," says another man from a few feet behind me. *Bren.* I recognize his voice, its low and threatening tone, like when he spoke to Grandmère.

I ball my hands, but don't turn around. "She's the mother of my children," I bite back.

"That doesn't change the fact that she wants nothing to do with you. She's chosen me, and I've promised to take good care of her. I'll never lay fists on her, for starters. Save your wrath for someone who deserves it."

Rage builds inside me, churning from the pit of my stomach until it boils like hot acid. I whirl and stalk toward Bren. "Someone like *you*, then, you filthy blacksmith?" I throw a swift punch at his face, but never see it land.

I'm hurled into a different body . . . not a human body. I prowl on four legs and leave huge paw prints in my wake, just like I leave the lifeless figure of an old woman on the ground.

I'm the Grimm wolf, and I've been possessed by my grandmother.

The comet still shines in the sky. It's the same night.

Dread coils inside me—the Clara watching, but unable to change anything—though it's fury that's overtaken Grandmère. I feel it in the low rumble from the wolf's chest, in the way her lips pull back to bare her fangs.

I'm on Solace Trail and heading for the linden tree, like Grandmère was when she spoke with Bren. Why is she going back? Didn't he leave? Or did she see him return?

Please, Grandmère, don't do something you'll regret.

The vision flashes to someone else's memory, someone else's body. It takes me a moment to figure out whose. All I absorb is my throbbing jaw, aching fist, and pained stomach like I've been kicked by a plow horse. My eyesight blurs, my head spins. I'm Rudger, and he's in the middle of his fight with Bren.

I stumble and swing my fist, but my arm sails through nothing. I aimed for the wrong head. Three Brens swim in and out of focus. They raise their right arms.

Slam! My head whips to the side. Fresh pain pounds through my skull.

I roar, feeling all of Rudger's hatred. I draw a knife from my belt.

Nearby, the bushes rustle. Three men with short blond beards burst out from the underbrush. They merge into one man. My heart lurches. "Kellen?"

The scene spins. At first I mistake it for another bout of lightheadedness. But when it stops and I'm locked in a steady mind and painless body—a body that is running to defend his brother—I realize I've become Kellen.

My stare fixates on the knife in Rudger's shaking hand. "Watch out!" I warn as Bren tackles Rudger from behind and wrenches the weapon away.

I barrel into Bren before he has a chance to attack. As we collide, something silver flies out from my jacket. The pocket watch.

Now I'm back on four legs. Back in the Grimm wolf. I pass the linden tree, spy the men fighting and a knife flash between them. I pounce forward.

My bones shake as I release a terrible growl.

I stumble on my human legs. The Grimm wolf isn't shaking. *I* am.

My eyes—Clara's eyes—struggle to see beneath the layer of the vision to the real world.

As if looking through clouded water, I make out my traveling companions several yards away. They're sitting rigid and tall like they've just woken up.

This isn't a nightmare or a trick of my visions.

I know what I just heard, how loud it was, how close.

I slowly turn my head as the remnants of the vision realm ripple away in a pulse of rapid blackness and silence. I brace myself for what I'll see right behind me—a massive wolf with canine fangs, five inches long. All I can wish for is that her eyes are the color of my grandmother's.

Please be violet, please be violet, please be violet.

I gaze into her giant eyes.

And they're brown.

CHAPTER 45

"Adiah," I whisper, my breath like white smoke on the chill morning air. "Don't hurt me. Grandmère wouldn't want that."

But I know in my heart it doesn't matter what Grandmère wants. Just as she told Bren in my vision, she can't control the Grimm wolf's instincts when she isn't in her body.

The wolf holds her head high, her neck arched, her ears jutted straight up. Her stare is direct and challenging. It's too late to make a submissive move by bowing my head and lowering my eyes. The wolf is ready to snap her jaws. Her nose bunches up, and her fangs fully bare.

"Over here!" Axel shouts, and then whistles shrilly.

The wolf turns her head briefly, but doesn't bolt. I don't dare look away, so I can't tell if my friends have untied themselves and are gathering weapons. Last time, Axel scared the Grimm wolf away by throwing his hatchet.

The wolf growls, her breath hot and gamey. Adrenaline flashes through my veins. My body screams, *Run!* But that would be a death sentence. I have to show I'm not easy prey.

I stand tall. Spread my arms wide. Shout in the wolf's face.

Her fur bristles. She unleashes an ear-shuddering growl that steals the marrow from my bones. Vaguely, I hear Harlan and Axel approaching. But I can't wait for them.

I fist my hand over the pocket watch and slam it into the

Grimm wolf's snout. She doesn't whimper or back away, but I've stunned her.

Too quickly, she recovers.

Her fangs gleam. She snaps.

I drop and curl into a ball, protecting my face and neck. My last defense.

I brace for sheer pain. For teeth to tear into my flesh.

Nothing comes.

Thud. The wolf yelps and crashes over.

The shaft of a crossbow arrow protrudes from her side. Blood soaks her fur.

I jerk to my knees. "No!"

I press my hands over the wound. I can't let her die. It doesn't matter that she almost killed me.

Harlan and Axel race over. Harlan casts the crossbow aside and raises his dagger.

"Don't you come near her!" I drape my body over the wolf.

"I have to finish this." He stalks closer. "She might survive that wound."

"Stay back!" I shout.

Axel drops his hatchet and grabs Harlan's shoulder. "Listen to Clara."

"That isn't your grandmother," Harlan tells me. "And it's not the first time she's hunted you."

"She's my family!" I stroke her face, frantic to alleviate her pain. She's panting, softly whining. I set my brow against hers. "I'm so sorry."

Her eyes shift to violet.

I gasp. "Grandmère?"

Another whine.

I fumble for the red rampion in my pocket. It's withered, but maybe it doesn't matter. I feed it to the wolf, and her guttural, pained noises smooth into a human voice. Grandmère's voice.

"C-Clara . . ."

"I didn't know—" I lose my breath. "Your eyes were brown and—"

"You did what was necessary," she rasps. "I felt an echo of Adiah's wound and came to her. Our lives are . . ." She wheezes. ". . . intertwined."

"What do you mean?" I'm shaking all over. She never told me this. "You have to go, then! Leave her body!"

"Do not worry. We have a little time, *ma chère*. I won't let myself die in Adiah. My soul must be in my own body when I leave this life, or it won't find rest with Rosamund."

Terrible understanding washes over me. She's saying her death will be absolute if she dies separated from her human body. Her *soul* will die. "Please go! You shouldn't have come! Go back to the cottage and get well! *Live!*"

A mournful grin flickers at the corner of her mouth, so humanlike, so true to my obstinate grandmère, even in her suffering. "I was already dying, dear heart."

I choke back a sob, hearing her speak my mother's term of endearment.

"Adiah's wound only hastened the inevitable," she explains.

"No!" I clutch fistfuls of her fur and bury my head against her neck.

"I am sorry I could not help you more on this journey . . ." She inhales, another pained wheeze. ". . . but I must fulfill my fate."

The cards she drew for herself flood to mind: the Fanged Creature for an untimely death and Fortune's Cup, turned down, foretelling a tragedy. It's all coming to pass.

"I must go now," she says. "I have no more strength to stay in the wolf."

My tears flow faster.

"Take courage, Clara. I believe in you."

I want to thank her or offer some words of comfort, but my throat won't open.

"Adiah will be drawn to me now," Grandmère murmurs. "She has some vitality left. Let her come."

I nod. "I love—"

Her violet eyes shift to brown. A fresh sob rips from my chest. The Grimm wolf stands up gingerly.

"Wait." I reach for the arrow shaft. Should I pull it out? Will that help, or quicken her death?

Before I can decide, she lopes away.

I wipe my nose on my cape, my shoulders falling.

Axel tries to set his hand on my arm. I move away. I can't have anyone pitying me right now, or I'll come undone.

"We have to hurry." I rinse my bloody hands in the stream, fingers trembling. "Grimm's Hollow is a four-day journey. We need to make it in three. I won't let Grandmère die alone."

Ghosts watch me across the stream. Even with all that's happened, their stares are as impassive as ever.

Someone kneels beside me. Lila.

Her expression holds none of the usual contempt she reserves for me. It's lucid, gentle. Even understanding.

She hands me a withered stem of red rampion that must have fallen from my pocket.

"White for a pure heart," she says. "Red for a blooding."

Feeling a strange and disturbing kinship with her, I accept the flower. She rises and helps the boys start packing.

CHAPTER 46

As we rush homeward, my S-curve throbs, berating me no matter how I adjust my bodice or rearrange my wedge-lift. But I can't slow down. Axel checked his pocket watch after I announced we needed to make the journey in three days. The gilt hands shifted from twelve o'clock to three o'clock. It has to be a sign. That's truly all the time I have left to make it home to Grandmère before she passes.

I don't care if she is the murderer . . . or at least I won't let myself care right now. I don't know how the events in my vision ended—how Bren finally died.

During the first day of our hastened travel, neither Axel nor Harlan asks what I saw in my last vision, though they must know I had one. They're tiptoeing around me. I wonder if it's out of respect because my grandmother is dying, or from fear I'll bite off their heads for trying to talk to me in the state I'm in.

We journey all day and through half of the night, not stopping until I finally come to a halt, worn to the bone. I lie on the grass to sleep, forgoing a bedroll. I barely even wake when Axel ties our ankles together.

At dawn, he nudges me until my eyes crack open. "I wish you could rest longer," he says, "but I'm worried you'll never forgive me if I let you."

I drag myself up and pull mulch from my hair. "Thank you."

"I'm here if you want to talk about your grandmother or the

vision you had . . . or anything else." He picks at the knot of the rope binding us.

I consider it for a moment. "To be honest, you're not the easiest person to talk to about visions. Especially when they involve your father."

"You saw him, then?"

"Among others."

He worries at his lip, searching my face as if it will offer any clues of what I've discovered. "Well, if you feel like sharing, I promise to try my best to be calm and rational."

I laugh wearily and scrub my tired eyes. I'm more exhausted than I should be. I've had too many visions, too soon again. "How about I tell you and Harlan as we walk? I don't want to have to repeat myself or waste time." I sound curt, but I have to keep a shield over my heart right now. It's one blow short of shattering.

As we follow the stream, just a day and a half away from Grimm's Hollow, I carefully tell the boys *most* of my vision. How Kellen was holding the pocket watch when he approached Grimm's Hollow and saw the comet. How Bren and Rudger got into a fight over Fiora. How Rudger drew a knife. How Kellen emerged onto the scene and joined the scuffle, losing his pocket watch.

I leave out the parts involving Grandmère. How she blamed Bren that my father was missing. How he denied it and warned her not to threaten Fiora's children as the Grimm wolf. How she tried to strike a bargain with him for his silence, but he dismissed her. How she shifted into the wolf and rushed to break up the fight.

How she *did* have motive to kill Bren Zimmer after all.

"I never saw how the fight ended," I finish, leaving Axel and Harlan to believe only Rudger and Kellen were involved in the skirmish.

They're quiet as they take in all I've said. I tug on the strings of my cape, too tight around my neck. A few yards away, the ghosts stare with their usual disinterest, which counters the fact that they must be interested or they would stop following me.

"I'm not even sure if my visions are true anymore," I confess. "This one felt very real—I was actually in the bodies of Rudger and Kellen and . . ." I trail off before saying *Grandmère*. "But obviously there were discrepancies. Kellen wasn't holding the knife when he charged toward Bren; it was in Rudger's hand. And Kellen didn't lose the pocket watch before he joined the fight; it fell out of his jacket during the fight."

"You never saw Lila at the scene, then?" Harlan asks, and I shake my head. "Well, that's encouraging—for Lila, anyway." He averts his gaze from Axel.

As usual, Lila doesn't realize we're talking about her. She walks beside Harlan, sneering at a frog leaping into the stream. "Beware enacting your wish, lest you make a mistake." She hurls a rock at it.

Axel finally speaks up, striving to be calm. "My father was only defending his brother." That tells me which vision he prefers—this latest one, not the one where Kellen is Lila's accomplice and under the spell of her love potion. "So if the knife got shuffled around in the fight, and he had to . . ." He waves a hand to fill in the blank. "Then it wouldn't have been murder, and it wouldn't have set off the curse."

Harlan frowns. "But if this new vision is true—if either Rudger or Kellen killed Bren—then how do we account for Lila ending up with the missing page in her caverns?" He casts a nervous look at her, and she hisses at him. "Clara learned about that in her other vision, when Lila and Kellen were—"

"My father couldn't have been under a love potion that long," Axel interrupts, losing some of his patience. "We've been over this."

"Unless he became Lost," I pipe in quietly.

Axel's face reddens, and his jaw muscle works.

He may not like that idea, but I pray it's true. If Kellen lived to follow Lila to her caverns, it would mean my grandmother, as the Grimm wolf, didn't kill him when she jumped into the fight.

"Look, I don't know what's real in my visions anymore. And part of me doesn't care. We have the missing page. Let's hope it's enough to break the curse."

Once it's broken, all the Lost Ones will return to the village. And with any luck, Axel's father will be among them.

CHAPTER 47

hen night falls, the pocket watch's hands reach one o'clock, and I calculate we're a half day's journey from Grimm's Hollow. I'm frantic to reach my cottage. Grandmère has to be alive. I'd know if she died, just like she knew when Adiah became fatally wounded. But I can barely keep walking. My crooked back hasn't hurt this badly since I lost my shoe on my last journey.

Axel keeps offering to help, but every time he does, I refuse. I can see in his twisted brow that part of him still resents me for not giving him conclusive answers about his father. Or maybe it's me who's the problem. Maybe I can't bear his touch when I continue to lie by not revealing that Grandmère could have killed Bren too.

When we come upon a little dell in the woods surrounded by aspens, I drop my pack. My energy is spent, and my back throbs like my spine will snap if I take another step.

Lila splays out on the grass. "Have we found our kingdom yet?"

"For the night, yes." I'm about to lie down beside her—I'm that desperate to rest—when someone calls, "Clara?"

My heart skips a beat. I whirl around and find my best friend racing toward me across the darkened dell. "Henni?"

It really is her, rosy-cheeked, even by the light of my lantern, her hair in two braids, her red kerchief wrapped over her head like a band.

I throw my arms around her, crying and laughing all at once. "What are you doing here?"

Her smile wilts. "I stayed in the village for as long as I could."

Four other people hurry over. Ella and Fiora, each holding the hand of a child. Hansel keeps close to Ella, and Gretel sticks right beside her mother. They all have scraps of red wool pinned to their clothes—pieces of Henni's kerchief.

Axel embraces everyone with me, and then we all stare at each other in wonder.

"This is Harlan Oswald and Lila Sommer," I say. "You might remember them from the village. Lila goes by the *eldest princess,*" I add with emphasis, and from my friends' slow nods, I see they understand she's Lost. "Harlan was a frog and . . . it's a long story."

Ella smiles, impossibly beautiful in a simple brown dress and her chestnut hair tossed into a loose bun. "Come and join us around our fire."

Axel perks up. "A fire with real firewood?"

"Yes." Her voice trills with lovely laughter. "We brought a cartful. Fiora and I take turns sneaking back to Grimm's Hollow for supply runs whenever we . . ."

I don't catch the rest of her words as they wander ahead into the campsite, Hansel swinging on Ella's arm. Harlan lifts Lila to her feet, and they follow, Lila walking proudly as if she's about to enter a court decorated in her honor. The ghosts who trail me wait for my lead, but I sense Fiora wishes to speak with me.

"I'm glad to see the bodice is holding up," she says.

I pull my gaze from Axel and Ella and smooth my hand down the sage-green brocade. "Yes, thank you. It's helped a great deal."

Gretel squeals and chases a firefly. Henni darts after her, unknowingly plowing through two ghosts. I'm left alone with Fiora, who tugs her lower lip between her teeth and studies my face. "Have you had any luck solving who murdered Bren?" Her voice catches when she says his name.

Show the murderer no mercy, she said when I left Grimm's Hollow, gripping my wrist like a vise.

"Not with any certainty," I answer carefully. If I confess it could have been Lila, Fiora might retaliate, or if I mention my suspicions about Axel's uncle or father, she'll bombard him with questions. And I won't betray my grandmother by admitting how she could be implicated. "But we found the missing page. That may fix everything."

Fiora swallows thickly. "I suppose we'll find out tomorrow."

I wrap my arms around myself. "Have you checked on my grandmother?"

"Not since we came here, although my parents give me updates." She adds gently, "I don't know how much longer she has, Clara."

I blink back a rush of tears. This isn't anything I don't know, but it tugs heavy at my heart all the same.

I let Fiora guide me to the others, who sit around the campfire. "I'm sorry," I announce, "but this hello is also going to be goodbye." Voice hitching, I explain how Grandmère has less than twenty-four hours to live, according to the pocket watch. "Afterward . . ." I squeeze my eyes shut. I can't comprehend an afterward. ". . . we'll regroup and make a plan to—"

"Clara, you need to rest," Axel says. "We'll rise early. You'll make it to your grandmother in time, I promise."

"No, I can't—"

"I've been watching you for hours," he presses. "I can tell how much pain you're in."

I rub my forehead. I hate my crooked back, my shaking legs, my ravenous stomach, my blistered feet, my powerlessness to save the last person in my family. "I'll have a quick meal, and then—"

"You'll *lie* down," he insists. "You'll sleep. Your grandmother would want that. And you'll want to be strong and alert when you're finally with her."

I find myself scowling at him. I don't want to admit he's right, and I don't want him to be the one telling me.

Henni rises and takes my hand. "Come, Clara." Her eyes shimmer with deep affection. "You can start by eating something."

I relent and sit on the grass with them as she brings me mushroom soup, made by Ella, and cheese toasted over bread. I try not to let Ella see me sniff and poke at the broth before finally daring to taste it. The last thing I need is to hallucinate any dreaded midnight weddings.

Henni explains how she had been living in Rudger's abandoned home, but as the village council became more paranoid when the curse worsened, they kept a closer watch on Fiora and Ella, suspicious of them as the only Lost Ones who had ever returned to the village. Soon the council caught wind that they were working to hide Henni, so the three friends, along with Hansel and Gretel, escaped into the forest before anyone was arrested.

Harlan clears his throat. "I want to apologize if my father has treated any of you wrongfully." Lila rests her head on his shoulder, mouthing words over and over, like she's invoking a dark spell. "I don't know how he's changed since I've been gone, but nothing excuses cruelty."

"I don't believe any council members are cruel at heart," Henni replies. "They're just afraid." Which is a noble thing to say since she's taken the brunt of their discrimination.

Harlan grins at her. "Once you've broken the curse, I expect you'll become Grimm Hollow's favorite citizen."

"That's what I said," Ella chimes in. "They'll hold festivals in Henni's honor."

Harlan nods. "The council will regret their poor treatment of you."

Henni rubs her blushing cheeks. Knowing my best friend, she can't endure any more praise or attention, no matter how much she secretly craves it.

A thought springs to mind. "Do you want to see the missing page?" I ask her.

Harlan sits up taller. "You think it will answer her one wish?"

That's what I'm hoping. Harlan pulls it out of his pack and passes it to her.

Henni excuses herself to speak her one wish privately, but a few minutes later, she returns with an apologetic expression. "It says it won't give me the answer until it's reunited with the book."

I slump, which sends a sharp twinge through my S-curve. "Well, it was worth a try."

Harlan seems even more disappointed, though he spares Henni a kind look when she hands him back the page.

I'm about to tell her she can keep it for now when Axel throws a log on the fire and abruptly changes the subject. "Tell me more about your supply runs to Grimm's Hollow," he asks no one in particular. "Who's chopping all this wood?"

Henni brightens. "Mostly Fiora's father. He and my parents established a secret place near the border where they leave us food and things."

"That's very good of them," I say. "Especially your father, Fiora. I imagine it isn't easy for him to leave his orchards." He's a hermit whom I, for one, have never seen in the village.

"He's ashamed he didn't do more for me before I went Lost," she replies, keeping a grip on Hansel's shirttail so he can't get too close to the fire. "And he'd do anything for Hansel and Gretel."

"As would any of us." Ella kisses Gretel's cheek. The little girl sits on her lap while Ella weaves her pale blond hair into a pretty four-strand braid.

Axel scoots around the fire and gives Hansel a stick to poke the embers with. "Did you know I'm your cousin?"

Fiora drops her bowl, and her soup splatters on the ground.

I throw Axel a pointed look. He squeezes his eyes shut, realizing his mistake. "Sorry, it's hard to keep track of who knows what from Clara's visions."

Henni spins on me. "You've had more visions?"

She's the only friend we've reunited with who knows about my ability, and as they all stare at me expectantly, I explain in the simplest terms what my gift is and how it helped us find the missing page, though I don't mention Axel's father or Lila. Or anything more to do with murder suspects.

"We promise not to tell anyone your secret, Fiora," I say, careful not to mention Rudger's name in case Hansel and Gretel don't know he's their father.

Her smile is pained, though her shoulders relax. "Thank you. I know I can't hide the truth forever." Her gaze warms on Axel. "It's nice for the children to know they have a kind cousin at least."

"What's a cousin?" Gretel purses her rosebud mouth.

"A very special friend." Axel winks.

"And Axel will be the best of friends," Ella adds, sharing a look with him that has a past I don't ever want to see in a vision.

I stand against the protests of my throbbing back. "Goodnight, everyone."

"Wait," Ella says. "Shouldn't we form a plan for getting the Book of Fortunes? It's protected by six night watchmen now."

"Can't we just tell them we have the missing page?" asks Harlan. "The village *wants* Henni to break the curse."

Ella levels him with a Cinderella-worthy glare. "I don't think you realize how dire her circumstances are. If anything goes wrong, and she can't break the curse again . . . All it would take is another mob to . . ." Her lips press into a razor-thin line. "Henni needs to break the curse alone."

"I agree," I say, although I haven't given much thought to how we'll gain access to the book. "Can we make a plan after my grandmother . . . ?" My voice goes hoarse.

"I'll go with you to your cottage," Axel says. Our eyes lock briefly before he lowers his gaze and brushes soot off his boot.

Harlan's jaw muscle spasms, and I swear for a moment he looks jealous, but he quickly masks it with a flash of his dimples. "Lila and I will come too. She isn't much use to anyone until the curse is broken." He cringes. "That came out wrong. I only mean it's best if I stay with her until then."

Lila breaks free from her daze and silent chanting. "Is it time to dance yet?"

Harlan winces, like he's embarrassed. "Not yet."

Henni chews on her fingernail. "What if we find a way to steal *Sortes Fortunae* while you're with your grandmother, Clara?"

Ella narrows her eyes. "Who is *we*?"

"You, me, and Fiora."

"I want to help!" Hansel cuts in.

Gretel shoves him. "Stealing is bad!"

Ella drops her face in her hands. "This is a terrible idea."

"We shouldn't delay," Henni implores her. "Once Clara and the others enter the village, someone is bound to find out. We should be getting the book at the same time."

"Henni is right," Fiora says. "We need to leave the forest as quickly as possible. We're lucky to have stayed here for this long—even with these." She touches the scrap of Henni's kerchief pinned to her dress. "None of us wants to become Lost again."

Red rampion can't protect us forever.

It's something we all know too well.

"If it helps, I've seen the night watchmen evaded before." I explain how, in visions, I've observed people trick the watchmen with their feminine wiles or other distractions that have lured them from their posts.

Again, I don't mention Grandmère or Lila, and Axel and Harlan don't share what I've left out. It seems we three have made a pact to keep the people we care about safe from scrutiny until I deduce what's true in my visions.

"We'll find a way to get the book," Fiora assures me.

Henni shares a curt nod with Fiora and sits taller.

Ella casts me a weary glance. "When we've all become ghosts, Clara, be sure to tell my mother and father that I *tried* saving my sister."

I offer her a sympathetic grin, looking past the ring of our campfire to the throng of ghosts watching my every move.

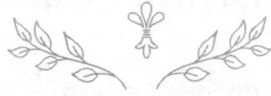

CHAPTER 48

That night, I tie my ankle to Henni's, which is a welcome change. I snuggle close and fall asleep within seconds, ignoring all the ghost eyes on me. My sleep is visionless, also wonderful. The only thing that wakes me is the snap of a twig near our campsite.

Just a ghost, I tell myself.

Then my fatigued mind realizes a ghost wouldn't trigger a loop only to do that.

I open my eyes. Past a line of thick bushes, I glimpse a shadowy figure with a wide-brimmed hat, and my stomach clenches.

I sit up and hiss, "Leave us alone, Rudger! We've already solved your riddle!"

He startles and races away.

Axel steals over to me, lantern in hand. "I heard you. Is Rudger really back?"

"Yes." My limbs shake, though the worst of it ebbs to have Axel close. A lock of hair at the back of his head stands on end, and my hand twitches against the urge to smooth it down. "But I don't think he's interested in me and you. What he lost is in the forest now."

"Hansel and Gretel?"

I nod. "It's a good thing they're leaving in the morning."

Axel squares his jaw. "I'll warn Fiora and give her the crossbow. And I'll sleep by the children for the rest of the night."

"Good idea."

Our eyes meet, and my heart strains.

Axel lowers his gaze. "Goodnight, Clara."

"Goodnight."

In the morning, everyone wakes before sunrise, and I hurry to help Henni take down clothes from a wash line. "Why do you keep staring at me like that?" I ask, catching her side-eyeing me.

She folds a pair of Hansel's trousers. "What's going on between you and Axel?"

"What do you mean?"

"Whenever you two are near each other, you fold your arms across your chest, and he keeps his hands in his pockets. You barely look at each other."

I release a long exhale. "It's complicated."

Henni angles her head. "It's me, Clara. You can tell me anything."

I fold another shirt as I think through where to begin. "We promised we'd trust no one else in the forest, but then I met Harlan, who wasn't Lost, just trapped in the body of a frog, and I got to know him through visions of his past . . . and, well, I kissed him." When Henni's eyes round, I add, "But only to break his spell and turn him back into a human."

"Oh, dear," Henni says. "You don't have feelings for Harlan, do you?"

"Not really. He's dashing and thoughtful, but none of that compares to what I feel for Axel."

"Have you told Axel that?"

"I don't think he's so upset about Harlan anymore." I shift from foot to foot. "I've seen Axel's father in visions, Henni. He may be alive. He may also have been involved in Bren's murder."

I share everything from my visions, and the purging of it to someone unbiased is such a cleansing release that I even share the visions that implicate my grandmother.

"Oh, Clara." Henni sits on a large root after we untie the wash line. "What a tremendous weight you've been carrying. But you can't really believe your grandmother is involved? She's your *grandmother*. She knits sweaters and feeds stray kittens."

"She also embodies the Grimm wolf and reads dire fortunes." I sigh and lift Henni up, despite my sore back, so we can keep hurrying. "In any case, Axel feels just as certain his father could have never stabbed Bren. It's hard for him to even stomach the idea that Rudger could."

"What about Lila?"

I sneak a glance at the eldest Sommer girl. As Harlan folds up a bedroll, she dances alone around the stamped-out campfire, her head tossed back, her hair wild. "She was awful to me in her caverns. I convinced myself she must be the murderer. But my visions haven't always lined up . . . and now I wonder if she's become my scapegoat."

Henni cinches shut a bag of clothespins. "I don't know how to solve who the murderer is, but as for you and Axel, I don't think you'll be able to heal your relationship until you're both willing to accept that the people in your family could have done wrong. The past is already lost, Clara. Don't lose what you can still save."

I sniff and bring her into my arms. "What have I done without you?"

She laughs. "You don't need me, Changer of Fate. Though I would have preferred traveling with you over hiding in Rudger's awful house."

"Sorry about that."

"I forgive you."

She kisses my cheek, and in my periphery, I glimpse a little ghost watching us with large elfin eyes. "Ollie," I gasp.

Understanding he's here, Henni lets me go, and I walk over to an aspen Ollie is playing with, jabbing a finger at its black spots.

He knows just when to halt his hand so it looks like he really touches the tree.

"The ghosts are all talking about you," he says.

"I know."

"If you don't break the curse, they won't be happy."

"Actually, Henni will be the one to break it, but, yes, I know that too."

"What if *I* don't want you to break it?"

"Why would you say that?" I shift around to see him better, but he ducks his head and pretend-kicks the trunk. "Then I'd be able to use all my time looking for your pennies."

Ollie gets frustrated with the aspen and shoves it, but of course his hand sails right through. "I want you to leave my dad alone."

So this is why Ollie is back. "*He's* the one who isn't leaving us alone."

"Stop trying to have visions of him. My dad didn't kill that man in the stream."

I've never mentioned the stream to Ollie. "Did you see it happen?"

"No," he admits.

I shrug off a wave of disappointment, but I'm glad Ollie didn't see the murder. No child, even a ghost child, should have to witness that. "It's hard to imagine someone you love doing something terrible, isn't it?"

"You should tell Axel that. Then maybe you two could stop having your stupid fight."

I suppress a grin, although it stings that even a seven-year-old knows how to fix my problems. "Have you ever seen Axel's father in the forest? He goes by Kellen. He's your father's brother, which makes him your uncle."

"I know who he is."

"So you've seen him?"

Ollie blows out a dramatic huff. "You don't want to know what I've seen," he says ominously.

I soften my voice. "As hard as it is, it's always better to tell someone the truth."

His somber mood breaks, and he snorts with a giggle. "You're funny."

"Why?"

"You keep telling me to do things you should do yourself."

"I told Henni the truth," I say, feeling color rise to my cheeks.

"Good. Now that you've practiced, you can tell Axel."

"Why are you so concerned about Axel?"

"He's my cousin. Plus, I'm tired of watching him mope around and stare at you like *this* when you're not looking." He makes an exaggerated frown and widens his eyes so they're huge and pitiful.

I try not to laugh. Does Axel really look at me like that? I glance at him in the middle of a deep conversation with Ella. My chest wrenches as he pulls her into a close embrace. Surely I'm the one looking sad and pitiful now.

"Goodbye, Clara," Ollie says. "I'll try to stop begging, but please don't forget about my pennies."

"I haven't. I won't. I thought maybe if you and I . . ."

He turns, already starting to disappear.

"Wait!" *Why does he always do this?* "You didn't tell me why I shouldn't break the curse."

"Because . . ." He looks over his shoulder. My last glimpse of him before he fades away is of his eyes, glossy with tears. "I don't want to be left all alone in this forest."

CHAPTER 49

We follow the stream until it forks with another one close to Grimm's Hollow, and in the late afternoon, we separate. Axel, Harlan, Lila, and I journey toward my sheep farm, and Henni and the others take the path that leads to the meadow pavilion. The plan is to join up again at midnight, hoping that allows enough time to accomplish what we need to do.

We'll meet at the tree house a couple of miles from the Dantzer farm. It's in the forest where Henni can make her one wish undisturbed from a potential mob of angry villagers.

Axel chose the spot. I tell myself it's because the tree house is conveniently located between my farmland and the meadow, not because it's where he and Ella shared their first kiss.

I tell myself many things . . . that their embrace this morning was platonic, that the way they walked together all day was also friendly, that Axel doesn't love her anymore, that he still loves me. That Love Lost is a fortune-telling card that doesn't have to mean forever.

Mostly, I try not to think of Axel. The closer we approach to my farmland, the more my chest tightens with urgency.

I'm almost there, Grandmère. Live awhile longer for me.

I smell the sheep before I see the land . . . a livestock aroma only farmers truly appreciate, and sheep farmers are best at discerning among it a blend of musky lanolin and wool.

For me, it's the scent of home.

I move past a dense thicket, up a little rise in the path, and my cottage comes into view. Tears prick my eyes.

Our farmland has decayed with the worsening of the curse, but my cottage still stands like it's stood throughout all the hard years Grandmère and I have already suffered through, made harder because we lost my mother and father and learned to rely on each other.

This is a precious place. A sacred place. I wouldn't want any other haven. Lila dreams of a kingdom, jeweled and mystical, but all I want is this half-timbered, three-bedroom cottage and all the history within its walls.

I press forward until I reach the ash-lined border that separates the village from the Forest Grimm. Like the meadow on the night of the autumn festival, the border has shrunk inward. It used to lie beyond the stream along the hedgerow, but now it falls within the boundary of our twig-woven fence and several yards into the north sheep pasture.

Relieved that the horde of ghosts can't follow me anymore, I cross the ashes with Axel, but Harlan and Lila hang back. He wrestles with her as she shrieks and batters him.

"What's wrong?" I ask.

He grits his teeth as Lila claws his neck. "She's afraid of the sheep."

A ram in the distance gives a deep-voiced bleat, and Lila screams. Harlan clamps a hand over her mouth, but she bites his fingers.

"Grimm wolves!" Lila gapes at the animals in the pasture.

"There is only one Grimm wolf," I assure her. "And she's wounded. You saw that for yourself."

Harlan nurses his bleeding finger. "She's probably confused, remembering the wolf in the meadow after she tore the page from *Sortes Fortunae*."

I think back to that vision. Lila had seen the Grimm wolf lurking nearby, its large tail flicking over the top of the wild grass. "Maybe it's best if you two wait in the forest," I say. "I'm sorry, but—"

"I understand," he says. "We'll stay back. I'll play her some music to help her settle down."

"Thank you."

He crosses the ash line and gives me an affectionate hug. "I'm sorry about your grandmother, Clara. But I'm glad you get to say goodbye."

I muster a shaky smile. "If I'm not too late."

"You won't be." He lifts my palm like he's done before—like he's also done with Lila—and brazenly kisses it right in front of Axel. My skin prickles, and I don't know if I like the feeling.

"Wait." I catch his sleeve as he turns. "Could I have the missing page?"

His eyelid twitches. "Hmm?"

"The missing page. Don't you have it in your pack?"

He nods slowly. "Sometimes I show it to Lila. It calms her. She associates it with her caverns. I was going to show her again, see if it helps. I haven't seen her this agitated in a while."

Behind him, Lila whimpers and flinches, her wild eyes on the sheep.

"She'll be all right, won't she?" I ask, trying to stifle my guilt. "I was really hoping to show the page to Grandmère. She probably won't live to see the curse broken, even if it happens soon." The pocket watch has reached twelve o'clock, which means today is the end. Sometime before midnight, I'll lose my grandmother. "But at least the page can assure her it will be broken."

The rigid line of Harlan's shoulders eases. "Of course." He slides off his pack and pulls out the page. A small laugh escapes him. "It's funny how attached I am to a piece of paper. It's like I've become its guardian."

"Don't worry, I'll bring it back. We *will* defeat this curse."

He struggles to return my grin as I clutch a folded edge of the page while he grips the other side. Finally, he lets go and flashes his dimples. "We'll be waiting past the hedgerow, then. Come back as soon as you can."

"We will."

"It could be several hours," Axel cuts in, coming to stand tall beside me. "You don't need to feel rushed, Clara, not about this."

My throat tightens, and I muster a little nod.

We part ways. As Harlan and Lila retreat into the forest, Axel and I advance toward the cottage. As soon as we're alone, the silence between us grows thick and heavy, like the air when clouds are a breath away from rainfall.

He stuffs his hands in his pockets, and I want to know why, remembering Henni's remark this morning. Is he still insistent on keeping emotional distance from me? But then why do his arms brush mine, why do his lowered eyes keep sliding in my direction, even if they rarely reach my face?

Some of the sheep amble over, recognizing me. One of the friendlier ewes nudges my waist with her nose. "Hello, Mia." I run my hand over her woolly head. She was my mother's favorite lamb, although Mother never saw her fully grown. In the same way, Grandmère will never see the new lambs become mothers, fathers. . . .

I flick away a bit of moisture from my eyes and roll my shoulders back. I need to stay strong. Grandmère will suffer more if she sees me falling apart.

"Would you like me to come inside with you?" Axel's voice is as soft as fleece, and his eyes are warm, his blue irises collecting all the gold from the sun as it falls toward the horizon.

I nod, unable to speak in case I start crying again. He belongs with me in my cottage too.

His hand comes out of his pocket and slips around mine, and my legs feel steadier. Approaching from the back of the house, our path takes us by Grandmère's bedroom window. I can't resist peering inside.

I see her in profile. She's lying on her bed, her eyes closed, but her chest rises and falls sporadically. Relief swells inside me. She's still alive.

The window is cracked open by an inch, and within the room, I hear a chair creak. I lean closer to the glass, expecting to see our farmhand, Conrad. So when I spy a different man's face, one that reminds me of Harlan, I startle and duck.

CHAPTER 50

A xel crouches low with me. "What is it?"

I don't dare whisper back, not until I pull him around to the side of the cottage. "Herr Oswald is in there, sitting comfortably in a chair like he's been with Grandmère for hours."

"Why is he keeping vigil?" Axel frowns. "They were never friends."

"I have no idea." The last time Herr Oswald came here was to deliver the news that my father was dead. The man is a bad omen. "We'll have to wait until he leaves to go inside." Herr Oswald can't know I'm back yet, not until the curse is broken and Henni and my friends are safe.

We sneak away to a spot in the pasture under an old hawthorn tree. It's down a slope and out of view from my grandmother's bedroom window, but if we peek above the incline, we can see the road leading from my cottage to the village. We'll see Herr Oswald when he leaves.

I pace around the tree. Creep up and glimpse the road. Listen for more noises from the cottage. A half hour passes, then an hour. The sun is setting. I wish the pocket watch could show me the time I have left, down to the minute. Will Conrad come? This is when our farmhand checks in with Grandmère before he turns in for the night.

She's too ill for a discussion, but perhaps the routine will bring him back all the same. When I see him, I'll ask him to shoo Herr Oswald away.

Tired of pacing and fretting, I gradually turn my focus to Axel. He's been patient, letting me mourn, or try to not mourn, allowing me room to feel whatever I need to. And when I really pause to pull down the walls around my heart, I realize I'm mourning more than my grandmother's impending death. I'm mourning her innocence.

I may never know before she dies what her role was on the night of Bren Zimmer's murder. Even if she did the worst, I want to hold space inside me for the love I've always had for her.

Axel is standing with his back against the trunk of the hawthorn, which is actually many thin trunks woven together to support the canopy, now leafless from the curse. Nevertheless, this hawthorn is still beautiful to me. "Do you know what happened here?" I ask quietly.

He looks up, surprised I've said something after my long spell of silence. "On your farm?"

I shake my head. "Under this tree?"

His gaze stretches to the branches above and the gentle dip in the surrounding grassland. It's secluded from even the view of the forest. His mouth curves up. "This is where you and I helped the ewe birth her twin lambs."

"You were helping Father that lambing season."

"He was busy with another ewe that night. So we had to face the task together."

I drift over to him. "The second lamb almost died, but we helped it breathe again. Then I burst into tears and sobbed for the longest time. You were fifteen, and I was thirteen, but you held me close. You didn't let go until my tears had dried."

Axel's eyes hold me now, as warm as when he embraced me

back then. "I still didn't let you go," he murmurs softly, like he's revealing a long-kept secret. "All that bravery I saw in you, all the love you gave a helpless creature, all the vulnerability you weren't afraid to show . . . it made a mark. Somehow, you became a part of me, Clara. I won't ever let you go." He lowers his gaze. "Not unless you want me to. And if you do, I understand."

I place my hands on the sides of his face. "Don't ever think that. You're my *home*. You're a part of me too. Soon, I'll have lost all the family that is blood to me, but I won't be lost. I'll have *you*." My breath hitches on a sudden sob. "You're my family, Axel. You're my forever." I search his eyes, wondering if I've said too much or offered more than he wants. "If you'll have me."

His eyes glisten. He takes one of my hands and presses my knuckles to his lips as his mouth trembles. He tries to speak, but his voice cracks. Tears spill down his cheeks. "I'm afraid my father is really dead, Clara."

My chest squeezes. "Oh, Axel." I brush away his tears and kiss the paths where they fall, crying with him. "We don't know that."

"But you sense it." His mouth quivers with a pained smile. "Deep down, I know you do. It's why you can't have the vision that will tell me the truth. You don't want to hurt me."

I shake my head, trying to deny it, but he takes me by the shoulders and bends his head to mine. "I'm not angry anymore. I'm sorry I ever was. I'm sorry I drove that wedge between us."

"No, I did. I broke your trust. I never told you about all of my visions. I never asked if you thought it was wise to break the spell over Harlan. We made a pact to make decisions together, and I left you out." A lump forms in my throat. "And there's more I haven't told you."

I finally share what I saw of my grandmother in my last vision, how she had reason to kill Bren, and how she came back as the Grimm wolf to join the fight between Bren, Rudger, and Kellen.

"She could have killed Bren," I confess. "Her human body was nearby. She could have returned after he was wounded and stabbed him. Or she could have been an accomplice in killing him."

"It doesn't matter." Axel cups my face and smooths his thumbs over my cheeks. "My uncle could have killed him too. Or my father." He exhales slowly. "I'm willing to accept that. The past is the past. We've let it tear us apart for too long. I won't do that anymore. I'm going to fight for *you* now."

I search his eyes. "You won't have any regrets about Ella?"

His forehead creases. "Ella?"

"You two seem close again. This morning, the way you hugged her . . ."

"No, that wasn't . . ." He sighs. "She'd just berated me for how badly I'd messed up with you. I hugged her to thank her for knocking some sense into me."

"Well, that's good." My chest warms. "What came of it, anyway."

"Yes." Axel chuckles softly, and his expression grows more earnest. "Clara . . ." He kisses my brow. "You're my whole world. My family, my soul. That forever you were talking about?" He smooths a lock of hair behind my ear. "If I could make a second wish on the Book of Fortunes, that would be it—a forever with you."

A small sob bursts out of me. I laugh and swipe my tears. "Stop making me cry." I shove his chest, and his strong arms come around me. I sink against him and release a slow breath. This is where I belong. We were fitted for each other, all the broken bits and the whole bits and the parts still growing inside us.

"I love you, Axel," I say against the steady beating of his heart.

His hand combs through my hair. "I love you too . . . and I loved you first."

"Maybe." I smile. "But the past is the past."

"Not when it comes to my feelings for you."

He pulls me higher and brings his mouth down on mine. His kiss is bold, filled with the fight he spoke of, the determination not to let anything tear us apart.

I surrender to it, swept away and dizzy on my feet, but then I find the fight within me too. I push back with my kiss, not by pushing him away, but by matching his strength, even urging him to show more.

My hands slide up his torso to his neck. He doesn't need his scarf, I realize. I unwrap it and cast it aside. His hands travel to the base of my throat as he also unties my cape. He pushes it off, and it ripples over my back. The wide neckline of my shirt slips off one shoulder, and Axel's lips find their way there in a trail of increasingly heated kisses. My neck arches, my toes curl. Shivers of warmth prickle over every inch of my body.

We tumble to the ground. I roll on top of him, untucking his shirt. My hands trace his hardened abdomen and the taut muscles of his chest. He gasps and spins me over, pinning my arms at my sides. His teeth slide up my neck and nip at my jawline and earlobe.

Then his breathing slows. His hold against me softens. His lips become pliable, tender. He pulls back to gaze down on me. His face is flushed, and his golden hair dangles over his brow. "You're so beautiful," he whispers, and swallows tentatively. "You're also precious to me, Clara. I never want to disrespect you."

I touch his cheek. "I trust you."

He kisses me gently. "Let's wait a little longer, all right? I don't want you to feel rushed or worried that at any moment your grandmother might . . ."

The grief I've been holding at bay swells fierce again. Tears leak from the corners of my eyes. Axel brushes them away and lifts me up so he can spread my cape like a blanket on the ground. He lays me down again and rests beside me. "I'm here for you," he murmurs. "I'll always be here."

He holds me as I cry, and the last rays of sunlight give way to the horizon.

CHAPTER 51

The sky is growing dark with velvety tones of blue. Henni and the others will be waiting for us at the tree house soon, and Harlan must be wondering why Axel and I haven't returned to meet him and Lila past the hedgerow of my farmland.

It's nearing midnight, but the pocket watch has changed time. Strangely, it shows the minute hand at *XII*, but the hour hand bounces between *XII* and *I*.

Has fate granted me more time?

It would be so easy to close my eyes and rest, secure in Axel's embrace and under the dome of the hawthorn. How fitting that a hawthorn symbolizes a healed broken heart. I've found that with Axel, and it's hard to leave here and face what's awaiting us. . . .

My dying grandmother.

A curse I hope can be broken.

A legion of ghosts biding their time to punish me if it doesn't.

I peer above the crest of the slope. A candle is lit in Grand-mère's bedroom. Behind it, a shadow passes back and forth. Herr Oswald is pacing. Why won't he leave? I've given up on Conrad returning to usher him away. Some errand must have taken him elsewhere.

"Do you think Adiah made it back here?" I ask Axel. She had a head start, but she was also wounded.

"Maybe not," he murmurs, tucked next to me. "Wouldn't the sheep be acting differently if she were on the land?"

I nod. I hadn't thought about that. It guts me to think of Adiah dying alone in the forest.

"I'm more surprised Harlan hasn't come looking for us," Axel says. "He was acting like you'd cut off a limb when he handed over the missing page."

"I'm sure he'd be here by now if it weren't for Lila. She was genuinely terrified of the sheep."

Axel props his head up on his hand. "Harlan mentioned something about how she saw the Grimm wolf after she tore out the page from *Sortes Fortunae*. What happened exactly? You never told me about that part of the vision."

"Oh, it wasn't anything very traumatic. All Lila saw was its tail . . ." I trail off, caught on what Axel just said. "Wait, I never told Harlan about that part of the vision either. He shouldn't have known Lila saw the Grimm wolf."

Axel studies my face. "What's wrong, Clara?"

A knot forms in my stomach. I sit up as I try to place why I'm agitated. "You said you thought something was off about my visions. Isn't it odd that Harlan knew something I saw but never told him about?"

"Maybe he *did* know, but was lying." Axel pulls up to sit beside me.

"But why would he lie?" I pick at my sleeve, thinking. "Harlan is the only person I've been able to talk to in a vision. Somehow he could break away from his memories, like he had the power to interfere."

"Then he could have interfered with other visions."

"Possibly . . . although I don't know how. But I'd trust any new vision over one I had when he was around."

"Whose memories would you want to see?"

"Rudger's, your father's, Lila's, my grandmother's . . . everyone's except Harlan's. I won't risk entering his mind anymore.

I'd want to see that night through the most unbiased perspective possible."

Axel scratches his jaw. "Could that person be someone we haven't considered yet?"

I ponder for a moment. Who would have eyes on everything that happened on the night Bren was murdered?

Then it comes to me. And it isn't a someone. It's an entity—alive and magical and all-powerful.

The Forest Grimm.

CHAPTER 52

Grounded with Axel beside me, knowing he'll keep me safe from sleepwalking or any present danger, I clutch my cape—dyed with forest-grown red rampion—and, using it as my token, I channel the memories of the Forest Grimm.

Like a hovering parent eagerly waiting to help their child, the forest welcomes me into its mind. I'm sucked into the black, the silence, then spit out into the sky, as if I'm a bird looking down on the vast landscape below me, lush with green trees and framed by beautiful mountains.

I stay floating as the forest waits for me to direct the vision. I consider everything I want to validate as true, and my first thought is Lila's one wish.

My perspective zooms toward the meadow on the outskirts of Grimm's Hollow, and I sense time rapidly reversing to a spring day before the curse: Lila's wish ceremony.

I'm amazed at how clearly I see whatever I focus on, especially since Grimm's Hollow isn't part of the forest. But then again, it once was, having carved itself out from the woodland as people settled here. In some sense, it still belongs to the forest.

Before it's time for Lila to make her one wish, Harlan kisses her palm and says, "You're astonishing," just as I saw in my other vision. But he's the one to kiss her on the mouth afterward, he's the one to whisper, "Our daydream won't be a fantasy any longer." Blushing, she returns his smile.

Now she's alone with the Book of Fortunes behind the pavilion curtains. She speaks the incantation and says, "I wish to share my one wish with Harlan Oswald, and we wish to possess the limitless magic of the Forest Grimm."

I should be shocked, but what pierces me is clarity. Lila's brand of Lostness makes perfect sense now. What she wanted in the forest was a prince to share limitless magic with, and this one wish, phrased exactly like she said, is why.

The book writes its answer in green ink, but it includes a new stanza:

> *Limitless magic brings limitless power,*
> *Limitless power brings limitless corruption.*
> *Beware the cost,*
> *For to sacrifice what is human*
> *Is to turn man to animal*
> *And mind to madness.*
> *Should you choose to pay the price,*
> *Here is the riddle:*

The rest of the reply is almost the same, though there is no stipulation on how many times Lila should attempt enacting her wish so as not to tempt fate:

> *White for a pure heart,*
> *Red for a blooding,*
> *Black for a faceless night,*
> *A kiss for a sacrifice.*

> *Beware enacting your wish,*
> *Lest your efforts tempt fate,*

And mind turns to madness
And love becomes cursed.

But do not despair,
For the tasks done right by another
Will undo the enchantment
And reverse the spell.

I'm thrown back into the sky in a bird's-eye view as the forest awaits what I want to be shown next. *Lila making her potion*, I think.

I remain stagnant in the sky.

I channel the thought again. Still nothing. I think through similar memories that perhaps don't involve a potion:

Show me Lila bewitching men.

Show me Lila performing rituals.

Show me other men falling in love with Lila.

Nothing elicits a memory I was shown before. Did they ever happen? I change tack.

Show me key moments on the night Bren Zimmer died that led to his murder and the curse.

Considering how events I've seen haven't always lined up correctly in visions, I add:

And show me them in order.

I'm taken to the meadow pavilion. Lila comes with her basket and a bottle of wine. Just like before, she distracts the night watchmen and tears out a page from *Sortes Fortunae*. The Grimm wolf prowls nearby, although her eyes are brown and she doesn't attack the watchmen.

I'm whisked away to a new location, now in the forest on Solace Trail and headed toward the village. Kellen travels alone, a smile on his face, the pocket watch in hand. Like before, he's awestruck when he notices the comet, the bad omen. He tucks away the pocket watch.

Now I'm closer to the trailhead, where Bren approaches from the village. His eyes are glazed over like the Sommer girls when they were drawn to the forest during the autumn festival. The only difference is Bren is following a sound . . . music. Pipe music. The song is the same one I've heard so many times in visions, whether whistled or played or sung.

Another man stalks Bren, not taking any pains to be quiet. It's Rudger, clearly drunk and unable to walk a steady course. Once Bren reaches the linden tree by the stream, Rudger catches up and shoves him in the back. The pipe music silences. Bren snaps from his stupor, and he and Rudger exchange heated words about Fiora and her children.

Rudger throws a punch that splits Bren's lip, but he quickly strikes back and gains the upper hand, landing more hits and eventually drawing a knife.

Kellen bursts onto the scene, not understanding the context of the fight, only that his brother is in danger. He joins the scuffle and loses his pocket watch.

At a critical point, when Bren and Rudger wrestle over possession of the knife, Kellen takes Bren in a chokehold. Bren's face purples, and a vein throbs on his forehead. His eyes lose focus. He won't make it much longer.

I watch in horror, thinking of Axel. *Don't kill him, Kellen!*

Emerging from the woods, the violet-eyed Grimm wolf bounds toward the men.

Bren finds a surge of strength and shoves Kellen, at the same time jumping and slamming his feet into Rudger's stomach. As Rudger buckles, his arms flying forward, Kellen and Bren fall back into the stream, and Bren seizes hold of the knife. He and

Kellen crash on the ground, and the momentum sinks the blade into Kellen's torso.

Bren rolls off him and gasps, seeing what he's accidentally done.

The wolf reaches the men, but there's no more fight to break up.

"Kellen!" Rudger howls, hurrying over to his brother. Kellen's eyes are wide with shock. Blood swirls like ribbons from his wound into the night-darkened water.

The wolf snaps her jaws at Bren. He startles, drags his hands through his hair, looking at Kellen, and rushes away. The wolf pounces after him, but soon pivots off the trail to Grandmère's prostrate body in the woods. She sits up, taking possession of herself, and the wolf's eyes shift to brown.

Grandmère pursues Bren and accuses him of harming my missing father. When Bren denies it, she says, "Do you expect me to believe that after I saw what you did tonight?"

A spasm cuts through Bren's brow, and he tosses a worried glance in the direction of the linden tree. But he won't be baited to talk about it. "I swear I don't know what happened to Finn."

"Don't lie when you've threatened me before!"

"*You*, Marlène. I threatened *you*. I wouldn't harm your family. That's your way of doing things."

Grandmère explains she wasn't in the wolf's body when it almost attacked Fiora's children, but Bren won't listen. "Keep the wolf away from the Winther orchards. If I see it there again, maybe I *will* come after you Thurns."

As he storms off, Grandmère calls after him to bargain for his silence.

Bren spits blood before answering wearily, "Ask me another night, Marlène. I've had enough of this one."

I'm swept to another place in the forest, a little ways off of Solace Trail. It's a spot I saw in the days before the curse, marked by a seven-foot boulder that's eroded to appear like it's balancing on a narrow base. I included it on my map and named it "Tilting Rock."

Rudger carries Kellen there, and Kellen groans as Rudger lays him on the ground. "We should be safe here for now." Rudger wipes his nose on his sleeve. "Don't worry, brother. You're going to be fine."

Kellen's forehead glistens with sweat, and he cracks a shaky grin. "Then why can't you stop crying?"

Rudger breaks into full sobs. "Why did you have to return on tonight of all nights?"

"Lucky for you, I did."

"But not lucky for you."

"Axel . . ." Kellen wheezes. "Is my son well?"

Rudger sobers, looking guilty, and answers with a small nod.

"I have a . . . pocket watch." With a trembling hand, Kellen motions to his jacket.

Rudger checks Kellen's inner pockets. "There's nothing here."

"I must have lost it . . . by the stream. Go back."

"I'll find it." Rudger starts to rise.

"Wait." Kellen grips his arm. "It's a gift . . . for Axel. Promise me, brother . . ."

Kellen's hand falls away. His eyes go glassy, vacant.

Grief surges inside me, threatening to wake me from the vision.

Axel guessed right. His father is dead.

I'm taken to a hill in the distance, where the violet-eyed Grimm wolf has watched a man die, though Grandmère must have not realized who Kellen was, likely having mistaken him for a traveler. Nevertheless, she lifts her head and releases a mournful howl.

The vision shifts. I'm brought back to the stream near the linden tree. I hear pipe music playing Harlan's signature song, though he must be hiding, because the only person I see is Lila.

She wears her mask with painted swirls of white, black, and red, and the hood of her deep blue cloak covers her hair. Bren Zimmer returns to the stream, his eyes glazed over again. Another luring spell is drawing him back, and I suspect it's emanating from Harlan's pipe.

"Come, my dear." Lila extends her hand.

"Fiora?" Bren speaks in a monotone voice. "Is that you, my love?"

Lila blinks twice, taken off guard, but quickly composes herself. "Yes, it's your loving Fiora who wishes to give you a kiss."

A faint grin appears on Bren's otherwise placid face. He shuffles near until the toes of his boots brush her fine slippers.

Harlan pockets his pipe, darts out from the trees, and snatches Rudger's bloody knife from the ground, even though his own knife hangs from his belt. Turning Rudger's knife over, Harlan spies two tiny carved initials, *R.F.*, on the base of the hilt. He smiles and creeps closer to Bren.

A terrible heaviness bears down on me. *Harlan, don't do this.*

Bren pulls back a step as the spell starts fading. "Is that really you, Fiora?"

"Now!" Harlan commands.

Lila grabs Bren by the shoulders. Plants her lips on his mouth. Harlan races over. Stabs Bren in the back. His eyes fly wide. He gurgles and gasps.

Lila screams. Bren coughs up blood. It sprays in her face and down the front of her dress. He plummets to the ground.

Lila drops to her knees. Shakes his body. He doesn't revive. She whirls on Harlan. "What have you done?"

"What was necessary," he says with unnerving calm. "This is why the deer blood didn't work last time. The blooding must be human blood—a human sacrifice."

He reaches for her as if to hold her, but she jerks away. "I never agreed to this! And it *wasn't* necessary! I tore out the page for you. You promised it would give you the power you needed if we didn't succeed this time."

"All that page does is answer questions. It doesn't have power to grant wishes."

"You never gave it a chance!"

"I did, Lila. I made a second wish on it tonight. I wished for limitless magic at any cost, hoping we'd be given clearer tasks. But all it replied with was what it already told you—beware the cost of limitless power and how it leads to limitless corruption."

"Then you should have listened!" Lila swipes away angry tears.

"I did this for us, our dream." Harlan's brows pull inward. "Even if the page *could* answer wishes, we don't want to be stuck deciphering riddles every time we want something. We're entitled to more than that, more than all we've been denied in this pitiful village. This forest once had a *castle*. There was a king, a queen. I'm sure I descend from them. I'm taking back what's rightfully mine, and I want you to share it with me."

He comes closer and brushes away her tears, even as she squeezes her eyes shut, repulsed by him. I feel the same disgust. He's deceived us all.

"Think of the kingdom you and I will create together—rule together." His smile broadens. "That is *true* power. No more farming, slaughtering pigs, milling grain . . . at least not by us. My mother deserved more than that, and I do too. *You* do. You'll be beloved by all your subjects." He smooths back a wisp of her black curls. "How could anyone not worship you?"

"Stop!" Lila pushes him away. "I don't want any part of your dream. Not anymore." She scrubs the blood on her dress. "You don't even know if we succeeded. I certainly don't feel powerful, and you look like the same sorry boy you've always been."

Harlan's jaw muscle flinches, but he laughs, confident. "Then I'll prove our power. What should I do with it?"

"Reverse time so none of this ever happened," Lila quips scathingly.

"How about I do the next best thing?" He raises his arms at his sides and draws a deep breath. In a booming voice, he shouts, "I command this forest to swallow up Bren's body and hide it forever!"

Despite her doubt, Lila turns expectant eyes on Bren. One moment passes. Then another. The earth doesn't shake or split open.

The forest doesn't stir at all.

Harlan's nostrils flare. He rolls out one shoulder. Nods to himself. "I see. We're supposed to call on the power together. You wished to *share* limitless magic with me, so we need to speak the command as one."

Half-heartedly, Lila repeats the words with him. Still, the forest doesn't comply.

Harlan curses.

Lila wrings her hands, breaking into more tears. "We've done something terrible! And it was all for nothing!"

Harlan wipes the perspiration off his brow and sets his jaw. He pulls Bren's body into the stream and leaves Rudger's knife in his back. "It's going to be fine," he assures Lila. "We'll try again. I promise we'll get it right."

"No, I'm done! Done with you too!" Lila yanks his pipe away and hurls it into the stream.

Harlan shoots her a deadly glare. He moves to retrieve the pipe, but something rustles, and he freezes. He hurries to Lila and clamps a hand over her mouth. "Someone is coming," he hisses, and then ushers her away.

Rudger appears, his eyes swollen from crying and his head downcast. He finds the pocket watch and picks it up before noticing Bren's body in the stream. He balks as he staggers closer and spies the knife. *His knife.*

From where she must have followed Rudger, the violet-eyed Grimm wolf watches from the tree line. Faint footsteps draw near. The wolf's ears perk. People are coming.

She barks at Rudger. He jumps and dashes away, unaware she's done him a favor by warning him.

The Grimm wolf bolts in a different direction as four men approach, one of them Herr Oswald.

"Did you hear that?" whispers a man with a scraggly beard. "I told you I saw the Grimm wolf heading this way."

"We'll hunt it down once and for all," Herr Oswald replies. But he doesn't continue down the trail. His gaze is drawn to the stream, and he gasps. "Is that Finn?"

He rushes over and lifts the body. "It's . . . Bren Zimmer." Shocked, he drops him and looks back to the other men. "Get help."

"Help?" The scraggly-bearded man frowns.

"Yes, help!" Herr Oswald yells, growing panicked. "The coroner, the undertaker, the rest of the council! We have to find out who did this!"

The others dash away, forgoing their hunt for the wolf.

Alone, Herr Oswald drifts closer to examine the knife, and his eye catches on something floating in the water. He picks it up. A double-reed pipe. "Harlan," he whispers, paling. He stuffs the pipe in his jacket and hurries away.

The vision shifts and blurs, but I'm not taken to a new place.

All that's changed is the arrangement of clouds in the night sky. A little time has passed.

Rudger returns to the now-abandoned stream. With a grimace, he pulls his knife from Bren's body and races off into the woods.

I'm thrown back into the sky like a bird overlooking the forest again.

I've seen enough, I tell it.

Blackness cloaks my eyes. Silence shrouds my ears. I gasp as I lurch back to the present.

Axel holds me steady. "Are you all right?"

I nod and tell him everything.

CHAPTER 53

My crooked back aches from how long I hold Axel, how tightly I wrap my arms around him. But my pain doesn't hold a candle to his. I would bear it endlessly if that could take it away. I know the heartache of losing a parent, but what he's going through is worse. It isn't fair. It's as if his father has died twice now. No one should have to endure that, especially him.

My neck is wet from his tears. Telling him his father died was the hardest part I had to share from the vision. Harlan being the murderer was a blow, as Axel had begun to trust him too, but it's nothing compared to this.

"I'm so sorry." I kiss the crown of his head. "I wish I'd never had the vision that made you believe your father was alive."

"I'm not sorry." His breath warms my collarbone. "I'd rather know how he lived the rest of his life than wonder. It's a gift to know he remembered me before the end."

I pull Axel's face up in my hands and press my lips to his.

"What about your father?" He rests his forehead against mine. "Do you think Lila was still involved in his death?"

I nod, swallowing hard. "Some of my past visions of her must be true, though I'm sure Harlan was her accomplice. From how she reacted when Bren died, I think my father's death was truly an accident."

Axel draws a long breath. "So what are we going to do about Harlan?"

I have no idea. "If we turn him in to the council, I'm not sure they'll believe us, not with his father as the chairman. At the autumn festival, Herr Oswald lied when he said Harlan was home with him the night Bren was murdered." I glance above the grassy slope to Grandmère's bedroom window. Herr Oswald's shadow still paces within.

"Maybe he's here out of guilt," Axel says. "The curse fell because of his son. It's why you're gone from home and can't be with your grandmother as she's dying."

My teeth set on edge. "Herr Oswald should be the one to confess his son's crime to the council."

One corner of Axel's mouth lifts with a sad smile. "As we've learned, it's not easy to admit those you love might have done something treacherous. But Harlan *will* have to face justice somehow."

"At least he won't be difficult to apprehend, between us and our friends. He never gained the limitless magic he longed for. Thankfully, the clause in Lila's riddle worked against him."

"The clause that turned him into a frog?"

"And sent Lila into madness."

"But Harlan isn't a frog anymore." Axel scratches the stubble on his jaw. "And he and Lila *did* succeed, as far as accomplishing the riddle's tasks."

I think over them:

White for a pure heart,
Red for a blooding,
Black for a faceless night,
A kiss for a sacrifice.

"The pure heart must have been Bren's," I reply. "He wasn't a perfect man, but he was a good man. He cared for Fiora and tried to protect her children."

Axel concedes with a begrudging nod. Regarding the blacksmith in a kind light must be hard for him, as Bren was ultimately responsible for Axel's father's death.

"The blooding was also from Bren," I go on. "He served as the sacrifice *and* the person Lila kissed. All those things happened on the night he was killed, except it wasn't on a new moon. At the time, Harlan and Lila believed 'black for a faceless night' meant she should wear a mask. The riddle wasn't fulfilled until five months later, when he turned into a frog and she went mad."

"On a new moon?" Axel asks.

"Yes, but it wouldn't have been the first new moon."

"So what was different about the final one?"

I think back to one of my visions of Harlan—a memory months after the curse fell. Lila was with him in his house. I didn't hear the words they exchanged, but she was weeping, and when he tried to comfort her, she lashed out at him. He endured it patiently and worked his way up to holding her and even kissing her. She melted against him for a moment, but then slapped him and ran outside.

I share the vision with Axel. "Harlan made me believe Lila was becoming irrationally jealous. I thought that's why she was upset. Now I know it was because she wasn't over him murdering Bren."

"Was that night on a new moon?"

"No . . . but the new moon must have come soon afterward."

"When it did, that's when her kiss turned him into a frog?"

I nod as my pulse jumps with another realization. "*Harlan* was the kiss for a sacrifice, not Bren. When Lila kissed him on the new moon, after completing the other tasks, she unknowingly finished enacting her wish."

Axel's mouth twists bitterly. "The same wish that *Sortes Fortunae* warned her would come with a price."

"To turn man to animal and mind to madness," I say, quoting part of the riddle's first stanza.

Axel tenses. "Clara, if Lila has completed all her tasks, what's preventing her from sharing limitless magic with Harlan? He's no longer an animal. She's still mad, but—"

"She won't be when the curse breaks." Cold sweat flashes up the back of my neck. "But we have the missing page. Henni can't break the curse without first restoring it to the book."

"Then we have to make sure that doesn't happen."

I spring to my feet. "We need to warn Henni."

Axel rises with me. "Do you think Harlan and Lila decided to go back to the tree house?"

"Let's hope not." I throw my cape around my shoulders, and Axel flings on his scarf. I look back to my cottage and the candle burning in the window. I check the pocket watch. The hour hand still fluctuates between *XII* and *I*.

Please wait for me, Grandmère.

No matter how difficult it is to leave her right now, I know she'd want me to.

I need to fulfill the fate she foretold.

Though I don't know if that means I should break the curse or make it final.

CHAPTER 54

Axel and I race for the tree house, taking a route in the forest that doesn't pass the hedgerow where we were supposed to meet Harlan and Lila. Just past the ash-lined border, over a hundred ghosts stand waiting for me. My nerves sting. What will they do if the curse isn't broken?

I rush past them—through them—and bolt for my destination. Several minutes later, Axel and I reach the tree house built in a maple tree. Henni and the others are already there. They've hung lanterns from the branches, illuminating the area with an amber haze that blends into the puffs of rising fog.

Henni takes one look at me and sees something is wrong. She hurries to meet us a few yards from the maple, and I blurt, "Harlan. Have you seen him?"

"I thought he and Lila were coming with you."

"I'm sure they'll be here soon. Do you have the book?"

"Yes. Fiora and Ella managed to—"

"Where is it?"

"Ella has it in a basket." Henni looks over her shoulder at her sister, who stands below the tree house, the basket at her feet.

Axel and I share a glance, and he rushes over to her. Nearby, Hansel and Gretel climb the ladder boards nailed to the maple's trunk, and Fiora pulls them down, saying, "It isn't safe up there. The wood is rotting."

Worry lines slice between Henni's slender brows. "What's going on, Clara?"

"We need to leave at once and return the book to the night watchmen. It's safer with them."

"What? Why?"

I yank her arm. "Henni, just come!"

"What about the missing page?"

I glance at the ghosts and think of my cursed village, all its starving and weary people. I'll have to face the consequences of what I'm about to do. I pull the folded page from my pocket. "I have to destroy it."

Henni's eyes pop wide. "Clara, no!"

I push past her and beeline for the nearest lantern.

"But we have the book *and* the page!" She sprints after me. "I could break the curse right now!"

I reach the maple. The lantern hangs above me. Henni tugs at my arm, but I shake her off. "I have to do this! Harlan murdered Bren!"

Everyone hushes. Ella freezes. Hansel and Gretel stare at me with huge eyes. Fiora looks like she could murder someone herself.

"I promise to explain more, but for now just know that if the curse breaks, Harlan will have unbridled magic. I can't allow that to happen."

I open the lantern's glass pane. Bring the folded page to the burning candle. Before its flame can lick the paper, a sharp blade presses against my throat.

"I wouldn't do that, Clara." Harlan's hot breath falls on my ear. He must have been hiding behind the trunk.

Axel reaches for the hatchet on his back.

"Careful, friend," Harlan says. "Your girl has only one pretty neck."

Axel's face goes ashen.

"Go ahead and throw that ax far behind you."

Stiffly, Axel does as he says. Harlan uses his free hand to ease mine down from the lantern. My body shakes from how badly I want to turn his dagger on him. But I have no clever moves. I'm at his mercy. "Where's Lila?" I bite out.

"Missing her already?" He pushes me farther away from the lantern, careful to keep me under his blade.

"I hope she's run off, never to return. You're nothing without her. Just a fool who plays a pipe that messes with people's heads."

Harlan chuckles. "I was wondering when you'd catch on. Should we count how many visions it took you? Though, to be clear, it's the song that has power, not the pipe. I learned that little fact once I no longer had a human mouth to play it. Turns out I could still send the tune through dreams to 'mess with people's heads.'"

"An ability that came from your one wish, no doubt. How else would someone like you have magic?"

Harlan laughs again, though it's lost a measure of its cool. "We're not all seers and changers of fate, Clara. But at least I have noble blood in my veins. I deserve power, and I have the cunning to take it."

"But the power to manipulate wasn't enough for you," I plow on, desperate to keep him talking, to do anything to stall him while I try to think my way out of this. All my friends are frozen, afraid to move for fear that Harlan will slit my throat, and the horde of ghosts surrounding us aren't helping either, only watching with hollow-eyed stares. "You needed limitless magic, and since you wasted your one wish, you turned to Lila to use hers."

"You're quick to criticize when you would claim more power in an instant. Think of what it could do for you. Heal your grandmother, for one thing."

My blood burns, and I thrash against him. "Don't you dare speak of her! You're a monster! You have no intention of using your power to help anyone except yourself!"

He scoffs, bringing his dagger closer to my neck. "Is that all it takes to be a monster?"

"You're corrupted and animalistic, like the Book of Fortunes warned Lila. To ask for magic at any cost is to have murder in your heart. And you did *more* than commit murder. You used innocent people. How many girls did you lure into the forest with your song, hoping they could break your spell?" It occurs to me that's what happened with most of the Sommer girls. "How many of them died after they became Lost? You may as well have killed them too."

Ella's mouth drops open. "I heard that song as well." Her gaze thins on Harlan. "You had the nerve to lure me away on the night before my wedding."

He *tsk*s. "A wedding that had already been called off."

"But you didn't know that." She stalks nearer, and Axel clutches her arm to hold her back. "You really are a monster."

Harlan sucks in a deep breath, releasing it with a dramatic sigh. "As much as this conversation has been a sheer delight, I'm afraid I need to get back to the matter at hand. Or, rather, we do, Henni."

Henni, who has been standing only five feet away, gulps hard. "P-pardon?"

"You know what your job is. You're the only one in Grimm's Hollow who can make a wish." The ghosts inch closer.

She twists her trembling fingers. "But I need a proper wish ceremony."

"No, you don't. All of that is pomp and formality. Clara has the page, and somewhere here must be the book. I bet Gretel can tell me where it is."

Fiora gasps, pulling Gretel to her side. "Leave the children out of this!"

Harlan snickers, too soft for the others to hear, but it seeps in my ear like poison. "Gretel, do you love your brother?"

She frowns, but nods slowly.

"I'll tell you what, then. I'll let Hansel live if you show me where the book is—the special book your mother and her friends stole tonight."

"Don't you dare threaten Hansel!" Fiora chokes out, shoving her son behind her.

"Stealing is bad." Harlan smoothly talks over Fiora. "Just like you said to Hansel the other night. But *you* don't have to be bad, Gretel. You can help me."

Gretel's eyes narrow in such a vicious way I'm reminded of how terrifying she was as a Lost One. "But *you* are a bad man. You want to cut Clara's throat."

Harlan's shoulder shrugs behind mine. "I can't save everyone tonight. But for you, I will save Hansel." His voice lowers to a growl. "Show me where the book is."

"Gretel, don't—" Fiora says, but it's too late. Gretel points to Ella's basket.

Harlan scoffs. "Not a very clever hiding place."

"I didn't think we'd need one," Ella spits.

He stands straighter, pressing my back taut to his chest. "Bring the book to Henni," he commands Ella.

She hesitates. Harlan's dagger slices my skin. I hiss as hot blood rolls down my neck.

"Ella," Axel warns.

She curses under her breath and gives the basket to her sister, setting it on the grass by her feet.

"Now, Henni, get the page from Clara," Harlan instructs.

Henni's eyes water. She advances one small step, then another. My heart stampedes. I can't let her take the page. I can't let Harlan get away with this.

I could drive my elbow into his gut and break free. Or would he only kill me faster?

Henni takes a third step. Tears splash down her cheeks.

But would Harlan really kill me? Why did he stay with me after I broke his frog spell?

He didn't really need me to find the missing page. He already knew where it was; he put the vision in my head that spelled out the place. He probably put a vision in Lila's head to hide it there. He didn't need me to persuade Jack either. He could have waited for one of his loops to tunnel a beanstalk to the caverns.

But Harlan kept me with him on the journey, even when he could have run off with Lila and returned as a hero to Grimm's Hollow, with the means to make the Book of Fortunes whole again. Henni wouldn't have had any qualms about making her one wish and breaking the curse.

She takes a fourth step.

Be my Changer of Fate, Clara, Harlan once told me. To him, I'm the girl who beat death, my own personal curse. The girl who elicited a reply from the torn-out page when he couldn't. The girl who broke *his* personal curse and changed him back into a human.

I've told him about the cards Grandmère drew, which foretold I will break the curse or make it final. He must believe I'm truly necessary to breaking it.

Now he needs me to unleash his greater power. Though I don't know what he expects me to do. Henni is the person who has to make the one wish. All I can trust is that he'll keep me alive until he's certain the curse is broken.

Henni reaches me. More tears stream down her face. "Sorry, Clara," she croaks, and lifts her open hand.

Adrenaline chases through my veins. I steel my nerves and unfold the page, as if readying it for her.

"Pass it over," Harlan snaps.

I don't. I rapidly tear the page into scraps and toss them in his face. The ghosts screech and howl.

"No!" Harlan grabs for the pieces. His dagger loosens from my neck. I tear free and run. Henni and Ella turn tail with me. Ella snatches the basket.

Axel springs for his weapon. It's closer than Harlan is. Fiora shoves Hansel and Gretel into the tree house. It's rickety, but it has four defensive walls.

Harlan's dagger flies past me. I flinch, but I wasn't the target. It sails toward Axel's back. I shout his name, but the blade pinwheels too fast.

Thud. He cries out as it sinks into his left shoulder blade.

I race to him. He's fallen to his knees. "I'm fine," he grinds out. "Stop him." He passes me the hatchet.

My pulse roars in my ears—do I really have the stomach to kill him?—but I take the weapon and wheel for Harlan. The ghosts leer at me. The soldiers among them look eager.

Harlan stands under a lantern. Warm light pools around him. The scraps of the page lie scattered at his feet. He isn't scrambling to pick them up like I expected.

He eyes me and the hatchet. Grins. Pulls something from his pocket. His double-reed pipe. "I wouldn't throw that, Clara. You're not practiced. If your aim isn't true, you might strike someone you'll regret."

What is he talking about? "All my friends are behind me."

"Are they?" He draws the pipe to his mouth and plays his manipulating song.

A few yards past him, on the fringe of our lantern light and the darkness, little figures in linen nightgowns emerge from behind the trees and walk through the ghosts.

My breath catches. They're children. Village children.

Four boys and two girls. Six altogether.

Six.

An unlucky number.

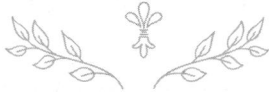

CHAPTER 55

Swayed by madness, Lila walks behind the children, herding them like a shepherdess, though I doubt that's necessary. The music lures them inexorably, their eyes transfixed but focused on nothing, their steps sure-footed but stiff like clockwork dolls'.

I can barely speak, I'm so horrified with Harlan. He premeditated this. He brought the children in advance in case he needed to force a terrible ultimatum. "Do you have no conscience? Even for you, this is unthinkable. Let them go!"

Coolly, he pulls the pipe from his mouth. "You know I won't."

The children remain entranced as they surround him. He must still be channeling his song to their minds.

I stand with my legs planted wide, my hatchet raised, though my bones feel ready to crumble. "What do you mean to do with them?" I demand. Lila holds no weapon, Harlan has lost his dagger, and none of the children are armed. One of the girls holds a rag doll by its limp hand.

"The options are limitless." Harlan pockets his pipe. "I could march them into the deep end of a stream, send them off a cliff, make them travel endlessly through the forest until they starve and perish. Their fate is in your hands, Clara."

"Or I could just kill you and end their spell. I might be better with this hatchet than you think."

Harlan's mouth quirks. "Even if we pretend that's true, killing me won't have the result you desire. It will trap the children in this state forever, even if the curse is broken."

I glance behind me at my friends, searching their faces for confirmation that Harlan isn't bluffing.

No one affirms or refutes it. Axel has removed the dagger piercing his shoulder, but also halts to attack. Henni and Ella only stare at me, speechless, their arms wrapped around each other. And Fiora stands like a watchdog under the tree house, hiding her children.

"I'll tell you what needs to happen," Harlan goes on calmly. "You'll put all the pieces of this page back into the Book of Fortunes and hope, for the children's sake, the book allows Henni to make her one wish."

Sick to my stomach, I set down the hatchet and cross to Harlan, kneeling to pick up the scraps. He kicks one I miss, and I bite my tongue and collect it with the others. The ghosts watch me with taunting sneers.

At Harlan's command, Ella brings the book and sets it on the ground. I stare at the cover, a wooden plate engraved with SORTES FORTUNAE and carved with trees and a border of red rampion. According to legend, the forest made the book and gave it to the villagers of Grimm's Hollow, who once lived so peaceably here.

I flip through the parchment leaves until I find the spot where Lila tore out the missing page. I hesitate, unsure if I should haphazardly set the scraps inside and close the book. Somehow, that seems disrespectful.

Sortes Fortunae is a sacred tome. Countless villagers poured their hearts out to it, including my parents and grandmother. Axel did too, wishing he could bring back his father from the dead. And while he couldn't save him, the book gave him the tasks that ended up saving me.

I carefully puzzle the scraps back together. Once I finish, delicate roots snake out from the binding and thread them as one again.

Awed by the book's ability to heal, I smile, but it falls the instant I spy Harlan's smug expression. "Stand back, Clara. Give Henni space."

Fists clenched, I retreat and Henni scuttles forward, wiping tears on her sleeve.

"If it helps, pretend you're in the meadow pavilion and this is your wish ceremony," Harlan says, like a kind brother instead of a heartless killer.

Henni spears him with a glare, but then her attention drifts to the village children, barefoot in their nightclothes, and she sniffles, kneeling before the book. "No one can hear me make my one wish, or *Sortes Fortunae* will reverse it."

Harlan crosses his arms. "I trust you can whisper softly enough."

Standing beside the little boys and girls, Lila swishes the skirt of her ragged dress. "When can they join me in the circle dance?"

"Soon, my love." Harlan spares her a tight smile.

Henni bends over the book and cups her shaking hands to her mouth to whisper. To her credit, I can't make out a word. She opens the book to the page that was sewn back in.

I creep forward. Harlan does the same. Even the ghosts encroach. Everyone wants to see what the book will write.

Leaf-green words scrawl over the page, but I'm not close enough to read them. Harlan must not be either, because he squints and frowns.

Henni shuts the book quickly, like she's frightened to touch it any longer. She looks up at Harlan, posture rigid. "I've been given my task."

"Which is?"

She mashes her lips together, delaying a moment. "To plant three red rampion seeds in the soil of Grimm's Hollow."

Relief courses through me. That means the curse might not break for several more weeks or months. Red rampion is rare.

"Ah," Harlan says with a small nod. "I can help you, then."

He reaches into his pocket and withdraws a tiny envelope. He doesn't seriously have red rampion seeds with him, does he?

"Remember the night we kissed, Clara? Red rampion was growing nearby, and in one of your sleepwalking spells, you crushed the petals and spread the juice on your lips." He lifts a shoulder. "I may have persuaded you to do that through my song." I realize why. He needed me to believe Lila's riddle meant "red for rampion-stained lips," and not "red for a blooding." "Anyway, I saved some of the seeds. I recalled what you said about red rampion being the seed of all magic. I thought they might come in handy."

I curse myself for ever trusting him with those words—*any* words or kisses or heartfelt confessions. "I wish you were still a wretched frog," I spit.

Harlan smirks and rocks forward to the balls of his feet. "Henni, let's go plant some seeds." Glancing at the rest of us, he adds, "It's best we all stick together, don't you think? For the sake of the children." He raps on the boards of the tree house. "You too, Hansel and Gretel. You're much too crafty to leave here on your own." He cocks a half grin at Fiora. "A trait of their father's, I'm sure, may his soul rest in the forest."

Fiora's body shakes with barely contained rage.

"Oh, and the hatchet and dagger, as well as any other sharp implements, will stay behind," he instructs us. Withdrawing his pipe, he casts a warm gaze at the boys and girls. "Come, children. Another adventure awaits."

He starts playing the tune, and Lila and the children take the path to the village, while the rest of us shuffle behind.

As fog rolls over the wild grass and ghosts emerge from their haunts to join us, Lila sways and twirls, singing along to the music:

"Come, my darlings,
Be you blackbirds or starlings,
Come, leave your nest for the night.
The primrose is blooming,
The evening is looming,
Come, take a wondrous flight."

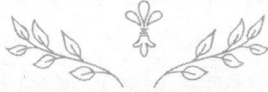

CHAPTER 56

We travel back to my sheep farm. Harlan must prefer its isolation. He wouldn't want to go to the meadow pavilion, where there are night watchmen, or anyone else's farm, whose number of inhabitants is unknown.

I hang back with Axel. He walks stiffly from the pain in his shoulder. It keeps bleeding and needs to be wrapped. I reach to tear a strip of fabric from the hem of my chemise, but Harlan shakes his head. "Keep your hands where I can see them."

"I don't sheathe hidden knives."

He ignores me and focuses on Henni, staying close beside her.

We pass the stream by the hedgerow, the twig-woven fence, and the ash-lined border, several yards into the north sheep pasture. We've reached the boundary of Grimm's Hollow.

Lila, who has been whimpering as we near the sheep, flinches and digs her hands at her scalp. Harlan wrestles to keep her from bolting. The children halt behind her, and the horde of ghosts takes vigil beyond the ash line.

"Henni, it's time," Harlan grunts, jostling as Lila thrashes harder. He pulls the envelope from his pocket and tosses it at her.

Henni picks it up and exchanges a nervous glance with me. I breathe tensely. Once she plants those seeds, the curse will break, and Harlan won't need me alive—or anyone else he's threatening.

She sets down the basket with the Book of Fortunes, kneels in the pasture, and starts scooping up dirt with her hands.

Think, Clara.

This is my land. What can I use to my advantage?

The cottage and barn, with everything in them, are too far away. A few sorry-looking haystacks dot the land, wilting and molding from the curse. Perhaps there's a scythe or a rake propped against one.

Henni scatters three seeds in the hole she's dug.

Axel and I move closer together. Fiora, Ella, and Hansel and Gretel pull into their own tight group.

Henni fills the hole with dirt and scampers back like she's lit a fuse.

My heart thunders. The task is done.

Harlan watches the soil feverishly.

Several seconds pass. Harlan's eyelid twitches. He shifts from leg to leg. Shoots a lethal gaze at Henni.

She blanches. "I did what I was supposed to do."

He reaches for his pipe. Just as his hand brushes its end, the ground starts to shake. The spot where Henni planted the rampion churns like a bubbling fountain of dirt. Green sprouts spring upward, quickly growing into leafy stems that blossom with clusters of tiny red flowers.

As the earth froths and quakes, the pasture grass changes color. It ripples outward from the rampion and across the rolling fields. The trees leaf out again. The evergreens pick up fallen needles. The ditches fill with spring water, and a nearby well sloshes as it brims.

For a moment, my chest is fit to burst with happiness. The sheep will thrive again, the hay will be sweet, and food will grow plentifully. But then my heart sinks. This gift has come at the cost of Harlan obtaining great magic. And he's done terrible things for it.

His eyes are wide with triumph. His smile is sickening. He

laughs to himself, watching the magic unfold, and turns to Lila, who has stopped shrieking and thrashing. She presses her hands to her chest like it's the only thing grounding her to reality.

"We've done it." He gazes at her with nauseating adoration. I don't believe his affection for one minute. He's a master manipulator, a great actor, and a deadly killer. Lila is merely a tool, the tether to their magic. He only gets it by sharing it with her.

"I don't understand." She shrinks back as the children also break from their spells. Two of them bolt across the pasture, running for the village road. Others scatter in different directions. The little girl with the rag doll starts crying. Fiora beckons to her and the others. Lila watches everything with growing understanding and horror.

She looks to the forest, clutching her wild and matted hair. "M-my sisters and cousins and friends . . . I think I left them back there somewhere."

"Don't worry, I'll help you find them." Harlan strokes her face. "But we'll have to use our magic together to do that."

As he murmurs of his love and what they can accomplish together, Axel pulls on my arm. "We need to go."

"There's nowhere to hide," I hiss. "Not quickly enough." I motion to Henni, and she hurries over.

"I'll be right back." Axel dashes away.

My gaze strays behind the line of ashes. "The ghosts are still here," I whisper to Henni. Their expressions twist in mounting rage; their souls still haven't been freed. "I don't think the curse has fully broken. Maybe Harlan and Lila don't have magic yet either. Did the book really only give you one task?"

"Mm-hmm," Henni squeaks.

I give her a pointed look. "Please, Henni."

She bites her quivering lip. "What it wrote is terrible."

"I understand." I was also given terrible tasks when I made my one wish.

She squeezes her eyes shut and blurts, "The book said the curse would break in stages, and for it to fully break, the Grimm wolf and your grandmother have to die."

My body jolts, and I stagger back. "What?" That's cruel—and horribly unfair. The reverence I feel for *Sortes Fortunae* vanishes.

"I'm sorry," Henni blubbers. "It had to do with fulfilling some promise made long ago."

The ground starts to shake once more. I look to the pasture, expecting the land to change again in some small way—maybe shoot up wildflowers or sprout a fruit tree—so I'm not prepared when a row of giant beanstalks bursts from the earth and tangles together to form a massive wall.

The sheep race away as more beanstalks launch into the sky, knitting into side walls and extending high above into towers.

This is a castle. A fortress.

It rises like a sentinel between us and my cottage. I whirl to scan the ghosts for Jack. He must be here. But how is he doing this? He works by triggering loops of past actions. But he never made a beanstalk castle before. Not on the Thurn farm.

Jack is nowhere in sight. I'm baffled until I spy Harlan and Lila holding hands and staring up at the castle together.

My heart rocks in my chest. They did this.

The curse might not be fully broken, but it broke enough for them to obtain power.

CHAPTER 57

"The castle should have flowers," Lila murmurs to Harlan.

He grins. "Then let's have flowers."

Hands held, they focus on the castle. Apparently no words of command or theatrics are required, for flowering vines spring from the earth and weave among the beanstalks. . . .

Purple wisteria. Blue morning glory. Yellow honeysuckle. Orange trumpet vine.

I note there is no white, red, or black. Lila must be over her obsession with those colors.

She laughs, gazing at the castle. Harlan kisses her cheek. "This is just the beginning," he promises.

"What are you doing?" I demand. Henni gives me a warning tug. "This is the Thurn farm! Take that down!" It's a foolish request, given their magic. I don't have any leverage over them. But I'm too furious to keep my mouth shut. My mother is dead because of the curse they wrought. My father died at their attempts to gain power. I won't let them take anything more from my family.

"I'm sorry." Lila flushes scarlet. "Tell me your name again?"

It stings that she doesn't remember me, even from her village days. "Clara Thurn."

"She's been working against us, Lila." Harlan grimaces as if I'm a fly buzzing around their dinner plate. "You may not remember, but she tried to strangle you."

My mouth drops open. "That's not—"

"We can't let her live." He talks over me. "She'll always be a threat."

Lila's shoulders curl inward. "But you promised no one else would have to die."

"This is self-defense. These people want to hurt us."

"That isn't true," Henni cries, but Fiora, for one, looks positively murderous. I turn around for Axel, but can't find him anywhere.

"They don't believe in the greatness of the forest," Harlan says. "They would quash us to live like peasants in Grimm's Hollow, to die inconsequential deaths after working ourselves to the bone, just like my mother. But this land wants more from us. It needs us to release its full potential. I can't do that without you. But first, we must do what's necessary."

"I don't know." Lila hugs herself. "This is all happening so fast. I'm worried about the other girls . . . my sisters." She makes a move toward the forest, but he catches her arm.

"We can't save them until we save ourselves."

I step forward hastily. "You'll be lucky if you find any of your sisters or friends alive, Lila. Last I saw, only four of eleven were still breathing. And Harlan lured all of them there."

"He lured me too," Ella calls as she helps Fiora with the frightened children.

"You can't trust him," I add.

Harlan laughs, scrubbing a hand down his face. "They're misconstruing the truth. I *did* bring a few girls there, but it was to aid us. I needed someone to break the frog spell over me. I had to become human before I could free *you*."

"*Seven* have died?" Lila asks, stuck on that fact. "Which ones? Were any of them my sisters?"

She's addressing Harlan, but he'll dodge the question. She deserves the truth. "Among your sisters, Geneva and Nixie were living, last I saw. So were your cousins, Viveka and Sibilla. But your other sisters, Ilsa and Liese, passed away in the forest. So have Edwina, Winola, Delia, Helene, and Tildy."

Lila buckles to her knees and buries her head in her hands.

"Harlan doesn't care that they're dead," I forge on. "He used them, like he used all these children. He didn't bring them here to dance with you. He would have killed them if Henni hadn't fulfilled her task."

Ignoring me, Harlan crouches beside Lila. "Do you feel this bruise?" He presses the base of her throat. "It still hasn't healed from when Clara throttled you. If I hadn't intervened, you'd be dead."

"He's not telling you everything," I snap. "I'd just learned you'd killed my father, Lila."

She pulls her hands from her face, remembering as fresh horror fills her eyes. "That was an accident! Harlan and I only meant to . . ." She chokes on another sob. "I'm so sorry!"

I hate to see her so pained, but at least she grieves what happened. "Can't you see all these terrible things point to Harlan?"

He places a gentle hand on her back. "Everything we've done has been for a greater purpose. I was born to be a king, and I've chosen you as my queen. How many people will we help live better lives? They can join us at our court. You will have ladies to attend you. We'll honor knights in great tournaments. It will be magnificent. Our people will prosper."

His delusions are beyond belief. "Before the curse that *you* caused," I say, "people *did* prosper. *Sortes Fortunae* granted them wishes. Everyone was content to live simple lives. Everyone but you."

His jaw muscle flinches. "Lila, she's poison. Take my hand, and we'll open the earth and bury her in it. You don't have to look. It will be over in an instant."

She glances between us, weeping harder. "I don't think . . . I can't hurt anyone else."

I motion to Fiora and Ella to take the children away. They slip off into the night, bringing Hansel and Gretel with them. Harlan doesn't notice. He's busy comforting Lila, telling her it will all be worth it. "I've put you before everyone." He enfolds her in his arms. "I love you."

"Stop!" She pushes back, crawling away. "I don't want magic anymore! I don't want *you*!"

Harlan goes as still as a corpse in a tree.

"Henni, leave with the others," I whisper, watching him carefully. She shrinks into the darkness and pads away. Axel still hasn't returned.

Harlan remains statuesque for a drawn-out moment, and then his mouth curves into a strained smile. "I understand, Lila. I love you, but I won't force you to live out our dream." He stalks toward her as she weeps on the ground. "If you don't want to share power, all we have to do is channel one more command together. We'll give all the magic to me."

I gasp. "Lila, don't do it!"

"Perhaps it's best you don't have magic." Harlan crowds in on her, his eyes heavy with sorrow. "I didn't want to tell you, but you were the one who killed your sisters, cousins, and friends. You starved them and made them dance without stopping."

"No." Lila shakes her head. "I wouldn't have done that!"

"You didn't know better," I say, coming nearer. "You were Lost. Don't listen to him!"

"Lost people fulfill their darkest desires," Harlan counters. "Which made you a very dangerous Lost One, Lila. You became a killer."

She balls her fists against her eyes. Her body shakes in full tremors. "Then take it! Take my magic! I can't hurt anyone else!"

"No!" I launch toward her.

Harlan pulls one of her hands away and grips it tight. A shared command must pass between them, because when he lets her go—when I barrel into him and shove him back—a thin vine bursts from the earth and coils to my leg. I fall forward, slamming to the ground.

Harlan laughs and steps over me. "Thank you, my love," he says to Lila. "Limitless magic will be so much easier without you."

"Lila, run!" I shout.

She scrambles to her feet and races away. Amused, Harlan watches for a moment before he opens a crevice in the earth at her feet. She manages to leap to the other side before it splits wider.

She keeps bolting. The beanstalk castle is close. She doesn't trust it. She pivots left of it, but flowering vines on one of the towers unravel toward her. They yank her up and weave her into the tower itself. She kicks and flails, but the vines hold her fast. One wraps over her mouth to silence her scream.

"There, my darling." Harlan cocks his head, his gaze sweeping up the length of her. "You make a lovely ornament."

The vines pull tighter around her body. He's suffocating her.

I uncoil the vine from my leg. Spring for the Book of Fortunes. It's a few feet away, where Henni left it in the basket.

Please, please, please, let me make another wish.

I crash to my knees. Rush through the incantation: "*Sortes Fortunae,* hear my voice. Understand my heart and its deepest desire. My name is Clara Thurn, and this—"

Thorns rip from the earth and snatch the book from my hands. They tear the pages and binding. The book is shredded to pieces. Some of my soul rends with it.

"How could you?" I whirl on Harlan. "That belonged to the village. It was a precious gift meant to bless people!"

"Not everyone is deserving, Clara." He saunters closer, clasping his hands behind his back.

My gut twists. I know why he's really done this. No one else will be able to make wishes now. No one will have a spark of magic to aid them in their lives. He's hoarded the power for himself.

I stand to face him. "The forest doesn't abide those who shed blood. It will turn on you."

"Hmm, I don't think so. The forest is tired of curses. It will enjoy my reign, and what I can do to make it thrive, like the jewel it's meant to be."

"You don't understand the forest's magic," I bite out. "It doesn't want grandeur. It wants to reward the selfless, the peaceful."

Harlan releases a low groan, rolling his eyes. "I'm *not* going to miss you, Clara. Though if I had to do everything over again, I wouldn't change a thing. The way you kissed me when you broke my spell . . . I'll cherish the memory. I so wish I had your power to revisit it."

"You're disgusting," I spit. "Corrupt and abominable."

"How about clever, resourceful, and romantic?"

He ambles nearer, toying with me, like killing me is something to savor. I retreat toward the ash line and look to the ghosts. "Help! I can't save you if he kills me."

Harlan scoffs. "Talking to your spirits? They can't hurt me from across the border."

The ghost of a woman with hollowed eye sockets glares at me. "The book is gone," she says in a scraping voice. "How can you still be a curse breaker, Clara Thurn?"

"But I am! There is one last task, and I must do it." The book never laid out that it had to be Henni. "Then you'll all be free."

"One last task?" Harlan's brow twitches.

Adrenaline surges inside me. "Henni didn't tell you the book's full reply. The curse is breaking in stages. Your power hasn't reached limitless capacity yet. If you kill me before I complete the last task, it never will."

He chuckles softly, but it mingles with a growl. "What is this last task?"

"I'll never say." I step behind the ash line, at the mercy of the ghosts. "And you can't force it out of me. The ghosts will protect me."

"Perhaps." He brushes lint from his sleeve. "If one of them has actually been on this land before and done something worth repeating." He *tsk*s and shakes his head. "Those chances must be slim."

I search the ghosts' faces. "Is there anyone who—?"

Wild grass blasts up from the ground, growing at an impossible rate. It snakes to wrap over me. I jump and catch the branch of a larch, but the limb swings and hurls me away. I turn furious eyes on Harlan. "What are you doing? You don't want me dead!"

"I'm not trying to kill you. Not yet." He paces on the other side of the ashes, treading just shy of the line. "What is the last task, Clara?"

The roots of the larch writhe toward me like a sea monster's tentacles.

"Help!" I beg the ghosts. I leap over roots and race around them. "Please, there must be someone who's been here before. This wasn't always my land. This village wasn't always here, but the forest has been. It's ancient. Someone must have—"

A man with kind eyes pushes through the horde.

"Conrad!" Gratitude overwhelms me to see my farmhand. But then I notice his blurring edges and otherworldly illumination. "You died?" I duck a flying branch. "H-how?"

He smiles sadly. "When the well went dry, I drew water from the old spring. But it was foul. I'm only glad I didn't give some to your grandmother before it caused the death of me."

"I'm so sorry." I dodge the wildlife seeking to plow me over. I wish I had time to be more thoughtful. "Would you mind—?"

"Of course." He looks around. "I *did* clear some of this land once."

"Wonderful! Do it again." I hope he can, although he was never Lost. Maybe that means he can't wield the forest's power. Unless being trapped as a ghost counts . . .

He strains his focus on the other side of the ashes. A moment later, trees and bushes pop up around Harlan like moles from burrowed ground holes. A fast-growing pine knocks him over, and he scrambles to avoid its wide-spreading boughs.

Relief sweeps over me. It seems any ghost can enact a loop.

Axel appears several yards away. *Finally.* Despite his bleeding shoulder, he rushes toward Harlan, a rusted scythe in hand. Lila is behind him with a hay rake. He must have cut her free. Herr Oswald is also barreling in our direction, just passing the beanstalk castle. The commotion must have drawn him outside.

Harlan curses. He sends a heavy branch from one of the new trees whipping for Axel.

"Conrad!" I shout.

The same tree cracks through at the base. At least that's how it appears. Conrad's loop moves so quickly there's no time to glimpse the marks of the ax that must have hewn it down before.

The tree topples toward Harlan. As he bolts for safety, Axel runs at him with his scythe.

"Stop!" Herr Oswald darts closer. "Don't hurt my son!"

"You know he's a murderer!" I yell to be heard above all the trees growing and falling. "He's responsible for many deaths! He wants to kill us too!"

"Let me talk to him! Give him a chance!"

"He's had enough chances!" Axel says.

Axel comes within reach of Harlan. Swings for his leg—a

blow that won't kill him. Axel still wants justice, for Harlan to face the council. But before his scythe strikes, wild grass sprouts and tethers to Axel's arm. Stunted, his blade only tears the cloth of Harlan's trousers.

Harlan runs past the stretch of land that's caught in a loop, only ten yards deep. Realizing nothing else is coming at him, he grinds to a halt and turns around, panting but smiling.

"I'm sorry," Conrad tells me. "That's all the land I've cleared."

Harlan laughs and wipes sweat from his brow. "Is that your full bag of tricks, then?" When I don't answer, he smirks. "Thought so."

More wild grass binds around Axel and yanks the scythe from his grip. Lila runs for Harlan, her rake lifted. He juts a thick root up from the ground. She trips over it and falls on the rake. Its tines pierce her leg. She shrieks in pain.

"Harlan, my boy." Herr Oswald hurries toward him, hands clasped in prayer. "Stop this madness. This isn't you."

Harlan sneers. "You never knew me, Father. And you didn't deserve Mother. If anything, you should be proud. Didn't you want a slaughterer for a son? Well, I've moved on past pigs."

The earth rips open in a great jagged line. Herr Oswald's foot catches on the edge. Roots lash to his ankles. The fissure tears wider. The roots drag Herr Oswald into the chasm, and he howls in terror. The sound cuts off abruptly as the fissure sews back together and fills in with earth.

I'm frozen to the bone, my mouth hanging slack. Harlan just killed his own father. His own blood.

He combs his hands through his hair to compose himself. "About that last task, Clara . . . now would be a good time to finish it. You may have noticed my patience is running thin."

Shaking from rage and revulsion, I cross the ash line and stalk toward him. Conrad ceases the loop. There's no point continuing it when it doesn't reach Harlan. "Let Axel and Lila go," I demand. "Then I'll tell you."

"I need you to do more than tell me."

"Fine. Let them go."

"Hmm." He crosses his arms, making a mock show of considering me. "No. I can't threaten you alone, Clara. I truly believe you'd let me kill you rather than allow me full power. I know you too well. And you have such a difficult time seeing the people you care about suffer."

The wild grass binding Axel squeezes tighter. His face darkens as his airway cuts off. Nearby, the thick root tangles over Lila and starts to drag her underground.

"Stop!" I cry. "I'll break the curse! I'll end it once and for all!"

"Do it now!" Harlan continues to strangle Axel and bury Lila.

I look wildly behind me at the ghosts, vainly searching for a way out of this. How can I reveal the last task to Harlan? I can't admit I have to kill my grandmother. She's on the brink of death, but I won't hasten it. And I can't let him kill Axel and Lila.

"I h-have to get the red rampion," I stammer, and rush back to where Henni planted it.

"Hurry. And don't try anything foolish."

I pluck up a few stems, sweat trickling down my spine.

Please let him believe this.

I return to where Harlan is waiting, but stop short where a skull-sized stone rests in the pasture. "The curse breaker is supposed to eat some red rampion."

"Eat it?" He frowns.

"I've seen it grant power that way. When my grandmother ate rampion as the Grimm wolf, she was able to speak." I take a breath. "And since the curse breaker is me, *I'll* eat it."

"And be granted power?" Harlan scoffs, shaking his head. "Give it here, Clara."

"No!" I shove the parsnip-like roots in my mouth.

He lunges at me. I drop the stems and pick up the stone. I swing for his head. He dodges the blow. The stone strikes his shoulder. He cries out and falls over, dragging me with him.

He rolls on top of me, straddles my hips, and throttles me. He roars like the monster he is. "You know what? I've changed my mind. More power isn't worth the pleasure of killing you."

He bears down on me, squeezing harder. I hit and kick, but can't break his hold.

My surroundings flicker, blacken, fade. Aside from the horrific sense of suffocating, it feels as if I'm slipping into a vision. I wonder if I might be, if it's some instinct to ease my suffering as I die. But I won't surrender to it. I need to fight. Live.

I claw the ground around me. Find the stone. I draw one last surge of strength and swing my arm.

Harlan is knocked over. But not by me. The stone never landed.

Disoriented, I gasp for breath, wheezing, dizzy.

I pull myself up. Clap eyes on the Grimm wolf. She has Harlan by the shoulder and thrashes him ruthlessly.

CHAPTER 58

"Adiah." My voice rasps, astonished, as I gaze into her brown eyes. "You made it home."

The arrow still protrudes from her side, wet with blood, though she somehow snapped the shaft shorter on her journey. Pus oozes from the wound. She's dying, but fighting.

She's a true Thurn.

Roots and grass whip at her, reaching to bind her—Harlan's desperate magic. She breaks through them. Sinks her fangs deeper into his flesh. He screams, but won't stop attacking.

Thorny vines shoot up and rake across her belly. They dig into her wounded side. She yelps, but won't let him go.

Shaky with lightheadedness, I grab the stone again. If Adiah can find strength, so can I.

I crawl to Harlan. He wraps thorny vines around Adiah's four legs. The whites show around her eyes. Her jaws shake. She can't hold him much longer.

I raise my arms to strike him with the stone. He sees me just in time. Roots writhe up and loop around my waist. They yank me back a few feet. The stone tumbles from my grip. My hand falls on the cluster of red rampion I dropped.

Adiah yelps again. She finally releases Harlan. He drags himself out from under her, his teeth clenched as his shoulder bleeds profusely.

I glance at my friends. Axel is being strangled afresh. Earth spills over Lila's face, the last of her to be buried. Adiah is about to die in a bed of thorns.

I can't let this happen. I won't. My fingers close around the red rampion. The forest won't let this happen either. It will not abide Harlan as its master.

I don't have *Sortes Fortunae* to make a wish upon. The book is destroyed. But it was made from the forest, its pages from the trees, its binding from the roots, its ink from emerald leaves. My land *is* the forest's land. Above all, red rampion is the seed—the heart—of all magic.

I press the rampion against the earth and channel thoughts of the forest that once loved its inhabitants, that once helped me and my father find a lost lamb with swaying branches pointing the way, the forest that worked in harmony with peaceful people and rewarded them with wishes.

The world was once rampant with magic, my father taught me. Only pockets of enchantment remain, places that are still reverenced and remembered.

"I haven't forgotten you," I assure the forest. "Don't forget us. Free the souls and save Grimm's Hollow from evil—from Harlan."

I think of the poem Ollie recited when I first met him, the one he learned from the ghost in the oldest tree:

When magic kissed the earth, it grew a red flower,
Which woke up the land and granted it power.
But a curse be upon those who wrong this domain,
For when blood soaks the soil, magic shall become bane.
Forgiveness comes slowly after such insurrection,
But the first to grow here will offer protection.

"Protect us with red rampion," I plead. "This is my wish."

The ground starts to tremble. Harlan meets my gaze, his brow twisted. He isn't doing this. "Is this the curse finally breaking?" he asks.

"Yes." I stand and untie my cape. Let it fall to the ground. I hope I'll never need it again. "But *you're* the curse, Harlan. This is your ending."

His mouth quivers like he's trying to laugh, but can't produce the sound. "You have no power over me."

"I don't need power. The forest has an abundance."

From the patch Henni planted, red rampion continues to seed, flower, and spread like a great crimson wave rippling over the land. It sprouts and blooms as the magic rolls toward Harlan.

He stumbles back and bolts at full speed for his beanstalk castle. The rampion springs up and flourishes faster, chasing him. He doesn't have time to run inside the walls. Instead, he leaps for one of the stalks and frantically climbs.

The red rampion pursues him, its lanky stems slithering up the beanstalk. It wraps around his ankle, leg, torso, head. It coils over him like he coiled Lila. More rampion surges up to cloak and twine around every beanstalk of the castle. Within seconds, the entire structure is dotted with crimson star flowers that dangle like bells.

The ground shakes harder. Lila surfaces, loose dirt falling from her face. The grass and vines tethering Axel and Adiah shrivel and recede.

Lila and Axel clamber to their feet and stagger to my side. We brace each other for support.

The trembling intensifies. As it peaks, the pasture around the beanstalk castle cleaves open. Like a net cast over it, the red rampion captures the castle and tows it downward into the crevasse in a thunderous implosion. Harlan roars furiously, straining for freedom. But he's dragged deeper into the fissure.

As quickly as it happens, fresh earth fills the hole and green grass sprouts over it. Bloodred blossoms adorn the pasture. The sheep that scattered now cautiously wander inward, bleating to each other, and the first rays of sunlight skim the land with buttery soft yellow light.

I look behind me to the forest. The ghosts smile and fade, rising to the sky beyond the towering trees, dozens of fireflies winking out of sight. The ash border transforms to sparks that glitter away on soft swirls of wind.

Axel stares at everything in wonder. "Can someone explain how all of this happened?"

I lean my head against him. "A wish came true."

"Then the curse is over—all of it?"

I begin to nod, but then my breath catches as I remember what Henni told me: *The book said the curse would break in stages, and for it to fully break, the Grimm wolf and your grandmother have to die.*

I turn to Adiah. The thorny vines have let her go and sunk back underground, but she lies motionless with blood-matted fur.

CHAPTER 59

*N*o, no, no! I dart over to her. Adiah's large brown eyes sluggishly capture mine. I kneel and pull her massive head onto my lap. I kiss her fuzzy brow. Stroke her thick fur. "It's all right, girl. Stay with me. We'll get you feeling better." I shouldn't make that promise. She's fatally wounded. But I can't let her go. I need her. Grandmère needs her.

A soft keening peals from her throat and wrenches through my chest. "I'm so sorry you're suffering. You were incredibly brave to help me. You saved my life."

She pants rapidly, her strong body limp and weak.

Tears slip down my face. "Don't die."

Her brown eyes shift to violet. I jolt. "Grandmère! No, you shouldn't have come. Adiah might die at any moment." I remember what she told me: *My soul must be in my own body when I leave this life, or it won't find rest with Rosamund.*

The wolf's eyes remain violet. I look desperately to Axel. He's already one step ahead of me and passes over a clutch of red rampion. I feed its roots to the wolf so Grandmère can find her voice.

"I am dying now too, *ma petite chérie,*" she rasps.

"No, please! I want to be with you in the cottage."

"There is no time. I need you to see a memory." She speaks on a pained breath. "Find me on the night Bren was murdered."

"I've already seen—"

"Find me when I spoke to *Sortes Fortunae,*" she insists. "Hear what I said. See what the book wrote. Do as I say, Clara. Do it *now.*"

I weep, hugging her tighter. I don't want to spend what's left of our remaining moments together by going to the past. But I can't refuse her dying wish. I close my eyes and try to concentrate, mend my broken heart long enough to enter the realm of visions.

Perhaps it's Grandmère who helps me make that leap, being the seer she is. Perhaps our abilities combine to forge the bridge faster than I thought possible. All I know is I'm suddenly taken to the black, the silence, and awakened to that summer evening over three years ago.

The Grimm wolf scares away the night watchmen from the pavilion, just like before, and Grandmère repossesses her human body. Rising from the meadow, she joins Adiah by the pedestal that holds the Book of Fortunes.

"Good girl, Adiah." She strokes the wolf's fur. Adiah nuzzles close as Grandmère speaks a sort of incantation: "*Sortes Fortunae,* hear my voice. Understand my heart and its deepest desire. My name is Marlène Thurn, and this is not a wish. It's an offer.

"My son-in-law is missing and likely dead, which I fear will be the catalyst to bring to pass my daughter's and granddaughter's grave fortunes. I know making a second wish isn't possible. If I tried, you would not hear me. All I ask is that you remember the one wish I made when my daughter was in my womb: I wished my bloodline would be protected.

"I will promise you anything, *Sortes Fortunae,* even my life, if you stay true to my wish. I will commit to any new tasks you may give to ensure it's done."

She opens the book, and green-inked words appear:

Answering your wish long ago,
I drew a red flower,

Pointing you toward its mysteries
And life-shielding power.

Now you ask me to recall
What I haven't forgotten,
Yet this plea shows your wisdom,
For the blessed have now fallen.

I bring this village a curse,
A bane for murderous malice,
But for the life that was stolen,
Your life amends the balance.

I grant you the grace to live
So long as the curse doesn't weaken,
But once its breaking has begun,
Your death must be its completion.

Swear this price to me now,
Daughter of seers, mistress of wolves,
And the bloodline with your magic
Shall be rightly preserved.

Grandmère takes a steeling breath. "I swear to your price."

Blackness falls, silence descends. I'm swept back to the present, to the dying wolf and the dying woman within her.

"Oh, Grandmère." I bury my head against hers. "What have you done?" The book would have granted her one wish, but she feared what she foresaw, the dire fortunes of her family and the curse that could undo the book's protection of them. So she struck a new and terrible bargain.

"I did what I could to save your life," she wheezes, "even if I could not save your mother's."

I weep against her. "I would rather have you live forever."

"You know that is not possible. I am old. I have walked this earth long enough. But *you* will live. And I will live on through you."

"How?" I sob.

"Don't you see, *ma chère?* You are how my bloodline and its magic will continue. You are my one wish come true."

My crying ebbs, and I pull back to gaze into her violet eyes. "Then everything I do, I'll do it for you and Mother. I will make you proud."

The wolf shakes her head ever so slightly. "You already make us proud. You must live for *you,* Clara. Live life so fully that your joy shines as bright as your sorrows weigh heavy. You are a daughter of seers and wolves. You were not made to restrain your heart. Embrace the pain that finds everyone in life, and live fiercely in spite of it."

"I will." Tears stream faster down my face. "I love you, Grand-mère."

"I love you too, my sweet, brave girl." The wolf shudders. "I must go now. Your mother, father, and grandfather are calling to me. And Adiah . . . she must rest."

I resist the urge to beg her to stay longer. I don't want to endanger her soul. My peace will come by knowing she's reunited with my family.

"Goodbye, dear heart," she says, her voice weakened to a gravelly whisper.

"Goodbye."

Her eyes fade to brown, and I choke on a sob. "Rest now, Adiah." I kiss her head. "I will bury you beside Grandmère."

The Grimm wolf pants her last breath, and her solemn eyes drift closed.

I wrap my arms over her and hold her close. In Grimm's Hollow, every villager knows that when someone dies, the windows of the house must be opened so their soul can escape. I will open the windows in the cottage for Grandmère soon enough, but first I must help Adiah. And as there are no windows in the pasture, I will be her window.

"Be free, wild spirit," I murmur. "Find your ancestors and run as a pack once more."

I feel the curse break fully. It's not something I can see or hear or taste or touch. The undoing is deeper, perhaps in my soul itself, a release as liberating as every window thrust open in every house of Grimm's Hollow, a widening that makes room for a world of enchantment to return.

Everyone is saved, though they will never know the cost. Grandmère wouldn't want that. She would hate being lauded and worshipped. She would want to be remembered as the kind neighbor whose door was always open if you dared to have your fortune read.

I pull back from Adiah and burrow into Axel's warm arms. Above his shoulder, I spy the trees of the Forest Grimm. Not everyone has been saved. Under an aspen, the ghost of a little boy with a mop of curls remains . . . a boy who is still missing his two pennies.

And I know exactly how to help him find them.

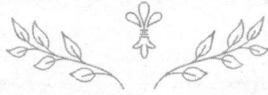

EPILOGUE

AFTER THE CURSE

To have a vision, Clara Thurn needed to touch a person. Failing that, she required a token, and since Ollie Furst was a ghost, a token was necessary. Luckily, Axel Furst, Ollie's cousin, knew which token was the most meaningful to him. It was in a jackdaw's nest up the chimney of an old shack on his uncle's farm. And Axel, being true to his princely nature, clambered up that chimney to retrieve it.

When he met Clara at the edge of her sheep farm near the forest, four days after the curse—during which time he'd helped her bury her grandmother and the Grimm wolf—Axel was blackened with soot and covered in cobwebs.

He had never looked more handsome to Clara.

She held the token, the lost drummer from Ollie's beloved set of tin soldiers, and had a vision. In it, Ollie's mother handed her son two pennies to give to a poor man in the village. Ollie had never told Clara the name of that man. It was Ralf Dantzer, Henni and Ella's father. But Ralf had never been poor in the sense of wealth.

"Poor Ralf Dantzer," Ollie's mother said. "Both of his daughters are sick. Give him these pennies, won't you? One for each girl, that they might have good luck."

Ollie was only seven at the time, old enough to comprehend

that two pennies could purchase him sweets at the market, but too young to understand how grave the girls' illnesses were. Somewhere on that pendulum of a conscience, he hesitated to spend the money and buried it in the forest while he contemplated what to do.

Fortunately, Henni and Ella, who must have been three and six years of age, recovered without the pennies. Unfortunately, the consumption they overcame was the same illness Ollie and his mother abruptly caught and passed away from.

When the vision ended, Clara and Axel met Ollie in the forest, though only Clara, as a Voyante of the Bygone, could see and hear him.

"You two look strange without your red cape and red scarf," Ollie said with his usual bluntness, which on this occasion Clara found endearing. "But sometimes strange can be good," he amended, and that was high praise indeed.

Clara beckoned him with a nod. "Would you like to join us for a walk?"

"Not if Axel wants to visit his father's grave again. His nose drips when he cries."

A fair observation, though Clara kept it to herself. "You'll appreciate this location," she promised.

The three of them journeyed all of ten minutes to a bridge made of simple planks that crossed a small stream. A flat stone rested in the grass just shy of the planks. Four-leaf clovers and red-spotted mushrooms grew all around it, and a lucky ladybug buzzed over to land on top.

"Do you remember this place?" Clara asked Ollie.

He shook his head, but maybe something felt familiar because his eyes rounded and his fingers wiggled as he glanced about.

Clara nodded at Axel. With a grin, he lifted the stone, brushing off the dirt that covered two shiny objects.

Ollie gasped. "My pennies!"

His smile was so broad it revealed something Clara had never noticed: a slight gap between his two front teeth, which made him even more adorable. She wished she could give him a hug, but showing him these pennies was even more rewarding.

Ollie divided a look between Clara and Axel. "Will you give the pennies to the poor man, then?"

"Of course," Clara replied. "Better yet, we'll give them to his daughters, who they were meant for. Believe it or not, those girls are Henni and Ella."

"And guess who we've invited to join us?" Axel said, taking up Clara's cue, although he wouldn't hear Ollie's answer.

The boy's smile dropped. "My . . . father?"

"No, not your father." Clara's brow wrinkled. "Why would—?" Then she saw Rudger trudging up the footpath. Clara and Axel hadn't seen him since the curse broke, but in that time, he must have found his way home and washed up, because he wore clean clothes, had no grime coating his skin, and had trimmed his beard and hair.

Despite his improved appearance, he was only the shell of the man Clara had once been acquainted with in Grimm's Hollow. He hunched as he walked, his head bowed, his chin almost touching his chest.

"I didn't invite him," Clara told Ollie. "But if you would like to say goodbye, I can share your message."

Ollie nibbled on his lower lip. "That's all right. It will only make Father sad about me again, and he needs to be sad about other things." He wagged a thumb at Axel.

Clara stared at the ghost, a little awestruck. "You're wiser than the oldest tree, you know?"

"I know."

She and Ollie waited quietly as Rudger approached Axel, and Axel scuffled closer to him.

Rudger scratched his beard, sniffed, and kicked a couple of rocks. "I can't remember much lately, but I do have a vague recollection of you getting back, um, a pocket watch?"

Axel nodded, crossing his arms.

"Which tells me you know some things about your, uh"—he cleared his throat—"father."

Another nod from Axel, stiffer than the last.

Rudger hiccupped back his tears. "I've been a coward, nephew. Worse, I've been cruel. I won't ask for your forgiveness, not until I've done enough right things in this world to stand a chance of earning it. For now, the best way I can apologize is by giving you something else that belonged to Kellen."

Axel's brows drew together, curious and cautious. Rudger pulled out a small leather book from his jacket. "He had this journal on him when he passed away. Something I'd meant to give you with the pocket watch."

With shaking hands, Axel took the journal and flipped through its pages. Clara couldn't read them from where she stood, but she saw that they were covered in tiny scrawl.

"Some of the entries are from before Kellen went on his journey through the mountain pass," Rudger said. "Some are from afterward. You're mentioned many times, although not as often during the years Kellen struggled to remember much of anything."

Axel's chin trembled. "Thank you," he croaked, roughly swiping beneath his nose.

Ollie gave Clara a pointed look. "I told you how it drips."

"Shh," she whispered, although no one would hear him. But they would hear *her* if Ollie made her laugh. The only thing that prevented that was the sight of two lovely sisters walking up the path. "Look." She gestured in their direction, and Ollie smiled his tooth-gap smile.

Henni and Ella passed Rudger as he was leaving, taking a double-glance at him before embracing their friends.

"Is everything all right?" Ella asked Axel, noticing his red eyes.

"Yes." He took a cleansing breath. "Better than it's been in a long time."

Henni bounced on her toes. "Is Ollie here?"

"He is." Clara grinned. Ollie told her something just then, and she shared it: "He says you and Ella better like your presents."

"Of course we will!" Henni looked to the spot where she presumed Ollie was standing. And he *had* been standing there two seconds ago, but Ollie was a child who didn't hold still. Now he was jumping around them—a group of friends who had the power to finally set his soul free.

"How will it work?" Ella asked, also addressing the Ollie-less spot. "Once the pennies are in our hands, will you suddenly disappear? I want to be sure we get to say goodbye."

"I don't know." Ollie laughs. "But I bet you two pennies I'll vanish right away to the happy place. Mama will be so surprised!"

Clara relayed what he said and told him to keep still for a moment. She showed the others where he was standing at the foot of the planked bridge.

"Goodbye then," Ella said. "Thank you for the gift I'll receive."

"Goodbye, Ollie." Henni bent to him, and he hopped to the left teasingly. "I'm going to paint a picture of you with your mother. I'll treasure it like I'll treasure your penny."

"Goodbye, cousin." Axel imparted a lopsided smile. "When you get to wherever you're going, ask around for your uncle Kellen. Tell him I said hello."

Clara repeated Ollie's answer: "He swears on his set of tin soldiers he will."

Now it was Clara's turn to say goodbye, which felt like losing another piece of her family. But she embraced the pain, just as she'd promised Grandmère. She wouldn't restrain her heart. Her sorrows would be as deep as her joy was bright. That was what it was to live.

"Thank you for helping me in the forest. You were the first person to tell me I had magic."

Ollie grinned crookedly. "Thank you for keeping your promise about the pennies."

"You're welcome. I'm glad we became friends."

"Me too." He leaped to swat a butterfly. "Do you think the Grimm wolf will be where I'm going?"

"I don't see why not."

"Then I'm going to play with her. She'll be my best friend."

"I think she'll like that."

"Goodbye, Clara."

"Goodbye, Ollie."

Clara blinked back tears as Axel handed her the first penny. "Ready?" he asked, looking in the general direction of Ollie.

"I've only been waiting almost fourteen years," Ollie said dramatically.

"He's ready," Clara replied.

Axel gave the second penny to Ella, and Clara gave hers to Henni.

Ollie tipped his head back, gave a whoop of joy, and ran across the bridge.

He vanished before he reached the other side, and the butterfly flitted away into the sunlight.

Two weeks later, the village held a festival to celebrate the breaking of the curse and the return of seven Lost Ones. Among them were Rudger, Lila, and three of the four Sommer girls Clara had danced with in the caverns, not so once upon a time ago. Sibilla, Lila's cousin, had perished, despite eating and drinking after Lila left. Her body had been too weak to recover.

The news had devastated Lila, but she'd found comfort among the villagers, who had also lost many loved ones during the curse. Lila offered them comfort as well.

Geneva, Nixie, and Viveka, the Sommer girls who returned, treated Lila with kindness and forgiveness. They had all been Lost like she was, but they were now found, and they determined not to shirk that gift.

They wore exquisite matching dresses to honor their sisters, cousins, and friends, and they danced at the festival, welcoming all to join their circle. Even Clara dared to dance with them, though she was grateful for the choice to stop.

Henni, as the hailed curse breaker, was crowned queen of the festival. Clara presented the wreath she'd made for her friend's hair, woven from the red rampion still growing in her pasture.

She never told the village council how the curse was broken in stages—she'd rather have Henni receive the praise—nor did she mention that Harlan Oswald was Bren Zimmer's murderer.

Harlan's body was gone now, and proof of his crime didn't exist beyond Clara's visions and Lila's witness. Clara had learned firsthand how much the council struggled to believe hard truths, and she wanted Lila to have a chance at a new life, free from the repercussions of the terrible things Harlan had involved her with.

Clara let the council believe Harlan was among the Lost Ones who died and never returned from the forest, and that his father, Herr Oswald, must have become Lost very recently in search of him, never to return as well. The village council was content to accept that one selfless wish had solved all their problems.

Axel gave Clara a bouquet of flowers. Red roses to remind her of her mother, mixed with forget-me-nots, cornflowers, and woodland phlox—blue blossoms. Clara had a new favorite color. And it wasn't red.

She and Axel danced around the bonfire that he in particular was drawn to, having chopped most of the wood with his hatchet. (Axel really loved his hatchet.) Clara's new hobby was teasing him about it, night and day.

"You should be my new farmhand," she said, thinking of the trees Conrad had regrown in the pasture as a ghost, which would need clearing again.

Axel twirled her around. "Aren't I already? You have me chasing lovelorn rams all day."

"They can't always be with the ewes."

"I know the feeling." He chuckled.

Clara poked him in the chest. "Tired of the barn?"

He spun her again. "The hayloft is more comfortable than a bedroll, but my ankle *has* been missing yours."

Clara had tried to persuade Axel to move into the cottage, but he'd insisted that it wasn't proper. He wouldn't have Clara's father turning over in his grave because Axel hadn't treated his daughter with every respect.

"Would you consider another arrangement?" Clara asked.

"In addition to being your farmhand?"

"That's a given."

"I'm all ears."

Her heart thumped. She didn't know all the adventures she wanted to experience in life, but she'd already had many, and what she yearned for most was what she'd yearned for from the beginning, and that had always led her back home.

"You're my family, Axel. We belong together."

He danced off beat, studying her face. "I-I feel the same way."

"I know I'm young, but there are some things I'm sure of." Her face heated, and she found it suddenly difficult to breathe. What was the matter with her? She'd been practicing this little speech all day. "I'm sure of *you*."

Axel tripped over his own shoes, and Axel never tripped. "I feel the same way," he repeated, caught in a loop of his own making.

"Did I say I love you?" Clara asked. "Tonight, I mean." Now she was the one wobbling on her feet.

Axel made a sort of nod-shrug-shake-of-the-head motion.

"Well, I love you." Clara had rehearsed lots of reasons why, but they fled her mind like she'd inhaled a heady breath of cavern vapors.

Gratefully, Axel wasn't any more eloquent when he sputtered for the third time, "I feel the same way." Clara laughed, and she was glad to look forward to more laughter in life.

"Will you marry me, Axel?"

His brows sprang up, and he laughed too, a moment made all the more beautiful when his eyes shone with tears. "Yes," he exclaimed, catching her in his arms. He spun her around and kept her aloft, her feet off the ground, as he gave her a kiss that promised he would always be her anchor, knowing she would forever be his compass.

Clara and Axel wouldn't need a map for the journey ahead. They, themselves, would be the rivers and the streams to guide their course.

They would forge their own fates, make their own luck, and conjure their own magic.

ACKNOWLEDGMENTS

I love this book all the more for how challenging it was to write. Weaving a new set of Grimms' fairy tale characters into *The Deathly Grimm* while tracking the ones I'd already introduced in *The Forest Grimm,* and then adding a murder mystery and several magical visions, was no small feat. My manuscript needed a hefty revision, as well as a lengthy chop off the word count before it was worthy of publication. I'm so proud of the result, and I have many people to thank for helping me along the way.

My deep gratitude goes to . . .

My editor, Sara Goodman, for her sharp eye in boiling down what needed to be fixed and showing complete trust in me to get the job done right.

The rest of the in-house team at Wednesday Books and St. Martin's Publishing Group: publisher Jennifer Enderlin, associate publisher Eileen Rothschild, assistant editor Vanessa Aguirre, jacket designer and creative director Olga Grlic, mechanical designer Soleil Paz, interior designer Devan Norman, marketers Rivka Holler and Brant Janeway, publicist Alyssa Gammello, production editor Melanie Sanders, production manager Gail Friedman, copy editor Christina MacDonald, managing editors Eric Meyer and Merilee Croft, audio marketer Claire Beyette, and audio publicist Isabella Narvaez. I'm in awe of the hard work and passion all of you contribute.

The audiobook narrator of this duology, Sarah Ovens. I've lost count of the number of people who have told me how exceptionally well you captured Clara, and I wholeheartedly agree.

My agent of nine years, Josh Adams of Adams Literary, and by extension Tracey Adams. Thank you both for the feeling of home you've given me and your endless championing of my writing career.

My wonderful family: my husband, Jason, for his patience and steadfast belief that I can do hard things; my daughters, Isabelle and Ivy, who embody the essence of Clara in their strength of character, and who also have scoliosis; my son-in-law, Ethan, who is the perfect Axel for Isabelle; my son, Aidan, for our deep conversations and his stage-fighting consultations—or, more aptly put, "page-fighting consultations"; my mother, Buffie, for her prayers and faith that I could accomplish the monumental task of completing this novel; and my angel father, Larry, who was the first to teach me how to wield words and who always leaves a mark on my stories, even from heaven.

My fantastic writing friends, especially Charlie N. Holmberg, who helped me throughout the revision stage; Emily R. King, who gave me invaluable guidance in trimming the length; and Sara B. Larson, who constantly checked in and cheered me along the way. You three are simply the best!

Holly Black and Rebecca Ross: reading chapters from your books was my reward after finishing my work for the day . . . and the weeks and months that followed. I will forever ship Jude and Cardan and Iris and Roman.

The Brothers Grimm, for collecting these fairy tales in the first place so I could play at inventing their origin stories in my duology. Let's be friends.

My Heavenly Father, for the gift it is to live, the dark days and the bright ones, and for the voice You've given me to weave my own creations.